Taken by You

*Also by Connie Mason
in Large Print:*

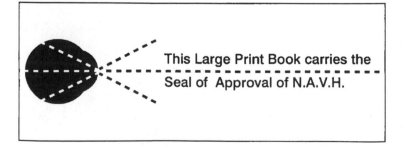

This Large Print Book carries the
Seal of Approval of N.A.V.H.

Taken by You

Connie Mason

Thorndike Press • Waterville, Maine

Published in 2005 by arrangement with Leisure Books, a division of Dorchester Publishing Co., Inc.

Thorndike Press® Large Print Romance.

The tree indicium is a trademark of Thorndike Press.

The text of this Large Print edition is unabridged.
Other aspects of the book may vary from the original edition.

Set in 16 pt. Plantin by Christina S. Huff.

Printed in the United States on permanent paper.

Library of Congress Cataloging-in-Publication Data

Mason, Connie.
    Taken by you / Connie Mason.
      p. cm.
    ISBN 0-7862-7233-3 (lg. print : hc : alk. paper)
    1. Pirates — Fiction. 2. Large type books. I. Title.
PS3563.A78786T35 2004
    813'.54—dc22   2004062029

2/05

Taken by You

As the Founder/CEO of NAVH, the only national health agency solely devoted to those who, although not totally blind, have an eye disease which could lead to serious visual impairment, I am pleased to recognize Thorndike Press* as one of the leading publishers in the large print field.

Founded in 1954 in San Francisco to prepare large print textbooks for partially seeing children, NAVH became the pioneer and standard setting agency in the preparation of large type.

Today, those publishers who meet our standards carry the prestigious "Seal of Approval" indicating high quality large print. We are delighted that Thorndike Press is one of the publishers whose titles meet these standards. We are also pleased to recognize the significant contribution Thorndike Press is making in this important and growing field.

Lorraine H. Marchi, L.H.D.
Founder/CEO
NAVH

* Thorndike Press encompasses the following imprints: Thorndike, Wheeler, Walker and Large Print Press.

Prologue

Somewhere in the Atlantic Ocean
1580

Morgan Scott poised briefly on the prow of the sinking galleon, arched his scarred, emaciated body, and dove into the dark, wind-tossed sea below. His arms and legs churning furiously, he struggled to escape the sucking wake of the sinking *Black Mariah*. He looked back but once, silently rejoicing when he saw the Devil's ship slowly sinking beneath the surface, taking her brutal Spanish master and crew with her.

Then he laughed.

Laughed until his sides ached and he was in danger of drowning.

Abruptly, he turned toward the English frigate whose guns were still smoking, and he swam like hell.

"She's sinking, Captain Dunsworth," First Mate Nickols reported as he lowered the spyglass and smiled at the captain.

"Good riddance," Dunsworth snarled. "That's one more Spanish bastard who won't interfere again with English shipping. His first mistake was taking us on, his second was thinking he could sink one of Her Majesty's finest. Any survivors, Mr. Nickols?"

Nickols raised the glass again to scan the whitecaps being plowed by the rising wind. "Doesn't look like it, sir."

Dunsworth nodded. "Just as well. Let's get out of here, there's a storm brewing. Set a course for England. We need to repair the damage done by the *Black Mariah*."

"Aye, aye, sir."

Nickols made one last sweep of the sea through the glass, lowered it, then suddenly swung it back up to his eye.

"What is it, Mr. Nickols, do you see something?"

"Aye, Captain. Looks like a man's head bobbing in the waves." He handed the glass to Dunsworth, who trained it in the direction in which Nickols was pointing. "Do you see him?"

"Aye. I've a notion to let the bastard drown, but I'm no barbarian. Lower a longboat and bring him aboard."

"He looks about done in, Captain," Nickols remarked as he stared down at the

8

half-drowned man sprawled on the deck. "Look at his back, poor devil. Whoever he is, he wasn't coddled aboard the *Black Mariah*. He's no more than a lad. I would doubt he's even a Spaniard with all that blond hair."

"Take him below and have the ship's doctor look him over. And for God's sake, feed him. I can count every one of his ribs. Until we hear his story, it won't hurt to treat him as decently as possible."

Morgan stirred, turned to his side, and spewed out some of the seawater he had swallowed. Then he lay on his back, staring up at the Englishmen who had pulled him from the sea. Despite his weakness and utter exhaustion, he smiled in genuine joy. It was the first time he'd seen an Englishman in five years, and the sight nearly overwhelmed him with relief.

"Do you speak English?" Captain Dunsworth asked.

Though his throat was raw from swallowing copious amounts of seawater during his desperate swim, Morgan answered without hesitation.

"I speak English very well, sir. My name is Morgan Scott. My father was Sir Duncan Scott. Five years ago he was appointed envoy to Italy by the queen. Our ship,

Southern Star, was attacked and sunk by the *Black Mariah*, and I was the only survivor. My mother, father, brother, sister — dead . . . all dead."

The captain looked incredulous. "The *Southern Star*! My God, man, I recall the incident very well. Nothing was ever heard from the ship, and it was assumed all hands and passengers were lost. Where have you been these past five years?"

"Consigned to Hell," Morgan said, struggling to rise. A sailor rushed forward to help him. "I haven't set foot off the *Black Mariah* in five years. I've been starved, beaten, humiliated, and forced into virtual slavery. I grew up fast, forced from youthful innocence and thrust into the bowels of Hell at the age of seventeen."

Captain Dunsworth shook his head in commiseration. "Thank God we crossed paths with the *Black Mariah* when we did. You're free now, Morgan Scott. I'm sure the queen will restore all your family's wealth and holdings to you once she learns you're alive."

"I suppose," Morgan said dully.

"I'm Captain Dunsworth of the Royal Navy. The ship's doctor will take a look at you directly. By the time we reach England you'll be in shipshape condition. You're young, you'll recover. In no time at all you'll be among your own kind leading a privileged life."

Hollow-eyed and gaunt, Morgan stared at Dunsworth. No one but he would ever really know how severely he had suffered at the hands of the Spanish. They could guess but would never know unless they'd experienced it themselves. Never again could he live the kind of useless life he'd been accustomed to before his years of captivity. His soul burned with hatred, his heart lusted for revenge. The cruel death of his family and his subsequent captivity had left an indelible mark upon him.

"I will use my wealth to avenge my family's death," he said in a voice so filled with menace that Dunsworth shivered and looked away. "From this day forward, no Spaniard — man, woman, or child — is safe from me. I will seek the queen's sanction, outfit a ship, and hunt them down on the high seas like the animals they are."

"I admire your ambition, Master Scott, but aren't you rather young to captain your own ship? Have you the skills needed to control men?"

Morgan's blue eyes blazed hotly with vindictive fervor. "After five years of captivity on the high seas I've learned all there is to know about ships and sailing. Just as I've learned to hate Spaniards. I think that more than qualifies me for taking them on. Nothing will stop me, Captain." He raised his fist toward the dark, threatening sky. "I vow on the heads of my dead family to become merciless and single-minded in my pursuit of Spaniards. I will hunt them down ruthlessly and give no quarter. So help me God."

1

Cadiz, Spain
1587

"I don't care how pious you are, daughter, the family honor is at stake," Don Eduardo Santiego stated emphatically. "You *will* leave the convent, and you *will* travel to Cuba to marry Don Diego del Fugo."

Shrouded in a shapeless gray habit, Luca Santiego stiffened perceptibly, and her chin tilted upward in an almost unheard-of act of defiance. Ten years of submission and obedience, drummed into her by the abbess and nuns at the Mother Of God convent, fled, for this was something she could not let go unchallenged. She would not be sacrificed to her father's honor.

"I do not wish to marry Don Diego, Father. Nor do I wish to leave Spain. I am quite content here at the convent. In another month I will take my final vows and happily serve God forever." If her zeal was a

13

bit too forced, she pretended not to notice. Becoming a nun was her ultimate goal in life.

"That is precisely why I am here, Luca," Don Eduardo told her. "I never intended you for a religious life. You were an incorrigible ten year old when I brought you here to be tamed and educated by the good nuns at the convent. Your mother had just died, and I could not handle one as spirited as you. I had all I could do to raise your brothers. But I never intended to leave you here forever. You have been promised to Don Diego del Fugo all these years, and he is growing impatient. The abbess has assured me that you are quite ready to become a wife."

Luca shuddered, imagining how repugnant it would be to submit her body to a man, especially a man she hardly knew. "Please, Father, why can't you see that I am meant for a life of piety and prayer? I wish to become a bride of Christ."

Don Eduardo sent his daughter a look that spoke eloquently of his contempt. "One has only to look at you to know how unsuited you are to a cloistered life."

He stared at her, at the sultry beauty of her face, at the lush curves of her body, barely disguised by her loose-fitting habit.

Her eyes, large, dark, and tilted up at the outer corners, sparkled with life, spirit, and passion. She could fool others, but she couldn't fool him; he was her father. He was convinced that once initiated to passion she would partake greedily, and he intended for Don Diego to be the man to ignite the flame burning within his daughter.

"I can't help the way I look, Father," Luca said with a hint of censure. "Outward appearance has nothing to do with piety. I wish to spend the rest of my days serving God."

"Bah! How can you know what you want when you have experienced nothing of life?" Don Eduardo chided impatiently. "I was remiss to leave you here so long. You will leave with me now, Luca. You must be ready to sail in two weeks aboard the *Santa Cruz* to join your intended. You will be pleased to know that Don Diego has been appointed governor-general of Cuba. He is a powerful man, much respected and admired. You are a lucky girl, Luca."

"Father, he is old and I . . ."

"Enough! I will listen to no more arguments. You will marry Don Diego and that is final. You will travel with a duenna and a priest. During the journey they will instruct you on your wifely duties. Don Diego will expect certain things of you," he said evasively. "An army of seamstresses will work night and day to provide you with a wardrobe fit for the wife of an important man like Don Diego. You must understand that I am doing this because I love you, Luca. You will have a good life with Don Diego."

Luca understood none of it. Why did she have to leave a place of peace and contentment to join a world torn asunder by strife and war? She wasn't completely ignorant of worldly matters. She knew of the tenuous coexistence between England and Spain and had heard about the simmering cauldron of political intrigue at the courts of Philip II of Spain and Elizabeth I of England. Visitors to the convent spoke in whispers about acts of piracy on the high seas. One name in particular made her shiver with dread whenever she heard it.

El Diablo. The Devil posing as an Englishman.

She shuddered, recalling the first time she'd heard the name. It had been several years ago. She'd overheard an overnight guest telling the abbess about the ruthless English privateer who attacked and sank Spanish galleons with almost manic obsession. *He's probably grown rich as a king on Spanish plunder,* she reflected, recoiling in revulsion when she tried to picture the cruel pirate who attacked Spanish ships almost exclusively.

"Did you hear me, Luca?" Don Eduardo repeated impatiently. "Say your good-byes to the abbess and pack your belongings. We must leave immediately."

Though twenty years old, Luca knew it would do little good to protest further. It was degrading to know that all aspects of her life were controlled by men. Her father, her two brothers, and now Don Diego, her betrothed. At least in the convent she had no one to answer to but God.

"I heard you, Father. Is there nothing I can say or do to change your mind?"

"No, daughter, I have your best interests at heart. With Don Diego you will have wealth and position. You will be the pampered wife of an important man. Do you not want children? Don Diego will give you children."

Not until Don Eduardo mentioned children did Luca feel any degree of longing for the kind of life her father had just described. Children of her own would be wonderful, but her mind couldn't picture Don Diego as their father. She had only seen him once. She had been ten years old, and even then he had seemed a stern older man, though he couldn't have been more than twenty-five at the time.

"Very well, Father," Luca said dispiritedly. "Only know that my heart isn't in this marriage."

Aboard the Santa Cruz

Bracing her feet on the pitching deck, Luca leaned into the wind, spindrift clinging to her ebony hair and stinging her luminous dark eyes. Her cheeks were blushing roses against the pale olive of her face, a charming result of the blustery wind. She'd been standing on the pitching deck for hours, staring moodily into the churning sea, wishing herself back at the convent, where life was serene and uncomplicated.

"Please return to the cabin, Luca. You must not catch a chill else Don Diego will be displeased with you, and with me for allowing it."

Luca sent Donna Carlotta an exasperated look. She liked her duenna well enough but thought her much too strict for one still young. Not much older than Luca, Donna Carlotta was a widow whom Don Eduardo had hired to act as duenna and traveling companion to Luca. Also accompanying her was the priest, Father Sebastian, who saw to her spiritual needs during the trip.

"I'm not cold, Carlotta. The wind is most invigorating."

"I find it revolting," Carlotta said. Her face had turned an unnatural shade of green, attesting to the seasickness she had suffered since boarding the ship at Cadiz. "I was hoping this wretched seasickness would pass after the first few weeks at sea, but it only gets worse."

"Go back to the cabin, Carlotta, I am fine. I'm sure Father Sebastian will keep you company."

"*Sí*, I will do that, Luca. He can read to me from the good book. His voice is so soothing."

Luca watched the woman stagger back to the large stern cabin they shared. She had to admit that Carlotta was a most pious and proper chaperon, but quite boring. As for Father Sebastian, the good priest was a stern disciplinarian who had been sent along to make sure Luca reached her betrothed as pure as the day she had left the convent. Each day the priest set aside a time for religious instruction and prayer, which Luca enjoyed. She hoped that once Father Sebastian saw how devout she was, he'd help her avoid this marriage upon which her father was so set.

Staring morosely into the distant horizon, Luca thought she spotted a sail. Squinting her eyes against the glare of the sea, she spied it again, then watched it disappear below the horizon. When it did not reappear, she assumed it was an illusion and turned her eyes in another direction.

Aboard the Avenger

"I see her, Captain. She's a galleon, all right. Riding heavy in the water, she is. Probably loaded with plunder."

Captain Morgan Scott trained his glass on the Spanish galleon just barely in his sights. He had spied her yesterday and had begun tracking her, keeping just far enough behind to avoid detection.

"You're right, Mr. Crawford, she's a big one. Probably carrying twenty or more cannon."

"We can take her, Captain. They're no match for the *Avenger*. Our men are seasoned fighters, itching for another go at the accursed Spaniards. Shall I prepare the men for battle?"

Morgan grinned in vengeful anticipation. "I agree, Mr. Crawford. Pass the word. Ready the ship for battle and distribute arms. Order the gunners to their posts. 'Tis time for El Diablo to take another prize."

"Aye, aye, Captain. We'll show those Spanish bastards what the *Avenger* is capable of."

Aboard the Santa Cruz

Inside her cabin aboard the *Santa Cruz*, Luca knelt beside Father Sebastian, fervently reciting prayers as the exchange of cannon fire exploded around them with a deafening roar. Captain Ortega had sighted the English pirate ship at dawn. As the day progressed it had closed the distance between them, until it came within cannon range. Riding heavy in the water, the *Santa Cruz* was no match for the swifter, lighter *Avenger.* When the shelling began, Luca could only imagine the terrible carnage to be visited on them by the pirate ship.

At the first hint of trouble, Father Sebastian had fallen to his knees in prayer, exhorting Luca and Carlotta to join him. But it seemed as if God was deaf to their entreaties, as the battle on deck continued unabated. After countless prayers, Luca could stand it no longer — she had to find out what was happening. She rose shakily from her knees and approached the door. Cracking it open, she peered outside. She spied Captain Ortega standing on the bridge amid the wreckage of his ship, and she stepped out onto the deck, determined to find out what their chances were of escaping the pirate ship.

"Luca, where are you going?" Carlotta's voice rose on a note of panic.

"To speak with the captain. I can't stay here and do nothing, wondering what's going to happen to us."

"You are doing something, child," Father Sebastian chided. "You're praying for a miracle."

"I'll be right back," Luca said, unmoved by the priest's words as she closed the cabin door firmly behind her. Flames and soot shot up from various places on the tilting deck, and noise from the roaring cannon was nearly deafening as she dodged debris and bodies to reach the captain.

Suddenly a cannonball from the *Avenger* ripped across the deck, slamming into the magazine located next to the cabin where Carlotta and Father Sebastian knelt in prayer. The resulting explosion sent Luca flying across the deck. Picking herself up, she cried out in genuine alarm and raced back to the shattered cabin. The door hung askew on broken hinges and she forced it open, throwing aside smoldering wood and rubble until she found the bodies of her two traveling companions amid the wreckage.

"Captain, help me!" she cried as she tried to find a spark of life in Carlotta's limp body.

But Captain Ortega had problems of his own. The *Avenger* was closing in fast, and his ship was sinking. He could see the pirates preparing grappling hooks and boarding planks and knew that he, his crew, and his passengers faced certain death.

To Luca's horror, Carlotta was beyond human help. Luca turned her attention to the priest. He still breathed, but barely. The rise and fall of his chest was so ragged that Luca feared his death was imminent.

Father Sebastian opened his eyes and saw Luca bending over him. He knew he had little time left on this earth but he was at peace with himself; he had devoted his entire life to preparing to meet God. His last few moments were spent in fear over Luca's fate. Her father had entrusted her into his care, and he prayed for enough time to impart important words of advice to her before death claimed him.

"The enemy, they are boarding?" he asked, his eyes already glazing over.

"*Sí, Padre,*" Luca said sadly. "Captain Ortega never had a chance."

"Listen carefully, child, for I have little time left." Luca bent close to hear Father Sebastian's dying words. "You must not let the pirates defile you. Choose death over dishonor. In time you will be ransomed, but only after you have been violated ruthlessly. You will lack the innocence Don Diego demands of his wife and the mother of his children, and unfortunately you will no longer be suited for a holy life among the pious at the convent. With my dying breath I implore you to think carefully, then do what your conscience demands."

Luca stared at him, aghast. "You would have me kill myself, *Padre?*"

Father Sebastian was beyond answering as he slipped serenely into death, but Luca knew that was exactly what he thought she should do.

Luca rose unsteadily to her feet, suddenly aware of the acrid stench of smoke and blood and of the fierce battle being waged between her countrymen and the English pirates. The ship was burning, listing to the starboard and in danger of sinking, yet Luca stood amid the smoldering shambles of the cabin with two dead bodies at her feet, unable to kill herself as Father Sebastian hinted. Had she not left the cabin when she had, she would have joined them in eternal rest.

Abruptly the terrible noise of battle subsided, and she heard the deep booming voice of an Englishman demanding surrender. Then she heard a name that sent chills down her spine. His name came to her on the smoke-filled winds of fear and dread, passed from mouth to mouth. El Diablo. Moments later that same deep voice ordered the ship searched for plunder, and Luca knew that she had little time left in which to make a choice between death or ravishment by the ruthless El Diablo. Neither choice was palatable. Fingering the small eating dagger she wore at her waist, she contemplated suicide. Two quick slashes across her wrists, and her life's blood would drain from her body before the pirates found her.

And yet . . . wasn't death the coward's way out? It had taken the nuns at the convent years to tame Luca's fiery disposition and subjugate her to their will, but it took only ten seconds for her to regain the stubborn pride and willfulness that her father had despaired of when she was a child. Had Don Eduardo seen her now, her eyes blazing defiantly, her expression neither meek nor submissive, his belief that Luca was not meant for a religious life would have been justified.

"I will not kill myself," Luca declared bravely, "nor will I submit to filthy pirates." Though her words were courageous, she had no adequate weapon save her small knife with which to defend herself, so she turned her thoughts in another direction.

Spying her trunk lying amid the debris of the cabin, she recalled that she had packed her gray nun's habit. She had foolishly thought that during the journey she could impress Father Sebastian with her piety and convince him how wrong it was to force her into a marriage, when what she really wanted was to spend her life serving God. But the priest had brushed aside her protests and adamantly refused to petition Don Eduardo on her behalf. He had been engaged by Luca's father to safely deliver Luca to her fiancé and see that she was properly wed, and he was a man of his word.

A commotion nearby moved Luca to haste; she pushed the sprung door shut and dug in the trunk for her habit. She pulled out the garment, tore off her own dress, and pulled the habit over her head, wrapping the wooden rosary beads around her waist to form a belt. Then she wadded up her rich finery and tossed it through the porthole. In minutes her long ebony hair was pushed beneath a linen headcovering, completing her transformation. She finished without a moment to spare.

Suddenly the door burst from its broken hinges, and a burly pirate covered with blood and grime appeared in the doorway, surveying the wreckage with grim satisfaction. He spied Luca and leered at her, revealing a mouthful of blackened, rotted teeth.

"Well, well, wot 'ave we 'ere?" He stepped inside, avoiding the bodies of Carlotta and the priest, and he reached for Luca. She backed away, tripping over wreckage. He stalked her relentlessly. "Don't be afeared, little gray dove. Old Pete ain't seen a woman since we left the Bahamas. Leastways not one as purty as you."

He lunged, snared Luca by the waist, and dragged her against the unyielding wall of his massive chest. The breath slammed from her lungs, but she quickly found it again, screaming at the top of her voice. Clapping his hand over her mouth, Pete bore her to the deck.

Morgan balanced himself on the listing deck, urging his men to make haste before the *Santa Cruz* sank. They had found riches beyond their wildest imagination aboard the

Spanish galleon, and the men were transferring it to the *Avenger* while he and Stan Crawford herded the Spanish survivors toward the quarterdeck. When Morgan heard the scream he stopped dead in his tracks and swung around to face the Spanish captain, his eyebrow quirked in honest surprise.

"Are there women aboard?"

Captain Ortega remained sullenly uncommunicative. Thinking he didn't speak English, Morgan repeated his question in flawless Spanish, having learned the language fluently during his years of captivity. When Ortega still did not reply, Morgan placed the point of his sword against the man's throat, needing little provocation to ram it home. Ortega's eyes bugged out, and he squawked in protest.

"Senorita Santiego, the shipowner's daughter, and her companion."

"What is your destination?"

"Cuba. Senorita Santiego's fiancé awaits her in Havana."

Morgan's eyes narrowed as he gazed toward the wreckage of the stern cabin, quite certain that that's where the scream had come from. "Take over here, Mr. Crawford."

Morgan strode across the burning deck, noting that all his men but for a few stragglers had already crossed over to the *Avenger* and awaited him there. The deck tilted crazily just as he reached the cabin, and he feared that any passengers remaining aboard would be trapped with the sinking ship.

Kicking aside the broken remnants of the door, Morgan's gaze moved quickly over the carnage inside the cabin, passing over two bodies and coming to rest on the couple grappling on the deck. One of his men lay atop a woman, having the Devil's own time subduing her. He was startled to note that the woman was garbed in the drab gray habit of a nun. Though he'd never held nuns or any other religious zealots in special regard, he grabbed the pirate by the scruff of the neck and flung him away.

"Go back to the *Avenger*, Potter, unless you wish to go down with the ship."

Pete Potter glared sullenly at his captain. "Wot about the woman, Captain? I want her. She's mine."

Luca's eyes widened with fear as she stared at Morgan. She knew without being told that this was the notorious El Diablo, the pirate feared and hated by all Spaniards. He was nothing like what she'd pictured in her mind. El Diablo was magnificently male, his face all hard lines and shadowed planes. In no way did he resemble the Devil, which made him even more dangerous. Golden hair, richly thick, and wickedly curved eyebrows were enhanced by the deep cleft in his chin. And those eyes, so keenly blue and assessing, roved over her with insulting intensity. His hard-muscled body rippled with unleashed power. The strong, rugged lines of his facial features were dominated by a generous mouth, which looked fully capable of being cruel and unrelenting, and a square, aggressive jaw.

"I'll take care of her."

Complaining bitterly, Potter gave Morgan a sullen look as he sidled past him and out the door. El Diablo was a fair master who expected his orders to be obeyed without question but did not hesitate to exact severe punishment if defied. No one aboard the *Avenger* would ever consider mutiny, not even Potter.

Moved by desperation, Luca scrambled to her knees, bowed her head, folded her hands, and prayed as fervently as she knew how. Morgan stared at her in dismay, her piety making him decidedly uncomfortable.

"What is your name?" he asked in Spanish.

A flare of stubborn resistance kept her mute in spite of her fear as she continued to pray most diligently.

Morgan spat out a curse. "Stop that gibberish and answer me! Who are you?"

Luca blinked up at him. "Sister Luca."

"What are you doing aboard the *Santa Cruz*?"

"Don Eduardo engaged me to act as chaperon to his daughter . . . Carlotta Santiego." She knew this one lie for which God would forgive her.

Morgan cast a dispassionate glance at the two bodies lying amid the wreckage of the cabin. "I suppose the dead woman is Carlotta Santiego."

"*Sí.*"

"And the priest?"

"He was sent to protect the virtue of Carlotta and witness the marriage between Carlotta and Don Diego del Fugo."

Morgan gazed into Luca's face, mesmerized by her sultry beauty. Never would he understand why so lovely a woman would choose to cloister herself behind walls, away from society and men. Though the drab gray habit did nothing to enhance her figure or beauty, neither did it detract from it. It would take a blind man not to see through the colorless trappings she wore to find the temptress within. Too bad she was Spanish, he thought, staring at her with barely concealed contempt.

31

Small of stature yet lushly fashioned and fair of face, there was something about her that made Morgan think deliciously lewd thoughts. Not even the loose gray habit stopped him from imagining how it would feel to thrust into the tight warmth of her virgin body. A dark noxious cloud of choking smoke brought Morgan's wayward thoughts under control.

"Captain, the ship's sinking fast! All hands are aboard the *Avenger* and awaiting us." Crawford's voice held a note of desperation.

"Coming, Mr. Crawford!" Morgan called back.

"On your feet," Morgan barked as he grasped Luca's arm and hauled her bodily from the cabin.

"Leave me," Luca insisted. "I'll take my chances with the survivors. I have no ransom value, it will earn you naught to take me with you. I am but a poor nun."

Morgan's cold blue eyes traveled the length of her body, boldly assessing her worth. "Perhaps I have something else in mind for you."

Luca sucked in a ragged breath. Did he mean to rape her despite her claim of being a virtuous nun? Would he pass her on to his men when he finished with her? For the space of a heartbeat she considered throwing herself into the sea to escape the terrible fate that awaited her on this Devil's ship.

Her conjecturing came to an abrupt halt when the deck tilted violently and she fell against Morgan. Cursing violently, he swept her off her feet and flung her over his shoulder like a sack of flour. Sprinting from the cabin and across the sloping deck, he approached the rail, where Mr. Crawford waited for him. Luca cried out in alarm when Morgan effortlessly leaped across the expanse of water separating the two ships, landing lightly on the deck of the *Avenger.* Mr. Crawford followed close on his heels.

Once they stood safely on the deck of the *Avenger* the sails caught the wind, carrying them away from the burning *Santa Cruz.* Luca's last glimpse of the sinking ship was of Captain Ortega and the surviving crew working feverishly to lower the longboat before the ship disappeared beneath the dark, swirling waves.

2

Aboard the Avenger

Morgan didn't dare release his hold on the trembling nun for fear she'd sacrifice herself to the sea. He had no idea why he cared, but he did. She was Spanish, and he despised her for that. Perhaps he should have left her aboard the sinking *Santa Cruz*, he reflected, since obviously she had no ransom value. His rather discerning tastes did not run to innocent members of a religious order. Logic told him he should give her to his men for sport and feel no guilt. But a spark of decency, instilled in him long ago by his parents, prevented him from doing so. She was far too fragile to survive even one night of rough handling.

"I am Captain Morgan Scott," Morgan said as he dragged Luca across the deck. "You are aboard the *Avenger* and at my mercy."

"Wh-where are you taking me?" Luca

asked, cringing beneath Morgan's devilish grin.

"To my cabin."

Luca balked, pulling against the force of Morgan's unrelenting grip. "No!"

"Aye, Sister, or whatever you call yourself. You will be safer there than out here. My crew are good men, but they hate the Spanish as much as I do. The drab rags you wear will not save you from them. If you speak English, I suggest you do so. Hearing your accursed language spoken aboard an English ship will likely incite them to violence."

With little effort Morgan dragged Luca across the deck to his cabin beneath the quarterdeck. Pulling open the door, he shoved her inside. He followed, closing the door behind him and leaning against it. He stared at her, his penetrating gaze as merciless as a sword thrust.

"What in God's name am I going to do with you, Sister Luca?" Morgan mused thoughtfully. "Shall I give you to my men to sport with? I assure you they would be most grateful. Perhaps," he continued in a voice so low and raspy it sent chills down Luca's spine, "I might find some use for you in my bed." Unexpectedly his eyes kindled, excited by the thought of tumbling the sultry beauty who claimed to be a nun.

"Why didn't I listen to Father Sebastian?" Luca lamented, wringing her hands in despair. "He told me it would be better to kill myself than submit to filthy pirates."

"Privateer, Sister, privateer. Sanctioned by the queen of England and sailing under the English flag. Why *didn't* you kill yourself?" he asked curiously.

Luca's chin rose a fraction, and her dark eyes glowed with defiance. "I did not want to die." She answered in English, not flawlessly, but with a charming accent. "I want to live."

He respected her honesty but little else. "You are an enigma, Sister. Your pretense of innocence does not impress me, for beneath those religious trappings lies a body ripe for bedding. Your earthy sensuality belies your piety. Your dark eyes smolder with fire and zest for life, and your beauty would tempt the Devil himself."

"I've heard that El Diablo *is* the Devil," Luca dared to say.

Morgan threw back his head and gave a bark of laughter. "There are few who would dispute that." The hellish gleam in his eyes pierced through the armor of her nun's robes.

He pushed himself away from the door, narrowing the space between them. She retreated, until the backs of her knees came in contact with the bunk. Morgan kept on coming, until he stood scant inches in front of her, a lazy smile stretching his generous lips, making his eyes crinkle at the corners. Intrigued by the smooth olive tones of her skin, he reached out and slid the back of a callused finger down her cheek, amazed at the satiny texture. Boldly his finger continued downward, coming to rest where her flesh disappeared beneath her neckcloth.

Luca exhaled sharply, fearing what he would do next, yet breathlessly excited by his casual caress. "Don't!"

Morgan went still. "Don't? You are my captive, Sister. I can do what I please with you. You are worthless to me as a hostage, you said so yourself. Who would ransom a penniless nun?"

"You could set me ashore on the nearest landfall. I will find my way back home somehow."

"You couldn't survive if I turned you loose. By your own admission you know nothing of the world outside your convent. I will think on what I will do with you."

To Luca his words were easy, deceptively

calm, deliberate. He appeared a man whose soul and emotions were under such rigid control they seemed encased in glacial ice. Had she known what Morgan was really feeling she would have been stunned.

For the first time in years Morgan felt oddly lost and confused. Never had anything like this occurred. He'd always been in control, knew exactly what he must do in any situation. Finding himself adrift in a pair of dark, smoldering eyes was a new experience. Though his hatred for the Spanish had not diminished, Morgan balked at turning the young nun over to his men for sport, or setting her free to be used by others even more cruel than his own crew. Nor did he feel the urge to harm the little saint himself. Indeed, the urges consuming him were far from protective. He actually felt desire for the woman, despite her religious calling and apparent innocence.

Never had another man looked at Luca like Morgan Scott dared to do. Indeed, she had seen few men at the convent, but she did recognize danger when she encountered it. And dangerous was precisely the word to describe the look in Morgan's blue eyes. She stared back at him, too innocent to realize what her sultry gaze was doing to him. Before she knew what was happening, he curled his fingers around her neck and dragged her against him.

Luca cried out in alarm when she felt the searing heat of Morgan's lips against hers and the wet slide of his tongue tasting her. The act was so blatantly intimate that she reared back in shock, covering her mouth with her trembling hand. It was her first kiss ever, and she felt a melting heat burst inside her, igniting some corner of herself that had remained untouched by human emotions. She felt vulnerable and fragile and . . . frightened. So very frightened. Did Morgan Scott intend to ravish her? Her answer became clear when his hands moved down her back to her buttocks and she felt a strange swelling pushing against her stomach when he pulled her tightly against him.

Driven by desperation and fear, Luca shoved Morgan away, dropped to her knees, and folded her hands in fervent prayer. She prayed aloud, raising her eyes and voice to heaven, hoping her piety would dampen the handsome pirate's lecherous intentions.

"Dear sweet Savior," she prayed, "keep me pure in mind and body. Protect me from these English heathens. If I am brutally ravished, give me the strength to kill myself afterward." She lowered her head and prayed silently while Morgan stared down at her, impressed by the strength of her faith.

There were few things that defeated Morgan Scott, yet Luca's piety was one of them. Desire left him as quickly as it had swelled his manhood only moments before. Lord knows he still wanted the sultry Spanish witch, but her unshakable faith had unmanned him.

"Stay on your knees, Sister, and pray to your heart's content," he barked hoarsely. "Ravishing an innocent zealot holds little appeal for me. I might not respect your religious calling, but I admire the way in which you use it to thwart my intentions." His eyes narrowed and his voice grew harsh. "You are amazingly brave, Sister Luca. I would like to show you what you are missing by hiding behind that ugly habit and coif. Perhaps I still will if you overset me with your constant prayers," he threatened.

Luca's prayers came to an abrupt halt. "I am no fraud. I have dedicated myself to God and the holy life. I know nothing of worldly things so I miss nothing. If I overset you, it is to remind you that my body is sacrosanct."

Morgan laughed harshly. "If I want your body I'll take it at my leisure. Or give you to my men. I haven't yet decided. I'll take my leave now so you can continue your prayers.

But know this, Spanish witch, the most fervent supplications will not save you if I decide you aren't worth the trouble."

Turning on his heel, he stormed out of the cabin.

Luca's small frame seemed to collapse inward once she was alone. She swayed on her knees, trembling when she recalled Morgan's fierce words and threatening manner. She touched her mouth lightly, remembering the softness of his lips on hers, feeling the lingering heat of his kiss. Her cheek still burned from the pressure of his callused finger, and she wondered not for the first time what manner of man he was.

Captain Morgan Scott hated Spaniards, that much was evident, and apparently he had no qualms about killing them. Would she be next? Obviously the man had no respect for religion or human life. Yet he had shown extraordinary restraint where she was concerned, which she attributed entirely to her piety. When he had looked at her with that wicked glow in his eyes, she had fallen to her knees in prayer and he had turned away from her in disgust. If that was what it took to remain unmolested, then she would play the role of pious nun to the hilt. She would rely on her faith to convince El Diablo to set her free.

★ ★ ★

"What do you intend to do with the Spanish wench, Captain? The crew are distracted by her presence. They have requested that you give her over to them when you're through with her."

Morgan's expression was thoughtful as he turned to acknowledge Stan Crawford, his first mate and friend of long standing. Similar in looks, build, and mind, they both held a healthy hatred for the Spanish. They had met shortly after Morgan had received permission from the queen to operate as a privateer under the English flag. Once Morgan's inheritance had been restored, he'd bought a ship, outfitted it with cannon, and hired Crawford as first mate. Crawford had tasted Spanish cruelty and hated them almost as much as Morgan did. Together they had made a formidable team, as well as become fast friends.

"I haven't decided," Morgan said slowly. " 'Tis our custom to ransom female captives."

"A Spaniard is a Spaniard whether they be male or female," Crawford intoned dryly. "Are you forgetting what the bastards did to you?"

Morgan's body tensed. "I've forgotten nothing." He paused, then said, "The

42

woman belongs to a Papist order. Are the men so eager to ravish a holy woman?"

Crawford grinned. "Beneath that gray rag is a woman like any other. And you have to admit she is comely. The men have been at sea for months, it matters little to them what the woman is."

Morgan looked away. "I freely admit the wench is most appealing, and endlessly vexing. Yet something about her troubles me. She seems sincere about her faith. But she is too earthy, too damn sensual to be what she claims. Hidden in the depths of those dark eyes is a fiery nature even she isn't aware of."

Crawford sent Morgan a troubled glance. "Do you fancy the wench, Morgan? If so, bed her and get her out of your system. Then give her to the men. It wouldn't do to keep her aboard too long; she'll cause trouble for sure. The entire crew will be fighting over her after you've finished with her."

"I do not fancy the witch, Stan," Morgan denied unconvincingly. "Man, woman, or child, I cannot abide the Spanish. You know that as well as I."

"Aye, but there is always a first time," Crawford warned. "Beware, Morgan, don't let the wench beguile you. Keep in mind that she is probably bald as an egg beneath that hideous headcloth she wears."

"See to your duties, Mr. Crawford," Morgan said with a hint of annoyance, "and I'll see to mine. Bald women never did appeal to me, but I admit the black-eyed witch intrigues me as none other has in a long time. Impress upon the men that she's not to be touched until I've had my fill of her."

Suppressing a grin, Crawford saluted smartly and walked away, leaving Morgan confused and undecided about his captive's fate. His men wanted the woman, and ordinarily he wouldn't balk at giving her over to them. He had no idea what was preventing him from doing what his conscience demanded. Was it the woman's piety? Her pleading dark eyes that spoke eloquently of mysteries he longed to discover? The hint of a passion even she was unaware of? Or could it be the lush promise of her virgin body? What was there about her that made her different from other women?

Morgan knew it wasn't the young nun's beauty alone, for he'd tumbled women even more beautiful and not been fascinated by them. And now he must decide what was to be done with her. His gaze swept over the deck, where his crew toiled to clear away wreckage inflicted by the Spanish galleon. Though fiercely loyal, most were rough men, crude of speech and manners. He winced at the thought of any one of them tearing into Sister Luca's innocent, virginal body. He knew if he gave her into their keeping that more than one man would claim her fragile body in the most violent ways imaginable. She wouldn't last the night.

Why should he care what happened to the Spanish witch?

Her Spanish blood should have made Morgan's decision simple, but it only complicated matters. Had he grown so callous, so heartless, so utterly devoid of honor that he would allow his men to ravish a holy woman? Or ravish her himself?

His grim thoughts were interrupted by the first mate, who had returned to report on damage sustained by the *Avenger.* "Captain, the men have discovered more damage from the galleon's guns than originally thought. We need to head to port for repairs. Shall we turn back to England or set a course for Andros?"

"Andros, Mr. Crawford," Morgan said succinctly. The answer he had sought concerning Sister Luca suddenly became clear. "The men are due for a short respite from the sea, and I certainly can use the time ashore to attend to my plantation."

Crawford cleared his throat. "What about the woman, Morgan?"

"The nun will come with us. Mayhap she can save a few souls on our island."

Luca paced the cramped length of the cabin, waiting for the pirate to return and announce her fate. After he had left she had tried the door to see if it was locked. It hadn't been, but an armed guard stood outside and leered at her when he saw her head poking through the opening. She had slammed the door shut immediately, her heart beating like a trip-hammer.

Luca had no delusions about the English pirate. He might look like an angel, but blackness and corruption lay hidden beneath his handsome exterior. If he turned her over to his men, she would find a way to throw herself into the sea first. Father Sebastian had been right all along, she reflected. An honorable death was preferable to being ravished by English pirates. But oh, Holy Mother, she didn't want to die!

Luca heard a footfall outside the cabin and braced herself for the worst. Scant moments before the door was flung open, she fell to her knees and bowed her head. Piety had worked before, and she intended to use it again and again in her future dealings with Morgan Scott.

"Still on your knees, I see," Morgan mocked sarcastically when he entered. "I am not impressed with your piety. Nor are my men. They see you only as a woman, fashioned for men's pleasure like any other woman."

Luca's head shot up. "You heartless brute! You've decided to give me to your men!"

Morgan grinned at her, enjoying the flash of defiance in her dark eyes. "Aye, after I've had my fill of you. But truth to tell, you don't appeal to me," he lied. "Are you truly bald beneath your headcloth?"

Thank God Morgan couldn't see the luxuriant fall of ebony hair concealed beneath her headcovering. Instantly Luca decided to cut off all her hair the first chance she got, before he discovered her secret. "*Sí*, as bald as an onion," Luca conceded. "Do you wish to see?" With shaking hands, she made as if to remove the headcovering. It was a bold ploy, and Luca prayed she wouldn't be sorry.

Morgan grimaced, visibly repulsed. He had no wish to see as beautiful a woman as Luca shorn of her crowning glory. He'd heard Queen Elizabeth was bald but could not credit it. He had never seen her without her lush red wig.

"Nay, I have no wish to look upon your bald head. 'Tis a sacrilege to defile a woman in such a way."

"Yet you would defile me in other ways even more vile," Luca countered. Her eyes challenged him to deny it. He could not.

"You are Spanish," Morgan bit out, as if that made his intentions perfectly acceptable. "I did not come here to argue with you."

"Why did you come?"

"To inform you of your fate." He watched her with brooding intensity. "Stand up, I don't like talking to the top of your head, and I'm growing weary of your prayers. Your knees must surely be raw from all that kneeling."

Luca rose gracefully, despite her stiff limbs. She faced Morgan squarely, her chin tilted upward. Her behavior was so militant that she could not credit how greatly she had changed in so short a time. Obviously ten years behind convent walls had not tamed her fiery disposition or the rebellious spirit her father had despaired of long ago. She blamed her lapse on a scurrilous pirate known as El Diablo.

"What have you decided, Captain?" There was an undeniable spark of challenge in her dark eyes.

Morgan quelled his sudden irritation with the Spanish vixen. Why did this proud Spanish nun make him feel like the lowest kind of cur? It was difficult to think rationally with her standing so close to him, and against his will he found himself admiring her spark of defiance. Then the sweet scent of roses drifted across the narrow space dividing them, and he frowned, more than a little surprised to discover that nuns wore perfume. He shook his head to clear it of thoughts far too disturbing for comfort, but it didn't work. His fingers itched to touch her. He wanted to mount her, pound himself into her, hear her gasping with sweet release.

My God, was he losing his mind? He should do what his conscience demanded. Ravish her, then let his men have her.

"The ship is in need of repairs. I'm taking her to our home port in the Bahamas. You will come with us."

Luca swallowed hard. "Why? Of what good am I to you?"

"Perhaps I will find some value in you. Do you come from a rich family? Would they be willing to pay ransom for your return?"

Luca stared at him. If she told him the truth, the nun's habit would no longer protect her. If he ransomed her back to her father, Don Eduardo would send her to Cuba to a marriage she did not want. But if she continued with her charade, the possibility existed that she might talk Morgan into letting her go. Then she could make her way back home, quietly reenter the convent, and take her final vows. By the time her father found out, it would be too late to do anything about it.

Luca knew she could place herself in grave danger if she gave the pirate captain the wrong answer. On one hand, she had no guarantee she wouldn't be ravished if she admitted to being Luca Santiego, and on the other hand, claiming to be a nun might not deter the pirate from any nefarious deeds. Yet, she had to say something. She made her decision in a split second.

"Alas, my family is poor, Captain. I was placed in the convent at the age of ten to relieve them of another mouth to feed. I was the only girl in our large family. The boys were useful to work our worthless piece of land, and I was given over to the church. I beg you to free me so I may return to the convent."

"I cannot do that. My men would mutiny

if I released you. They expect me to give you to them when I'm finished with you."

Luca swallowed visibly. Fear sent icy claws deep into her gut. "I beg you to spare me. I've done nothing to you. Why do you bear such hatred toward my countrymen?"

Morgan's expression hardened and he looked past her, stirred by memories she couldn't begin to understand. He could still feel the whip flaying his back and hear his Spanish tormentors laughing cruelly as they threw saltwater on his wounds and watched him writhe in pain. They had worked him excessively and kept him on starvation rations for five years, and he wouldn't have survived much longer under those intolerable conditions. If not for the Spanish, his parents and siblings would still be alive today. And the woman standing before him carried the accursed blood of Spanish murderers.

Luca recoiled in terror when she saw Morgan's fierce expression. Whatever her countrymen had done to him must have been terrible indeed, she reflected dimly.

Morgan noted her fear and gave her a lethal smile. "You are wise to fear me, Sister Luca. Your countrymen made my life a living Hell and destroyed everything I once held dear. I vowed no mercy for the Spanish, and now you must suffer for it. You will accompany the *Avenger* to Andros and submit to me in any way I want you."

Standing so close to the pirate, Luca felt overwhelmed by the solid, unyielding strength in him. The rush of his anger, the heat of his body . . . the tenacity and determination of this man, the sheer power he wielded flooded her with a dread so intense she felt utterly without hope. Yet despite all she knew about the English pirate, all the terrible things she'd heard that should have sent her swooning, what she felt was a heady sense of being alive after merely existing for many years.

"I will kill myself before I allow you or any of your vicious men to touch me," she vowed, sending Morgan a look of utter disdain. It was an empty threat, for she didn't think she had the courage to kill herself. Hopefully, though, it would make the pirate think twice about touching her.

Morgan's generous mouth curved upward in a smile that offered little comfort. "Oh, no, Sister, death is the easy way out, and you are no coward. Your eyes speak clearly of your love for life. It will be amusing to let you stew about your fate. Perhaps I'll take you tonight, in my bunk. Then again, I may wait until we reach Andros.

Or," he added with a careless toss of his head, "I may decide you're too much trouble and give you to my men immediately. You aren't really my type, but my crew isn't so discerning." His eyes raked the length of her body with insulting intensity. "If you've a mind to, you could change my mind."

Luca felt a choking sensation so fierce she could barely swallow past the lump that had formed in her throat. The well-defined angle of Morgan's jaw was clenched so tight she could see a muscle twitch convulsively beneath the tanned skin of his lean cheek. She didn't doubt his words for a minute. His hatred for the Spanish was too violent, too deeply ingrained and too long-standing for her to expect mercy from him. She could think of no way to change his mind, but that didn't stop her from falling back on a method that had worked in the past. Surely God wouldn't forsake her, would he?

Falling to her knees, she bowed her head and prayed as fervently as she knew how.

3

Luca prayed in earnest long after Morgan stomped from the cabin in disgust. The air around her still vibrated from his commanding presence, and she felt as if she had been caught up in a violent tempest. A tempest named El Diablo. She was shaking like a leaf when she finally rose from her knees. The vile rogue affected her in ways she didn't understand. Why hadn't she listened to Father Sebastian? Why was she too cowardly to kill herself? She trembled with the knowledge of what he would do to her tonight when he returned. That terrifying thought sent her onto her knees again.

Morgan stormed from the cabin, his temper dangling by a single thread. The little Spanish witch had him doubting the very motives that drove him so relentlessly toward his quest for revenge. She had him questioning his own sanity, wondering why he had allowed her to get to him. Why couldn't he just use her and be done with it? Or give her to his men if she didn't appeal to him? Trouble was, she appealed to him too much. Taking her to Andros was madness, he knew. It annoyed him that he didn't even know his own intentions where Sister Luca was concerned.

"Something bothering you, Morgan?" Stan Crawford asked once Morgan reached the bridge.

Morgan sent him an austere look. "Should there be?"

Crawford grinned. "Not as far as I can tell. What of the nun? Will you sample her yourself or give her to the men?" He thought he already knew the answer, but he wanted to hear it from Morgan. "Surely something so simple as a woman's fate shouldn't bother El Diablo."

"She's mine!" Morgan said with a fierceness that took Crawford by surprise. "I'm taking her to Andros. If and when I tire of her, you'll be the first to know."

Crawford did a poor job of disguising his amusement. "I'm surprised, Morgan. Innocent virgins normally don't appeal to you. What do you see in Sister Luca that I don't?" His eyes narrowed speculatively. "Or have you already sampled her and found her to your liking? Perhaps you'll share her."

Morgan stiffened. "Don't press your luck, Mr. Crawford. Our long-standing friendship doesn't give you leave to question your captain's judgment. I suggest you go about your duties."

"Aye, aye, Captain Scott," Crawford said, snapping to attention. It wasn't often that Morgan flaunted his rank, but when he did Stan knew enough to back off.

Crawford recalled the countless times he and Morgan had shared women without coming to blows over any one of them. Not only had they shared women but they also shared a mutual hatred for the Spanish. He too had felt the lash of a Spanish whip during the six months he had been a Spanish captive. What was there about the Spanish nun, Crawford wondered, that made Morgan so testy? If Morgan hadn't already sampled her, Crawford hoped to Hell he'd do it soon, or Crawford and the crew would suffer the brunt of Morgan's temper.

When it grew dark, someone brought Luca a tray. The rough sailor stared at her for a brief moment, then quickly left. Though the food looked appetizing enough Luca couldn't swallow a bite. The implied menace of Morgan's threats did terrible things to her mind. She pictured herself at his mercy. She couldn't look at the oversized bunk without imagining what a powerful man like El Diablo could do to her. She wasn't exactly sure how rape was accomplished, which made her vivid imagination all the more terrifying. If only she had a weapon.

With a burst of excitement she remembered the small eating dagger she'd placed in her pocket after she'd donned her nun's robes. Thrusting her hand into the pocket, she was comforted by the security of cold steel, meager though it might be. Did she have the nerve to use it in her own defense? Contemplating the consequences gave Luca the courage she needed when the cabin door burst open and Morgan Scott stepped inside, bigger than life and twice as terrifying.

He stared at her distractedly, noting the fear transforming her nearly perfect features. His gaze fell to the tray, which sat before her untouched.

"Is the food not to your liking?" he asked, unbuckling his sword as he strode across the room. "I thought religious disciples were accustomed to meager rations and poor fare. My cook does wonders with the food at hand, you should try it." He removed his sword and flung it onto a chair. His jacket followed.

Luca leaped to her feet and backed away. "Don't come any closer."

"Your virtue is safe for the moment, I doubt I could rouse myself enough to partake of your dubious charms." He sent her a look that made Luca wince. Was she so unattractive that she actually repelled him?

Good, she thought, awash in relief. That's exactly what she'd intended when she'd dressed herself in the drab garb of a cloistered nun. The abbess would be proud of her. Her expression must have reflected her thoughts, for Morgan gave her an impudent grin that sent her heart plummeting down to her heels.

"Smugness does not become you, Sister Luca. I didn't say I won't feel differently tomorrow, or even ten minutes from now. If I want you I will have you, but I'd rather keep you guessing. Besides, I want to be well rested when I attempt you." He leered at her. "I'm sure my patience will be amply rewarded."

Horrified, Luca gaped at him. "You're a monster, Captain Scott. I am neither frightened nor tempted by the Devil." She eyed his discarded sword with longing.

Morgan stepped closer, looming over her

small form in all his male splendor. "Are you not, Sister? As long as we're trading insults, I think you're a fraud. I've thought long and hard and come to the conclusion that you are no nun. The unholy fire in your eyes denies the very existence of your piety. You're too haughty by far to be the meek holy woman you claim to be. You are neither gentle-natured nor humble. Who are you, really?"

He was so close Luca could feel the hot rush of his breath against her cheek. She tried to retreat, but there was no place to go. She fingered the knife in her pocket and glared up at him defiantly. "I told you who I am. I am Sister Luca, recently from the Mother Of God convent. I was told by the Reverend Mother to accompany Senorita Carlotta Santiego to Havana. If you return me to Spain, I will remember you in my prayers until the day I die."

"I do not want your prayers, Sister Luca," Morgan said. His voice was low and rough, as if he was having great difficulty controlling his breathing. "Perhaps I want something else from you. Something that will make us both happy."

Luca's mouth went dry. The tip of her tongue flicked out to moisten her lips. She thought she heard Morgan groan but couldn't be sure. "I . . . I don't know what you're talking about."

Morgan's hand thrust forward to grasp her chin. "Don't you? I could show you. I may be too tired to attempt you, but I'd have to be on my deathbed to resist such a sweet invitation."

Luca went still, enthralled by the blue intensity of Morgan's eyes. She had thought them merely blue, but now she saw that they were the gray blue of a storm-tossed sea, tumultuous with glittering highlights of pure silver. She'd never seen eyes exactly like that before. Devil's eyes. She gulped in dismay and tried to form a reply to his daunting words.

"I offered no invitation."

"Ah, but you did." His head lowered a fraction, his blond hair brushing her forehead as his lips touched hers.

Fire. Pure fire. At first there was a burning sensation in the place where their lips melded. But when his mouth covered hers fully and his tongue slid wetly across the seam of her lips, the burning turned into a raging inferno that rushed through her veins to places unmentionable. When she tried to pull away he grasped her arms, holding her in place while he plundered her mouth. When he tried to force his tongue into her mouth, she gasped in shock, unwittingly giving his tongue free access to the sweet warmth within.

Never had Luca felt anything quite like the overwhelming magnetism of Morgan's kiss. She wanted to kiss him back! She ached to wind her arms around his neck and run her hands through the golden tangle of his hair. She wanted to. . . . The things his kiss made her want had no name. It was wrong. So very wrong. She shouldn't feel like this. The man was an enemy. He was a vicious pirate who had kidnapped her and intended to rape her. That thought brought a semblance of sanity to her scattered emotions even as Morgan's hands grew bolder, searching out places no man had a right to touch. She knew she had to do something, anything to break this man's spell upon her before she was completely at his mercy.

The knife!

Reaching into her pocket, she dragged the tiny weapon out and upward, pressing it into a vulnerable spot on Morgan's neck. His hands fell away as he abruptly ended the kiss, staring down at her with a perverse kind of admiration. The little saint wrapped her virtue around her like a damn holy shroud.

"Don't touch me. Don't ever touch me again."

A smile tugged at his lips. "That's going to be hard to do. Where did you get the knife?"

"It's mine. Back away or you'll not live to see another day."

It was all Morgan could do to keep from laughing outright. What did she think she could accomplish with that toothpick? With a flick of his wrist he could disarm her, even hurt her if he wished. It would take little effort on his part to throw her on the bunk, push her skirts up, spread her legs, and take his pleasure. All Spaniards were his enemy. Why should one Spanish witch who claimed to be a holy woman be different from the others?

"How fierce you are, Sister Luca," Morgan mocked.

"I mean what I say, Captain."

"Do you, now? Very well, do your worst. Slit my throat, I dare you." His eyes glittered dangerously. When the blade drew a drop of blood, he did not react as she expected. "Before you do," he added ominously, "perhaps you should consider this. My death will distress my men beyond reason. They will make you suffer, and I assure you it won't be pleasant."

Luca's hand faltered.

"Wouldn't it be preferable to submit to me rather than take your chances with my crew? My men are a brutal lot. I doubt you'd last the night."

"I will kill myself first!"

She said it so fiercely that Morgan did not doubt for a minute she possessed the courage to carry out her threat. He was also aware that he had allowed this game to get out of hand. Luca couldn't hurt him with her little toothpick, but for some unexplained reason he didn't want the feisty little saint who possessed more courage than sense to be harmed.

With a swift movement quicker even than the eye, Luca found herself relieved of the knife and encased in the prison of Morgan's arms. Tears stung her eyes when she realized what had happened, but she wouldn't let them fall.

"Now what, *Sister* Luca? Where is your courage now?"

"Contemptible, vile . . . pirate!"

"Privateer. There's a difference. I only attack and plunder Spaniards."

"Let me go!"

"Gladly." He released her instantly, and she stumbled before righting herself. "Go to bed. I've suddenly lost interest. But I'll keep this little toothpick of yours just in case you decide to gullet me during the night."

Luca glanced at the bunk in horror. Did he expect her to lie beside him? When she looked at him for clarification, she was stunned to see that he had removed his black silk shirt and stood clad only in tight black trousers molded to his strong legs and thighs, and leather boots. She blanched and looked away, but not before she caught a glimpse of his bronzed chest and shoulders, rippling with thick coils of ropy muscles. And the mysterious bulge straining the front of his trousers.

"Do you intend sleeping in that hideous coif?" Morgan asked disdainfully. "I assure you your bald head will not frighten me. Disgust me, mayhap, but not frighten me."

"I prefer keeping it on," Luca insisted. If she took it off and revealed her long hair, he'd see through her pretense. Though nuns normally did not shave their heads, they nevertheless kept their hair short beneath their headcoverings. She had not taken her final vows, and until she did she had been allowed to keep her luxurious fall of ebony hair.

"Get into bed," Morgan ordered crisply. He untied the lacings on the front of his trousers and bent to remove his boots.

"What are you going to do?" Her voice held a note of panic.

"Sleep." He leered at her. "Unless you have a better idea."

"I won't lie beside you." Her lips thinned stubbornly.

Morgan glared at her, then shrugged. "Suit yourself. The deck gets rather hard after the first couple of hours."

"I'm accustomed to hardship. The convent offers little physical comfort. We live a life of austerity and prayer."

He nodded curtly. "You may do as you please for now. I'll let you know when I desire your presence in my bed."

Luca tried not to stare at his bare chest, but it was difficult not to. She knew so little of a man's anatomy. Oblivious to her shocked perusal, he sat on the edge of the bunk and removed his trousers. Luca's cry of dismay brought his eyes back to her. He gave her a cocky smile. She whirled on her heel, her face flaming red. She heard his footsteps behind her but refused to look up.

Her relief was enormous when he dropped a blanket and pillow on the deck beside her and turned away. She didn't want to look at his nude body, but when she heard him moving about, she couldn't help glancing over her shoulder at him, keeping her gaze on his feet. He walked casually to the chair and retrieved his sword.

"This will be safer with me," he said, carrying the sword to the bunk with him. She heard a shifting of bedclothes, then silence. Then came sudden darkness, and Luca realized he had doused the lamp swinging from the ceiling above him.

Still she did not move, fearing he might change his mind and demand her presence in his bed. She stood motionless, scarcely daring to breathe, until she heard the even cadence of his breathing and knew he was asleep. Only then did she wrap herself in the blanket and lay down on the hard wooden deck.

Despite the pillow beneath her head, the coif made it nearly impossible to seek a comfortable position. Her head itched beneath the linen cloth, and she longed for a comb to run through her tangled hair. Or better still, a scissors to cut it all off. Her one concession to comfort was to remove her shoes and stockings. She fell asleep almost instantly, wearied from her encounter with El Diablo. Unfortunately her dreams were fraught with images of the virile captain, his nude body displayed in all its masculine beauty.

Without his trousers.

God help her.

Morgan did not easily find sleep despite the forced cadence of his breathing. He lay awake, fiercely aware of the woman who claimed to be a nun. She affected him in ways that made him uncomfortable. There had been many women in his life. He was a virile man, one who took sensual pleasure in women and the sexual relief they brought him. There were many ports and many women. None were like Sister Luca. What was it about the little nun that made him want her? He should just take her like his body demanded and promptly forget her. She was a Spaniard, wasn't she? He had never known a Spaniard he hadn't hated with consuming passion.

She was a nun.

He didn't believe her for a minute.

He wanted her. It would be so easy to disregard her holy calling and take her body. So easy . . .

Was she truly a holy woman?

He glanced down at Luca, curled up on the hard deck, stunned by the direction of his thoughts. He'd captured one or two Spanish women before and had promptly ransomed them. He had never felt desire for them despite their willingness to accommodate El Diablo. One in particular had made it quite apparent that she fancied him. But she hadn't appealed to him. He found no beauty in her dark, sloe-eyed features, and so he had rebuffed her.

Morgan sighed raggedly and turned toward the wall. Why should he worry about the comfort of a Spanish witch? Sleeping on the deck had been her choice. So be it.

Luca awoke to the morning sun slanting through the open port window. She gasped in shock when she realized she was lying in Morgan's bunk and leaped up as if burned, staring down at the rumpled bed in horror. How had she gotten from the floor to the bed? She had no memory of moving or being moved. Where was the pirate? What had he done to her?

Taking stock of her clothing, she appeared to be lacking nothing that she'd worn the previous day. Her body felt stiff from sleeping on the hard floor, but other than that she suffered no pain in unusual places. She had no time for further inspection, for the door opened and Morgan stepped inside, closing the door firmly behind him. He carried a tray from which delicious odors emanated.

"Ah, you're awake, I see. I've brought you something to eat. You must be hungry after skipping supper last night." He set the tray down on the desk, pushing a map aside as he did so.

Luca's mouth watered. "I have no appetite," she lied. But her stomach betrayed her, for it rumbled loud enough for Morgan to hear. "H-how did I get on the bunk?"

"I put you there," Morgan said. "I arose at dawn. You looked so uncomfortable I moved you to the bunk. You were still sleeping soundly when I left the cabin."

"You didn't . . ." She licked her lips, uncertain how to continue. "You didn't . . . take advantage of me, did you? Are you evil enough to defile a handmaiden of God?"

Morgan scowled so fiercely that Luca leaped back in alarm. "When I take you I want you awake to know it. I want you responsive in my arms, not unconscious and unaware of what I am doing to you. I may be a bastard, but there are some things even I will not stoop to. Eat now. I have a ship to run." He turned to leave.

"Wait!" Morgan paused but did not turn around. "May I . . . may I walk out on deck?"

"My men are loyal, but pirates nonetheless, Sister Luca. I cannot protect you from them once you step outside this cabin. They will assume that I have already tired of you and that they are free to satisfy their urges.

You may do as you please, but if you do not wish to submit to my crew, then I suggest you remain safely inside."

A shudder went through Luca. She believed him. Were all men so vile? So reprehensible? By the time he had proceeded out the door she knew that wild horses couldn't drive her out of the cabin. The captain's dubious protection was preferable to being ravished by the entire crew.

Morgan chuckled to himself as he strode away. He hadn't exactly been truthful with Luca. His men might want her, but they would obey his orders or suffer the consequences. After he had spoken with them this morning not one man among them would dare lay a hand on her without his permission.

Luca watched him leave as the delicious aroma drew her to the tray of food. She had to keep up her strength, didn't she? With that thought in mind she quickly devoured the contents of the entire tray, finding it amazingly palatable for ship's fare. She had no sooner finished than she heard a discreet knock on the door. She watched in trepidation as the door opened without invitation and the first mate stepped inside, carrying a pitcher of water and a stack of soft cloths.

"The captain thought you'd like some

water. 'Tis the closest thing we can come to a bath. That will have to wait until we reach Andros."

Crawford set the pitcher down on the washstand and boldly assessed her. He wondered if Morgan had taken her last night. Judging from the captain's vile mood, he assumed the virtuous little nun had managed to keep her virginity intact. It wasn't like Morgan to lust after a Spanish slut, no matter how beautiful or desirable. Yet this little gray dove had Morgan tied in knots. It puzzled Crawford. He thought he knew Morgan better than any man alive, and it wasn't like Morgan to deprive himself of something that was his for the taking, something he wanted desperately, as he obviously did this Spanish nun.

"Is something wrong?" Luca asked, smarting under Crawford's intense scrutiny.

Crawford gave her a cocky grin. "Are you aware of what you're doing to Captain Scott? Why don't you surrender and save you both time and trouble? In the end he'll have his way."

Luca bristled indignantly. "Surrender? No, never! I am a nun. To defile me is to defile God."

"God deserted Morgan when he needed Him."

71

Luca gasped aloud. "You blaspheme! How like the Godless English. You may tell your captain that I will fight him with my dying breath."

Crawford shook his head. "No one need die, Sister. I am but warning you that Morgan isn't a patient man, and the crew prefers to have him happy. I prefer him happy."

"You can go to the Devil, Mr. Crawford!"

"Where did you learn English? You have an excellent command of the language for a nun." Like Morgan, he also suspected the fiery Spaniard wasn't what she claimed.

"I had excellent teachers at the convent. My studies began at age ten, and I found I had a natural affinity for foreign languages. I also speak a smattering of French and German."

"No wonder you intrigue Morgan," Crawford intoned dryly. "Beauty and brains are rare in a woman. Are all nuns as well educated as you?"

Was he baiting her? She couldn't admit that her father had demanded that she be educated so as not to embarrass her future husband. Don Diego del Fugo was a very learned and powerful man who needed a wife as bright as she was beautiful. Don

Eduardo had been generous to his only daughter in regards to her education.

"I can only speak for myself, Mr. Crawford. Thank you for the water."

Crawford recognized a dismissal when he heard one, and he turned to leave. "Oh, by the way," he added before he stepped through the door, "there's a piss — uh — a chamber pot beneath the bed. You may use it. The cook's helper comes in and empties it once a day."

Luca's face flamed. In truth she was in desperate need of a chamber pot but was too embarrassed to ask the despicable Captain Morgan Scott for one. She wondered if Morgan had instructed Mr. Crawford to mention it. She did appreciate the water, though, for she hadn't had a decent wash since she'd been abducted from the *Santa Cruz.*

When she noted there was no bolt on the door, Luca did the next best thing. She wedged a chair beneath the door handle. Then she quickly washed, removing the upper part of her robe briefly, then pushing up her skirts to reach her legs. She debated about removing her headcovering and did so reluctantly, her eye on the door lest the pirate burst through the meager barrier and discover her secret. She wished she had her little eating knife so she could cut off her glorious mane of hair.

After she finished washing she eyed Morgan's desk with interest. A veritable treasure trove, she thought, opening the drawers in rapid succession. The best she could hope for was a letter opener, but if it was sharp enough it would do the job of cutting her locks. Luck was with her. In the bottom drawer Luca found a small grooming shears. She supposed Morgan used it to trim his hair. But when she lifted the scissors to her head, her hands shook. Her hair was her one physical attribute in which she took pride. She knew it would have to be cut when she took her final vows, but until then she had jealously groomed and preserved her long, lustrous locks. Now she was faced with a painful choice. Would she prefer dispensing with her virtue or her hair? It was no choice at all. She must protect her virtue against the virile pirate and his overwhelming power over her.

She worked quickly, efficiently, whacking off great hanks of hair without benefit of a mirror. Tears ran down her cheeks as the pile of shorn hair grew. She had no idea if she was cutting evenly, nor did she care. She only knew she had to finish and get rid of the evidence before Captain Scott returned.

The deed was finally done. Carefully gathering up the black locks she walked to the porthole, which had been left open to catch the breeze, and threw every last strand into the sea. She watched dispassionately as the dark locks hovered on the crest of a wave, then disappeared beneath the surface. Then she turned away and replaced her headcovering. And not a moment too soon. The door handle rattled, and suddenly the chair flew away as Morgan burst through the door.

"What did you hope to accomplish with the chair?" The sardonic tilt of his eyebrow told her just how ineffectual he thought her ploy to keep him out actually was.

"I needed privacy to wash."

"No one but me will ever enter this cabin without my permission."

"Is that supposed to make me feel better?"

Morgan smiled. "Soon, my little nun. Soon you will beg for my attention."

"When the moon spins and the stars explode!"

"I can make that happen," he promised. His voice lowered to a husky whisper. "When I bring you to pleasure you will catch the spinning moon and reach for the stars."

His seductive words sent Luca's senses

whirling. She had no idea what he was talking about, but somehow she suspected he could make it happen if she allowed it. "Your ego is severely overinflated, Captain."

"Is it, little witch? Perhaps we should test my theory." He walked slowly toward her. She turned to avoid him, but he was too fast for her. Besides, there was no place to go. He grabbed her and pulled her against him. She felt his incredible heat through his clothing and hers.

"What is it you want from me?" she cried. "Look at me! My behavior is neither seductive nor lewd. I'm wrapped from head to toe in drab gray, nothing is showing but my face. Surely there are more attractive women than me. I am a nun, a holy woman. I know nothing of worldly things."

"If you think those robes you're wearing will make you unattractive, you are sadly mistaken. I would teach you passion, little gray dove."

His mouth came down hard on hers, demanding, parting her lips. His tongue swept hotly into her mouth, creating a fire that threatened to consume her. She felt his heat against her, branding her. She moaned beneath the furious onslaught of his kiss, held spellbound by his taste and touch.

Morgan was acutely aware of the physical

contact between him and Luca. She was flush against him, and through the barriers of their clothing he could feel the length of her shapely legs, the seductive curve of her hips, and the soft fullness of her breasts. She may or may not be a nun but she was all woman. And ripe for the taking. Ripe for him.

Luca realized her danger, felt it with every fiber of her being and seemed helpless to stop what Morgan Scott had begun. If she truly wanted to know about passion, she felt certain that this English pirate could give her a forbidden glimpse of paradise. But she was made of sterner stuff than that. Being seduced and discarded by a virile rogue was worse than having to wed a man she didn't know. Neither choice was palatable. Some way, somehow, she had to convince El Diablo to send her back to the convent. And soon, before he made a mockery of her piety.

Wresting from his grasp, Luca used a ploy that had worked in the past with the pirate. She promptly fell to her knees before he could reach for her again. Grasping her rosary beads in her hands, she raised her eyes to heaven and moved her lips in fervent prayer.

Her devotion touched a responsive chord

inside Morgan, and he stepped away with a vile curse. How could he seduce one so pious? So reverent?

She is not a nun, a voice inside him argued.

But Morgan's ardor had cooled. Not because he held any reverence for her papist religion, but because she struck a chord deep inside him that spoke to his decency.

"Say your prayers, little nun," Morgan snarled. "But in the end they will do you no good. I will have you, in my own good time."

4

Morgan's fierce scowl prompted Stan Crawford to speak. "So the Spanish nun is still a virgin."

Morgan rounded on him. "What in the hell is that supposed to mean, Mr. Crawford?"

"Even the crew is remarking on your foul temper. 'Tisn't like you to deny yourself."

"Perhaps I don't want the aggravation of deflowering the woman." He shrugged expansively. "Virgins are rather inept creatures, hardly worth the trouble."

"Are you trying to tell me you don't want her? Any one of the crew would jump at the chance to take their sport with her."

"Including you?" Morgan asked sharply. "Forget it," he said, not waiting for Crawford's answer. "The crew will never have her. Even if I decide I don't want her for myself."

Crawford sent him a measuring look.

"Then I take it you will set Sister Luca ashore on one of the Spanish Islands to make her own way back to Spain."

"Good God, no! Are you daft, man? Have you taken a good look at her? Even wrapped in those hideous robes and headcovering she exudes sensuality. She's fooling no one by hiding her extraordinary beauty behind the trappings of a nun."

"You don't believe her? If you think she's lying, why don't you just take your fill of her and kiss her good-bye? You've done it before, many times, in fact."

Morgan stared out across the tossing waves, mulling over Crawford's advice. Lord knows he wanted the Spanish chit, nun or no. But for some reason he couldn't bring himself to defile her, on that rare chance that she actually was a holy woman. One way or another he was determined to learn the truth about her. Once she was ensconced in his island home, he would turn his talents to learning exactly who Sister Luca was and why she had lied about her identity. If indeed she was lying. Then he would seduce her. Slowly, with great expertise, until she could no longer hold out against him. He looked forward with relish to the day Sister Luca doffed her gray robes and admitted she had lied.

And that day would come. As assuredly as the sun rose in the east and set in the west.

"In my own good time, Mr. Crawford," Morgan smiled, "in my own good time. Right now it pleases me to humor her. I assure you, once we reach Andros I will learn the truth. Then I will teach Sister Luca what it is like to be a woman. 'Tis true I have no love for the Spanish, but perhaps I'll find some redeeming quality in her. Time will tell, Mr. Crawford, time will tell."

"What about Rouge? She won't be happy with the addition to your household."

"Rouge has no hold on me, therefore she has nothing to say about whom I invite into my home."

"Something tells me Rouge has other ideas about your relationship. She'd like to make it permanent."

Morgan gave a shout of laughter. "I'm rich as Midas. 'Tis the money Rouge loves. When she became stranded on the island three years ago, I offered her passage back to England. She preferred to remain on the island as my mistress. Do you think I'm her only lover? I know of at least three other men, pirates all, who put into port and service her during my long absences. I'm sure there are others I don't know about. When and if I decide to marry, it won't be to a sensuous tart like Rouge."

No, definitely not, Morgan thought silently. Incredibly, the auburn-haired Rouge LeClerc hadn't once entered his mind since he'd met Sister Luca, a woman whose Spanish heritage made her his enemy.

Luca paced the cabin endlessly, stopping occasionally to stare out the window. More than once her hand found her head, feeling the loss of her hair keenly. And all because of *him*. El Diablo. He was arrogant, overbearing, and . . .

Handsome as sin.

He tempted her. Made her think impure thoughts. Touched her in ways and places that were sinful.

Made her want more.

Perhaps her father had been right, and she was not meant for the religious life. She should have accepted her marriage to Don Diego as the will of God and taken comfort in any children born of their union. But when she tried to recall Don Diego's face, all she saw was Morgan Scott's devilish smile. She cried out in sincere alarm and willed his image away.

Actually, Luca looked forward to reaching the pirate's stronghold, but only for the opportunity it offered. Though she knew almost nothing about the Bahamas, she supposed Spanish ships arrived occasionally, and with God's help she would make her way back to the convent and take her final vows before her father found out and sent her back to Havana and Don Diego. What she didn't look forward to was being alone with Morgan Scott any longer than necessary. The dark, fierce emotions he aroused in her were completely outside her realm of knowledge.

Luca spent the entire day scheming and making plans for her escape from Andros. Unfortunately she had no idea that the Bahamas were uninhabited. Though technically owned by Spain, no country seemed interested in the more than seven hundred islands and cays.

A tray of food was delivered at noon and again that evening by Mr. Crawford, who didn't linger to engage her in conversation. Sometime during the day the cook's helper, a scruffy young man who said his name was Lester, arrived to spruce up the cabin and carry out the odious contents of the chamber pot. He seemed to take the chore in stride, paying little heed to Luca's flaming face. To Luca's vast relief, Morgan didn't return after leaving her kneeling in prayer earlier that morning.

When darkness arrived and the ship settled down for the night, Luca's eyes returned to the door again and again, aware that Morgan would return to the cabin soon and her torment would begin anew. She tried to ready herself mentally but still wasn't prepared when he stormed into the cabin. Arrogant, confident, commanding, the very air around him pulsed with the turbulence of his entrance. He searched her face, and once again Luca found herself cast too quickly beneath his spell.

The spell of a man who would ravish her, a man who hated her for her Spanish blood.

She stared back at him, stunned by the tempest in his eyes.

He smiled, and his blue eyes turned a peculiar silver, a mesmerizing silver. Was it desire she saw in them? She'd had too little experience with that emotion to know. She did not smile back.

"I'm surprised to find you still awake, Sister. No doubt you are accustomed to retiring early and arising with the dawn to begin your prayers."

Her tongue refused to work, so she nodded.

"Then I suggest you get into bed."

Her eyes grew wide. Her mouth went dry. Her voice was hoarse when she finally found it. "I will sleep on the floor."

Morgan unbuckled his sword and tossed it on the chair. He had removed his jacket earlier in the day since the air was quite balmy in the southern waters they now sailed. Hands on hips, legs spread wide, he could be the answer to any young woman's fantasy. But Luca's fantasy was for a saintly life among the nuns.

"You'll sleep in the bed . . . with me," he added, watching her closely. Her eyes were on his sword, and she looked ready to bolt for it. Morgan reacted swiftly. In two long strides he was beside her, his hands spanning her waist. He lifted her effortlessly and tossed her onto the bunk. She bounced once, then settled down.

He couldn't help but note how light she was, how incredibly tiny her waist, how small and defenseless. He could crush her with one hand had he a mind to. But he had other, more pleasant things he wanted to do to her.

When he followed her down on the bunk, she quickly scrambled off and fell to her knees at the bedside. Her prayers were loud and sincere.

"Damn your hide!" he cursed furiously.

"Do you think your prayers would save you if I truly wanted you? I'm a pirate, remember?"

"How can I forget?"

Another barrage of cursing followed her answer. "Lie down, I won't bother you. You may sleep in peace, just as I intend to do."

"In the same bed?" Her voice shook.

"In the same bed," Morgan answered. "Why should either of us be uncomfortable? I don't fancy you tonight."

Morgan's verbal denial tasted bitter in his mouth. He wanted Luca, more than he cared to admit. He couldn't decide if the Spanish woman was a saint or a witch. Fortunately he was no callow youth who couldn't control himself. Until he learned Sister Luca's secret, he'd bide his time. Meanwhile, he'd employ the art of subtle seduction to assault her senses and wear her down. Once on his island he'd have her all to himself.

"Into the bed, Sister," Morgan ordered as he began removing his clothing.

"No."

"If you don't I'll tie you there."

She sat gingerly on the edge of the bed then lay down. Her body rigid, she clung to the narrow edge to keep from falling off. When Morgan doused the light, she sighed audibly. The whisper of cloth told her that he had shed his clothing, then the mattress dipped with his weight and he stretched out beside her. She cried out in dismay when he pulled the blanket over them.

"Settle down," he complained. "If I have problems going to sleep I may be forced to find a way to amuse myself until I grow tired."

She went still, willing herself to relax, fearing she would not like the type of amusement he had in mind. When his arm came around her she held her breath, then slowly let it out when he did nothing more than pull her against him.

Morgan felt the furious pounding of her heart through the barrier of her clothes and knew she was frightened. But he did not remove his arm. Nor did he do anything further to frighten her no matter how desperately he wanted her physically. He wanted her to grow accustomed to his presence, to be comfortable with him sleeping next to her, to become familiar with his state of dress or undress. Then, when she least expected it he would tempt her innocence with a sensual assault upon her virtue.

Their brief association had shown her to be a tempestuous creature whose sexuality had not been fully explored, but he knew it was there nevertheless, hiding beneath her gray robes and false piety. One day he would ferret out the truth and force her to reveal her soul to him.

Luca awoke with a start and stretched, surprised at how rested she felt. The captain's bunk was much more comfortable than the wooden deck or the hard cot she had grown accustomed to at the convent. It would be even more enjoyable if the captain wasn't in the bunk with her. She turned her head slowly and found him staring at her; his eyes this morning glittered with silver highlights.

"Was that so bad, little saint?" he asked. There was a strange hoarseness in his voice that sent awareness shivering through her. "Was I the first man you ever slept with?" His arm tightened around her.

"Let me up," Luca said, trying to tug his arm from her waist. "What are you doing still abed? I thought you arose with the dawn."

"Are you trying to get rid of me?"

"*Sì.*"

"I'm much too comfortable to move."

"Well, I'm not!"

He chuckled in amusement when she

leaped from the bunk, but he did nothing to stop her. "Perhaps you're right, it is time I got up. The Bahamas are just over the horizon. We'll make landfall by midday."

Luca's dark eyes sparkled with excitement. "Really? Are the Bahamas inhabited? Is there a village? A harbor? Do other ships put into the port?"

"You're full of questions this morning, aren't you, Sister Luca? I see no reason not to answer them. The Bahamas are uninhabited but for the Arawak Indians, a peaceful, friendly people. It is a Spanish possession, but they have yet to claim it. The Indians work my plantation and care for my home. As for a village, if you can call a collection of huts inhabited by natives and pirates a village, then I suppose there is a village of sorts. There is a natural deep water harbor but no docking facilities, no port. Few ships visit Andros except for pirate ships putting in for fresh water and fruit. Occasionally an English or Spanish ship will reach our shores, but it quickly leaves. An uninhabited island is of little interest to any country."

"There are no settlers on the Bahamas? No harbor? No port?" Luca repeated, dismayed.

"More than seven hundred islands and two thousand cays make up the Bahamas," Morgan informed her, "and very few have enough fresh water or plant life to support inhabitants. Andros has an abundance of both, but we have few visitors. I intend to keep it that way. When El Diablo isn't operating in the Atlantic he's at home either on Andros or his ancestral estate in England. If you're thinking about escape, forget it."

"Let me go, Captain," Luca begged, her eyes luminous with unshed tears. "Put me ashore on Spanish territory, and I'll find my way back to the convent. I'm well aware of your hatred for my countrymen, and I can't imagine why you want me when I'm of no earthly value to you."

"No value?" Morgan repeated in disbelief. "Don't sell yourself short, little saint. 'Tis true the only hostages I keep are those that are ransomed back to their relatives, but in your case I'm keeping you around for my amusement." Then, with a nonchalance that stunned her, he arose from bed as gloriously naked as the day he was born.

Embarrassed fury exploded inside Luca. "What you're doing to me is not amusing, you arrogant, wretched blackguard!" She flew at him, her fists flailing his chest like one possessed. He grasped her wrists, confining them in one of his large hands while he pulled her against him with the other.

"You're sorely testing my good nature, Sister," he growled. He could feel the heat explode in his groin, filling him near to bursting. Didn't she know what she was doing to him?

It wasn't until Luca felt the hard ridge of his manhood rising against her stomach that she realized her danger. His face was so close to hers she could see his pupils, dark circles rimmed with silver, and feel the rampant beating of his heart. He bore her backward toward the bunk.

"Please, oh, please, don't do this to me. I'm sorry I made you angry." She closed her eyes and uttered a frantic prayer. "*Dios* in heaven, save me from this fate. Do not allow me to be dishonored in such a violent manner."

"Dishonored!" Morgan roared. "When I make love to you, dishonor will have nothing to do with it. It will be for pleasure and mutual satisfaction. When that day arrives, I vow you will be willing and compliant. And you will wonder why you ever feared our joining."

"I will kill myself first!"

"You will die a little, as will I, but it will

not be a permanent death, this I promise you. You will wish for it again and again."

Then his mouth crushed down on hers, fevered, urgent, sucking the breath from her. Oh, *Dios,* the seduction. She tried to keep her lips tightly sealed against the prod of his tongue, but he easily breached that meager barrier. He searched out her tongue, moved within her mouth, stole all reason. She breathed in his scent, savored the taste and feel of him, and willed herself not to respond. Then suddenly he released her, and she fell backward onto the bunk. She expected him to fall upon her, but he didn't. To her surprise and gratification, he glared at her with bored indifference and began pulling on his trousers.

"Why are you doing this to me?" she asked shakily. "Do you enjoy corrupting nuns?"

His smile was grim. "I don't know, I've never tried it. As I said before, you might provide amusement. You must be aware that I bear no love for the Spanish. Why should I care what happens to a Spanish nun? Or a woman who claims to be a nun."

He strapped on his sword and paused at the door. "Be prepared to go ashore later today. You will like my home far more than the bleak convent you came from, if indeed you came from a convent at all."

Luca looked out from the window as the island of Andros came into view. She watched as the *Avenger* maneuvered into a deep water channel between two thickly wooded islands. As they veered toward Andros, she noted that a river bisected the forest and flowed into the sea. At one point she swore they were going to run aground, but then the shelf fell away into an open harbor, wide enough to accommodate three or four ships at one time. Her heart leaped with hope when she saw another ship riding at anchor a short distance from shore. There were no docking facilities, but Luca saw both dark-skinned and White men engaged in various activities on shore.

Shortly after the *Avenger* dropped anchor, Morgan came for Luca. They boarded a longboat, accompanied by several crew members to man the oars, and then were winched into the water. The water was the clearest blue Luca had ever seen, and when she trailed her hand in it she found it warm to the touch. She gasped in appreciation when she caught sight of a flock of long-legged birds standing in the water along the shoreline. Their glorious pink plumage was in vivid contrast to the lush green foliage and blue water. A flock of wild birds of every description took flight over the mangroves that stretched along the shore.

"Those are flamingos," Morgan informed her, pointing to the brilliant pink birds. "They breed on Andros and feed on small shrimp. There are hundreds of species of birds here but no wild animals to speak of. Timber Ridge lies just over the rise."

"Timber Ridge?"

"The name of my plantation."

"What kind of plantation? What can you grow in this soil?"

"Trees, Sister Luca. Caribbean pine, to be exact. We harvest and export pine logs to England. See, it grows all around us in abundance. The Indians also dive for sponges, which are bountiful around the islands. They are popular items in England and Europe."

Effortlessly, he lifted her from the longboat and deposited her on the white sand that was littered with hundreds of colorful shells of all sizes and shapes. Luca's gaze wandered toward the ship riding at anchor beside the *Avenger*.

"What ship is that?" she asked, trying to hide her excitement. Perhaps its captain would be willing to help her escape.

" 'Tis my ship. She carries lumber to

England and staples on the return trip. I have several like her in my fleet. The *Avenger* is the only ship I use for privateering."

She felt her disappointment keenly. Was there no escape from El Diablo?

"Remain here while I speak with Mr. Crawford," Morgan ordered when he saw his first mate step ashore from a second longboat. He hurried away, and Luca immediately turned her attention to her surroundings. Lush with vegetation, surrounded by sparkling water, the island would have been a paradise in any other circumstance.

Morgan hailed Crawford, and they met several yards down the shore from where Luca stood.

"What are your orders, Captain?" Crawford asked.

"It will take a solid two months to return the *Avenger* to her former good condition. Set the men to work immediately. There is plenty of wood about to complete the repairs. Once she's beached the men can careen her hull. Meanwhile, I have a special assignment for you, my friend."

"And what could that be, Morgan? It wouldn't have anything to do with Sister Luca, would it?"

"Exactly," Morgan said, casting a surreptitious glance at Luca, who was now kneeling on the sand examining shells. "I want you to take the *Queen's Glory* to Cuba and find out all you can about the *Santa Cruz* and her passengers. By now the surviving crew have surely been rescued by a passing ship and reported the sinking. I want to know how Don Diego reacted to the news of his fiancée's death. Find out all you can and report back to me."

"Should I leave right away?" Crawford asked, eager to carry out his captain's orders.

"I'll let you know when you're to leave. You may have a passenger."

Crawford looked stunned. "Sister Luca? You want to send her to Havana?"

"Never!" Morgan denied vehemently. "At least not yet," he added more reasonably. "If Luca is who I think she is, I have special plans for our little nun. And if she isn't . . ." His words skidded to a halt. He had no idea what he would do if Luca actually turned out to be a nun.

"If it isn't Luca, who in the hell will my passenger be?"

"Morgan! *Mon amour, mon cheri,* how I have longed for your return."

Morgan and Crawford turned as one to watch a voluptuous auburn-haired woman sprint from the trees toward the two men. Crawford turned to Morgan, his brow quirked in askance. "Rouge? You wish to send Rouge to Cuba?"

"I have a feeling she'll be happier there," Morgan said evenly.

"My God! The Spanish witch truly has beguiled you. I thought Rouge pleased you."

"She did, but one must move on, and I have a feeling Rouge is tiring of this island paradise. There is not enough here to keep her occupied during my long absences. Besides, I intend to return to England soon to give the queen her share of the plunder, and I do not relish bringing a French whore with me. Our agreement when she became my mistress was that either of us could move on whenever we wished with no strings attached."

Squealing in delight, Rouge reached Morgan. The men working on the beach to unload the *Avenger* of her plunder watched in amusement as the fiery-haired vixen threw herself into their captain's arms. Dismayed, Luca watched the open display of affection between the woman and Morgan. She seemed to kiss him endlessly, with great affection. His mouth, his cheeks, his throat, wherever her lips could reach. A dull pounding began in Luca's temples, and she squeezed her eyes closed against the pain. Why didn't Morgan tell her he had a wife?

"Rouge, take it easy," Morgan laughed as he tried to defend himself against the onslaught of Rouge's passion. "This is no place to display your affection. You are providing my men with quite a show."

"I don't care, *mon amour*," Rouge pouted. Her sultry gaze devoured him. "But if it bothers you, come with me to the house. A bed is far more comfortable than hot sand beneath one's back."

She sensed Morgan's distraction and followed his gaze down the shoreline to where a woman clad in a shapeless gray dress stood watching them.

"Who is that woman, Morgan?"

"Come, I'll introduce you." He grabbed her hand and pulled her across the sand.

Luca was mesmerized by the fiery-haired beauty. Why would he want a drab gray dove when he had a woman like that in his bed? The woman regarded her with hostility, which Luca found puzzling. She could think of no reason for the woman to dislike her.

"Who is this black-eyed witch, Morgan?" Rouge asked. "She looks like a nun. Don't tell me you've suddenly found religion."

"Rouge, meet Sister Luca, recently from a

Spanish convent. Sister Luca, this is Rouge LeClerc, a . . . friend of mine."

"A very *good* friend," Rouge purred. "But tell me, *mon amour*, what is a nun doing on your *island?* Dieu, a Spanish nun, no less."

"She is my guest. Now, shall we all proceed to the house? I'm sure Sister Luca is anxious for a bath and a comfortable bed." He flashed Luca an impudent grin. "My bunk offers scant comfort."

Rouge's eyes widened in anger, but before she could vent it Crawford drew her away. Luca found herself being guided up the beach by Morgan, whose grip on her elbow was unrelenting.

"The house is several hundred yards through the forest, in a clearing hewn out by my men. I hired Arawaks to build my house, importing all but the lumber from England," Morgan continued conversationally. "The house isn't lavish, but you'll find it comfortable."

Luca had not yet found her voice. The appearance of the beautiful Rouge had rendered her speechless. She should have known that one woman couldn't satisfy Morgan. He probably had an entire stable of mistresses scattered in all the ports of the world. Actually, finding a woman residing in Morgan's home eased Luca's mind. With

Rouge in residence he couldn't possibly want another woman carnally, which suited her perfectly. She didn't want Morgan to think of her in that way.

But Morgan's possessive hold upon her arm seemed to defy logic. Nothing was simple or straightforward with Captain Morgan Scott.

Entering the coolness of the forest, Luca would have liked to have stopped along the way to examine the various flora and fauna, but Morgan would not allow her to stray from the beaten path along which they walked. Abruptly they came upon a clearing, dominated by a large house built entirely of pine logs. It was two stories high, and a wraparound porch on each level kept out the rain and allowed the windows to remain open to catch the breeze. The windows themselves were made of glass, no doubt imported, and tiles covered the roof. On the whole, the house was quite impressive for a wilderness abode.

They climbed the steps onto the porch and proceeded through the doorway. Luca stood in the foyer, amazed at the coolness that greeted her. They were met by a handsome middle-aged woman with strong Indian features. She was barefoot and dressed in a colorful sarong.

"Welcome home, Captain." Her smile was genuinely fond.

" 'Tis good to be home, Lani. Has all gone well in my absence?"

"As well as can be expected," Lani said, sending a somewhat disgruntled glance at Rouge.

"Is your family well?"

"Prospering, Captain, thanks to you."

"I bring a guest to Timber Ridge, Lani. Please make Sister Luca welcome and see that she is comfortable. Give her the room overlooking the garden. I think she will enjoy that. Her trunk will arrive shortly."

Luca sent him a startled look. "I have no trunk."

"I took the liberty of having Senorita Santiego's trunk removed from the sinking galleon. Surely there is something inside you can wear. Anything at all is an improvement over the gray sack you've been wearing."

"What I'm wearing is the approved dress of my order," Luca said with a hint of reproof. "I take great pride in my nun's garb. Those who serve God forsake bright plumage and worldly trappings."

"Too bad," Morgan said softly. "They would suit you."

During this exchange between Luca and

Morgan, Rouge had been listening carefully, growing suspicious of the rare tenderness in Morgan's voice and the way he looked at the little gray mouse. What did he see in her?

Once Lani led Luca off and Stan Crawford sought his own quarters in the large rambling house, Rouge rounded on Morgan.

"What in the hell was that all about? You are no more religious than I, yet you flaunt this little nun like . . . like you're planning to seduce her."

The look on Morgan's face was enough to convince Rouge that she was right. "*Dieu!* That's exactly what you plan, isn't it, *mon amour?* Or have you already succeeded?"

5

Morgan glared at Rouge. He recalled with alacrity the times he'd returned to Andros and spent amorous days and erotic nights in bed with Rouge, eating and sleeping sporadically. Sporting with the feisty French wench had been fun and satisfying, but suddenly she no longer appealed to him. Their time together had run its course; he was tiring of her, it was as simple as that. And she could deny it all she wanted, but he knew she was ready to leave the island.

"Well, Morgan, *mon amour*, answer my question. Have you already seduced the woman? She's a nun! I can't believe it of you, even knowing your hatred for Spaniards."

"Looks are often deceiving," Morgan said, admitting nothing, denying nothing. Rouge was too astute not to realize his ultimate goal.

"What do you mean by that? The girl is a nun, isn't she?"

"As far as I know," Morgan said blandly. "And for your information, I haven't seduced her. I can't get her off her knees long enough to lift her skirts."

Rouge laughed lustily. "Ah, *mon amour,* if you want her bad enough you'll find a way. Come," her voice grew husky as she grasped his hand and pulled him toward the stairs. "I've missed you dreadfully. If I have my way we won't leave the bedroom for a full week. I intend to have my fill of you before you leave again."

Morgan hung back. "I've duties to attend to."

Rouge sent him a heated glance. "Let Crawford see to them."

"Crawford is busy. He'll be leaving the island soon."

"Alone?"

"No. Not necessarily. I thought you might like to accompany him to Cuba. I'm willing to settle a sum on you that will allow you to live independently for the rest of your life. If you don't fancy Cuba, you can take a ship from there to France."

Stung, Rouge reared back, her eyes narrowed in disbelief. "You're sending me away? *Dieu!* You're tossing me aside for a

Spanish bitch who claims to be a nun? You're mad! What has she done to you?"

"Consider it, Rouge," Morgan said placatingly. "Don't you think I've noticed how restless you've grown in the past few months? Admit it. Life is too tame on Andros."

"Not when you're here, *mon amour*." Her voice grew sultry, her eyes dark and luminous. She placed her hands on his chest, working their way inside his shirt to tease his nipples. "You've always enjoyed what I do to you."

"I can't deny it," Morgan admitted, "but our association has run its course. When you leave with Mr. Crawford, I'll see that you want for nothing."

"Bastard!"

"Have you forgotten our agreement? Each of us is free to go our own way whenever we please."

She hissed her displeasure. "I expected more from you. I expected to go to England to meet your queen. In time . . . who knows what our relationship would have led to."

Morgan tensed. "It would have led to nothing. When I marry, if I ever marry, it will be to . . ." *Someone he loved.* "Never mind."

"If that's what you want, Morgan," Rouge said bitterly.

"You'll not suffer for our relationship. I wish you good luck and Godspeed." He turned and walked from the room.

Rouge wanted to scream in frustration. She had known from the beginning that nothing permanent would come from her relationship with Morgan Scott, but she'd had high expectations nevertheless. Morgan was filthy rich; she loved that about him. They got along well together in bed. He had never taunted her with it, but he knew she had been a whore in her homeland and had left with a ship's captain who had promised her handsome compensation for warming his bunk during his voyage. A storm had sent the ship aground on Andros, and she had remained as Morgan's mistress.

Still, she had her youth and her beauty, and if Morgan was as generous as he'd hinted, she'd have wealth, so she couldn't complain. It had been fun while it lasted. But truth to tell, Morgan was right. Andros was beginning to bore her. Not Morgan, never Morgan, but between homecomings she roamed the island like a caged animal. Even bedding pirates whose ships occasionally anchored in the cove did not cure her restlessness. Yet, it still hurt to be dismissed so casually. She knew instinctively that Luca was to blame. What she didn't understand was what El Diablo wanted with a drab little Spanish nun.

Luca felt strange in the lovely room assigned to her. All the furnishings had to have come from England, she thought as her appreciative gaze took in the large canopied bed hung with mosquito netting and the ornate furniture polished to a high sheen. She walked to the bank of windows and the double door leading onto the wraparound porch on the upper gallery. The curtains blew inward, admitting a cool ocean breeze. She couldn't recall such luxury since she'd left her father's villa at age ten.

Luca's trunk had been delivered earlier, and she had sorted through it, finding nothing appropriate for a nun to wear. The clothing had been made for Don Eduardo's daughter. Nothing inside was proper for Sister Luca.

After a long, luxurious bath, Luca washed out her habit and donned a robe she'd retrieved from the trunk. She wrapped her head in a towel and hung the habit over the balcony railing to dry. She was more than ready for a nap and stretched out on the bed to wait for her clothes to dry in the hot sun.

Morgan rapped lightly on Luca's door.

He wanted to ask if she was pleased with her room. When he received no answer he grew alarmed. Fearing she had foolishly tried to find a way off the island, he turned the knob and entered the room. He saw her immediately, sleeping peacefully on the bed. The tub of used bathwater still sat in the center of the room. He wondered what she had done with her clothing; a visual search of the room located the gray habit draped over the balcony railing. The white headcovering was spread out beside it.

Smiling mischievously, Morgan quietly gathered up the drab gray garment and left the room as quietly as he had entered. He carried the offending garments all the way to the kitchen behind the house, where he tossed them into the cooking fire. He waited until they burst into flame before returning to the main house and his own bath.

A loud rapping on the door awoke Luca. Dazed from sleep, she gazed at the unfamiliar surroundings and suddenly remembered where she was. On Morgan's island, in his house, at his mercy. The rapping continued.

"Who is it?"

"Rouge. May I come in?"

"If you like."

Rouge entered, her hips undulating sensuously. "It's getting dark. Why haven't you lit a candle?" Without waiting for an answer, she struck a sulfur match and lit a nearby branch of candles.

"Thank you. Is there something you wanted?"

Rouge looked at her curiously. "Are you really a nun?"

Luca regarded her squarely. "*Sí*, I am a nun." She hoped God would forgive her small lie.

"What are you doing with a man like Morgan Scott? He's probably one of the most godless men I know. He hates Spaniards, you know. Do you think your nun's garb will save you from him?"

"I had no choice in the matter. I begged him to set me free or leave me on the sinking ship, but he refused."

"He abducted you? I don't believe it. You have no ransom value, whatever could he want with you?" Her eyes narrowed speculatively. "Morgan is a handsome man. Any woman would want him."

"Not I," Luca denied vehemently.

"Obviously he wants you. He's sending me away."

"What! No! It cannot be. You must not go and leave me alone with him."

Rouge shrugged. "It wasn't my decision to make. Besides, I don't believe you're as innocent as you pretend. I know Morgan Scott too well. No woman alive could hold out against him for the length of time you've been together. Did you tell him to send me away?"

"No! I didn't even know you existed until we reached the island."

"You lie," Rouge charged viciously. "This pretense of innocence does not fool me. You want Morgan all to yourself so you told him to send me away. I will go, Sister Luca, but you haven't heard the last from me. Morgan would never send me away if not for you."

"Rouge, what are you doing here?"

Morgan stood in the doorway, a fierce scowl on his features.

"I was merely speaking with Sister Luca, *mon amour*," Rouge said sweetly. "It isn't often I get to converse with a holy woman."

"Perhaps you should change for dinner. I know how particular you are about your appearance."

His subtle hint was not lost on Rouge. "*Oui*, you are right, Morgan. I will see you at dinner. I asked Lani earlier if she'd serve the meal out on the patio. It will be very romantic."

"Sister Luca and Stan Crawford will join us."

Rouge sent Morgan a sour look. "Of course. Whatever you say, *mon amour.*"

She left in a huff, and Morgan turned his gaze on Luca. "That robe is the most becoming garment I've seen you in."

Luca shifted self-consciously. "It isn't mine."

"Funny, it looks as if it should belong to you."

"I won't be joining you for dinner tonight. I doubt that my habit will be dry by then."

"Habit? What habit?" His eyes were hooded like those of a hawk.

"I washed it out and hung it on the railing to dry."

Deliberately Morgan walked out onto the gallery. "I see nothing."

"What! Where could it have gone?" Luca rushed onto the gallery and peered frantically over the rail into the yard below. Morgan was right, her habit was nowhere in sight. "Well, that settles it. I cannot leave this room until my habit is found."

"You have a trunk full of clothing. Beautiful clothing, unless I miss my guess. They are yours to wear."

"I cannot."

"You will."

Before Luca knew what Morgan intended, he grasped the towel and pulled it from her head. Shock shuddered through him. Her dark hair, which probably had been beautiful at one time, now curled against her head in uneven hanks that barely covered her ears.

"Who in the hell did this to you?"

Luca fought to keep the tears from rolling down her cheeks. " 'Tis the custom. All nuns have their hair shorn."

"By a butcher? By God, it's a sacrilege. I'll send Lani up to help you dress. Hopefully she can do something with that dreadful mess atop your head. I'll see you at dinner. If you fail to appear I'll come up here and dress you myself. Is that clear?"

Luca fumed in impotent rage, suddenly certain that Morgan was behind the disappearance of her habit. She felt naked and vulnerable without the protection of her gray robes. Scrambling to her knees before the trunk, she searched for something less attractive than the elaborate dresses her father had ordered made for her trousseau. At the bottom, beneath the layers of silks and satins, she found some of Carlotta's widow's weeds. She recalled permitting Carlotta to use a section of her trunk to pack her scant belongings.

Perfect, she thought, pulling out the somber dress and shaking out the wrinkles. She even located a mantilla to cover her shorn hair. By the time Lani arrived she had donned corset, stockings, and petticoats, and was struggling into the dress.

"Is that all you have to wear?" Lani asked, eyeing the dress with distaste. "And your hair," she wailed. "You poor thing."

"I am a holy woman," Luca said by way of explanation. "If my habit hadn't mysteriously disappeared, I would be wearing it instead."

"The captain said you needed help. It is a sin to cut off hair as beautiful as yours. I will see what I can do with it."

"No, it is fine, really. I am not a vain creature."

"I dare not disobey the captain," Lani said, seating Luca at a bench before a low, mirrored dressing table. She pulled out a scissors from a small basket she carried and began clipping Luca's hair, trimming away the ragged edges and shaping it into a semblance of order. Mesmerized, Luca watched as Lani created a cap of lustrous black curls that covered her head in tiny ringlets. The effect was charming. Luca hardly recognized herself.

While Lani wielded the scissors, Luca

plied her with questions. "Have you been working for Captain Scott long?"

"Since he arrived on our island," Lani replied. "He takes care of us. Some of our women have married his crewmen. They live in the small cluster of huts at the north end of the beach. He taught our people how to speak English and how to deal with ships that come to our shores seeking water and slaves."

Luca mulled that over, then asked, "What about Rouge? Has she been with Morgan a long time?"

Lani thought a moment before answering. "Yes, a very long time. But I think she grows tired of the solitude. Do not worry, now that you are here, I do not think she will remain."

Luca's cheeks flamed. Lani sounded as if she expected Luca to take Rouge's place in Morgan's bed. It wasn't going to happen. Not now, not ever. "It matters little to me if Rouge stays or leaves. If you're finished I will join the others on the patio for dinner."

Luca was the last to arrive. All conversation stopped when she walked onto the patio lit by hundreds of candles. The black dress fit poorly, since Carlotta was much larger than she, and her cap of curls was discreetly covered with the mantilla to cover her shorn hair.

"Good God!" Morgan said with a hint of disgust. "You've been transformed from a gray mouse into a blackbird. Was there nothing more flattering in the trunk? I find it hard to believe a grandee's daughter would go to her fiancé dressed in widow's weeds."

"This was the only thing in the trunk that suited me," Luca said primly.

"Of course," Morgan bit out, "I should have known."

Nevertheless, he was disappointed. He was looking forward to seeing Luca in something other than gray or black. Something that fit the curves he suspected lay beneath her saintly garb. "Shall we eat?" he asked, seeking distraction.

Morgan and Stan kept the conversation going throughout the meal. Rouge was sullen and Luca uncommunicative. Whenever Luca looked at Rouge she pictured the flamboyant beauty in Morgan's arms. The image shouldn't bother her, but it did. Why, even tonight they would . . . in his bed . . . *Dios!* Why was she torturing herself with such sinful thoughts?

"Stan, why don't you escort Rouge out to the ship and let her select whatever she wants from the plunder? Don't forget to show her the jewels we removed from the *Santa Cruz.*"

My jewels, Luca thought angrily. They were part of her dowry.

"Oh, Morgan, how generous," Rouge cooed, batting her long lashes at Morgan. "I'll have to think of an appropriate way to thank you."

"No need, Rouge. Consider it part of your going-away present. Take your time, select whatever pleases you. Meanwhile, I'll take Luca for a walk on the beach."

Stan sent Morgan an amused look. He knew without being told that Morgan was giving him permission to take his pleasure with the lusty Rouge if he so desired. He wouldn't mind. It had been a long time since he'd had a woman, and he'd had Rouge once or twice before and found her delightfully entertaining in bed.

"Come along, Rouge, there is truly wondrous plunder aboard the *Avenger*," Stan said, pulling back her chair. After a searching look at Morgan, she twined her arm in Stan's, and they set off together through the trees. Morgan's curt dismissal stung, but she'd have the last laugh yet.

Morgan turned to Luca, his smile predatory. "Shall we, Sister? The night is warm and inviting. I bet you've never seen a lovelier sight than moonrise over the islands."

Luca's knees went weak. The last thing

she needed was to be alone with the handsome pirate. "Some other time, Captain. I'd prefer to seek my bed."

His grin widened. "So would I. Your bed would suit me just fine." He offered his arm. "Shall we?"

Luca's breath slammed against her breast. "On second thought, a walk would do me good after being confined in your cabin."

"As you wish. Take my arm, the path can be treacherous at night unless you know it well."

They reached the deserted beach, and Morgan led her away from where the *Avenger* rode at anchor. The moon hung over the water like a huge shimmering globe. The sight was as impressive as Morgan had said. The breath caught in Luca's throat as she paused to admire the play of a million sparkling moonbeams dancing on the water.

"Oh, it's beautiful," she breathed appreciatively.

"I know. Sometimes I think I'd rather be here than at Scott Hall in West Sussex. The hall is my ancestral home, but Andros is the home of my heart." He stared at her, at her luminous dark eyes, at her lush lips, and knew a hunger that went beyond mere lust.

Luca felt the consuming heat of his gaze

and lost the ability to think. She said the first thing that came to her mind. "I feel the same way about the convent. It is the home of my heart."

Morgan's brow quirked upward. "Is it now?" Clearly he didn't believe her.

"The peaceful days I spent within those walls were the happiest of my life."

He took her arm, and they continued their stroll. Suddenly he stopped and pulled the mantilla from her head.

"Wha . . . what are you doing?"

"I merely wanted to see Lani's handiwork. She's quite skilled, don't you think? You look enchanting, Luca, utterly enchanting. If not for that dress . . ."

"*Sister* Luca," Luca reminded him. "I think we should leave."

"No." He took off his coat and spread it on the sand beneath a swaying palm tree. "We'll rest here a while before I take you back to the house."

If Luca knew her way back to the house she'd have turned and run. Every instinct bespoke danger. The kind of danger with which she was totally unfamiliar. Morgan had taught her about kissing, and she greatly feared there were other things he wanted to teach her.

She sat down gingerly, keeping a wary eye

on Morgan as he pushed her skirts aside and plopped down beside her. "Don't you think Rouge will miss you if we stay here too long?" Luca asked in an attempt to dampen the heat emanating from the molten depths of his blue gray eyes.

"Stan Crawford is more than capable of keeping Rouge occupied for a few hours. They'll be leaving aboard the *Queen's Glory* soon." He shifted closer. Luca tensed. His arms went around her, pulling her against the scorching heat of his body.

"Captain, this isn't proper. I told you, I'm a . . ."

". . . nun, I know. I promise I won't do anything you don't want me to do."

His hands slid upward, through the crisp black curls hugging her head. "I've wanted to do that all evening. Your hair feels like silk. I'm sure it was lovely when it was long, but it's captivating just the way it is now."

A master of seduction, Morgan knew exactly what to say and when to say it. He intended to wind a spell around Luca's senses until she forgot all that nonsense about being a nun, or else told him the truth.

"You have no right to say those things to me."

"I suppose I have no right to do this, either."

Her eyes grew wide as his face came closer, closer still, until she felt his lips caress hers. His touch was light, teasing, and Luca felt a melting sensation deep in her core. A shiver traveled down her spine when he slid his tongue along the seam of her lips, seeking entrance. When she refused to grant it, he thrust boldly past her lips and teeth, forcing them apart until his tongue darted inside. She sighed as he held her head between his large hands and ravished her mouth.

Luca felt the heated hunger of his kiss spiral through her. Felt it pushing down into her core, between her legs. His lips left hers, then pressed against her throat, his tongue licking the pulse beating at the base of her neck. Without conscious thought, her head fell back against his arm, giving him easy access. And suddenly the sweet flesh of her neck wasn't enough. With his free hand he unbuttoned the front of her dress, pushing the edges open, baring the upper curve of her breasts above the corset to the heady pleasure of his kisses. He pressed his mouth there to her rounded flesh, tasting, arousing, wet, feverishly hot. His touch was demanding, seducing, evocative.

He slipped her right breast free of the confines of her corset, his fingers curling around it, stroking the fullness. His thumb flicked over the nipple and she cried out. "No, oh no!"

She felt the hardness of his body pressing against hers. Then his mouth covered the place where his thumb had just been, and she quivered in response. *What was he doing to her?*

Morgan had never tasted anything as sweet as Luca's flesh or felt anything so soft and silken. His desire spiraled out of control, hot, aching, hungry. God, he didn't want to stop, wasn't sure he could. He wanted to carry this through to its natural culmination, wanted her to open her legs in joyous welcome, wanted to attain paradise.

Her mouth parted to form a protest; nothing came out but a rush of breath. His hands grew bolder, lifting the hem of her dress and pushing upward along the inside of her leg. His torment increased when he found the enticing bare skin above her stocking. He stretched farther, his fingers brushing against the soft, inviting warmth of her maidenhair. His hand inched higher, seeking a more intimate reward, while the hot suction of his mouth pulled at her breast.

Frenzied excitement shuddered through Luca's body, leaving her feeling hot and cold at the same time. She knew this couldn't go on, that it had to stop now or she'd be forever damned, joining the ranks of those countless women seduced by El Diablo. She suspected that once he had his way with her a holy life would never satisfy her. That thought alone broke the spell of Morgan's intoxicating kisses and gave her the strength to twist from his arms.

Morgan stared at her blankly. She was panting, her eyes luminous, her face a white oval in the moonlight. "No! I won't let you do this to me. Tonight I will pray on my knees for the salvation of your soul."

"Goddamn!" Morgan was so aroused by the Spanish witch he could have tossed her on her back, spread her legs, and taken his fill of her. The fact that he didn't both surprised and angered him. "If you truly were a nun, Luca, I'd respect your religious calling, though I consider it a senseless waste of womanhood. But from the first, I doubted you. I want you, I think you know that. I can't recall when I wanted a woman more.

"I'm going to learn the truth about you. And when I do, you may or may not be safe from me no matter what I learn. Do you understand me, Luca?" When she nodded, he raised her to her feet and helped her fasten her dress. "I'll take you back to the house."

Luca's knees were still shaking when they

reached the house. To her vast relief, Morgan left her at her door and bid her good night.

Painfully aroused, Morgan stormed into the parlor and gulped down several fingers of strong brandy before he felt calm enough to plan his next move. When Crawford and Rouge returned from the *Avenger*, Morgan sent Rouge to bed, indicating that he wished to speak privately with his first mate. Once Crawford was sitting across from him sipping a brandy, Morgan instructed his first mate to take the *Queen's Glory* out at high tide the next day, setting a course for Havana. He wanted to know who Luca really was, and he wanted to know as soon as possible.

"I'll see that Rouge is ready to leave on time," he added. "A fortnight should see you there and back. Cuba is no great distance away. Let's hope you can find the information I desire in Havana."

"I'll do my best, Captain," Crawford assured him.

"And Stan," Morgan warned, "I'm sure Rouge will be content in Havana. There is no need to bring her back to Andros with you."

Rouge glared sullenly at Morgan. She had been in her room preparing to retire when

Morgan knocked on her door and entered without being invited. Without preamble he told her she was leaving aboard the *Queen's Glory* on the morning's tide.

"So this is how it is to end. Did you succeed in seducing the nun tonight? I've never known you to be so singularly minded about any woman. You really do want her, don't you?"

Morgan ran a hand distractedly through his hair. "That's beside the point. I had decided long before I met Luca . . . er . . . Sister Luca, that the relationship between you and me had run its course. Admit it, Rouge, you're not unhappy to be leaving Andros."

Rouge hefted the heavy sack of gold coins Morgan had given her and smiled. "Not exactly unhappy, *mon amour*. 'Piqued' is a better word. A woman should be the one to break off a relationship, not the man. But I am resigned to leaving. Perhaps we will meet again one day. Besides," she said, smiling coyly, "Crawford is a handsome man, he might prove amusing for a few days."

"It has been enjoyable, Rouge, and so I bid you adieu." He raised her hand and kissed it.

Rouge's eyes sparkled. "It doesn't have to

end so impersonally. Spend the night with me, *mon amour,* for old time's sake. I promise you won't be sorry."

Morgan was almost tempted. Luca had roused him beyond endurance tonight, and he craved relief. Unfortunately there was only one woman he wanted in his bed tonight, and he couldn't have her, not yet. . . . *Soon, little nun, soon,* he swore to himself.

Luca was too unnerved to sleep. Morgan had tempted her beyond reason. She'd had to summon all her religious fervor in order to resist the powerful lure of his seduction. After slipping on her prim white nightgown, she stepped out onto the gallery. She ambled along the walkway, past darkened rooms, trying to come to grips with the strange emotions Morgan aroused in her.

The sound of voices made her pause before a particular room. Candlelight lit the interior. Inquisitiveness made her sidle closer when she recognized Morgan's voice. She went still, hovering in the shadows, listening, praying she wouldn't be discovered and accused of eavesdropping. She knew she should turn around and walk away, but curiosity got the best of her and she peered inside.

She saw Rouge and realized that Morgan was in Rouge's room. There was only one reason a man would visit his mistress's bedroom. Instead of turning away she moved closer, looking directly into the dimly lit room and its occupants as Rouge moved into Morgan's arms, twining her hands into the thick richness of his hair and bringing his lips down to hers. Luca saw it all, the scorching kiss, the intimate caress, the possessive manner in which they held one another, as if their bodies were long accustomed to each other.

Luca's heart beat wildly, angry with herself for the jolt of jealousy stirring her blood. She didn't want Morgan, yet she hated the thought of another woman having him. What was wrong with her?

Stifling a cry, she turned and fled to the safety of her own room. The lovers deserved privacy, and she was an unwanted interloper in a highly intimate moment.

Morgan broke off the kiss abruptly and stepped away, strangely unmoved by his former mistress. His instincts had been right. He knew now that sending Rouge away was right. "Good night, Rouge, I wish you nothing but the best."

Glancing into her eyes, he noticed they were suspiciously moist. "Good-bye, *mon*

126

amour, I wish you luck with your little nun. Something tells me you'll need it," she whispered as he turned away.

6

When Morgan wasn't tempting her to sin, Luca found life on Andros quite pleasant. Fortunately for her peace of mind, Morgan was occupied most of the following days with his ship. They ate dinner together each evening, and she could find no fault in his behavior. Still, she didn't dare deviate from her method of dress, continuing each day to don the oversized black widow's weeds and mantilla. She did it to remind Morgan that she was off-limits to him. Despite his exemplary behavior, Luca felt that Morgan was toying with her.

Since there was virtually no means of escape, Luca was allowed to roam the island at will. She spent long hours studying the island's unique flora and fauna and watching the natives fish from canoes fashioned from hollow logs.

Luca made friends with Lani and learned

much about Morgan and his island. She discovered that Morgan returned to Andros for infrequent intervals. During his long absences he was either plying the high seas in search of Spanish galleons or in England. During his absences his island home was looked after by Lani and her relatives. There were a number of permanent residents on Andros; trusted men who had married native women and opted to remain behind to oversee the logging industry owned by Morgan.

During the two weeks of Stan Crawford's absence, Morgan waited and watched and speculated. And kept himself busy. If he didn't, he'd go mad from wanting. The little Spanish saint was driving him crazy. Just thinking about her was exquisite torment. Despite his conviction that she was no proper nun, he forced his thoughts elsewhere, for she continued fervently to invoke God every time he attempted seduction. He had no idea why he didn't just send her away and be rid of her. He didn't need the kind of aggravation she provided with her sultry beauty and tempting dark eyes.

Two weeks and four days after he left, Crawford returned from Havana. Morgan met him on the beach.

"Welcome back, my friend. Come to the

house and you can tell me what you learned over refreshments."

Stan Crawford nodded, wondering how Morgan would react to the information he brought back from Havana. He hoped he was doing the right thing by telling his captain, for he hated the thought of Morgan harming his captive.

Seated comfortably in his large office, Morgan waited anxiously for Stan to speak. " 'Tis just as you suspected, Morgan. The name of the grandee's daughter is Luca, not Carlotta. The captain of the *Santa Cruz* and her surviving crew were picked up by a Spanish galleon and taken to Havana, where they reported the sinking and abduction to Diego del Fugo, the governor-general of Cuba."

Morgan tented his fingers in front of him and nodded thoughtfully. "Luca Santiego. No nun at all. I knew the witch was lying all along."

"Part of her story is true, Morgan. Luca was raised in a convent and removed against her wishes to marry del Fugo. The governor-general was eagerly awaiting his innocent bride. There's a new price on your head, my friend. One thousand gold doubloons."

Morgan whistled. "So much? They must want me badly."

"Very badly, especially del Fugo. You abducted his intended bride. A ship was dispatched immediately for Spain to inform Don Eduardo Santiego, Luca's father. Rumor has it that del Fugo is furious over the loss of Luca's dowry. Not to mention his intended's virginity. It is widely assumed that El Diablo will ravish the girl before ransoming her back to her family."

"How astute of them," Morgan said evenly. His face held a sharp edge that did not bode well for Luca.

"I know I advised you to take your fill of the chit, Morgan, but that was before I came to know her story. She's innocent in all this. Don't hurt her."

Morgan's thoughts turned grim. "Hurt her? You know me better than that, Stan. We'll play this little game out to the bitter end, but I assure you I will win. Eventually the bogus little saint will be returned to her bridegroom, but not before I relieve her of her virginity. When I do, I assure you she will be a willing participant."

"Don't do it, Morgan, don't do that to Luca. She doesn't deserve such shabby treatment. What if you plant your child in her? What kind of life will await her at home if you ravish her? You know how rigid those Spanish bastards are about such things."

Morgan tried not to think of his child growing inside Luca. He knew he could claim no child carrying Spanish blood in its veins. What he did concentrate on were his years of forced slavery on a Spanish galleon, of daily beatings and starvation rations, and being tortured beyond endurance. No one had pitied him during those years he was made to feel less than human, so why should he spare Luca? But there was a more pressing reason for demanding his pound of flesh. One he had never shared with anyone before.

"I have never told you this, Stan, but the galleon that attacked the ship carrying my family was a ship of the Santiego line. I even saw Luca's father once when he visited the ship while I was a slave. I must do what my pride demands," Morgan returned shortly. "Go about your business and leave Luca to me. I will not hurt her physically, if it will ease your mind. She is a very good actress, and I'll let her play her game for awhile longer, but in the end I will have my way."

He smiled then, a genuine smile, one that bespoke his pleasure for the task he set for himself.

Seduction.

If a twinge of regret lingered somewhere in the vicinity of his heart he tried to ignore it. He would not hurt Luca, oh, no. He would wind a sensual web around her senses and bring her pleasure, more than she had ever known before. When he finished with her she'd forget all that nonsense about wanting to be a nun. Later, when he sent her back to her family in shame, he would count it as one more act of vengeance against his Spanish enemies. If he was a brutal man he would have slain Luca immediately, just as her countrymen had killed his family. But as Crawford said, Luca was truly innocent in all this, and he didn't wish her harm. Truth to tell, if he didn't want her so badly he would leave her untouched and ransom her for an enormous sum. But he had lost that option the moment he kissed her and felt desire.

"Enough about Luca. Did Rouge seem content when you left her in Havana?"

"Content enough with the money and gifts you gave her," Stan said, "but angry at the abrupt way in which you sent her away. She'll land on her feet though, her kind always does." He gave Morgan a placid smile. "She made the voyage to Cuba quite pleasant for me. She's good, Morgan, damn good. I'm surprised you sent her away. Once Luca is gone it will be damn lonely on Andros. You should have kept Rouge

133

around to amuse yourself during your visits to the island."

In his mind's eye Morgan pictured Luca, her dark eyes sparkling with anger, her cap of black curls hugging her head in charming disarray, her lips lush and swollen from his kisses, and he knew he could never want Rouge in the same way he once did.

" 'Tis for the best," he said without offering further explanation.

Luca and Morgan ate dinner that evening in the formal dining room. The rain which had begun during the afternoon looked to continue well into the night. Luca fidgeted nervously, leery of the way Morgan was staring at her, as if he wanted to devour her along with the meal. She thought he had given up on trying to seduce her, but something in the depths of those blue gray eyes told her otherwise. Had he been merely biding his time all these weeks? She took a deep breath and began her mealtime prayers, a ritual she had grown accustomed to at the convent and continued on Andros.

Morgan waited patiently while she prayed, unaware that she had deliberately launched into a lengthier version than customary. Something told her she was going to need all the help she could get tonight.

"Are you finished, *Sister* Luca?" Morgan asked, stressing the title. "The food grows cold."

"*Si,*" Luca said, concentrating on the food on her plate. She picked up her fork and began eating.

Morgan watched her, his gaze hot and hungry.

"Is . . . is something wrong?" she asked nervously.

"No, you look lovely tonight, though I'd prefer seeing you in something more colorful. Nevertheless, black suits you. It is far more fetching than drab gray. Too bad it's raining. A walk on the beach would be a perfect end to an enlightening day."

"Enlightening? How so?"

"You wouldn't be interested. Let's just say I learned something today that pleases me."

Luca didn't like the direction of the conversation, so she changed it. "I saw the *Queen's Glory* arriving today. Is Mr. Crawford back? Why isn't he joining us?"

"Mr. Crawford is busy tonight."

"Oh. Have you decided to set me free? You'll be leaving soon to be about your business of pirating. I'll just be in your way."

"In my own good time, Sister, in my own good time. Are you finished eating?"

Luca set down her fork. "*Si.*"

135

"I'll see you to your room."

"There is no need."

His eyes turned pure silver. "Oh, but there is. Come along, Sister."

Luca knew they were alone in the house; after preparing dinner, Lani left to be with her own family in the village. She would not return until early the following morning.

"Good night, Captain," Luca said when they reached her room.

Morgan quirked a tawny brow and opened the door. Lani had lit a brace of candles within before she'd left for the night; they bathed the room in a golden glow. When Luca stepped inside and tried to close the door in Morgan's face, he pushed past her.

"Excuse me while I say my prayers," Luca said. Her voice held an unwelcome tremor. The way Morgan was looking at her made her tingle and burn. She approached the bed and dropped to her knees, praying more fervently than she ever had before.

Morgan sat on the edge of the bed, watching her with a predatory gleam in his eyes. She prayed long and hard, until her knees hurt and her back ached. Morgan appeared unmoved by her lengthy prayers and more than a little impatient while Luca renewed her vows to keep herself pure for

God, asking for strength to avoid Satan's evil temptation. Morgan smiled without humor during her recitation.

"Enough, Luca," Morgan said impatiently after a lengthy period of time.

"Please leave the room so that I may retire."

"This is my home and you're my . . . guest. I go where I please."

"Your prisoner, you mean."

"Call it whatever you like. I've been more than patient with you. You know what I want."

"What you want is to rape a woman intended for God."

His eyes glittered dangerously. "I've never raped a woman in my life and I don't intend to start now. How do you know you are meant for a religious life? That kind of life seems singularly unappealing. A fool can see that you're a sensual creature, as unsuited to a religious life as I am. And I am no fool."

Luca sucked in a ragged breath. "I don't know what you're talking about. Until I met you I had never been kissed. I hated being kissed by you." There, Luca thought smugly, now he knew exactly what she thought of his attempts at seduction.

"Did you now?" Morgan said. "Perhaps I

didn't try hard enough." He grasped her arms and pulled her from her knees onto his lap.

"Don't touch me, I'm a servant of God!"

Morgan merely laughed. Maybe she wasn't saying it with enough conviction. "Did you hear me? I'm a nun, a holy woman."

"And I'm a saint." His mouth slammed down on hers, teasing her lips with the tip of his tongue before covering them completely.

Luca breathed in a ragged sigh. Morgan's kiss made a mockery of her words. She didn't hate his kisses; she loved them. Loved the taste of him, the moist heat of his mouth, the scent of his sweet breath, his arousal. She was surely going to Hell!

He pressed her back onto the bed and leaned over her, continuing the assault upon her mouth with renewed fervor. Luca summoned her anger and tried to break the sensual hold he had upon her senses. Morgan broke off the kiss and flashed her a predatory smile. "Ah, *Sister* Luca," he said, once again stressing her title, "I don't think I could stand it if you *liked* my kisses. Forget all that nonsense about being a nun and submit to me. I'll give you pleasure; so much pleasure you'll beg for more."

Finding her mouth suddenly free of Morgan's electrifying kisses, she called forth her piety to protect herself against the handsome pirate. When Morgan moved his kisses to her neck and began unfastening the front of her dress to reach her breasts, she loudly invoked God's name, praying for deliverance.

Morgan laughed mirthlessly, aware that she was fighting to preserve her virginity for her Spanish bridegroom. Morgan had her measure now. She feared that once he took her innocence she would no longer be suitable for the great governor-general of Cuba. She and her family would be shamed beyond redemption, losing all prospects for a prestigious marriage. He decided it would be amusing to play out her game to the bitter end. But he would only be pushed so far.

"Is your virginity so important to you, little saint?" Morgan mocked.

"It's all I have to offer God," Luca said fervently.

"Then keep it a little longer." He pushed himself to his feet, wondering how long he could stand to play out this game. His loins burned, his manhood throbbed painfully. "Guard it well, little nun, for as long as I allow you to keep it. Only know that soon it will be mine."

Luca watched him stride from the room, fear and desire warring within her. Morgan Scott was the Devil incarnate. He tempted her beyond reason, promising things of which she could only guess, making her ache with wanting. How much longer could she resist the powerful lure of his seduction? Why couldn't she convince him to free her? Why didn't he believe she was a nun? Did he see something in her that proclaimed her a liar?

Morgan's subtle seduction continued endlessly. He was charming, attentive, a master of sin and sensuality. He intended to dishonor her, and she couldn't do a thing about it. Soon, she knew, he would have his way and she'd fall into his arms like a ripe plum. Then what would become of her?

Several uneventful days passed. Morgan knew the exact moment he had reached the end of his tether. It happened while she was praying over her food. He had waited as long as he could and longer than he would have thought possible. If Luca hadn't continued to flaunt his lust with her piety, he would have had her a long time ago. But now that he knew she wasn't really a nun, there was nothing preventing him from gorging to his heart's content on her succulent flesh. The sooner he bedded Luca the faster he could send her back to her family in shame. He tried to convince himself that seducing the daughter of Don Eduardo Santiego would satisfy his lust for revenge against those he hated so passionately.

After dinner that night Morgan suggested a walk on the beach. Luca refused, recalling what had happened, or almost happened, the last time they had walked together in the moonlight. But Morgan refused to take no for an answer. They reached the beach just as the moon was rising over the water. He led her a short distance into the trees where they couldn't be seen and spread his coat down on the sand.

Luca hesitated. "I . . . I think I'll return to the house. I suddenly feel the need to pray."

He grasped her wrist and pulled her down beside him. "It won't work this time, Luca. I know."

Luca stared at him. "Know what?"

"Luca Santiego, daughter of Don Eduardo Santiego. You were traveling to Havana to marry Diego del Fugo, governor-general of Cuba. Your bridegroom was livid when he learned you were abducted by El Diablo. There is a large reward on my head."

Luca stared at him. "No, it isn't true!

Carlotta was Don Eduardo's daughter. I was merely her companion."

"There no longer is a need to lie, Luca. I sent Stan Crawford to Havana because I felt you were lying from the beginning. The fate of the *Santa Cruz* was widely discussed in Havana, including the fact that the governor-general's bride-to-be was abducted by El Diablo. So you see, Luca, your playacting only delayed the inevitable."

"It wasn't playacting," Luca denied hotly. "I truly want to become a nun. I would have if my father hadn't removed me from the convent before I was able to take my final vows. The marriage between me and Don Diego had been arranged years ago, but I was hoping for a reprieve. Unfortunately, Father did not see it that way."

"I commend your piety," Morgan said, "but I will have you, despite all those hours you spent on your knees in prayer."

"Please, I beg you. You can demand a higher ransom from my father if you leave me untouched."

He laughed harshly. "Do you think your bridegroom will believe that I did not bed you?"

"I don't care what he believes. I will know and God will know. I wish only to return to the convent and live out my life serving God."

"I don't believe you." His voice was low, seductive, coaxing. "Kiss me, Luca. Kiss me with all the zeal and fervor you devote to your prayers."

"No."

"Are you afraid?"

"*Sí*." It was true, she was afraid.

She feared the pirate would reach that private place deep inside her that she'd held sacrosanct. A place no one else had touched. She'd already had a taste of desire, of wanting. If she allowed Morgan to show her paradise she'd be forever damned. He wanted her only to dishonor her and her family. His hatred for her people demanded that he ravish her and send her home in disgrace. He didn't care for her, she knew that. Revenge was the driving force in his life, it controlled every aspect of his existence.

"I won't hurt you, Luca," Morgan said, pulling her into his arms. "I have nothing against you except your nationality. You'll be ransomed back to your father in good time."

"After you dishonor me," Luca said bitterly.

He rose and pulled her to her feet. "Come, I don't want your first time to be on the ground, no matter how soft and yielding the sand. I want it to be memorable, something you can remember with pleasure when you return to your bridegroom."

Luca laughed harshly. "Don Diego will not have me after you defile me."

"Then you can go back to the convent as you wish. I will be doing you a favor."

"They will not have me."

That startled Morgan. He should have known that the rigid Spanish mentality would punish a woman for a man's sin against her. But he couldn't let that sway him. Don Eduardo deserved to suffer, to have his pride deflated, even if Morgan had to use the man's daughter to accomplish it. The shame would not only be Luca's but her father's as well.

They reached the house too soon, much too soon. Luca hung back, but Morgan swept her from her feet and carried her up the stairs into his room. Once he stood her on her feet, he locked the door and placed the key inside his pocket. Then he turned to Luca, his face stark with hunger.

"Do you know how long I've looked forward to this?"

Speech deserted Luca. She saw the predatory look in his eyes, felt the heat of him reach out and surround her, and knew no amount of argument would turn him from the course he had chosen. She was doomed.

She took a step backward, another. He stalked her relentlessly. He reached for her. She froze. His arms came around her. She melted. His touch was like fire, stirring her blood, dissolving her bones. He kissed her. She could think of no prayer that would dispel the torrid heat building inside her. The master of sin and sensuality had finally succeeded in breaking through to that inner part of herself that had denied her sexuality.

"Sweet Jesus, Luca, but you're sweet, so damn sweet. I could go on kissing you forever. But there is more, so much more I want to do to you, with you. Let me, little nun, let me."

She exhaled raggedly as Morgan molded her body to his. His hands settled on her shoulders, his eyes probing deeply into hers. "You don't know how long I've wanted to peel these damn widow's weeds from your sweet body." The front of her dress opened to the tugging of his fingers as he undid the fastenings. She grasped his hands, but he pushed them aside. Then he slid the dress down her shoulders and over her hips, where it caught briefly before pooling at her feet. Her petticoats followed. When she stood in corset and shift, she finally found her voice.

"Morgan, one last time I beg you, don't

do this. God will punish you. I belong to Him."

"You belong to that bastard del Fugo. You would freely give to him what I'm claiming for myself. Now you will belong to me."

Morgan frowned. Where in the hell did that come from? He had no desire to own any woman, let alone a Spanish witch.

"I don't want to belong to anyone but God."

"I'm going to prove differently."

He kissed her then, melding their lips in fire and longing. His fingers worked frantically to strip the corset from her. It loosened, and he tugged it free. She moaned, surrendering to his kiss like one starving for his heady touch. Rather than release her mouth, he ripped the shift in two and pulled it from her body. Then he lifted her from the pile of clothing at her feet and carried her to the bed. He laid her down gently, finally freeing her mouth. Luca cried out.

He stood back and stared at her, at the beauty and perfection of her body. Her breasts were sized to fit a man's hand, full yet firm, with large nipples that tempted a man's sanity. She was of small stature but rounded in all the right places. Her hips curved enticingly from an incredibly tiny waist. Her thighs were long and supple, her calves and ankles as shapely as any he'd ever seen. When he finally allowed himself to look at the one place he wanted to be above all others, he nearly lost control, something he'd never done before. The dark curling triangle of hair at the juncture of her thighs covered a treasure beyond imagination.

Slowly Morgan began to undress. Shock shuddered through Luca. She never imagined how arousing it could be to have a man look at her nude body. Or that she would ever be in a position to look at a man's nude body. She wanted to turn her gaze aside but couldn't. Something perverse inside her made her want to look her fill. When he started to remove his trousers, Luca could no longer bear the spiraling tension building inside her, and she lowered her eyes.

Morgan grasped her chin and tilted it upward. "Are you afraid to look at me, Luca?" Morgan asked. "Don't look away. I want to please you just as you please me. Your body is perfection, just like I knew it would be."

He dropped his trousers and Luca shuddered and gasped in shock. It was the first time she had ever seen an aroused nude male. He was magnificent. He was frightening. He was too big.

"Do you know what I'm going to do to you, sweetheart?" The endearment startled

Luca. She shook her head. "Has no one told you what to expect from the marriage bed?" She shook her head again. "Jesus! Just relax, I'll explain as we go along."

He lay down beside her and stroked and kissed her breasts. He licked her nipples, and she jerked convulsively.

"There are many ways in which a man can arouse a woman." Morgan's voice was lyrical. "This is but one of them. Before the night is over we'll explore other options."

Disbelief flickered in her eyes. "Why does a man wish to arouse a woman? I thought they merely took their pleasure."

Morgan chuckled. "Some men, perhaps, but not I. Half the pleasure is bringing a woman slowly to climax."

His words confused her, made her realize just how far out of her element she was. She also realized that she had to make one last effort to stop El Diablo from ruining her.

"I don't want this . . . this climax you're talking about. This is sinful. Let me go now and I'll see that my father doubles whatever ransom you ask for me."

"It's too late, Luca. Now, where were we? Ah, yes, the climax. When you reach it, it's like a little death. That's what the French call it. The feeling is difficult to explain, you'll have to experience it yourself to know."

His head fell to her breasts, and this time instead of merely kissing and licking her nipples, he took one into his mouth and suckled while rubbing the other between his finger and thumb. Luca cried out and arched against him. This couldn't be happening to her. Being a nun was all she'd ever wanted. How could she let an arrogant pirate seduce her? The answer was shocking in the extreme. Suddenly nothing else mattered but this man and the sinful feelings he was arousing in her. And the climax . . . she wanted to experience it in the arms of Morgan Scott.

Pirate.

Despoiler of women.

Master of sin and seduction.

Lover.

Were those soft cries coming from *her* mouth, or did she dream them? Did she imagine the shaft of fire that shot through her as he feasted on her breasts, devoured her nipples? She stiffened against him, stunned by the flames consuming her. She felt as if her bones were melting, her blood boiling. When she thought she had experienced the ultimate pleasure, he added a new dimension to his loving torment. His hands trailed liquid fire over her hips, her stomach, down her thighs, moving unerringly into the soft moist place between her legs. His fingers parted her, sliding along the slick cleft, testing her readiness.

Morgan groaned from the effort it took to contain his ardor while he aroused Luca. Luca moaned in response, need spiraling from the very center of her being. "Don't do that, I . . . I can't bear it."

"It's all part of arousal, sweetheart. It's supposed to continue until you're ready."

Luca jerked violently as his finger found a particularly vulnerable spot hidden in the wet folds of her womanhood. "Ready for what?"

Morgan sighed. Lord spare him from ignorant virgins. "When you're wet enough and hot enough to take me inside of you." The hard knob of his sex prodded her stomach, letting her know exactly what part of him would fit inside her.

"*Dios,* no! I can't! You're too . . ." she blushed furiously, "you're too big. You'll kill me."

"Trust me."

Taking her mind off of what he was doing, he kissed her, thoroughly, demandingly, thrusting his tongue into her mouth.

Dios, Luca thought, did decent women feel such powerful emotions? With a will of their own, her fingers wound into thick hair, moving down over powerfully muscled, taut shoulders. The flesh beneath her fingertips felt vibrantly alive, just like the man himself.

Dios save me, she prayed, as she prepared to surrender her virtue to the Devil.

In another moment El Diablo would destroy her innocence, justifying the name he had taken in his quest for vengeance.

El Diablo.

7

The languid sweep of Morgan's tongue moved hot and slow over the flesh of Luca's stomach. Luca moaned, twisting away, yet somehow finding herself closer to the sweet torment of his mouth. She tried to deny the feelings building inside her but lacked the will. His hands were between her thighs, probing higher, his fingers wet with her moisture.

"What are you doing to me?" Luca cried out in dismay. The heady seduction of his hands and mouth destroyed her senses and reconciled her to the fact that Morgan was determined to have his way. And when strange yearnings overwhelmed her, she was curious enough to want to know everything he was doing to her, everything that was happening between them.

Morgan groaned and lifted his head. "You ask too damn many questions." He slipped a finger inside her, moving his kisses downward along her thigh.

"Morgan! What are you doing? Tell me."

He sighed heavily. "I'm arousing you. The wetter you are, the less it will hurt when I finally come inside you. You're very small, sweetheart, try to relax."

Luca choked on a sob. "If you don't want to hurt me then don't do this."

"You may as well tell me to stop breathing."

She felt his kisses tease the inside of her thigh. His touch spread liquid fire, so intimate, so demanding she began to tremble. His finger began to move, in and out, slowly at first, then faster. She moaned and writhed against the searing pressure of his hand as wondrous shards of rapture speared through her.

"Soon, sweetheart, soon," he crooned. Then he found with his tongue the sensitive button hidden within her lush folds and she surged upward, crying out his name in ragged supplication. Nameless splendor soared through her. "Now," he breathed raggedly. "Oh, yes, now."

He rose above her, staring into her stunned face. "I'm going to come inside you, Luca. This part may hurt, but I'll be as gentle as possible."

At first his words failed to register. But when they did she shook her head back and forth. "Nooooo! You're too . . . I'm too . . . it won't work."

"Trust me," he reassured her. "It's done all the time. Girls are married as young as thirteen and live through it. Most come to enjoy it. Now, look at me, sweetheart, I want to see your face when I come into you."

He melded their bodies together, his flesh taut and slick as he carefully parted her. His silver gaze locked with hers as he wedged his great strength between her spread thighs. He thrust the throbbing knob of his sex inside her, paused, then thrust again. Luca stiffened, trying to heave his weight from her, desperate to avoid impalement.

"Relax, sweetheart," he whispered against her lips. Then he flexed his hips and thrust again, driving himself through her maidenhead. "I'm all the way in!" he cried, exultant.

Pain. Relentless. Enduring. Tears stung her eyes; she tasted salt. "S . . . stop! You're killing me." She stiffened and arched, trying to buck him off her.

"Easy," he crooned, "easy. I promise it won't hurt for long." He moved experimentally, and Luca shuddered. Was there no way to escape this agony?

"It hurts, oh, God, it hurts."

"I can't stop now, sweetheart."

He smoothed the dark hair from her damp forehead and kissed her tenderly, waiting for her to grow accustomed to the intrusion into her virgin's body. He kissed her until she began to relax and kiss him back, then he thrust forward, slowly, then out. She moaned but did not protest this subtle rocking.

Luca was stunned at Morgan's gentleness, at the tender care he was taking of her. She doubted her intended husband would be so caring, so gentle with her on their wedding night. It was almost as if she were Morgan's bride.

Morgan's forehead glistened with sweat, his body drenched in it as he fought the urge to thrust himself to completion. He shouldn't care so much about Luca's comfort or pleasure, he told himself. He should do what his body demanded and to Hell with the woman. She was Spanish. She was the daughter of the man he had every reason to despise.

She was a sweet innocent he was using to slake his vengeance as well as his lust. Jesus! There were times he hated himself.

"Morgan . . . ?" She exhaled slowly.

He knew what she wanted to ask. "I want

to bring you to climax," he told her. "I want to give you pleasure. Is the pain still bad?"

She felt the fullness of his manhood inside her, endured the subtle movement as he deepened his thrust. So slow, so careful, so gentle. So seductive. The pain still hovered at the edge of her consciousness, but it was swiftly fading. "It's not so bad now, but I . . . I don't know how to reach a climax."

"I'm going to give it to you. Don't fight it, and it will come. You're hot-blooded, Luca, I suspected you were from the beginning. Move against me. Ah, that's it," he said, grasping her hips and thrusting deeper. "Keep moving, don't stop."

Suddenly he touched something inside her. Something she didn't know existed. She gasped and arched against him, inviting the hardened length of him deeper as he shuddered and tensed, in and out, again and again. He moved slowly, then rampantly, then slowly, thrusting, withdrawing, swift, sure, masterful.

The pain was gone, Luca realized, replaced by a newer, sweeter ache. An ache that burned like fire through her veins. She closed her eyes and let the feeling rush through her, overwhelm her. It was coming. It was close, so close. Rising, spinning, whirling. Sweet splendor rose from the point of their joining in rippling waves. It was coming. . . . She screamed and exploded in a burst of something so incredible it defied description. Merely calling it pleasure wouldn't do it justice.

Morgan began thrusting urgently now, his tension stretched so taut his arms felt like bands of steel. He raised her up against him, bringing her breast to his mouth. He seemed dimly aware that something astounding had happened to her, but he was focused now on his own pleasure. He shuddered against her, slick and damp, shuddered again and gave up his seed. Then he went still.

Morgan felt something shoving at him, and he groaned. He was weak and limp as a kitten. Still stunned from the most incredible climax he'd ever achieved, Morgan realized he was still laying atop Luca. Reluctantly he removed himself from her body and stretched out beside her.

"Are you all right?" he asked solicitously. "Did I hurt you excessively?"

"*Sí,* you hurt me," Luca told him. Her face burned with embarrassment. "But . . . but it did not hurt for long. What happened? I've never felt anything like that before. What did you do to me?" Would Don Diego have been as tender a lover as Morgan? Somehow she doubted it.

Morgan gave her a wolfish grin. "I gave you a climax. Was it not as wondrous as I said?"

Luca grew thoughtful. "It was . . . pleasant." He was far too arrogant, she decided. "Does it happen to every woman? Can any man give me a climax?"

Morgan scowled fiercely. Just pleasant? The thought of another man, any man, giving Luca pleasure annoyed him. No, it angered him. He had been the first with her, she belonged to him.

"Morgan?"

"Ah, yes, your questions. Well, all women are capable of achieving climax, but it doesn't always happen. Much depends on the man. As for your second question, I don't know. It's possible another man could give you pleasure."

"Are you saying you're better at . . . at this than other men?"

"Jesus, you're innocent."

"Not anymore," Luca said ruefully.

"No, not anymore. I've never had any complaints about my technique. Most women seem to enjoy my lovemaking."

Luca didn't want to hear about the other women Morgan had bedded. "Will you be sending me back to my father now? Have you already contacted him about my ransom?"

"Not yet, but soon. Meanwhile, I'm going to enjoy you while the negotiations are in progress. After I've had my fill of you I'll return you to your father."

Luca sat up abruptly. "You've done your worst. I'm no longer an innocent. Of what possible good am I to you now? Let me go home and repent my sins in peace and solitude. I cannot marry now nor can I retire to the convent. I hope my father will allow me the sanctuary of his home to repent my sins."

Morgan felt rage building inside him. "*Your* sins! You did nothing. You never had a chance against me. You knew it was just a matter of time before I had you."

Luca hung her head in shame. "The sin is mine. I didn't have to enjoy it."

Morgan's tension eased. A smile hovered at the corners of his lips. "You're truly an innocent, Luca. You had no choice in the matter. I was determined to wring a response from you, and I did. Beyond my wildest expectations."

She looked at him doubtfully. She wished he weren't looking at her with those keenly intelligent eyes. They had the ability to probe deep inside her, to find that vulnerable place no man had ever touched before. She couldn't stand it. Deliberately, she turned her back on him.

"Go away, let me contemplate my sins in private."

That angered Morgan. He forced her around to face him. "No, from now until I release you, my bed will be yours and I will be in it. I've had enough of your infernal prayers. I want to love you again. Now."

"Haven't you hurt me enough?"

"I told you it wouldn't hurt again."

"I'm not talking about physical pain."

Morgan's brow creased. "You can't deny I gave you pleasure."

"You don't understand, do you? *Sí*, you gave me pleasure, but it is nothing compared to the cost to my pride. I am nothing to you but an instrument of revenge. You'll take your fill of me and send me away. Pleasure! Ha! You could give me pleasure every night, and it wouldn't compensate for what you've stolen from me."

"You place considerable value on your virginity. I never wanted to hurt you personally. You're Spanish," he said, as if that explained everything.

"Why do you hate Spaniards so much? What have they done to you?"

Her question seemed to release a dam inside him. "What did they do, you ask? They stole five years of my life. They killed my parents and younger sister and brother. They enslaved me, beat me, and starved me. That one act of piracy thrust me into a living Hell. The ship upon which I was imprisoned was one of your father's line."

Luca's eyes grew round in disbelief. "No! He wouldn't allow such a thing aboard his ship."

"You're so damn naive," Morgan snarled. "It happens all the time. Would you like to see some of your countrymen's handiwork?"

He presented his back to her, revealing thick scars crisscrossing his flesh in a pattern only a whip could have produced. And it had to have happened more than once. Luca's hand flew to her mouth.

"*Dios!* No!"

"Look your fill, Luca, and wonder no longer why I hate Spaniards."

Unable to bear the sight of Morgan's severely abused flesh, she turned her gaze aside. "I'm sorry."

"So am I. Can you blame me for wanting to use you to punish your father?"

"I blame you for involving me in your vendetta against my country and my father.

Since you have succeeded in ruining me and humiliating my family, I suggest you let me go."

"No, not yet. Revenge is a small part of the reason you're in my bed. I want you. From the moment I saw you kneeling in prayer I wanted you. I know you hate me, but I can't help myself. You must be a witch to affect me like you do. I'm not ready to send you back, sweetheart."

She turned to face him, her dark eyes glittering with emotion. "You're wrong, Morgan, I don't hate you. I pity you. I can understand your hatred of my people and even forgive you, as God would do. You may have given me a taste of passion, but I still yearn for the peace and contentment of the convent where worldly matters cannot touch me. When I return, perhaps I can convince my father to donate generously to the order. If he does, they will accept me despite my sinful state. I will pray to that end."

She pitied him? The last thing he wanted from her was pity. "You don't belong in a convent."

"Where do I belong?"

Taken aback by her question, Morgan carefully considered his answer. "For the time being, right here in my bed. The *Avenger* is ready to take to the sea again. I'm sending her out with Mr. Crawford in command while I remain on Andros and take care of business. He will carry a ransom demand to your father and wait for him to deliver the payment for your release. Shouldn't take more than a couple of months."

"Morgan, I . . ."

"Luca, there is nothing more to say." He didn't want to think about the day he would have to send Luca home. He knew that day would arrive sooner than he liked, so he preferred focusing on the woman in his arms. He would have her again, and again, and when the *Avenger* returned he'd send Luca back to her father well used.

Luca squawked in protest when Morgan pulled her tightly against him. He silenced her with his mouth, kissing her until she no longer had the breath to deny him. Then she was kissing him back, responding with renewed ardor, shocked that she could want this again. Morgan had given her a glimpse of something she'd never expected to experience.

He had shown her soul-wrenching pleasure. And something deeper. Something she was reluctant to acknowledge. Then all thought ceased as his hands and mouth wrought their magic upon her. This time there was no pain when he slid inside her and moved with exquisite tenderness. There was only a splendid awakening of her body and a shattering climax that held her spell-bound.

Stan Crawford and a full crew took the *Avenger* out the next day, leaving behind Morgan and the men who spent their days on the island attending to the plantation. Two days after the *Avenger* left Andros, the *Queen's Glory* sailed for England with a load of lumber.

During the long, hot days Morgan worked alongside the natives, providing Luca ample time alone to think of him and the carnal pleasure he gave her. Her sins were many, but the most serious was the sin of enjoying her nights in Morgan's bed. Despite his hatred for the Spanish he hadn't been brutal with her; quite the opposite. He was always gentle and careful of her, and always mindful of bringing her pleasure before seeking his own. She was no longer the innocent she once was. She learned volumes about kissing and arousal and climax. Especially climax, which she'd discovered was a state all men and most women aspired to above all others.

Did she still hate Morgan? Sometimes,

she admitted. But more often, another emotion left scant room for hatred. An emotion that gave her insight into the intricate relationship between men and women. She learned that what she felt for Morgan was something on a higher plane than physical satisfaction. Luca preferred to give it no name. Besides, how could she hate a man who had ample reason to despise those responsible for taking the lives of his family? He must have been very young when his family was killed and he was forced into slavery. His hatred was so deeply ingrained that he had devoted his life to visiting vengeance upon his enemy.

Making love with Morgan during those soft, balmy nights on Andros gave Luca a glimpse of paradise. But afterward, when he finally fell asleep, curled around her in exhausted contentment, she was plunged into the deepest Hell imaginable. She knew that once he sent her back to her father he would forget her as if she had never existed. She meant nothing to him. He was using her to humiliate her father. And yet, when he turned to her in the dark of the night, she went willingly into his arms, aware that she would have long, lonely years ahead of her in which to repent.

8

Cadiz, Spain

"Give us a ship, Father, and we will bring El Diablo's head back to you in a basket," Arturo Santiego swore.

"*Sí*, Father, it is rumored that the pirate makes his home on Andros when he isn't on the ocean, sending Spanish ships to the bottom of the sea or in England boasting of his accomplishments," Cordero said, echoing his brother's sentiments. "If King Philip wasn't involved with gathering, arming, and provisioning a great armada to send against England, he would commission an expedition to Andros to destroy the pirate. Unfortunately our king is financially strapped and unable to afford more than one expedition."

"We will rescue Luca and her dowry without King Philip's navy and personally send El Diablo to perdition," Arturo vowed.

The sons of Eduardo Santiego were hot-tempered Spaniards eager for blood. They had just received word from Havana that the *Santa Cruz* had been sunk and Luca abducted by El Diablo. Both Luca and her dowry were missing. Now the brothers were hot for Morgan's blood and for revenge.

"Let's not be hasty. Perhaps we should wait for a ransom demand," Don Eduardo suggested.

"We cannot wait that long," Arturo spat. "While we sit here doing nothing that bastard is defiling our sister. Don Diego will no longer want her, we all know that."

"Surely the pirate knows how valuable our sister is," Cordero, the more level-headed of the pair, said. "It is possible that he will not take her virginity, knowing that it will reduce her value to us. That's why we must act swiftly and strike when he least expects it."

"*Sí,*" Arturo agreed eagerly. "Give us a ship and fifty men and we will rescue Luca and deliver her to her bridegroom in Havana, with her dowry intact," he added.

"What about her reputation?" Don Eduardo asked. "Don Diego might no longer want her even if by some miracle El Diablo has spared her innocence. There will be rumors and gossip about her abduction that not even the governor-general will be able to quell."

"Double the size of her dowry," Cordero advised. "We will take it with us. Don Diego is too smart to turn down so great a fortune."

"Are you sure you can find Andros?" Don Eduardo asked sharply.

"Give us a captain who knows the area and we will find it," Arturo assured him. "We will slip in on a moonless night and strike when he least expects us."

"Hmmm, it could work," Don Eduardo mused after giving the matter careful thought, "if he's on Andros. But instead of killing the bastard, take him to Havana. The pleasure of killing him should be left to Don Diego. Luca is his intended bride; he is the one most affected by her abduction."

"*Sí,* Father, we will do as you say," Cordero concurred. "I feel certain he is still on Andros. He won't leave until a ransom demand is delivered or an answer received. When may we depart?"

"I will make all the arrangements. The *Santa Maria* is in port now. Give me a day and a night to provision her, find the men you require, and gather additional funds from my coffers to increase Luca's dowry enough to make her still palatable to Don Diego."

"We will not fail, Father," Arturo promised. "We will rescue our sister and deliver her to her intended."

Andros Island, the Bahamas
Three weeks later

Spreading her thighs with his knees, Morgan pressed into Luca, filling her with his strength, bringing a soft sigh to her lips. His mouth took hers, fevered, urgent, as he moved his hips in seductive invitation. Luca responded by arching against him, bringing him deeper into her honeyed sweetness. Morgan groaned, the taste and heat of her making him wild for release. His bronzed shoulders glistened with sweat, and his face was drawn into stark lines that bespoke the high degree of control he was exerting.

What was there about Luca that made him want her so desperately? he wondered, not for the first time. He never tired of thrusting into her tight sheath, making her his again and again. He had merely to look at her to want her. Once he had discovered her real identity, she had taken to wearing her own beautiful clothing, and sometimes the sarong Lani had given her. He loved her best in the sarong, with her feet and shoulders bare, her magnificent breasts unhampered by bone and steel. Even with her shorn hair she was an outstanding beauty. And though he tried desperately to deny the spell she wove around his senses, his body reacted in typical male style.

Moaning softly beneath her breath, Luca felt herself spiraling out of control. Morgan's lips moved from her mouth to her breasts, licking and suckling her nipples, bringing her closer and closer to that moment of ecstasy toward which her body strained. She no longer feared that suspended moment of splendor when she exploded in shattering climax. She was not the innocent she once had been, for her virtue had been thoroughly compromised. Morgan had seen to that. Despite her inexperience, she knew beyond a doubt that Morgan was an incredible lover. An insatiable, demanding lover who held her spellbound in the web of his seduction.

Morgan lavished tender care on Luca's nipples, loving the way she moaned and arched against him. He raised his head from his succulent feast, watching her face intently.

"I love your nipples." His voice was raspy, his desire rampant against her. "All plump and rosy, just begging for my attention.

You're exquisite, Luca, I couldn't ask for a better mistress." He thrust deeper, withdrew, in and out. Sweat dripped from his face onto her breasts. "Now, sweetheart, now!"

Luca barely heard his words. She was already reaching for that high plateau of pleasure only Morgan could give her. She was convinced that no other man had the power to raise her to such awe-inspiring heights. Somewhere along the way her traitorous body had betrayed her high ideals. Her sins compounded each time she lay in his arms, reveling in his lovemaking. The day would arrive, she knew, when she must repent her sins. And face the fact that Morgan was merely using her. He was a sensual, lusty pirate who took women when it suited him and discarded them just as easily, as he had discarded Rouge.

Suddenly Luca's thoughts scattered as Morgan's hips pumped vigorously, sending her over the edge. She clutched his shoulders and screamed, her body shuddering as wave after wave of pure bliss washed over her. When Morgan had wrung from her all she had to give, he raced toward his own climax, releasing his seed in a violent rush toward ecstasy.

Several minutes passed before Morgan

eased himself to Luca's side. He didn't speak; he couldn't. As always, making love to Luca affected him in ways that alarmed him. He could recall no time since reaching adulthood that a woman had such an impact upon his life. Yet even as he listed the many ways in which Luca inspired and aroused him, he knew she would be leaving soon. Stan Crawford would return with the ransom, and he would send Luca on her way. No matter how many oceans separated them, he'd never forget the Spanish woman who aspired to sainthood but settled for paradise.

Luca felt Morgan withdraw from her and turn away. She felt his rejection keenly. She was astute enough to realize that he wanted her physically while utterly rejecting who and what she was. Nothing could change her Spanish heritage, or the fact that she was her father's daughter. She chose not to break the tenuous peace between them, so she turned her face to the wall and gave herself up to sleep. Sometime during the night Morgan pulled her naked body into his arms, holding her close, as if he feared she would be torn from him.

The *Santa Maria* sailed into the cove under the cover of a moonless night.

Andros lay sleeping and secure. No one stirred on the beach. The ship anchored a short distance from shore, and two long-boats were launched by a landing party of armed men. Arturo and Cordero led the party ashore, the oars slipping noiselessly through the water. They beached the boats and pulled them into the protection of brush and trees.

Arturo led half the men in one direction while the rest followed Cordero in another. Since little was known about Andros, each group was to search for El Diablo's lair. The Spaniards found no ships in the small cove, which could be either a good or a bad omen. It could mean that El Diablo was no longer on the island, which was bad if Luca was with him. If they were lucky it meant that El Diablo had dispatched his ship without himself at the helm and was sleeping soundly in his house. Finding the beach un-guarded puzzled the brothers, but it did not stop them from pushing forward into the in-terior of the island.

Arturo was the one who found the path leading through the trees. He led his men quietly through the murky night and was re-warded when a rambling house loomed be-fore them in a clearing. No guards were visible, and Arturo thought El Diablo stupid for not protecting himself against invasion. But then, how could he have known that the Santiegos would invade his island to retrieve what had been stolen from them? Andros was off the beaten path and rarely visited by ships.

Arturo found the door unlocked and motioned his men inside, scoffing anew at such carelessness. Slowly he negotiated the stairs, his men close on his heels. They were very quiet, very careful. A branch of candles that Lani habitually placed on a table at the top of the stairs each night lit their way. Arturo opened the first door he came to and looked inside. The hinge squeaked, and he froze. The room was empty and he moved on.

Arturo cracked open a door further down the hall and peered inside. He saw a shadowy figure in the bed and slammed the door open with a resounding bang. One of his men had removed the branch of candles from the hall table and now thrust it into the room, providing enough light to see two naked bodies intimately entwined on the bed.

"Bastard! Rapacious bastard! You will pay for dishonoring my sister!"

Morgan jerked upright. It took a moment for his head to clear, and when it did he cursed himself for a fool. He reached for his sword, which he never left far from his side, but it was too late. More men than he could count were on him instantly.

Luca screamed and tried to pull the sheet up to her chin. She could see the intruders leering at her, and panic seized her. Had the island been invaded by brutal pirates or unfriendly natives? She gasped in recognition when she saw her brother, and she guessed that he had been sent to rescue her.

"Cover yourself," Arturo snarled, sending Luca a virulent scowl. "What has happened to my innocent sister?"

Then everything happened so quickly that Luca barely had time to think, let alone speak. Arturo's men charged Morgan, and Arturo dragged her from the bed at the same time. She watched in growing horror as Morgan was pummeled and beaten unconscious.

"Take him to the ship," Arturo ordered his men. Then he turned his attention to Luca. "Where are your clothes?"

"There's a trunk in my room." She pointed to a room down the hallway. "What are you going to do to Morgan?"

"You won't have to worry about him hurting you again," Arturo said curtly. "He'll be safe enough chained in the hold

until we reach Havana. El Diablo has corrupted his last woman."

"Havana!" Luca looked stunned. "Why
are we going to Havana? I wish to return to
the convent."

"That is out of the question. You're to be
taken to your intended." He glared at her
through narrowed lids. "What in the hell did
you do to your hair?"

"I cut it. But forget that. You know as well
as I that Don Diego won't have me now."
She had expected to feel crushing shame for
the sin she had committed with Morgan,
but to her surprise she did not. "You found
me in Morgan's bed. Don Diego will spurn
me, he's a proud man."

"You did not go willingly to the pirate's
bed," Arturo said craftily. His expression
turned grim when he realized what must be
done to save his sister's reputation. He and
Cordero had already discussed what would
happen if El Diablo had indeed ravished
their sister. "Don Diego will take into account that you are a widow and accept you
along with a generous addition to your
dowry."

"A widow? I . . . I don't understand."

"There is no time now for explanations.
Get dressed. We must return to the ship before we are discovered."

"Leave Morgan on Andros," Luca begged. "You have me, there is no need for further bloodshed."

"Leave El Diablo behind? Are you mad? Cordero will have my head. There is a hefty reward out for the pirate. He has defiled you, an innocent young girl on her way to her bridegroom. El Diablo will die for his many counts of piracy against Spain. I'm sure Don Diego will make it a slow, painful death."

He dragged her to her room and pushed her inside. "Hurry and dress. I will wait right here for you. One of my men will carry your trunk aboard the *Santa Maria* when you're finished."

Morgan came to his senses slowly, aware of his aching head and bruised body. Santiego's men had beaten him senseless then dragged him naked to the ship, where he was chained to the bulkhead in the dank, musty hold. It was dark, he could hear rats scurrying about and felt them brush against his bare legs. He kicked out, cursing viciously when one of the rodents sank sharp little teeth into his ankle. His only consolation was that Luca wasn't suffering. Her brother would never harm her.

Not for the first time Morgan cursed his

carelessness. He had been so besotted with Luca that he had never considered the possibility that Santiego would send his sons to invade his stronghold on Andros. Before he had passed out he had heard someone say that the caskets containing Luca's dowry had been located in a storeroom and were being transferred to the galleon. He didn't care about the plunder, they could have that. What really hurt was losing Luca before he'd had a chance to tell her. . . . Too late. Too damn late.

While Morgan bemoaned his fate, Luca sat in the captain's spacious cabin with her head bowed as her two brothers roundly castigated her. A priest, sent along to counsel Luca after her rescue, stood nearby, his expression as disapproving as Luca's brothers'. All three considered her behavior with the infamous pirate outrageously wanton.

"How could you beg mercy for the bastard after what he's done to you?" Arturo raged.

"He did force you, didn't he?" Cordero questioned more reasonably.

"At first . . . not exactly . . . it was more like . . . seduction."

"You went willingly to his bed?" Arturo thundered. "Are you telling me that you were the willing mistress of El Diablo?"

"Not exactly," Luca hedged. "Not at first, anyway. I begged him to send me back home. I even pretended that I was a nun, but in the end Morgan had his way."

"You should have killed yourself," the priest said sternly, stepping forward into the circle of light. "But what is done cannot be changed. We must rectify this terrible wrong immediately."

Luca raised her eyes, looking directly at the priest. "I did not wish to die by my own hand. As you say, what's done is done. Unfortunately nothing short of a miracle can change what has already happened. If the convent will have me, I will devote what remains of my life to God."

"That won't be necessary, Luca," Cordero assured her. "The scoundrel seduced you, and we will see that he does right by you before he dies. You have been promised to Don Diego, and Father's honor is at stake. Arturo and I will take steps to make certain Don Diego doesn't look elsewhere for a bride."

Luca's brow furrowed. "I don't understand. How can you make things right? Nothing is the same. Don Diego expects an innocent bride."

Cordero and his brother exchanged knowing glances. "Don Diego's pride will be restored when he learns he is wedding a widow instead of a dishonored virgin. Widows remarry all the time."

"But I'm not a widow. Don Diego wouldn't believe such an outrageous lie."

"Ah, my dear sister," Cordero informed her, "you will indeed be a widow after you are married to El Diablo and he is put to death for his vicious acts of piracy on the high seas. A very wealthy widow, at that."

Luca's mouth flew open. "That's ridiculous! Morgan will never agree to that. Nor will I."

The priest stepped forward. "You are distraught, my child. It distresses me that you have been duped by the pirate to become his mistress. Your family won't be satisfied until his sin against you is avenged. A marriage between you and El Diablo is the only way to make this thing right. Once the pirate is put to death you can get on with your life. You will be a respectable widow. A rich one. Don Diego will be pleased."

"We don't need your compliance, Luca," Arturo warned. "Father Ricardo will marry you and the pirate no matter how much either of you protests. He will do it because it is what God would want."

Father Ricardo nodded sagely.

Cordero walked to the door, opened it,

and called to a sailor working nearby on the rigging. Cordero removed a key from his pocket and tossed it to the fellow. "Bring the pirate topside, Julio. Give him something to wear — we don't want him offending his bride on his wedding day."

"*Dios.*" Luca's plea ended on a sob. "If I agree to marry him, will you spare his life?"

"Then you wouldn't be a widow, would you?" Cordero said. "Fear not, sister, we wouldn't kill our own brother-in-law. We will leave that unpleasant chore to Don Diego. Father will be pleased with the way we've handled things."

The brothers were very similar in looks. Both darkly handsome with slim bodies and elegant features. Arturo, the younger and more explosive in nature, was somewhat more muscular than Cordero, the more levelheaded of the pair. Luca loved them both dearly, but right now she could have gladly wrung their necks.

Morgan kicked out ferociously when one of his furry companions boldly attacked. He pulled at the chains binding him, cursing his captors and all Spaniards in general. In all the years since he'd escaped his forced slavery, he'd never imagined himself a captive a second time. He swore that if he ever got himself out of this predicament it would never happen again.

Morgan tensed, suddenly aware that someone was approaching from above. A dim light appeared through the grill at the top of the ladder. He heard a grating sound, then a man popped into view. The dark-skinned sailor stared at Morgan, his contempt palpable.

"You are no longer pretty, El Diablo," Julio said in rapid Spanish.

"I never was," Morgan replied in the same language.

Startled, the sailor sent Morgan an appraising glance. "I see you speak our language. It is good that you will be able to participate fully in the marriage ceremony held in your honor."

He moved cautiously to the bulkhead, releasing Morgan's chains from where they had been attached to an iron ring. Then he stepped back, holding his sword at the ready.

A few moments later a second sailor started down the ladder, carrying a bundle under his arm. "Are you down there, Julio?"

"About time, Matteo. Give the captain the clothes. It wouldn't be proper to attend a wedding dressed inappropriately." Matteo proceeded down the ladder and offered

Morgan the clothing on the outstretched tip of his sword.

Morgan hesitated only a moment before accepting the tattered pair of trousers and threadbare shirt. He stared at them a moment, then he shrugged, nodding toward his chained ankles and wrists. "Remove the chains."

"First the leg irons," Matteo advised. "I do not trust the bastard."

Julio approached Morgan gingerly. "Keep the sword at his throat, Matteo. He is one dangerous hombre." When Julio reached Morgan, he bent and unlocked the leg irons. "There," he said, stepping back, "you may put on the trousers now."

Morgan stepped into the soiled, ill-fitting canvas trousers and tied the strings together at his waist. When he was done, Julio reattached the leg irons and unlocked the chains at his wrists.

"Now the shirt," Julio said, prodding Morgan with the tip of his sword. "And do not try anything courageous. We are well out to sea; there is no escape."

Morgan shrugged into the shirt. It was loose and flowing and fit his muscular build without splitting the seams. When he was dressed Julio clasped the irons on his wrists and prodded him up the ladder.

"Your presence is required in the captain's cabin, pirate," Julio smirked. "A woman cannot become a widow until she is properly wed and her husband departs this world for the next." By now everyone on the ship knew what the Santiegos were planning for El Diablo.

Morgan shuffled stiffly up the ladder, his bruised body protesting the brutal treatment he had suffered. Hampered by the chains, his dragging steps were slow and measured. When he reached the deck he blinked repeatedly, nearly blinded by the bright light. Morning had arrived while Morgan had lain unconscious in the hold, and with it came the knowledge that he was on a ship bound for God only knew where.

Morgan was pushed roughly across the deck and into the captain's cabin. He stumbled on his fetters then fell flat on his face. He raised his head and saw Luca. She looked haggard, sad and exhausted.

"What have you done to Luca?" he asked harshly.

Arturo lunged for Morgan, but Cordero held him back. "We have done nothing to our sister. It is you who have done her injury. You raped her. She was innocent until you abducted her and made her your mistress."

Morgan's gaze settled disconcertingly on Luca. "Did she say I raped her?"

"There was no need. She was found in your bed," Arturo answered. "You will pay with your life, Captain. But first you will make amends to our sister. Get up!"

Luca's heart went out to Morgan, feeling keenly his anger and confusion. She wanted to reach out to him, to help him to his feet, but she didn't dare. Any move she made toward him now would only further antagonize her brothers. Later, after she went through with this forced marriage and their tempers cooled, she'd try to find a way to free Morgan before they turned him over to Don Diego. The thought of his death made her physically ill.

Morgan raised himself painfully to his feet, his face set in grim lines. "What do you want of me? It would take a miracle to restore Luca's innocence."

Arturo lunged at Morgan again, but Cordero stepped between them. "You will marry my sister, Captain," Cordero informed him coolly. "Father Ricardo is willing to perform the ceremony."

Shocked, Morgan's gaze flew to Luca. "Marry? You want me to marry your sister? Bloody Hell!"

"You will be married immediately, Captain," Cordero continued smoothly. "But fear not, the wedding will be of short duration. And there will be no honeymoon. Fortunately for Luca, your execution in Havana will leave her a widow so she and Don Diego can marry as originally planned. But not before you have made out a will leaving all your worldly goods to your bereaved widow. It is rumored that you are enormously wealthy."

"If I am to be executed, why bother with a wedding at all?" Morgan asked evenly.

"You have dishonored our sister. Santiego pride demands that you right the wrong done to her. Widowhood will suit her, I think. Don Diego's honor will be assuaged, and all will be as it should be."

Morgan sent Luca a contemptuous look. "I'll admit she wears black well. What if I don't agree to a marriage?"

"You will agree, for you have no choice," Arturo threatened, clenching his fists beneath Morgan's nose. "I know you care little for Luca's welfare, but she deserves happiness. Widowhood is much more palatable than admitting she was a man's whore."

Luca blanched. "Arturo!"

Morgan's face tautened with rage. Calling Luca a whore was blasphemous. If he hadn't been chained he would have torn into Luca's brother.

"It is true, Luca," Arturo returned. "Everyone will consider you a whore. Marrying the pirate before he is put to death is the only way to redeem yourself." He motioned Father Ricardo forward. "You may begin the ceremony, Father."

Luca glanced apologetically at Morgan, but it had little affect on his fierce scowl. They were both pawns in her brothers' scheme to restore her respectability, and there was nothing either of them could do about it. When Father Ricardo called for her response, she answered without hesitation. She agreed to take Morgan Scott as her lawful husband. Morgan's reluctance was plainly evident. Only when Arturo pricked Morgan with the tip of his sword did he agree, albeit sullenly, to take Luca as his lawfully wedded wife.

In a shockingly short time he was a married man. He stared at Luca, more than a little surprised that he felt scant regret at making Luca his wife. Immediately following the brief ceremony he was forced to sign a will, written and witnessed by Father Ricardo, leaving all his worldly goods to Luca, his beloved wife.

"Don't I get to kiss the bride?" Morgan asked, slanting Luca a sardonic grin.

Cordero sent him a fierce scowl then

opened the door and summoned Julio. "Take him back to the hold and guard him well."

"Wait!" Luca cried. Was this how it was going to end? How could she live knowing she had caused Morgan's death? She'd rather die along with him than marry Don Diego. "I wish to speak to Morgan alone."

"Impossible!" Arturo snorted. "The bastard has ruined you beyond redemption. Be grateful that we have salvaged your reputation."

"Morgan is my husband," Luca insisted.

"Not for long," Cordero replied. "We have done our duty by you, little sister. We want only what is best for you. Accept your fate graciously. Your future is with Don Diego. Once the pirate is dispatched to Hell you will forget that he ever existed."

Luca thought it highly unlikely that she'd ever forget Morgan.

"Take him away," Arturo repeated. Julio nudged Morgan with his sword. Morgan hesitated, sent a scorching look over his shoulder at Luca, then shuffled out the door.

The utter hopelessness of Morgan's situation nearly broke Luca's heart. When had these powerful emotions invaded her heart? she wondered dismally. When had she stopped thinking of Morgan as a loathsome pirate?

When had she begun to love him?

9

Havana, Cuba

The deep water of Havana harbor permitted the *Santa Maria* to drop anchor at the seawall and lower a gangplank directly onto the quay. Throughout the years the town had seen numerous attacks from English, French, and Dutch pirates. In 1537 the city was sacked and burned, and a half century later in 1586, just the previous year, it had been threatened by Sir Francis Drake. It was no wonder that King Philip II of Spain had just recently ordered the erection of La Punta and Moro castle in defense of the city. With the population of Havana pushing three thousand, the residence of the governor-general had just been moved from Santiego de Cuba to Havana.

Standing at the rail of the *Santa Maria*, Luca saw the skeleton of Moro castle rising like a grim specter against the brilliant blue sky. It wasn't completed yet, but when it was she knew it would be an effective deterrent against marauding pirates and invaders. Luca's dejection was evidenced by the slump of her shoulders and glazed expression. They had been at sea for nearly a week, and she had failed to find a way to free Morgan.

Her husband. She closed her eyes and savored the taste of the word on her tongue, until she recalled that Diego's plans for Morgan would make a widow of her.

Luca had found no way to help Morgan. Both Arturo and Cordero guarded her like a hawk. The only time she was let out on deck was in the company of her brothers. Pleading for Morgan's life had earned her naught but their contempt.

"Are you ready to go ashore, Luca?" Cordero asked as he came up to join her.

"As ready as I'll ever be, Cordero. Is there nothing I can say that will persuade you to take me back to the convent? I don't want to become Don Diego's wife. I never did."

"It is for your own good, Luca. Arturo and I want your happiness. Don Diego will take care of you." His gaze settled on her hair, and he sighed heavily. "Be sure you cover your head. Your shorn hair is a disgrace."

"I explained why I cut it," Luca said. "It

will grow back. You haven't told me what you're going to do with Morgan."

"His fate has already been decided. His death will ensure your future. Don Diego can't marry you until you are a widow. Don't fret, things will work out."

Luca's eyes took on a haunted look. "You don't understand, do you, Cordero? I . . ." she bit the tender underside of her lip, ". . . love Morgan."

Cordero looked at her as if she had lost her mind. "The bastard ruined you. How can you love him? You are truly innocent, Luca, if you believe the scoundrel cares for you. You fancy yourself in love, nothing more. Don Diego is older, wiser, he will guide you in the right direction."

"No, I . . ."

"Ah, there's Arturo now. He will take you to Don Diego. I will follow at a slower pace with the prisoner. We will meet at the governor-general's mansion." He hurried away, ignoring Luca's pleas in behalf of the pirate. His sister was young. She knew nothing about life's trials and tribulations, or men who took advantage of innocents. He felt certain Don Diego would help Luca forget the pirate and what he had done to her.

Luca was already on the quay with Arturo when Morgan was brought up from the hold by Julio and Matteo. His fetters clanked noisily as he shuffled up the ladder and stepped onto the deck where Cordero was waiting for him. But the brief glimpse he had of Luca was enough to satisfy him of her well-being.

His wife. The thought brought him a certain amount of satisfaction, improbable as it sounded. Soon he would die, and she would be his widow and the wife of another. Bloody Hell!

Prodded forward by Cordero and his men, Morgan walked through the narrow, crowded streets to the governor-general's mansion, dragging his chains behind him. He was the object of much speculation as people stopped to gape at him. When Julio boasted that their prisoner was none other than the infamous El Diablo, an outcry rose up against the vicious pirate who had plundered the Spanish Main without mercy these past years.

"Fear not, good people," Cordero promised. "The pirate will be turned over to the governor-general. I hear Don Diego is a man who doles out punishment harshly. Justice will be done."

Luca and Arturo were shown into Don Diego's office immediately. He greeted them effusively, his dark, intelligent gaze probing Luca relentlessly. When his secretary had given him the names of his visitors, he could hardly credit the fact that his intended bride had been released by the infamous El Diablo and was here in Havana. As far as he knew no ransom had been requested. After one look at Luca he knew why El Diablo had abducted her. Luca Santiego was an astonishing beauty. What man in his right mind would willingly release her once she had graced his bed?

"Arturo, how good to see you again," Don Diego said, grasping Arturo's hand in welcome. His gaze slid almost insultingly over Luca. "You have changed, *querida*."

"I was ten years old the last time you saw me," Luca said sourly.

"Sit down, sit down. You must tell me everything. I did not expect you in Havana. When I learned the *Santa Cruz* had been sunk and you abducted by El Diablo, I despaired of ever seeing you again. You must have suffered greatly. Your father must have parted with a fortune to get you back."

Arturo cleared his throat. "There is a great deal you don't know, Excellency. Perhaps it would be best if Luca is allowed to rest while we discuss the matter at hand."

"Forgive me, *querida*," Don Diego said,

turning to Luca. "You must be exhausted." He reached for a bellpull and summoned a footman, instructing him to conduct Luca to one of the guest rooms and summon a maid to see to her needs. When Luca was gone, Don Diego turned his glittering black gaze on Arturo. "You may begin now, Senor Santiego. Tell me everything."

Arturo studied Don Diego in silent contemplation. He hadn't seen the man in years, but he'd changed little over time. Of medium height, his slim, aristocratic build and arrogant stance gave scant hint of his volatile temperament and cruel nature. Only those who dealt closely with him knew of his dark, vindictive side. The mouth beneath his slim mustache revealed perfect white teeth and a sensuous, self-serving nature. Few people were allowed a glimpse of the real Don Diego. He revealed only as much of himself as served his purpose.

But to Arturo, a man known more for his explosive temper than for his good judgment, Don Diego appeared a dignified, sensible man who would deal gently with his sister. Having come to that conclusion, Arturo launched into a lively account of his sister's rescue, leaving out the fact that Luca was discovered in the pirate's bed. Nor did he explain the reason for the hasty wedding aboard the *Santa Maria.*

"Father thought it best to bring Luca and the pirate directly to Havana," Arturo explained when he came to the end of his story. "Once you've seen to the pirate's death Luca will be free to marry again." Arturo smiled, thinking he'd handled the situation quite sensibly in Cordero's absence.

Don Diego wasn't so easily deluded. "Why did you and your brother deem it necessary to force a marriage between El Diablo and Luca?" His face was rigid, his voice taut.

"We thought it necessary in order to stem gossip that is bound to stir up around Luca's abduction. Since she will soon be a widow, I can foresee little problem on that score."

"Hmmm," Don Diego said, drumming his fingers against his desk. "Perhaps you are right. Still, you haven't told me what I really want to know." He stared intently into Arturo's eyes. "Did the pirate defile my intended bride?"

Arturo swallowed visibly. He had hoped the delicate subject wouldn't be brought up. Unfortunately it was something Don Diego had a right to know. "We have good reason to believe he did. But Father anticipated just such a disaster and provided for it. I already told you we have recovered Luca's dowry in its entirety. What I didn't mention is that in view of what has happened Father generously doubled the amount upon which you originally agreed. Every gold doubloon, each precious jewel and silver plate is intact aboard the *Santa Maria*. It will all be yours when you and Luca marry."

Don Diego's eyes gleamed with avaricious pleasure. "Doubled the dowry?" he repeated, his eyes dark with excitement. Luca's dowry was generous even before being increased by her anxious father.

It was at that point that Cordero was announced, requesting an immediate audience with Don Diego. The governor-general granted it. His expression darkened when he saw Morgan being dragged into the room by Cordero and his men.

"So this is the infamous El Diablo," Don Diego said with cool disdain. "The nemesis of the Spanish Main. You don't look so dangerous now, pirate."

"His name is Morgan Scott," Cordero explained. "He is one of the queen of England's courtiers."

"Too bad he must die an ignoble death in Havana." Don Diego smiled thinly. Death would not come easily for El Diablo. "He has defiled my betrothed bride and grown rich on Spanish plunder. I will see him in Hell for what he has taken from me."

Morgan's lips stretched in wry amusement. "No man, including you, will have from Luca what she willingly gave to me. If you or her brothers care for her at all you will return her to the convent. It is what she wants."

"Bastard!" Don Diego aimed a vicious blow to Morgan's middle, sending him reeling backward. "I intend to make Luca a widow very soon and wed her as Don Eduardo and I planned. But first I will make you suffer for corrupting my bride-to-be. A quick death is too easy for a rapacious abuser of Spanish womanhood."

Before Morgan could gather his wits, Don Diego summoned the guards and had Morgan taken away to the prison. Located near the waterfront, the foul air, filth and dampness soon tamed the most recalcitrant prisoners, if they didn't sicken and die first.

After Morgan was dragged from the room, Diego turned fiercely to confront the Santiego brothers. "Was your sister the pirate's willing whore? I want the truth."

Arturo flew out of the chair, but Cordero wisely held him in check. "Our sister was forced, Don Diego. Luca was an innocent, gently reared in a convent. Surely you don't think she invited ravishment."

"Of course not, I do not blame Luca at all," Diego lied smoothly. "She is young. Fear not, we will deal well with one another once she learns her place. About the dowry," he reminded Cordero. "You have it with you? Arturo wasn't lying when he said Don Eduardo graciously doubled the amount agreed upon, was he?" He was nearly salivating.

"My brother spoke the truth. Father increased Luca's dowry in hopes of making Luca's 'small indiscretion' easier to disregard."

"Very generous," Diego said, "though unnecessary. Luca is a treasure. You were wise to marry her to the English scoundrel. It will put many a tongue to rest. Once she is a widow people will forget her shame. You can leave Morgan Scott in my care, he will be executed with all due haste. You may leave Havana with the knowledge that Luca is now under my protection."

"*Gracias,* Don Diego," Cordero said. "We should leave immediately. King Philip needs every ship he can get his hands on for his Expedition. A great armada is gathering at Lisbon and is to sail soon for English waters.

The heretic queen will be destroyed for the greater glory of God. Hopefully the *Santa Maria* will return in time to join the armada."

"Make haste, my friends. I will send my most trusted men to the *Santa Maria* to transfer Luca's dowry into my keeping. I will also authorize my secretary to turn over to you the reward for bringing in El Diablo. Whatever you need to provision your ship for the journey is yours."

"Shouldn't we say good-bye to Luca first?" Cordero asked, suddenly not so certain of Don Diego's intentions toward his sister. He hadn't mentioned marriage. The man was too smooth, too cool and calculating. Vaguely he wondered if he and Arturo had made a mistake in bringing Luca to Havana.

"It is best that you do not upset your sister more than she already is. I will tell her in the kindest way possible of your departure."

"I don't know . . ." Cordero said doubtfully. "Luca will expect to see us tonight."

"Don Diego is right," Arturo concurred, looking forward with relish to the reward money. "We should leave Luca to her fiancé. He will do what's proper. We have accomplished what we set out to do. Father will be pleased."

Cordero wasn't so sure but pushed his doubts aside. After all, Diego del Fugo was a respected and honest man.

Diego had extended every luxury and amenity to Luca. She had soaked in a much needed and appreciated bath, then tested the comfort of the bed. She had promptly fallen asleep and was awakened later by her maid, who told her Don Diego expected her presence at dinner. The usual dinner hour was nine o'clock.

Luca wanted to look her best and donned one of the beautiful gowns from her trousseau. The silk was a particularly lovely shade of yellow, fashioned with a high neck and wide ruff that circled her throat and framed the delicate beauty of her face. The maid had clucked her tongue disapprovingly at the unfashionable length of Luca's hair, but by the time the lace mantilla was draped over a turquoise comb atop her head, her lack of hair was barely noticeable.

There was a compelling reason why Luca wanted to look her best. She still had hopes of persuading her brothers and Don Diego to spare Morgan's life. Slim hopes, but hopes nonetheless. If she failed, she hoped to convince them to allow her to spend the remainder of her days in a convent atoning for her sins. If Morgan's life was to end in his prime, her own life meant nothing to her. She'd rather let another woman have him than contemplate his death.

At the stroke of nine Luca swept down the long curving stairway to the main floor below. Don Diego was waiting for her at the foot of the stairs.

"You're punctual; how refreshing." His penetrating gaze traveled the length of her form, then upward to her face. Admiration shone in the shimmering depths of his eyes. But beneath the admiration lurked something else, something deep and dark and disturbing.

"I'm always punctual," Luca murmured.

He offered his arm and she graciously accepted, suppressing a shudder of revulsion. She hardly knew the man but had already judged him harshly. No man could compare favorably to her handsome pirate. They entered the dining room, ablaze with a bank of branched candles. Luca searched the room and was dismayed to see that the table was set for two people.

"Won't my brothers be dining with us tonight?"

His eyes gleamed darkly. The smile that curved his lips appeared sinister in the candlelight. "Your brothers returned to Spain.

They were quite anxious to return in time to add the *Santa Maria* to King Philip's armada." He seated her in the chair at his right and took his own place at the head of the table.

"Without saying good-bye to me? They would not do such a thing. What have you done to them?"

That seemed to make Diego angry. "You will learn to hold your tongue! Why would I wish to harm your brothers when they returned my soiled bride-to-be to me? Am I not fortunate?" he mocked. "By now all of Havana is gossiping about the intended bride of Diego del Fugo becoming whore to the infamous El Diablo."

Luca drew back in shock. "If you felt that way why didn't you send me back to Spain with my brothers?"

Diego laughed nastily. "And have your brothers return your dowry to your father? I am not stupid, Luca. Besides, you are a beautiful, desirable woman. It would be foolish of me not to keep your dowry and let you pleasure me with that enticing little body of yours. I'm eager to see what the pirate has taught you."

Alarm shuddered through Luca. "Did my brothers know how you felt?"

"Your brothers think I am the soul of

kindness and generosity for taking their ruined sister off their hands. Few men would be so forgiving. Besides, the reward they collected for El Diablo greatly eased their consciences."

Luca drew herself up defiantly. "I will not marry you. You may keep my dowry. I will return home on the next ship."

"And destroy my reputation as an honorable man? Oh, no, *querida,* this match has been planned a long time. Your father expects it."

"You still want me after . . . after . . ."

". . . after you have been thoroughly corrupted by El Diablo?" he finished crudely. "Your body interests me, Luca, I cannot deny that. You look so innocent, but, ah, such fire beneath the surface. I want to explore that fire, *querida.* But marriage?" He laughed harshly. "Women like you are good enough for a man's bed but not to bear his name or children. You shall serve as my mistress."

"I will not!" Luca spouted indignantly.

Don Diego eyed her narrowly. "I wonder," he mused, "if you protested as much when the pirate made you his whore."

She rose abruptly, intending to leave his vile presence.

"Sit down, *querida,* do not make a scene

before the servants." He picked up his napkin, shook it out, and lay it across his lap. "We will discuss this further after our meal. I do not wish to have my digestion upset."

"I am no longer hungry, Don Diego. If you'll excuse me I will go to my room and pack. I will be leaving on the next ship available."

He grasped her wrist in a brutal grip; the pain wrung a cry from her lips. "Sit down, I said."

Luca sat abruptly, rubbing her wrist where his fingers had bruised her flesh.

He smiled. "That's better."

The servants filed in then, serving the elegant meal with all the pomp and ceremony due the governor-general's lofty status. They ate in silence, Diego gustily and Luca hardly at all. Surprisingly Luca's fears weren't for herself but for Morgan. If Diego thought so little of her, how was she ever going to convince him to spare Morgan's life?

"We'll take coffee in my private chamber," Diego said, pulling out Luca's chair.

Luca wished herself anyplace but at Diego's mercy. How could her father do this to her? How could her brothers leave her at this man's mercy?

"Come, *querida,* there are things we need to discuss."

Luca preceded him up the stairs, her heart pounding, her knees weak and rubbery. The only thing she wanted to discuss with Don Diego was Morgan's release. And she didn't need the privacy of his chambers to do that. What would she do if he wanted her in his bed tonight? She couldn't do it! She couldn't.

The sitting room of Diego's personal chamber was small, private, and richly furnished with dark, heavy furniture. The night was warm, and the windows facing an outside gallery were open to catch the ocean breeze. She caught the scent of flowers wafting upward from the walled garden below. She perched gingerly on the edge of a small love seat, watching warily as Don Diego sat down beside her.

"Now, where were we?" Diego remarked. "Ah, *sí*, I remember." He reached out and caressed her cheek with the back of his finger. Luca stiffened. A gesture that was meant to be tender felt ugly and vile. "I will enjoy having you for a mistress."

"Don Diego, you cannot mean it. My father trusts you. He would be appalled at the way you are treating me."

"Don Eduardo left you in my care, Luca. He insulted my pride by offering a dowry I could not refuse. He suspected you were

206

ruined, but he wanted to be rid of you in order to save himself embarrassment over your shameful behavior with the pirate. What I do with you now is entirely up to me."

"No, that's not true! Father expected you to marry me, not shame me."

"How can I shame someone who is already a whore?"

Luca's face flamed. Unfortunately everyone would judge her the same way Diego had. Yet she felt shockingly little guilt for giving herself to Morgan. That little bit of happiness she'd found in his arms was probably the only happiness she'd ever know in her life. But perhaps, she thought slyly, something could be salvaged from this gross travesty.

"If I become your mistress will you grant me something in return?" Her bold request caught him by surprise.

"You are in no position to ask for anything, *querida*."

"Would you prefer a willing mistress? Or one who fights you tooth and nail?"

He stared at her. "What is it you wish of me? Fancy clothes? Jewels? Gold?"

"None of those. Free Morgan Scott. I'll do anything you say, just don't kill him."

Diego sent her a speculative glance. Then

he laughed, laughed until his eyes watered. He wiped his eyes and shook his head. "Willing or unwilling, I will take you when it pleases me. As for your infamous El Diablo, his fate is sealed. Tomorrow I will sign the papers for his execution. Within the week Spain will be rid of an enemy."

Luca blanched, fighting to remain conscious. "I want to see Morgan before . . . before . . ."

Diego smiled nastily. "How touching. The man must be an amazing lover. But I am better." He pulled her into his arms, but she struggled violently. He picked her up and started toward his bedroom, but her kicking and punching angered him and he snorted in disgust. "*Caramba!* Perhaps you will appreciate me once your pirate is consigned to Hell. I am a patient man, I can wait." He dropped her abruptly. "Get out of here! I'm not in the mood to fight for your favors tonight."

Luca picked herself up from the floor and stumbled to the door. "Wait!" he said slyly. She paused to look back at him. His dark eyes narrowed cunningly. "I have changed my mind. You may see your damn pirate. My carriage will be waiting outside at three o'clock tomorrow afternoon." He turned away, and Luca fled the room.

Morgan shifted uncomfortably on the hard dirt floor. His aches and pains were many and varied, and the vile stench of the straw beneath him made him physically ill. Last night his jailers had come to torment him. His ribs were on fire from their vicious blows, and his face was black-and-blue. There was a cut over his right brow that leaked blood into his eye.

Chained and helpless, he could not adequately protect himself. When the jailers had finished their sport, he had curled up into a ball and tried to sleep. He awoke this morning feeling as if every bone in his body had been broken. But they hadn't taken the cat-o'-nine-tails to him and he was grateful.

It was noon before a meal of sorts was delivered, which Morgan pushed aside with distaste. He knew he was going to die, and he would rather die hungry than eat slops. Death. How final it sounded. If there was anything in his life he would repent of, it was his treatment of Luca. He should have sent her back to the convent like she wanted instead of using her in an act of misguided vengeance against the Spanish. She didn't deserve his callous treatment. She had been an innocent until she had fallen into his hands, where she had become a victim of his lustful revenge.

He recalled their hasty wedding aboard the *Santa Maria*. Luca was his wife; his until death parted them. That thought gave him little comfort.

He prayed that God would forgive him for taking her against her will. But God knew he couldn't have kept his hands off her even if he'd wanted to. He had wanted her fiercely, more than any other woman of his acquaintance. And she had desired him. Her passionate response to his loving had proven her need for him. After his demise she would become the bride of the governor-general of Cuba. He'd give his life to save her from such a fate, but it seemed his life was no longer his to give. Soon it would be snuffed out as easily as a candle.

Morgan's musings came to an abrupt end when he heard the sound of footsteps approaching his cell. He rose unsteadily to his feet, moaning from the effort it cost him. The door flung open and Diego stepped inside. He wrinkled his nose, as if offended by Morgan's foul stench combined with that of the filthy straw. The thin mustache above his lip quivered in disgust. He stared at Morgan in open hostility.

"Good afternoon, Captain. Did you sleep well?"

Morgan's lips curled sardonically. "As well as can be expected."

"I slept amazingly well. One usually does after a fulfilling night in the arms of a passionate woman. I must commend you on Luca's performance. Quite spirited, most inventive. You taught her well."

"You bastard!" Morgan reached for Don Diego's throat, but his chains hampered his movement. Don Diego stepped back, well out of reach.

"Did I tell you Luca became my mistress last night? I'm sure you will understand why I cannot marry her after you defiled her. You rendered her unfit to bear my name. But she will do nicely as a mistress. When I find a respectable woman to marry I will give Luca to one of my men, or send her to a brothel."

Morgan knew del Fugo was goading him, and it was working. The thought of the Spaniard's hands on Luca made him want to vomit. "Luca is too good for you."

Diego smiled. "Do you think so? Perhaps you'll change your mind after learning how sweetly she begged me to punish you for ruining her for marriage. She despises you for corrupting her, Captain. If not for your untimely intervention she would have become my wife. Anything she could possibly wish for would have been hers."

"Luca never wanted to marry you."

"You think not? Perhaps Luca will tell you herself how much she hates you. Do you think I'd trouble myself to have you beaten when you are already under sentence to die? It was Luca's wish that you be punished and made to suffer for your sins against her. She pleased me so well last night I can deny her nothing. Cortez, bring the cat!"

A man appeared in the doorway, holding a cat-o'-nine-tails. He handed it to Diego, then stepped aside.

"Strip the shirt from his back and fasten his chains to the wall!"

Cortez moved with alacrity, tearing off Morgan's shirt and affixing his chained wrists to a ring halfway up the moldy wall while Diego held his sword ready should Morgan resist. Morgan barely had time to catch his breath before he heard the cat swish through the air. He braced himself for its bite but still wasn't prepared for the agony when the separate thongs cut into his flesh. He stiffened and bit his lip to keep from crying out. His back was on fire; he could feel blood dripping down into the waistband of his trousers.

Diego delivered another vicious blow before Morgan had time to recover from the first. After that he never knew where one left off and the next began. Then abruptly the lashing stopped. Morgan slumped against the chains, scarcely able to lift his head.

Diego pulled out an immaculate white handkerchief and wiped the sweat from his brow. "I think Luca will be satisfied with your punishment for one day. We don't want you to die prematurely. All of Havana is looking forward to your execution tomorrow. A great holiday has been declared. If Luca wishes it, I will visit again tomorrow before your execution and make sure you are properly repentant before you go to meet your maker."

Diego's words burned into Morgan's brain. The pain of the beating chased all the tender thoughts of Luca from his mind. Luca wanted him punished. Luca was the cause of his unbearable pain. Luca hated him. It wasn't enough that he was going to die. Bloody Hell, no! The bloodthirsty little witch enjoyed making him suffer. If he got out of this alive, which was highly unlikely, she'd pay, and pay dearly. His last thought before he passed out was that while he may deserve to die for his acts of piracy, he didn't deserve to suffer this agony for the sake of a vindictive woman.

It was all so humorous. He had actually begun to love the little witch!

10

Luca stepped through the ornate entrance to the governor-general's mansion at exactly three o'clock. The coach Don Diego had promised her was waiting. Her heart was pounding in fear and anticipation as the coachman handed her into the lavish rig. Diego was nowhere in sight, which pleased Luca. She wanted to be alone when she spoke to Morgan. This might be the last time she'd ever see him alive.

The ride to the prison was very short; Luca realized that she could have walked the distance with no difficulty. The jail was housed in a low building crudely constructed from stone blocks. The only windows were placed high up in the wall where prisoners could see nothing but a speck of sky. She knew how miserable Morgan must be, which served only to strengthen her resolve to find a way to help him.

The coachman flung open the door, and Luca stepped down from the coach. A moment later the door to the calaboose swung wide, and Diego stepped out to greet her. Luca's composure shattered.

"Punctual as usual, *querida.*" He smiled blandly.

"What are you doing here?"

"Interrogating the prisoner." His smile grew wider. "The pirate was proving most difficult. I'm afraid my men and I were somewhat overzealous in subduing him."

Luca's gaze shifted downward, to the whip held loosely in his right hand. He had kept it hidden behind his back, and she hadn't noticed it until he had drawn her attention to the weapon. He seemed to take unholy pleasure in taunting Luca with what he had done to Morgan.

"*Dios!* You've beaten him! How could you?"

Diego's voice was taut with menace. "How could I not? He stole something from me that cannot be replaced. Before he goes to the gallows tomorrow he will be beaten again, and yet again, until I am satisfied that he has suffered sufficiently. Come along, *querida,* he should have revived from his swoon by now and is ready to take more punishment."

"Please, no more beatings," Luca begged. "Hasn't he suffered enough?"

Diego gritted his teeth. "No, not nearly enough." He gave her a brutal stare, then smiled slyly. "It is within your power to help him."

"Tell me what I must do! I'll do anything. Anything."

"Then you must tell El Diablo that you have willingly become my mistress. That you hate him and begged me to punish him for ravishing you. You will say that you are glad he is being put to death."

A gorge rose up in Luca's throat. "No! That's not true!"

"Nonetheless, you will repeat everything I just said. Otherwise the pirate will be beaten hourly until his death. Is that what you wish for your lover?"

"Why are you doing this? What can it possibly gain you?"

"Satisfaction," Diego said grimly. "I would prefer to dismember him slowly, loping off his hands, his feet, his limbs, making him suffer the agonies of Hell for what he has done to Spain and to you. King Philip cares not how he dies, only that he does so. I am being merciful."

Luca swayed, dangerously close to fainting. Diego was a clever fiend. He didn't know the meaning of mercy. He knew she wouldn't allow Morgan to be cruelly tortured, that she'd say or do anything to save him from further agony. Even lie.

"If I do as you say, will you release Morgan?"

Diego looked at her as if she had two heads. "Release him! Never! What I will do is order the beatings stopped and allow him a dignified death."

A sob caught in Luca's throat. It was so little. Too damn little. But for the sake of a peaceful death she would lie. Then, before Diego took her to his bed, she would join Morgan in death. Living without Morgan was no longer an option.

"Very well, I will do as you say. May I see Morgan alone?"

"I do not trust you, *querida*. We will go together." He handed the whip to one of the guards and led Luca into the building.

The fetid odor of death and suffering assailed Luca as she walked through the guard room into the dim, dank corridors of the calaboose. Heavy wooden doors were barred from the outside and thick stone walls separated the individual cells. A small grille low down on each door enabled the guards to pass food through to the prisoners. Diego stopped abruptly before a closed door, and one of the guards hastened to raise the bar.

"Bring a light," Don Diego ordered. A light appeared and the door was kicked open.

The light revealed a tableau straight from Hell. When Luca saw Morgan, a scream hovered at the back of her throat. He was still chained to the wall, just as Diego had left him earlier. His back was a mess; livid bruises and numerous cuts slashed deeply across his shoulders and rib cage. Diego squeezed her arm in warning, and her outcry died abruptly in her throat.

Morgan turned his head slowly toward the light. His body was afire, his head pounding. Cloaked in a haze of stabbing pain, he saw Luca standing beside Diego. She stared at him, saying nothing, and his pain turned into red-hot rage. He wet his lips, trying to summon enough saliva to ease his parched throat.

"Why did you bring your slut with you, del Fugo? Wouldn't she take your word that her orders were being obeyed?"

Diego laughed nastily. "I told her you would not be a pretty sight, but she insisted upon seeing for herself that your punishment was all she wished it to be." He turned to Luca. "Tell him, *querida,* tell the good captain exactly what you think of him."

Luca closed her eyes and summoned the courage to say the words that would stop Morgan's torture. "I hate you for what you did to me, Captain."

"Come, Luca, isn't there something more you wish to say?" Diego's hand tightened brutally on her arm.

Luca winced. "I am Diego's mistress. Thanks to you I am not fit to become his wife. He is . . . he is a wonderful lover." The last was added more for Diego's benefit than for Morgan's. Anything to appease the demented monster and ease Morgan's suffering.

Diego sent her a pleased smile. "Ah, you are a treasure, *querida*. I am well pleased with you, in bed and otherwise. Do you think El Diablo has suffered enough for corrupting your life?"

"Oh, *sí*," she said quickly, too quickly to suit Diego. "I am satisfied. His death is all I desire now."

Diego's smile turned sour. "You are too tender, *querida*. Let us leave this foul place. There are better things we can do with our time than converse with a condemned man."

When he reached out a slim, manicured hand and caressed Luca's breast, Morgan wanted to kill the man. Then he wanted to kill Luca. He knew he deserved her hatred for his callous disregard for her innocence, but didn't she realize that he truly did care for her? He freely admitted he had used seduction to win her, but she had been a willing participant. He thought he knew Luca, but evidently he hadn't scratched the surface of her perverse nature.

Luca shied away from Diego's vile caress and put all her emotions into the look she gave Morgan, but he had already turned away and did not see it. His mind and heart had already dismissed her. She had no choice but to let Diego steer her out the door. But as the door clanged shut behind her, his name left her lips on a ragged sigh. Diego clapped a hand over her mouth and dragged her away.

Morgan's head shot up. He could have sworn that he'd heard Luca call his name. His imagination must be working overtime, he chided himself. It had sounded as if her heart was breaking. He shook his head to clear it of such foolish thoughts. Hadn't Luca just admitted that she despised him? That she enjoyed seeing him beaten and tortured? She had freely admitted that she had become del Fugo's mistress. Funny, he mused dimly, he never thought he'd be brought low by a woman.

★ ★ ★

An unnamed ship slipped into Havana under cover of darkness and dropped anchor in the deep harbor. A short time later, a longboat slid away from the ship and glided through the water toward the shore. The longboat reached its destination, depositing its men on the deserted quay. Five men remained inside the boat while two others slipped away and disappeared in the shadows. The two men separated by mutual consent, each choosing a different direction. Two hours later the men returned separately to the place where they had left the longboat. They crouched in the vessel, imparting the information they had gleaned to their leader.

"Did you learn anything, Pierre?" Stan Crawford asked.

Pierre, a dark-skinned Frenchman who spoke both French and Spanish fluently, spat out a vicious oath. "The captain's here, just like you suspected. He is to be executed tomorrow."

"Bloody Hell!"

"The governor-general declared a holiday so the entire population of Havana can watch the execution. The whole town is talking about El Diablo. Finding out where he is being held was easy. What did you learn, Ramon?"

"*Dios,* the whole damn town is eager to see him strung up," Ramon revealed. Ramon was the only Spanish member of Morgan's crew and had good reason to hate his countrymen. He had nearly lost his life in the Inquisition. "The captain is in the local *calabozo* awaiting execution."

Stan gazed at the moon, calculating the hours left before dawn. "We don't have a helluvalot of time to rescue Morgan and return to the *Avenger.* You men were chosen for your ability to work under pressure. Are you with me?"

"Aye, Mr. Crawford," the men echoed in unison, "we're with ye."

"What about the woman?" Crawford asked his spies. "Do either of you know what has become of her?"

Pierre aimed a dirty stream of tobacco juice into the water. "Forget the little slut. Rumor has it that she is already warming the governor-general's bed. It's amazing what you can learn in an alehouse. There ain't no talk about a wedding, either."

"It's just as well," Crawford said bitterly. "We'll be lucky to get Morgan out alive, let alone the woman. Where's the *calabozo?*"

A short time later, seven armed men crept through the dark to the squat building that served as a jail. They traveled in single file, darting from doorway to doorway. Crawford led the way, his hand curved around the hilt of his sword. He halted the group within sight of the calaboose, where they squatted behind some thick bushes, sizing up the situation. Crawford counted two guards lounging against the door, their weapons hanging loosely in their hands. After a silent signal from Crawford, Pierre and Ramon crept stealthily toward the inattentive guards. Sneaking up from behind, they swiftly put the guards out of commission, then dragged them off into the bushes, where they exchanged clothes and took their places.

Crawford cautiously opened the jailhouse door and peered inside. The flickering light from a single candle revealed only two men seated at a table playing cards. They had timed it perfectly. Obviously the other guards were out making rounds and weren't expecting company. And if by chance unwanted company did show up, the guards posted outside the door were expected to dispatch them.

Crawford paused in the doorway and motioned his men to follow him. One by one they slipped through the door into the guardroom. Crawford did not have to tell them what to do, for they knew instinctively what was expected of them. The guards seated at the table must have heard something, for they jumped up and reached for their swords. Crawford's men were on them instantly. The battle was fierce but of short duration. The Spaniards were quickly subdued, bound and gagged, and left lying on the floor. Crawford found a ring of keys hanging on a hook in the guardroom. Two men remained behind in case the absent guards returned while the others followed Crawford.

Morgan heard scuffling in the passageway but paid it little heed. There were always comings and goings of one kind or another in this evil place. If they were coming for him he hoped it was to end his life, not torture him further with the cat. Or worse yet, taunt him with the knowledge that Luca had ordered his beating. That cut him deeper than the leather thongs plied to his back.

"Morgan, psst, answer me if you're in there."

Morgan swiveled his head toward the locked door. He feared that the severe beating he had endured was causing him to hallucinate. Mayhap the Devil had come to claim him.

"Morgan, it's Stan Crawford. Answer if

you're able. God's blood, man, we must flee quickly before we are discovered."

"Stan?" His mouth was so dry he could barely speak above a whisper. He prayed it was enough. "In here, Stan. Do you have a key?"

Relief shuddered through Stan. He had no idea when the guard changed or how many hours were left before dawn. "Aye, I have a key."

"I'm wearing shackles, Stan. I hope you have a key for those too."

The door opened with a resounding crash. Stan held a candle aloft, waiting for his eyes to adjust to the darkness. The candle nearly flew from his hand when he saw Morgan slumped against the wall, supported by the chains binding him.

Stan sucked in his breath as he took in the pitiful condition of Morgan's lacerated flesh, his swollen face, and his split lip. He swallowed convulsively. "Bloody Hell, you're lucky to be alive."

"I'm not feeling very lucky, my friend. Do you have the key, Stan? Quickly, there's much to be done before taking the *Avenger* home."

Trying one key after another, Stan finally found the one that sprung Morgan's fetters. Once he was free, Morgan fell against him, unable to support his own weight. "Can you walk?" Stan whispered. "Lean against me."

Morgan staggered and grit his teeth against the stabbing pain of his lacerated flesh. One eye was swollen shut, but his good eye was focused and steady. He nodded grimly. "I can walk."

"Let's go then." Stan took the lead. Morgan followed close behind. The passageway was quiet. When they reached the guardroom, Morgan's lips twisted into a parody of a smile when he saw that his crewmen had the situation well in hand. Stan, Morgan, and the crewmen slipped out the door and were joined by the two men who had stood guard outside.

Crawford moved purposefully toward the waterfront where their longboat waited. He urged Morgan forward, but Morgan balked, refusing to accompany Crawford to safety.

"Bloody Hell, Morgan, what is it? Do you need help?"

"There is something I need to do first," Morgan said in a voice so filled with venom Crawford was glad he wasn't the recipient of Morgan's anger.

"Shit, Morgan, you can't get to del Fugo. Forget the bastard, he isn't worth your life."

Morgan's eyes grew flinty; his face was stark with an emotion Crawford had never seen in him before. "It isn't del Fugo I want."

"Not del Fugo? Who?" Suddenly it dawned on him. "No, forget her. Leave her to her lover."

"Luca is my wife, Stan. I cannot leave Havana without my 'loving' bride." He laughed harshly when he saw the stunned look on Crawford's face. "Prepare the *Avenger*. If I don't return by dawn, sail without me."

"When did Luca become your wife? Rumor has it she's del Fugo's . . ."

". . . Mistress. I know. Nevertheless, she's my wife. We were married by a priest aboard her brothers' ship. I'll tell you all about it when I return from my 'rescue' mission."

"Those beatings must have addled your brain, Morgan. The governor-general's mansion is well guarded, you couldn't possibly get inside without being seen or heard. You are in no condition to rescue anyone but yourself."

Morgan's lips thinned in determination. "I'm still captain, Mr. Crawford. Are you going to obey orders?"

Crawford stared at Morgan in consternation. The longer they stood there arguing, the greater their risk of being caught. But he could see that Morgan was determined, and that was putting it mildly.

"Very well, Captain, I suppose there is no stopping you. But I'm going with you."

"I'm going alone, Mr. Crawford, is that clear?"

"Perfectly," Crawford grit out from between clenched teeth.

"Remember, if I'm not back by dawn, you're to sail without me. Give me a sword." Someone thrust a sword and scabbard into his hand, and he strapped it around his waist.

"Not bloody likely," Crawford muttered beneath his breath as he watched Morgan disappear around a building. When Morgan was out of sight, he spoke briefly to his men and took off after his captain. He never considered the consequences for disobeying orders, for he thought Morgan had lost his sense of reason. A man in Morgan's weakened condition had to be out of his mind to storm an enemy stronghold single-handedly. And Crawford was crazier still to think he could save his misguided captain from self-destruction.

Luca spent the entire evening in prayer. If God performed a miracle and spared Morgan's life, she would never ask another thing for herself again. She would accept whatever fate dealt her and be grateful that Morgan's life had been spared. On the other hand, if God allowed Morgan's death, she prayed for the courage to end her own life and join him in eternity.

After she had returned from the calaboose, Don Diego had left her to her own devices. He coolly informed Luca that he had decided to restrain his lust for her until after her husband had been put to death. A weeping woman would spoil his pleasure.

Luca was grateful for that small reprieve and had spent the rest of the evening at her devotions. If prayer alone could save Morgan, she reasoned, his salvation was assured. Unfortunately God worked in mysterious ways, ways she didn't pretend to understand. God had made her love the pirate, hadn't He?

Ignoring the tray of food sent to her room after she failed to appear at dinner, Luca remained on her knees far into the night. When exhaustion left her swaying dizzily and in danger of toppling over, she left her prayer bench and staggered through the open door to the gallery overlooking the garden. How peaceful it looked, she thought, stretching her weary muscles. Her insides were coiled as tight as a corkscrew; not even prayer had dispelled the tension gripping her. But the crushing thought of Morgan's impending death sent her back to her prayer bench.

Morgan climbed the garden wall and dropped heavily on the ground below. Pain splintered through him; his body felt as if it was being torn apart. Setting his teeth, he forced himself to his feet and tried to gather his scattered wits. Glancing upward, he saw a flank of dark windows facing a gallery on the second floor. He assumed most of those rooms were bedrooms, and wondered how in Hell he was going to find Luca's room. If she was in bed with del Fugo he'd take great pleasure in killing the bastard. He prayed for strength.

He was still staring intently at the second-floor windows when a small figure appeared on the gallery. The breath slammed against Morgan's ribs and he blinked repeatedly, fearing his eyes were playing tricks on him. Luca! Mesmerized, he watched as she stretched, stared into the garden for a brief moment, then turned and disappeared into the room directly behind her. If Morgan had ever doubted there was a God, he no longer did.

Morgan crept toward the house with grim purpose, noting with satisfaction the thick vines clinging to the walls of the brick mansion. They appeared stout enough and strong enough to support his body. He neither hesitated nor considered the consequences as he grasped a handful of vines and climbed painfully upward, unaware that Crawford was close on his heels, having scaled the garden wall in time to see Morgan cautiously ascend the vines to the second-floor gallery. Crawford crept through the dark garden, watching with bated breath as Morgan reached the top safely.

Morgan stepped lightly over the rail onto the gallery. He could see directly into the room where Luca had disappeared. A votive light flickered dimly before a statue of the Blessed Virgin, illuminating Luca's kneeling form. Her eyes were closed, her head bent piously. If Morgan didn't know better, he'd think she was the most holy of women. She had fooled him once, but it wasn't going to happen again, he vowed. Nun, indeed! She was a hot little witch who couldn't wait to get another man between her thighs once she had been relieved of her virginity. She had fallen into del Fugo's bed like a ripe plum while awaiting her husband's death. Hatred shimmered through him, alive and pulsating. He was tempted to wring her lovely little neck. But an emotion he preferred not to confront prevented him from throttling his own wife.

Morgan stepped into the room. Despite his exhaustion, regardless of his weakened state and brutally abused body, his footsteps were light and noiseless as he approached Luca. He was so close now he could smell the sweet scent of her flesh, feel her heat radiating outward to engulf him. Lust slammed through him, and he suppressed a groan. This was the woman who wanted his death, he reminded himself. This was the woman who fell eagerly into del Fugo's arms.

"Luca." He bent low, whispering her name.

Luca heard and turned her head. Shock shuddered through her. She exhaled sharply, her face suffused with incredible joy when she saw Morgan standing behind her. When she realized she wasn't fantasizing, that Morgan was indeed flesh and bone, she reached out to him. "Morgan, how . . ."

Morgan acted swiftly, before Luca could cry out and alert del Fugo. He clipped her on the jaw, and she went out like a light. He regretted resorting to physical violence, but he had no choice. If Luca hated him as she'd indicated during her visit to the calaboose, she wouldn't have hesitated to scream for help. He would have had no chance at all against del Fugo's guards.

Morgan let out a grunt of pain as he tossed Luca over his shoulder. Despite his weakness, adrenalin flowed through his veins now, suffusing him with desperately needed strength. He realized belatedly that carrying Luca down the vine-covered wall in his condition was going to drain what was left of his vigor.

Poised on the gallery, Morgan stared down into the dark garden, wondering if he had the fortitude to make it to the bottom with his burden. One foot was already over the rail when a man stepped out from the shadows beneath the gallery. Morgan knew a moment of panic. Then he recognized Crawford and dared to breathe again. So much for his men following his orders, he thought — not that he wasn't damn glad to see his first mate.

"Pass her down to me," Crawford hissed, indicating that Morgan should drop Luca into his arms.

Morgan hesitated but a moment before lowering Luca's inert form over the railing and dropping her handily into Crawford's arms. Morgan followed swiftly, lowering himself over the rail and clambering down the vines.

"Go ahead, I'll carry Luca," Crawford whispered, alarmed by Morgan's pallor. It surprised him that Morgan had accomplished so much after the brutal beatings he had endured. It must have taken enormous will and fortitude.

They reached the garden wall, and Crawford handed the still unconscious Luca to Morgan while he scaled the rough stone edifice. He had checked the gate earlier and found it securely locked against intruders, forcing them to leave the same way they had arrived. Crawford reached the top, let out a low curse, and scrambled down again. "A patrol," he hissed, urging caution as the sound of footsteps grew louder.

They crouched at the foot of the wall until the patrol passed. Then Crawford rose cautiously and lifted himself atop the wall. Indicating that all was clear, he held out his arms for Luca. Morgan passed his fragile burden to Crawford, who waited for Morgan to join him. Morgan reached the top and dropped to the ground on the other side, holding his sides as pain jolted through him. Then Crawford transferred Luca into Morgan's arms and lowered himself to the ground.

Safely out of the walled garden now, both men moved stealthily among the shadows toward the quay. They had one close call and were forced to take cover when the night watch passed so close they had to hold their breath until he was out of sight.

They reached the quay just as Luca stirred in Morgan's arms. She moaned softly, and he placed a warning hand over her mouth. "If you cry out, I'll wring your bloodthirsty little neck."

The longboat was waiting where Crawford had left it. All hands had arrived back safely and were anxious to return to the *Avenger.* The moment Crawford, Morgan, and Luca were aboard, the men shoved off. All hands knew it would be only a matter of minutes before Morgan's escape was discovered and the alarm given. With cannons from shore aimed at them, the *Avenger* would be a sitting duck in the water.

Once they were a good distance from the shore, Morgan removed his hand from Luca's mouth. She rubbed her jaw and glared at him. "You didn't have to hit me."

"I had to make certain you wouldn't cry out for your lover. If I had found you in del Fugo's bed, I would have killed him."

"*Dios!* Why would I warn Diego? I would have come with you willingly had you the courtesy to ask." Her eyes softened when she looked at him. "I prayed for a miracle but didn't expect one."

"If I didn't know you for a lying little witch, I would be inclined to believe you. The miracle you spoke of was no miracle at all. I don't know yet how Stan knew where to find me, but I'm grateful he arrived when he did."

"If you think so little of me, why didn't you leave me instead of risking your life to return for me?"

"Don't tell me you've forgotten already that you are my wife? My faithless wife," he clarified. "You wasted little time welcoming del Fugo into your bed. Did your brothers know the bastard had no intention of marrying you?"

"They never would have left if they had known Diego's intentions. The man is deceitful and utterly without scruples."

"He must have had something you liked," Morgan hinted crudely.

"I lied, Morgan, to save you from further beatings. Diego forced me to admit to things that aren't true in order to save you from torture. Everything I said was a lie."

"Including what you're telling me now." His face was hard, implacable, his voice cold and unrelenting.

Abruptly the longboat bumped into the hull of the *Avenger*. Several men began scurrying up the rope netting while others attached the boat to lines being lowered from above. When no one but Morgan and Luca remained in the boat, it was winched aboard the *Avenger*. In a very short time the sails were unfurled to catch the breeze, and the *Avenger* scudded before the wind, away from Havana and danger. The faintest of mauve streaks colored the eastern sky, heralding a new day.

Morgan clung to the rail and stared at the shore receding in the distance. He recalled vividly his brief sojourn on the hostile island. If not for Stan, today would have been his last on earth. His bruised and battered body would have turned to dust and ashes on foreign soil. But the memory of Luca's words hurt far worse than the torture he had endured. She had told him she hated him, that she wished for his death. She had become del Fugo's willing mistress. She had taken great pleasure in his suffering. Releasing the rail, he rounded on Luca, his eyes blazing with fury.

As the *Avenger*'s sails filled with air, Luca tried to remain calm, hoping that once Morgan's temper cooled he would see things more clearly. How could he not know that she never meant those hurtful things she said? Didn't he realize she would do and say anything to save him from torture? But when he swung around to face her, the fires of Hell burned in the depths of his blue gray eyes. Her heart thumped wildly. What was he going to do to her?

Grasping Luca's arm, Morgan pulled her roughly toward his cabin and shoved her inside. He followed, slamming the door behind him. His unrelenting hatred for her was awesome to behold. She didn't deserve this kind of treatment from him.

"Wha . . . what are you going to do?" she asked, backing away from his implacable fury. "I've done nothing to hurt you."

"I haven't decided yet on your punishment. When I do decide you'll be the first to know. I never wanted a wife, Luca, but now that I have one I will do whatever is necessary to keep you in line. Your brothers did neither of us a favor when they insisted we wed."

"Is there nothing left between us then? Nothing to build upon?"

He sent her a leering grin. "There is lust, Luca. Neither of us can deny that." Then he turned and stormed from the cabin.

11

Morgan flinched involuntarily as Stan Crawford cleansed his lacerated back and applied a salve he'd retrieved from the medical supplies.

"Hold still, Morgan. I'm trying not to hurt you."

"You're not hurting me, Stan." Morgan's glazed expression made a mockery of his words. "Tell me how you learned where to find me." He hoped Stan's explanation would take his mind off Luca, who was waiting in his cabin, contemplating her punishment. "When did you return from Spain?"

"We arrived on Andros two days after you and Luca were abducted. Lani was frantic when we arrived. She saw signs of a fierce struggle and knew you hadn't gone willingly with your captors. Who were they, Morgan? You mentioned Luca's brothers."

"Aye, Luca's brothers. They came in the dead of night and caught us sleeping."

Crawford's brow shot up. "Together?"

"Aye, together. It was foolish of me not to place guards around the island. I assumed no one had the courage to invade Andros. Did you contact Luca's father in Cadiz?"

"Funny thing," Crawford said curiously, "Santiego refused to negotiate. Now I understand why. He had already dispatched his sons to Andros. We returned as quickly as possible, never expecting to find the island in an uproar."

"The wily old bastard," Morgan muttered beneath his breath. "How did you know where they were holding me? I shudder to think what would have happened had you arrived a few hours later. I'd not be here to tell the tale."

"We have Lani's husband to thank for that. He had fallen asleep on the beach and awoke to the sound of voices. The Spaniards passed within a few feet of him but failed to see him. The night was dark and moonless. He understood little of what they said except for one word. Havana. He told Lani, and she put two and two together. We stayed on Andros only long enough to replenish our water supply and stow away enough fresh fruit for the journey."

"I can never repay you for saving my life. Thank you, my friend."

Crawford grinned. "I was appalled when you insisted on returning to the governor-general's mansion for Luca. I would have thought you'd be thrilled to get her off your hands. According to rumor she'd become del Fugo's mistress. 'Tis not like you to want another man's leavings."

Morgan stood abruptly, pulling on the shirt Stan had given him. "Luca and I have unfinished business. One doesn't discard a wife so easily. When I'm finished with her she'll regret begging her lover to torture me. She wanted my death but has steadfastly denied it. She said she was forced to say those things in order to save me from further torture." He whipped his fingers through his tousled hair. "Bloody Hell, Stan, she told me to my face that she ordered my beatings! She seemed pleased at becoming del Fugo's mistress. What in the Hell am I supposed to believe?"

Crawford shook his head in consternation. "Why did you risk your life to take Luca away from del Fugo? Unless," he mused thoughtfully, "you think she truly was forced to lie."

Morgan deliberately turned away lest he reveal more of his soul than he intended. "I don't know what to believe. I can't trust my common sense where Luca is concerned. There is something between us, something even I don't understand, something deep and disturbing. She's mine. A priest joined us in marriage, and by God she's going to remain my wife!"

Crawford was stunned by the grim purpose behind Morgan's words. Morgan Scott was a driven man. Crawford almost pitied Luca, given Morgan's frame of mind and volatile disposition.

"I didn't tell you the most important thing about the voyage to Spain," Crawford said when an uncomfortable silence stretched between them.

Morgan swung around to face Crawford. "What is it?"

"There is a great armada forming off the coast of Portugal. We saw ships gathering in the harbor at Lisbon; all kinds of crafts, galleons, galleys, vessels of all sizes and descriptions. It appears that King Philip is financing an expedition against England."

"So the Spanish monarch is finally showing his mettle. Queen Elizabeth knew something was brewing and even ousted the Spanish ambassador from England when she heard he was conspiring against her. 'Tis time to return home, Mr. Crawford. Set a course for England."

★ ★ ★

Luca paced the small cabin restlessly. Her nerves were raw, her composure shattered. It hurt to think that Morgan believed all those lies she'd told him. Even when she denied them, explaining why she'd said them, he seemed disinclined to accept her word. He was angry. Both at her and at her brothers. In a way she couldn't blame him. He had suffered horribly on her account. Not satisfied with merely ordering Morgan's death, Diego had derived great pleasure from using the cat on Morgan. And afterward Diego had insisted that Luca take the blame for the beatings.

During the following days Luca languished in abject boredom. She saw no one save for Stan Crawford, who delivered her meals, and the cook's helper, who saw to it that the cabin was kept clean and that Luca was provided with water for bathing. Neither man seemed inclined to engage in conversation. She saw nothing of Morgan, whom she supposed was still too angry to confront her. She recalled his injuries and feared he hadn't been properly treated for his numerous wounds. When she sought to question Stan, he refused to tell her anything about Morgan's condition, leaving her to stew and fret over Morgan's injuries.

Morgan was told of Luca's inquiries about his state of health, and he felt nothing but contempt for her mock concern. Did she expect to gain his sympathy by pretending remorse? He wasn't that gullible. Why then was he deliberately avoiding her? his conscience asked. Because he still wanted the Spanish sorceress, he answered truthfully. Despite all the lies she had told him he remembered how sweetly she had responded to his loving, how exquisitely she had moaned and writhed beneath him; the heat and tightness of her body when he buried himself deep inside her. Bloody Hell! He was nearly mad with wanting.

Take her, a little voice inside him urged. *She's yours.* He had every right to bed her when and where he pleased. *No,* that same voice warned. *She will bewitch you. Her Spanish blood will taint you. She will beguile you with her sweet body and tempt you with her flawless beauty.*

"She is my wife!" Morgan said aloud, forgetting that he was standing at the helm of his ship where others could hear him.

"Did you say something, Captain?" a sailor standing nearby asked.

Startled, Morgan shook his head. "Sorry, Stiles, just muttering to myself. Go about your work. Wait," he called as the sailor ambled off. "Find Mr. Crawford and tell him I want him to take the wheel. There is some unfinished business I have to take care of in my cabin."

"Unfinished business, indeed," Crawford chortled as he took the wheel and watched Morgan stride purposefully toward his cabin. He hoped Morgan had finally come to grips with his feelings for his Spanish bride. Either that or he'd finally decided on a fit punishment.

Morgan flung open the cabin door. It crashed against the wall, and he slammed it shut. Luca started violently and jumped to her feet. Had Morgan finally come to punish her? He was strong enough to snap her in two if he wished. She prayed to God he didn't.

"Morgan . . ." His name slid past her lips on a shaky sigh.

He grinned mirthlessly. "You were expecting someone else?"

Her throat was as dry as dust. "I'm not afraid of you. I spoke the truth. I was not Diego's mistress. I would have killed myself before allowing him to . . . to . . ."

"You expect me to believe that?"

"I don't care whether you believe it or not, it's the truth."

"Ah, Luca, ever proud and defiant. Do you still want to be a nun?"

"*Sí*, if I had a choice in the matter. But since I am a married woman it is no longer feasible. Unless, of course, you pay them to take me off your hands."

"You would make a terrible nun." He stepped closer, closer still, forcing her to look up at him. "How can I punish you if you are locked away in a convent?"

He touched her face, so tenderly, yet she felt the steel beneath his caress. "I've done nothing to deserve punishment."

His eyes took on a silver glint. "What do you deserve, little nun?"

"Your consideration. I am your wife."

"My wife." Though he'd never admit it, the word tasted sweet on his tongue. "I can't recall wanting a wife. If anyone had told me that one day I'd have a Spanish wife I would have cut them down with my sword. Yet to my regret I find myself lusting for you, my fiery Spanish bride."

Luca reached out to him; her sultry eyes hinted of promise, and hope. "Is that so bad, Morgan? Does my Spanish blood render me unfit to be your wife? It didn't seem to matter to you on Andros when you seduced me." Her eyes darkened with the pain of rejection. "Seducing me was nought but a game, wasn't it?" she charged. "A game you were determined to win. Once you took my innocence I became dispensable."

"You were merely my hostage on Andros, not my wife."

"You destroyed my virtue," she contended.

Morgan gave her a leering smile. "And enjoyed every minute of it. So did you, Luca, admit it."

"Unlike you, Morgan, I do not hide the truth. You risked your life for me, you can't be completely immune to me."

She was standing so close he could feel her sweet breath brush his cheek. Her chin rose defiantly, placing her lips near enough to . . .

He groaned, succumbing to the sweet seduction of her lush lips. His mouth captured hers, his tongue playing teasingly upon her lips, unwilling to deepen the kiss for fear he'd lose his soul. When Luca opened her mouth to his kiss, she denied Morgan the choice of withdrawing before his senses deserted him. He was drawn into her web of seduction just as thoroughly as a fly was enticed into a spider's web. His kiss deepened, growing almost savage in its intensity as his arms came around her. The moment their lips touched, a strange madness seized him.

Fire. A jolt of liquid, scorching flame seared through Morgan. He felt exhilarated, more alive than he'd been since the last time he'd held Luca like this. He wanted to shout at the pure pleasure of her body melding and shaping to his.

Luca strained against Morgan, savoring the taste and feel of him. His mouth was hot, persuasive, demanding. He tempted and conquered, coaxed and took, but also gave. Luca trembled with desire as his lips devoured hers. The heat of his body and strength of his desire overwhelmed her senses.

"Witch," Morgan whispered against her lips. "Spanish witch." Then he swept her from her feet and laid her on the bunk. "You drain me of the will to resist you."

Luca caught his hand and drew it to her breast, placing it so he could feel the wild tattoo of her racing heart. "If I'm a witch, you're a warlock, for you make me tremble with need."

"You hate me," Morgan reminded her.

"No, never! Well," she amended, "maybe at one time."

"You derived great pleasure from my pain."

"A lie!"

"You lay with Diego del Fugo."

"*Dios!* You are the only man I've ever known intimately."

He wanted to believe her. "You are Spanish."

"*Sí.* And you are English. That will never change."

"Bloody Hell! Do you know what you do to me?"

Morgan's eyes glittered dangerously as he placed his hand on her throat, applying slight pressure. Luca's eyes widened, waiting for his next move. He could kill her so easily.

His hand left her throat and slowly, deliberately moved downward until his palm cupped her breast. Luca released her breath in a harsh sigh, unaware that she had been holding it.

"Did you think I would kill you?"

"It had crossed my mind."

He gently explored the shape of her breast, flicking the nipple with his thumb. "I've never killed a woman in my life and I don't intend to start now."

"Damn you for your inflexible attitude!" Luca pulled away from him, her eyes flashing with anger. "You believed what Diego wanted you to believe. Why is it so difficult for you to believe me?"

"I truly want to trust you, Luca, but at the

moment it doesn't happen to matter. I want you." He pulled her against the hard ridge of his need, letting her feel how much he wanted her. "Are you going to help me remove your clothing or must I do it myself?"

His long fingers trembled as he pulled roughly, impatiently, at the ties, laces, and buttons fastening her clothes. Luca searched his face a moment before pushing his fingers away and finishing the job herself. "This is the only dress I have, I don't want it ruined." He helped her tug the dress over her hips then turned his attention to her petticoats and corset. He touched her bare thigh, and thick desire pounded through him.

Within moments she was gloriously nude, a tempting feast spread out before him, and suddenly he wanted to taste every luscious inch of her. His sword fell to the deck with a clatter. His clothing followed. Luca stared at him. Tall, broad-shouldered and muscular, he radiated a sense of power, strength, and masculine vigor. His features had been molded with boldness and originality. There was no subtlety and only a hint of refinement. He looked like a pirate, one who took what he wanted and hang the consequences.

He was her husband. Luca convulsed with

longing. She feared that if he couldn't overcome his hatred for Spaniards there would be nothing more than this between them. Lust. She might love him desperately, but she realized it would never be enough to overcome his hatred for her and her countrymen. But she could try. *Dios,* she could try.

She took his face between her hands and kissed him with a wild, sweet passion that swelled him with pounding desire. She could feel his sex, thick, heavy, fully erect, throbbing against her thigh, and reveled in the power, no matter how fleeting, she had over him. He groaned and grasped the lush curve of her buttocks, grinding himself against her in a frenzy of need.

His mouth found hers again, licking, tasting, as if he couldn't get enough of her honeyed essence. His tongue searched out all the tender places inside her mouth, scattering her wits. Leaving her mouth, his lips traveled down her body, closing around a dusky nipple. He nipped gently. Luca cried out, clinging to his shoulders and arching against him. He lifted her breast more fully into his mouth, suckling her vigorously as she shuddered and trembled beneath him.

"Morgan . . . I want you inside me."

"I'm going to taste you, Luca. Every

single inch of your delectable flesh. I'll give you what you want, but not until I'm ready."

His mouth slid downward, searing a path of fire over her breasts and stomach. He paused on his sensual journey to explore the sweet indentation of her waist, the rise of her hips, licking and kissing the satiny insides of her thighs. His fingers sifted through the dark triangle of hair at the juncture of her legs, coming close but deliberately avoiding that place where she ached for his touch. She felt herself swelling with need as his tongue moved desperately near, then abruptly withdrew. She smelled the acrid scent of her own desire and felt the gathering wetness between her legs.

Shocked by the journey his lips were taking, Luca cried out in protest. "Morgan! What are you doing? You can't . . . you don't mean to . . . oh, *Dios,* it's sinful."

He tugged her legs apart and touched her gently with his fingertips. She was slick and wet and hot. Her hands clawed gently at his shoulders. He entered her with his finger; she tightened around him, her heat scorching him. He lowered his head, parting her with his tongue. He found what he was looking for as his lips closed around the sensitive, dewy pearl nestled between her legs. Luca screamed and nearly bucked him off of her.

"Morgan! *Dios!*"

"Relax, little nun," he crooned against her flesh. "Nothing is sinful between husband and wife."

His tongue touched her again, that sensitive place between her thighs, and she nearly shattered. He tasted her boldly, his tongue and mouth working its magic upon her flesh as his fingers continued to torment her.

"I can't stand it!"

He lifted his head. "I know. Don't hold back. You're hot and wet and ready. Submit to me now."

Then he was tormenting her again, his hands, his mouth, his tongue, all working in unison to drive her insane. He showed no mercy, demanding her response, her body, her very soul. Luca could feel it building inside her; a great pressure demanding release. Intense pleasure radiated through her, and suddenly she was there, soaring to a shattering climax. A strangled cry slipped past her lips as her body jerked and vibrated in tempo to Morgan's thrusting tongue. A kind of splendor few people were privileged to experience rippled through her, and she seemed to die a little.

Morgan was brittle with urgent need. His hunger was profound, he was desperate to thrust himself into the woman writhing in ecstasy beneath him, to stroke himself to completion. He slid upward along her slick body, panting as if he'd just run a great distance as he positioned his thick manhood at the moist opening of her body. The heady scent of her desire teased him, lured him, held him spellbound.

"Luca, look at me."

Luca came to her senses slowly, still drugged from the powerful response Morgan had wrung from her. She heard him calling to her as if from a great distance and opened her eyes.

"I'm coming into you now and I want you to know who is making love to you. Concentrate, Luca. I want you to come with me."

He grasped her hips, lifting her off the bed and sliding the hard knob of his sex into her. He flexed his hips and pushed forward, filling her with his incredible strength.

"Move with me," he urged hoarsely as his shaft drove in and out of her tight sheath. The accelerated tempo of his thrusting and withdrawing sent renewed fire spilling through her veins, and she rotated her hips to match his rhythm.

"Good, so good," Morgan groaned, forgetting everything but the way his body was reacting to the woman beneath him. For a brief moment in time it no longer mattered that Luca was Spanish, that she may or may not have slept with Diego del Fugo, that she hated him enough to wish for his death.

Luca was rushing toward another explosive climax. No, not rushing, hurtling. Hurtling so fast she couldn't catch her breath. She gazed up at Morgan, noting that he was as caught up in passion as she, and at that moment she couldn't have loved him more.

"Morgan, I feel . . . *Dios*, I *feel!*"

Her words sent Morgan plunging over the edge. He shattered explosively, violently, stiffening and crying out her name as he spilled his seed into her. Luca held him tightly, soaring with him to paradise . . . and beyond.

When Luca came to her senses, she found that Morgan's comforting weight had shifted and he now lay beside her. She felt the heat of his gaze and turned to look at him. His expression was unreadable; his eyes glittered like shiny silver coins.

"I almost believe . . ." His sentence fell off, fearing to bare too much of his soul.

"What do you believe, Morgan?"

He hesitated a moment then said, "That

you really do feel something for me. No one could make love like that and not mean it."

Hope soared in Luca's breast. But Morgan's next words sent them plummeting. "You're a damn good actress, Luca. You know exactly what to do and say to make me want you. I intended to punish you but ended up making love to you. I'm aware that you have many reasons to hate me, but I had hoped . . . you truly beguiled me on Andros. Now I see you clearly for what you are."

"What am I, Morgan?"

"A Spanish sorceress who had no knowledge of your own sexuality until I showed you. Once I relieved you of your virginity you couldn't get enough. You . . ."

Red dots of rage exploded in Luca's brain. She had heard enough of Morgan's insults. Drawing back her hand, she slapped him viciously. Morgan's head snapped sideways with the force of her blow. When she would have slapped him again, he reared up and pinned her hands to the bed above her head. He glared down at her, his face a mask of fury.

"Don't ever do that again!"

"You know I was an innocent until I met you," Luca charged. "You taught me to enjoy sinful things that I would never have learned in a convent. I know you still believe

I bedded Diego, but you're wrong, dead wrong."

She flung herself from bed and crossed to the desk, pulling out drawer after drawer until she found what she was looking for. She turned back to Morgan, her face flaming from the injustice of his insults. Morgan watched her carefully, ready to react forcibly should the need arise. He relaxed when he saw what she held in her hands. It was a Bible. It had belonged to his mother, and he had made a habit of taking it with him wherever he went. It occurred to him that Luca had occupied the cabin long enough to become acquainted with every object within it.

Gloriously naked and rosy from Morgan's loving, Luca walked back to the bunk and fell to her knees. She held the Bible beneath his nose, placing her right hand on it. "Heed me well, Morgan Scott. I swear on the good book that everything I told you in Havana was a lie."

Morgan sent her an amused look, took the Bible from her hands, and tossed it aside. Then he picked her up and settled her atop him. "You've lied to me so many times in the past I don't know what to believe. You addle my brains and tempt me to perdition. Regrettably I don't have it in me to punish you, for I always end up making love to you, and your punishment becomes my pleasure."

He stroked her buttocks, lifted her slightly, and thrust up into her.

"It's frustrating to know that I could want a Spanish sorceress who beguiles and seduces me." He shoved all the way inside her, pushing her down onto him at the same time. "Bloody Hell!"

She pulsed around him hot and wet, and Morgan knew that the only way he could keep a clear head and not succumb to the wiles of the Spanish witch he had married against his will was to remain unemotionally involved. He thrust upward again, wringing a moan from her throat. Aye, that's what he'd do, pretend indifference. But later, not now. Oh, God, not now.

He lifted his head and took her breast into his mouth, his moan of pleasure eclipsing hers. He sucked vigorously, moving his loins into the cradle of her thighs. *Don't fool yourself into falling under her spell,* his brain repeated while his body reacted violently to the woman straining above him. *Don't let yourself become dependent upon the pleasure you derive from her body. Any woman would do,* he told himself. He thrust into her again, swifter, harder, wildly, his mouth urgent against her nipples. He felt himself approaching climax and moaned against her breast. Then he shoved all the way inside and lost the will to think.

Luca felt the initial spurt of his seed and surrendered to the magic of Morgan's loving. She came in a rush, throwing her head back and crying out. Morgan clamped his jaw and raced after her. When it was over he carefully set her aside and rolled away. So much for his resolve, he thought ruefully.

"Did you mean what you said, Morgan?" Luca asked hesitantly when she saw he wasn't going to initiate conversation.

"What did I say? Men say many things they don't mean while caught up in their pleasure."

"You said you'd rather love me than punish me. You said my punishment became your pleasure."

"So I did."

"It's my pleasure, too."

Morgan turned abruptly to confront her. "Then we shouldn't let it happen again, should we?"

"Why not? I'm your wife."

"Aye, my *Spanish* wife."

"Will you abandon me? It would take little effort to declare our marriage invalid, since it was forced upon us."

"We spoke our vows before a priest. It's

legal, little nun. Don't get any ideas that it's not."

Luca sent him a puzzled look. It sounded as if he was glad they were married. "Can't we live like a normal married couple? We could be happy on Andros."

"There is nothing normal about our relationship. You're my enemy." That rather disturbing statement gave him a moment's pause. One did not enjoy making love to one's enemy, did one? He pushed that confusing thought aside and continued. "Do you have any idea how my friends in England will react to you? The queen will be furious with me for marrying without her permission. I've always enjoyed the queen's good graces and don't intend to lose them now."

Luca heard nothing beyond England. "If you're thinking about taking me to England, I won't go! I'd prefer to live on Andros."

"Andros is out of the question at this time."

He rolled out of bed, gathering his scattered clothes from the floor, where he had thrown them in his haste to make love to his wife. He dressed quickly, securing his sword firmly in place.

"I think it would be best if we avoided one another in the future. I'll provide adequate

261

support, but we won't be sharing a bed. I've hated the Spanish far too long to change for your sake." What he didn't say was that he feared what she did to his sanity.

Luca sent him a startled look. "Not share a bed? You're a lusty man, Morgan Scott."

He shrugged. "There are women aplenty."

"And men aplenty," Luca reasoned calmly.

Morgan whirled around, nearly choking on his rage. "If you take a lover I will kill him! And maybe you."

Luca's chin rose defiantly. "If you take another woman into your bed I will kill her! And maybe you."

Morgan's lips twitched in amusement. "I believe you would, my fiery Spanish nun. Indeed, I believe you would."

His laughter lingered long after he was gone.

12

Morgan's restraint deserted him within a few short days. Just thinking about Luca sleeping in his bed filled him with fierce longing. The ship was his prison and his Hell. There was no escaping her magical allure. It beckoned him, tempted him, lured him, and he lacked the strength to resist her magnetism. He fought a magnificent battle, and lost.

Luca heard the cabin door open and sensed Morgan before she saw him. "Bloody Hell, Luca, you've bewitched me!" He stormed into the room like a maddened bull, his nostrils flaring at the scent of a female. He removed his sword, and by the time he reached the bunk he was naked.

The mattress groaned beneath his weight, and his boots hit the deck as he flung them off. When he slid into bed beside her, the scalding heat of her body seared the length of him as he pulled her into his arms.

"I did no such thing," Luca whispered, shivering in response to his purely male domination. *Dios,* Morgan had but to touch her and she burst into flame.

"I tried my damnedest to resist you, but this ship isn't big enough to escape my desire for you. I have no will where you are concerned. You're a sickness I have to purge from my body. Before we reach England I intend to have my fill of you."

Luca smiled inwardly. If she didn't love the arrogant pirate she would have found the strength to resist. But if Morgan had no will where she was concerned, she could almost pity him, for she felt the same. She opened her arms and welcomed him eagerly, hungrily. They were husband and wife; she would make him love her.

After their passionate encounter, Luca was allowed the freedom to roam the deck. The crew knew she was off-limits and, between Morgan and Mr. Crawford, she was rarely out of someone's sight. The weather had grown colder now that they were in northern waters; it was December, and the blustery winds blew sleet and rain against the windows. The men were bundled up to the eyebrows, and there were days Luca had to remain in the cabin to keep warm. It was difficult to believe that a few days ago she had been in the tropics, enjoying sunshine and warm breezes.

The weather was dismal and rainy a few weeks later when they sailed past Plymouth and entered the English Channel. Luca stood in a sheltered spot on the deck, staring in dismay at the large contingent of ships gathered in Plymouth harbor. She was about to search for Morgan to question him on the activity, when he appeared at her side.

"What do you suppose all those ships are doing in the harbor?" Luca asked curiously.

Morgan debated telling her the truth and decided it could do no harm. "I suspect the queen is gathering a force to meet the armada your king is sending to strike against England."

Luca looked at him guardedly. "If King Philip is sending an armada it is to rescue the Catholic Queen Mary."

" 'Tis too late, and well they know it. Queen Mary was executed at Fotheringhay in February of this year."

Luca paled. "Executed? How barbaric. What manner of woman is your queen?"

"A cautious woman wise in the ways of the world," Morgan replied.

What he didn't say was that she was also

vain and possessive. She wanted her courtiers around her at all times and demanded their full attention, love, and devotion. Few if any of the gallant men orbiting around her bright star brought their wives to court unless ordered to do so. She even demanded that her courtiers join her summer progress when she traveled from estate to estate, visiting her domain. And woe be to those who married without her consent. Elizabeth's reaction to his own misalliance was bound to earn him a harsh reprimand, Morgan thought dimly.

"If Queen Mary is dead, I doubt King Philip is considering a move against England."

Morgan sent her a quelling look. "You know little about politics, Luca. I'm anxious to reach London and find out what is transpiring. Being at sea for weeks and months at a time has its disadvantages."

"I thought you said we were docking at Portsmouth." During one of his more talkative moods Morgan had revealed that they would debark at Portsmouth and travel by coach to his home in West Sussex.

"We are. Mr. Crawford is to remain with the ship and sail it with the queen's portion of our plunder to London. He had the foresight to load it aboard the *Avenger* before he left Andros. After I escort you to my country estate I must hasten to London and present myself to the queen. I admit I'm anxious to learn what is taking place between Spain and England and place my ship at England's disposal."

"You're going to leave me in West Sussex?" Luca swallowed a lump of panic. "I . . . I don't know anyone there. What will I do?"

"You'll do what other wives do in your situation. Stay home and see to the servants and estate. And raise our children, should there be any," he added, thinking how miscrably he'd failed at keeping himself from her bed. She could be carrying his child right now. The thought left a sour taste in his mouth. Never in his wildest dreams did he imagine a Spanish mother for his children.

With Luca in West Sussex and him in London, it would be a hell of a lot easier to forget he had a wife, let alone a Spanish one. There were any number of hot-blooded court ladies who would jump at the chance to ease his loneliness.

Before Luca could form a suitable reply, Morgan was called away, leaving her to stew in silence. Did Morgan intend to leave her to languish in boredom on his country estate while he danced attendance upon his queen? And what about those months he'd spend at sea plundering Spanish ships for England's glory? What would become of her in a hostile country with no friends to sustain her?

The ship docked with little fanfare. Before Morgan and Luca went ashore, Morgan sent Crawford out to hire a coach to carry them to Haslemere in West Sussex, which Luca learned wasn't too great a distance from Portsmouth. When he reappeared at her side he was fashionably attired in trunk hose, knee-length satin breeches, and brocade doublet. He cut a handsome figure, she thought, admiring the curved length of his long legs. But she much preferred him in the trousers, flowing white shirt, and high boots he wore aboard the *Avenger*.

Unfortunately her own attire left much to be desired. And there was nothing she could do to improve her shorn hair. Though it had grown somewhat, it was still indecently short, hugging her face and head in a riotous mass of ebony curls.

Shivering beneath the voluminous folds of one of Morgan's capes, Luca huddled in the seat beside her husband as their hired coach rattled along the rutted road. Noting her discomfort, Morgan pulled her into his arms, all too aware that once they reached his estate any intimacy between them must necessarily end. Luca was becoming too important for his well-being; he needed to put his forced marriage into perspective. Once he was at court among his own kind he expected Luca's hold on him to diminish.

"What do you think of the English winter?" Morgan asked in an effort to turn his dangerous thoughts from the warm body nestling against the curve of his own.

"I do not like it," Luca said truthfully. She gazed through the window at the passing scenery. The grass was sere and brown and the trees had lost their lush foliage. A misty rain obscured her view of the land, and a bone-chilling dampness had settled over her like a dismal gray curtain. It was very depressing. She sighed wistfully. "Spain's gentle climate is much more hospitable. And Andros is a virtual paradise compared to this."

Morgan laughed. "I'm inclined to agree with you. Nevertheless, this is the country of my birth, and I must report to my queen periodically and see to my estates."

"What will happen to me when you return to sea?" Luca asked, aware of how little he valued her as a wife.

Morgan scowled. *What indeed?* he asked himself. Bloody Hell, what a muddle. He hadn't intended to marry until he was ready to give up the sea and settle down. Then he'd planned to make the rounds of those boring social affairs and find a bride among the young hopefuls offered on the marriage market. He'd hoped for a rich one, who would be content to be sequestered in the country, raising his children, while he attended to the queen and took a mistress in London to keep boredom at bay.

Unfortunately he had been married against his will to a spirited Spaniard whose fiery disposition and sultry beauty kept him in constant turmoil. The simple truth was that he wanted her, but her question unsettled him.

"When I return to sea you will remain at Scott Hall."

Luca opened her mouth to protest, but Morgan stopped it with a kiss. He couldn't help himself. Her lips, slightly wet and glistening, were tempting him. So disturbing and yet irresistible, like forbidden fruit. He pulled her onto his lap, clamping his mouth over hers in a heart-stopping kiss. His lips were anything but gentle as he nudged her mouth open with his tongue so he could savor her sweet essence. He loved the taste of her, the feel of her in his arms, so solid and warm and giving. It was almost as if she . . .

No, he wouldn't think about that. His life was complicated enough without wondering if Luca felt anything special for him. Lust, certainly, but other than that he dared not contemplate. Of course there was no question of his own lustful craving for his fiery Spanish bride. His weakness for Luca was reason enough to distance himself from her before he was irrevocably lost. His vendetta against Spaniards made it impossible to care for her, didn't it?

But with Luca squirming provocatively on his lap it was difficult to recall the bitter dregs of revenge. Her hands clung to his shoulders, pulling him close as his mouth plundered hers. Her whimpers of strangled delight drove him nearly wild.

He broke off the kiss and stared at her. Her eyes were so dark and filled with erotic promise that he tumbled headlong into their depths without a care for the consequences. "Witch," he whispered hoarsely, truly convinced she had bewitched him. How else could she shatter his senses, if not by witchcraft?

"Not a witch, Morgan," Luca replied on a

breathless sigh. "Just a woman who . . ." She bit her tongue. She had nothing to gain by telling him she loved him and everything to lose. She had to convince him she wasn't his enemy before admitting to such a thing.

"A woman whose hot blood and tempestuous nature answers a need in me," Morgan finished. "A woman whose own need matches mine."

He kissed her again, his mouth hot and demanding as he slowly drew her skirts past her thighs, providing himself free access to his most fervent desire.

"You enjoy what I do to you, sweetheart." His hand found the soft nest between her legs, his fingers caressing the tender, slick flesh of her innermost self. His head dipped to her breast, making a wet circle on the material of her bodice. "I enjoy it, too."

Luca caught her breath and held it. His intimate caress was making her giddy. "Your arrogance is appalling."

His fingers moved unerringly into the sweet warmth of her sheath, and he groaned as his rod hardened and nearly split the lacings of his codpiece. "Damn clothing is fashioned by men without vision," he muttered, shifting to accommodate his rather daunting erection. " 'Tis nearly impossible to do justice to both of us in this uncomfortable contraption, wearing layers of constricting clothing."

Luca moaned in disappointment. Morgan heard and chuckled. "That doesn't mean I can't pleasure you." He shoved his finger deeper and Luca jerked convulsively. Once her heart settled down she began thrusting against his stroking fingers, driving him even deeper inside her. When his thumb found the throbbing pearl of sensitivity, she erupted in violent climax. He stayed with her until the last tremor left her body. Then he pushed down her skirts and cuddled her close.

"Did you enjoy that, sweetheart?"

Luca blushed furiously. "You know I did. But what about you?" She groped for him, determined to do for him what he had just done for her.

Morgan gasped when her hand curled around his rod, still painfully erect, still throbbing. His control dangled by a slim thread. It would take so little to join Luca in ecstasy. Gathering his scattered wits, he shoved her hand aside. He decided that this was as good a time as any to test his willpower and prove that he could resist Luca's seductive allure. It would be the challenge of a lifetime. When he spoke, his voice was a strangled parody of frustration and thwarted desire.

"No, Luca!" His words came out harsher than he had intended. Luca drew her hand away as if scorched.

"I did not mean to . . . to . . . offend you. I wanted to please you."

Morgan's heavy lids came down to shield his anguish. He couldn't afford to let Luca know how difficult it was to protect his heart from her. Abruptly he plucked her from his lap and set her down on the seat beside him.

"We'll pass the night at an inn," he said coolly. "Normally the journey from Portsmouth to my estates is not overtaxing, but we left the *Avenger* late in the day, thus necessitating a stop. I don't like being on the road at night without outriders. Highwaymen abound in the area. I've sent someone ahead to engage rooms for us and arrange for a meal and baths."

Luca regarded Morgan in consternation. What had she done or said to make him change so abruptly? He went from lover to stranger in the blink of an eye. Except for that brief interlude a few moments ago, it appeared as if Morgan was deliberately discouraging further intimacy between them. He had as much as told her he was going to leave her in the country while he pursued his interests in London and cavorted outrageously at court. Well, she admitted, he hadn't used those exact words, but she could read between the lines.

Darkness hovered at the edge of dusk as the coach clattered into the courtyard of the Hoof and Feather Inn. The innkeeper came out to greet them, wiping his hands on his stained apron.

"Welcome, Captain," he greeted effusively, having been already informed of Morgan's visit. " 'Tisn't often we get so distinguished a guest at the Hoof and Feather. Sit ye down while me wife prepares a right proper meal for ye. Nothing's too good for El Diablo and his lady wife."

He turned to Luca, and the smile died on his face. "Yer pardon, Captain Scott, I understood ye would have yer wife with ye."

Luca shrank back against Morgan. Obviously the man expected a peaches-and-cream English miss instead of a dark, sultry Spanish senorita. Was this just a sample of the kind of reaction to her marriage she could expect in England?

"You have the right of it, innkeeper," Morgan said with a hint of annoyance. "This is indeed my wife."

"But . . . but she's Spanish, Captain. I thought, that is, everyone in England knows . . ."

"Bloody Hell!" Morgan muttered when he saw the stricken look on Luca's face. No matter what he felt for vile Spaniards, he didn't enjoy seeing Luca hurt by his countrymen. "It matters little what everyone in England thinks of my marriage. The subject is not open for discussion. I'm starved. My wife and I would like our meal served immediately."

"Aye, Captain," the innkeeper said, bowing obsequiously. He knew he had gone beyond the bounds of common courtesy, but he was so stunned by the sight of El Diablo's Spanish bride that he had allowed his mouth to run away with him.

"Pay him no attention, Luca," Morgan said once they were seated at a private table before a roaring fire.

Luca stared into the dancing flames, feeling the warmth soak into her chilled bones. After several moments of silent contemplation she turned to Morgan. "You need not apologize for your countrymen. It is all very clear to me. They feel as you do about my country. But they are wrong. King Philip would never send an armada against your queen. With Queen Mary dead there is no reason."

"That remains to be seen," Morgan said dryly. Then the food arrived, and all conversation stopped while they concentrated on the feast placed before them.

Luca set down her fork and yawned hugely. Noting her exhaustion, Morgan snapped his fingers. The innkeeper appeared at his elbow, scraping and bowing.

"Show my wife to her room," Morgan said. "See that a tub is prepared so she may bathe before she retires."

The innkeeper, a short, rotund man with lively blue eyes, turned stiffly toward Luca. "If ye will follow me, yer ladyship. Me wife will see to yer bath."

"Thank you," Luca said softly. Before she turned to follow the innkeeper, she asked Morgan, "Are you coming up?"

"I'm going to sit before the fire a while longer and finish my brandy. But you need not worry that I will awaken you when I retire, for I have my own room."

Luca sent him a puzzled look. "You've engaged separate rooms for us?"

He stared moodily into the fire. "I thought it best."

"I see," she said with subtle rancor. "Good night, Morgan." She refused to show her crushing disappointment as she followed the innkeeper up the narrow stairway, her head held high despite her flagging spirits. Once on English soil Morgan had changed. She hardly knew this distant stranger. She didn't relish spending her days buried in the country while the man she loved sought his pleasures elsewhere. That thought darkened her eyes in splendid fury.

Morgan sat staring into the fire long past the time when he should have retired. He hated his weakness where Luca was concerned and renewed his vow to maintain strict control over his dealings with his wife. He was strong; he fully expected to win his fierce struggle to contain his hunger for Luca no matter what the cost to his heart. Once he lost his need for the Spanish vixen he would be free to live the kind of life he had been accustomed to before being forced into this marriage.

The innkeeper breathed an audible sigh of relief when Morgan finally sought his bed. Morgan's eyes were blurry and his gait wobbly when he passsed Luca's door. He did not linger but continued on to his own room, pleased with his ability to ignore the pounding of his heart.

The next morning Morgan was waiting for Luca when she arrived downstairs. He was somewhat pale, and his hands shook as he quaffed a cup of ale. Luca tried to over-look his sour disposition. If he was suffering from overindulgence it served him right after deliberately ignoring her the night before.

She ate her breakfast of cold mutton, cheese, bread, and fresh milk in silence, all too aware of the disturbing way in which Morgan studied her through bloodshot eyes. Why was he looking at her like that? she wondered, trying to maintain her dignity despite his heated gaze. She shifted uncomfortably several times before Morgan realized he was staring.

God, she's beautiful, he thought dully. Her dark, sultry beauty was exotic and innocently seductive. She wore her Spanish heritage with pride, he thought. With that sobering thought he hoisted himself to his feet. "Are you ready, Luca?"

"*Sí,* Morgan." She rose in one graceful motion. He escorted her into the waiting coach, and they rattled off down the road.

Morgan slept until they reached the village of Haslemere. Then he came abruptly awake, as if sleep had merely been a pretense to avoid communicating with her. Luca wondered how he could run hot one minute and cold the next.

"We're nearly at Scott Hall," he said with an eagerness that surprised her. "You'll like it. It's a lovely estate with orchards, a small forest, and a river flowing through the acreage. My parents loved the place, and I can understand their feelings every time I return."

"If you like it so well how can you stand to be away months at a time?"

He was silent for so long that Luca thought he hadn't heard. When he finally spoke his voice was distant, as if his thoughts were focused elsewhere.

"London society and political intrigue amuse me, and my estate requires a good deal of my time, but after a short visit on land the sea always beckons to me. I've made a home on Andros; an environment far removed from London and its dissolute society."

Luca fell silent. No wonder Morgan had no need for a wife. He was married to the sea. Her being Spanish by birth complicated the situation between them. Her brothers had done her no favor by insisting she and Morgan marry. Then again, they had no idea Morgan would live to lay claim to his wife. Her mistake had been falling in love with the pirate.

Luca gazed appreciatively at the mellow brick mansion rising tall and imposing on a grassy knoll surrounded by a vast expanse of manicured lawns and formal gardens. An orchard stretched from the west edge of the gardens to the river, which wound placidly through the forest beyond. Luca thought that whoever had charge of Morgan's estate in his absence did a magnificent job of maintaining it. It had retained a patina of elegance despite Morgan's long absences.

"It's lovely," Luca said. Morgan was strangely pleased by her sincerity.

"It's rather small," Morgan said as the coach stopped before the tall, slim columns standing guard at the front entrance. "Only thirty rooms, but I think you'll find it comfortable. You may redecorate in any way you wish. Very little has been changed since my parents lived here."

The coach door opened, and Morgan stepped down. With an economy of motion he swept Luca from inside and set her down beside him. His hands dropped away from her waist abruptly when the front door opened and a tall, gaunt man somberly dressed in unrelieved black livery stepped out to greet them.

"Captain," he said, bowing stiffly. "On behalf of myself and the staff, I would like to welcome you home." His piercing gaze settled on Luca, and he sniffed disdainfully. "We were told you were bringing home a wife."

The man, servant or not, was intimidating, and Luca took a step backward, bumping into Morgan. He placed his hands on her shoulders to steady her.

"Forsythe, you old reprobate." Morgan laughed, slapping the man on the back. " 'Tis good to see you. You never change. I still remember the day you swatted my behind when I teased my sister unmercifully."

Forsythe's face twisted into what could have passed for a smile. "And well you deserved it, Captain." Once again his gaze found Luca, as if having judged her and found her lacking.

" 'Tis fitting that you should be the first to meet my wife," Morgan continued. "Luca, this rather dour-faced individual is Forsythe. He runs the household with an iron fist and has done so since my parents engaged him as a young man. He's kept the household running smoothly since I was a young lad. I couldn't do without him."

Forsythe's gaunt frame swelled with pride. And love. Luca could see that the majordomo felt more than passing affection for the daunting El Diablo.

"Thank you, Captain." He gave Luca a stiff-legged bow. "I'm pleased to meet you, Lady Scott." Forsythe's voice was coolly polite yet distinctly disapproving, nothing like

Luca would expect it to be if he were welcoming an English wife to Morgan's home. She felt the rejection keenly.

Luca murmured an adequate reply while Morgan looked on, frowning.

"Please summon the rest of the servants to the foyer. I want them to meet their new mistress," Morgan instructed Forsythe with a hint of censure.

"Right away, Captain," Forsythe said, his attitude unbending as he turned to carry out Morgan's instructions.

Morgan started to follow him inside, but Luca touched him lightly on the arm. He paused and looked askance at her.

"He doesn't like me," Luca said, trembling. "All your servants will find reason to hate me. All your friends will despise me because they distrust anyone who is Spanish. Even you hate me!" she cried in growing panic.

"Luca, stop imagining things. It's not Forsythe's place to like or dislike his mistress. He will follow your orders because he is loyal to me and mine."

Morgan could temporize all he wanted, but he was astute enough to realize that Luca would have difficulty fitting into his traditional English household. But there was no help for it. Everyone knew of his consuming hatred for Spaniards. Bloody Hell! How could he explain bringing home a Spanish bride?

Luca stepped into the foyer, intimidated by the large group of servants gathered to greet her. To her chagrin, she could not find one friendly face among them. What she did see was curiosity, hostility, and cool disdain.

Forsythe introduced the cook first; a large woman wrapped in an immaculate white apron who looked down her long nose at Luca and sniffed. Next came the cook's helpers and pot scrubbers. The maids, all young and pretty, curtsied with much the same condescension as the cook. There were twelve servants in all, and every one of them made known in one way or another their lack of respect for their master's Spanish bride.

For Morgan they displayed love and respect and awe-inspiring loyalty. The pretty maids giggled and ogled him shamelessly, their eyes rolling in blatant invitation. If Morgan noticed their brash perusal he chose to ignore it. One in particular, a saucy wench named Daisy, looked at Morgan in a brazen, suggestive manner that thoroughly disgusted Luca.

After everyone had been introduced except the steward, gardeners, stablemen, and coachmen, whom she would meet in due time, Morgan surprised Luca by choosing Daisy for her personal maid. Of all the servants, Daisy was the one Luca was least likely to have chosen for herself. Once dismissed they drifted away, gossiping among themselves as servants were inclined to do. Luca felt as if she could reach out and touch their animosity.

Morgan spoke privately to Forsythe for a few moments, then joined Luca at the foot of the stairs. "Tomorrow will be time enough to acquaint you with the house. I suggest you rest for an hour or two. Later this afternoon a dressmaker from the village will arrive to measure you for new clothing. I can't have my wife running about in rags. We eat promptly at eight o'clock. I'll wait for you at the bottom of the stairs." He offered her his arm. "I'll show you to your room. Daisy will help you disrobe. Tell her if there is anything you wish. If you're hungry she'll bring you something light to eat to hold you till dinner."

"Morgan, about Daisy. Isn't there another just as capable to serve as my maid?"

"What is wrong with Daisy?"

"Nothing, really, except she seems somewhat brazen and forward."

"How can you say that when you don't

even know her? Give her a chance, Luca. If she doesn't suit you, you may choose another. Life will be much easier for you if you learn to get along with the servants in my absence."

Luca stopped abruptly. "You're not thinking of leaving already?"

"Yes. Tomorrow, in fact. I want to be on hand when the *Avenger* docks in London. I'm on my way now to confer with Clyde Withers, my steward. He'll take good care of things in my absence."

It saddened Luca that Morgan was so anxious to leave her. Obviously he couldn't wait to sample the exciting nightlife of London and join the dissolute court of Queen Elizabeth. He'd been at sea so long he must be eager indeed to immerse himself in political intrigue.

Morgan's abrupt departure left Luca with the dismal feeling of being abandoned.

13

Luca thought her room lovely. It was light and airy and furnished with a delicate, feminine hand, prompting Luca to believe that it had once belonged to a woman. A small door led to a dressing room, which she had yet to explore. The windows overlooked a rose garden that in summer would be magnificent with colorful blooms. Beyond was the orchard, whose lofty branches gave hint of a fruitful bounty. A fire blazed merrily in the hearth, for which Luca was grateful. The inhospitable weather chilled her to the bone. She would never become accustomed to the English climate, she reflected dismally.

Luca was still contemplating the dancing flames when Daisy entered the room without bothering to knock. "Captain Scott said I was to be your maid." She eyed Luca's hair and clothing with distaste. "If your trunks have arrived I'll unpack and select something appropriate for you to wear tonight. But I doubt there is anything I can do about your hair. Is that the style in Spain? You have the dark, Spanish look about you and your accent is atrocious. I can't believe Captain Scott would marry someone like you."

Luca drew herself up proudly. She felt no shame in being Spanish. "*Sí*, I am Spanish. I was born in Cadiz. As for my trunks, I have none. I own nothing but the clothing on my back. If you'd like something to do you may take the dress I'm wearing and make it presentable until others can be made. I will see to my hair myself since I am accustomed to grooming it."

Instead of helping Luca with her toilette, Daisy stood with folded arms and stared at her with contempt. "The servants are wagering that you're the captain's whore, not his wife. Everyone in the household, in England, for that matter, knows how much he despises Spaniards."

Luca stepped back as if struck. "How dare you! Get out of here and don't come back."

Daisy dropped Luca a clumsy curtsy and fled. She didn't regret her words. She was but repeating the widespread rumor circulating among the servants. She happened to be the only one bold enough to confront the Spanish woman about her role in their master's household. Rushing down the stairs, she careened headlong into Morgan, who had just entered the house. His arms closed around her to keep them both from falling.

"Daisy, you must be more careful," Morgan warned as he steadied her. Absently he noted her flushed cheeks and overbright eyes. "Is something amiss? It's not your mistress, is it?"

A consummate actress, Daisy trembled and wrung her hands in mock distress. "I fear I upset your lady. She dismissed me and told me not to come back." Boldly she pressed herself against Morgan and squeezed a tear from her eye. "I tried my best to please her, Captain." She blinked up at him through a curtain of long golden lashes. Daisy knew she was pretty and her figure winsome, and she used her assets to her advantage as she openly flirted with Morgan.

Morgan scowled, wondering what in the Hell Luca had done to upset the little maid. Daisy was shaking like a leaf in his arms and seemed truly distraught. He patted her back clumsily. "Don't fret, Daisy, I'll talk to your mistress. Meanwhile, show the dressmaker upstairs when she arrives. My wife is in desperate need of proper clothing, and the sooner the dressmaker gets started, the better."

"I'll take care of it, Captain," Daisy said, dimpling prettily. "If there is anything else I can do for you, anything at all," she stressed, rolling her eyes suggestively, "let me know. I'd be most happy to oblige you in any way."

At first Morgan didn't catch Daisy's meaning, for he was too upset over Luca's unpopularity with his servants. But when it became clear what she was hinting at, he gave her a startled glance. Daisy noted his enlightened expression and lowered her eyes coyly. Then she dropped a curtsy and hurried off to tell the rest of the household about her encounter with the master's wife, if indeed she was his wife.

Morgan stared at Daisy's twitching rump as she walked away, chuckling in amusement. What in the world gave that little piece of blond fluff the idea that he'd want her when he had someone like Luca?

The dressmaker arrived on time, and before she left she promised that the first of Luca's dresses would be ready the next day. Luca was grateful that the woman had included a large assortment of velvet and wool, for the winter days promised to be colder than any she had ever known. She had selected a deep red velvet, dark blue wool, and two other gowns of equally warm and sturdy fabric. Morgan had instructed the dressmaker beforehand to include appropriate nightwear, fur-lined cloaks, and lightweight capes. She was also to include gloves and petticoats in assorted colors.

If the talkative dressmaker had any negative feelings about Captain Scott's Spanish wife she knew enough not to voice them. Business in the small village of Haslemere was not brisk, and Morgan's patronage was much appreciated. Still, Luca couldn't help but notice the strange way in which Mrs. Cromley and her helper stared at her when they thought Luca wasn't looking.

After Mrs. Cromley and her shy little helper left, Luca brushed and shook out her gown as best she could and laid it across the bed in readiness to wear to dinner. Briefly she wished she had something elegant to wear, until she recalled that not too long ago she had been more than satisfied with her gray habit and white headdress that covered everything but her face. Morgan had changed her in so many ways she couldn't begin to count them. And in her opinion not all of them were good.

A short time later servants arrived with a

tub, and Luca took a leisurely bath. Afterward she dressed herself and ran a brush through her short curls. Daisy did not return, which did not overset Luca much. She didn't need Morgan's uppity servants criticizing her speech or comparing her to English womanhood. When the hall clock struck eight, Luca started down the stairs. Her heart nearly stopped when she saw Morgan waiting for her on the bottom landing.

She thought him outrageously handsome in a blatant masculine way with his bold, rugged features bronzed by sun and wind and his lithe, muscular body toned by physical activity. He was dressed casually in trunk hose, jerkin, and knee-length breeches. Had he been dressed to the nines she would have been put to shame in her shabby gown. When she reached the bottom stair, he offered his arm.

"I thought we'd dine informally in the library on trays before the fire," Morgan said. "The dining room is large and rather intimidating. It can accommodate fifty people easily."

Luca looked at him through a fringe of inky lashes. "*Gracias*, Morgan, I appreciate your thoughtfulness. In Spain we are not so formal as you English. In my father's home, in good weather, we often dined on the gallery or patio."

They entered the library, a cozy room lit by a blazing fire. The room was lined with bookshelves, all of them filled with leatherbound volumes. She sniffed appreciatively the scent of leather and furniture polish, deciding that no matter how elegant the other rooms, this would always be her favorite. Morgan led her to one of two upholstered chairs placed side by side and seated her with a flourish. Then he pulled up two small tables and eased himself into the chair beside her.

As if on cue, servants entered and served the meal. The food was rather bland English fare and Luca ate sparingly, washing it down with several glasses of excellent wine. Morgan picked at his food but drank copiously, his heavy-lidded gaze never leaving Luca. Luca boldly met his eyes, finding traces of anger, sorrow, and desire in his silent regard.

"Daisy said you sent her away," Morgan began after the meal had been cleared and the servants dismissed. "Did she displease you in some way? Should I choose another to serve you? Perhaps I should dismiss her."

The last thing Luca wanted was to give the servants another reason to hate her. "I was overwrought and tired. Do not dismiss her on my account."

Morgan nodded sagely. " 'Tis just as I thought. As I said before, you must learn to get along with the servants. If they don't respect you you'll get little work out of them. They all come from good English stock and are trustworthy. I won't always be here to act as a buffer between you and the staff. If trouble arises you'll have to fend for yourself."

The thought of being left on her own gave Luca a sinking feeling in the pit of her stomach. "Morgan, perhaps you should send me home to Spain. I don't belong here. You don't want me, and your people hate me. Why do you insist on torturing us both?"

Morgan's blue eyes grew hard as diamonds. "We're married. Or have you forgotten? I'm not letting you go, Luca, forget it."

"I don't understand." She was thoroughly confused.

"Nor do I," Morgan replied, staring morosely into the leaping flames. His frankness startled her. "Witchcraft," he muttered to himself. "Nevertheless," he said more clearly, "you are mine and shall remain mine. Do you really think your father wants you back after leaving your betrothed?" He laughed harshly. "I think not. At least I can keep you safe and see that you want for nothing."

Except your love, Luca thought silently. *You can't give me your love and that's the only thing I want from you.*

Luca rose abruptly, intending to leave, but Morgan grasped her arm and pulled her back into the chair. "Do I have your word that you'll try to get along with the servants?"

Luca nodded. Satisfied, Morgan released her. Touching her was pure torture. He felt himself being drawn again into her seductive web, and past experience with Luca had proved he wasn't strong enough to resist the overwhelming power she had over his senses. Reminding himself that Luca was Spanish and recalling his hatred for those bearing Spanish blood failed to quell his clamoring need for his sultry wife. He wished he could just let her go and forget her.

It would be a simple matter to return her to her father, or send her to a convent with enough blunt to ease her entry to their order. A seething cauldron of resentment boiled inside him. Something was happening to him he didn't like and couldn't control.

"I'm leaving in the morning, Luca. I don't know when I'll be back. London is but a short distance from Scott Hall. I'll keep in touch with Withers and Forsythe. They in turn will keep me informed of your welfare. Should you need anything, ask Withers, he'll present himself tomorrow to meet you. You may shop in the village if you wish. Charge anything that you fancy to my account."

His words sounded so cold and impersonal. Did all husbands and wives in England lead separate lives? She knew so little about marriage. Couldn't Morgan see how much she loved him? She could tell he was attracted to her. How could he make love to her with such tender feeling if he didn't care for her? He wanted her; she saw his hunger for her in the hot depths of his blue eyes, in the torrid heat emanating from his pores. It was the same with her. *Dios!* Just looking at him turned her to cinder.

"I wish you a good journey, Morgan." Her cool words belied her seething resentment. "Will you be home for Christmas?"

Luca's chilling gaze left Morgan bruised. Bloody Hell, it took every ounce of his willpower to resist her.

"Go to bed, Luca," he said gruffly, fighting for survival of his soul. If he lost the battle, the life he knew and had grown comfortable with would be lost to him forever. "There is nothing more to discuss. As for Christmas, 'tis unlikely I'll return for the holidays."

"You are a fool, Morgan Scott," Luca hissed from between clenched teeth. "Avoiding me will accomplish nothing, and lying about your feelings is dishonest. You are fooling no one but yourself."

Morgan closed his eyes, suffering the blast of her accusations with stony calm. God, how could she be so wise? When he opened his eyes, Luca was gone.

Luca's words hit a raw nerve inside Morgan. Damn her! Was she deliberately making him feel like a fool? His gaze found the brandy and glasses Forsythe had thoughtfully left on his desk, and he poured himself a generous measure. It went down so smoothly he poured another. By the time he finished his third he was wallowing in self-pity. Bloody Hell! His life had taken a surprising turn. He'd never asked for a wife, and now that he had one he didn't know what to do with her.

He knew it would be courting disaster to arrive at court with a Spanish wife at his side. He'd be foolish to imagine the queen would welcome Luca without reservation. It was going to take some doing to explain Luca to Elizabeth. By now the queen had already been informed of the marriage and was anxiously awaiting his explanation. During his last visit to London the queen had hinted that she was seeking a suitable heiress for him to wed. Morgan sighed. Right now his head hurt too badly to think about Elizabeth's reaction to his sudden marriage.

Staggering to his feet, Morgan sought his bed.

Luca stripped to her chemise and climbed into bed. She tried to sleep, but her heart was heavy, her mind too beset by her insurmountable problems, and, despite the fire in the grate, she was shivering from cold. Life in the convent had been so simple and uncomplicated, she sighed, recalling those happier days. Why hadn't God seen fit to leave her there to live in peace? Why had He thrust her into a world of strife and turmoil and given her an annoying man like Morgan Scott to love? If God wanted her to love Morgan Scott, why didn't He make Morgan love her in return? It was all so confusing.

Flipping to her back, Luca stared at the mingling of shadow and light upon the ceiling. Somewhere in the distance she heard a scraping sound but paid it little heed. In a house this size there was always activity of some kind, even in the dead of night. Luca couldn't pinpoint the exact moment she knew she wasn't alone. Raising herself on her elbow, she squinted at the door. Nothing. Swiveling her neck, she glanced toward the dressing room.

The door was ajar. Morgan stood in the opening, limned in a flood of light from a lamp behind him. Vaguely Luca realized that Morgan's room was connected to hers through the dressing room. She could see past him into his room beyond.

His name left her lips on a trembling sigh. She couldn't see his face, for the light behind him obscured all but the muscular outline of his body. He was balanced on the balls of his feet, his muscles flexed, his hands fisted at his sides.

"You are right, Luca, I am a fool," he rasped, slurring the words. Luca's heart soared, but his next sentence laid her high hopes to rest. "A lackwit for allowing you to affect me in ways I'm not strong enough to resist." He walked more fully into the room, and Luca sucked in a ragged breath. He was nude. Totally, gloriously nude, his aroused manhood fully distended.

Luca's mouth went dry, and she licked moisture onto her lips. "That's not what I meant, Morgan. I called you a fool for denying something that's inevitable. Something we both want. Can't you see what's beneath your nose? Don't you realize that I lo . . ." Her sentence fell off. What good would it do to tell him she loved him? He still couldn't see anything past his hatred for her Spanish blood. "I had nothing to do with the deaths in your family."

Twice Morgan tried to turn back to his room, and twice he failed. He was drawn toward the bed and Luca like a bear attracted to the scent of honey, aching for the sweet delicacy despite the risk. The promised reward made the effort well worth it.

When Morgan staggered slightly, Luca was quick to realize he wasn't sober. "You're drunk!"

Morgan grinned. "Not too drunk."

The bed shifted beneath his weight. He gave her a wobbly grin and ripped away her shift. The worn material gave way easily, and he tossed it aside. He pulled her into his arms, letting her feel the hard ridge of his desire. "At least this is always good between us," he vowed. "Losing myself in your sweet flesh makes me forget who you are and what I am." He groaned as he ground his arousal against her stomach and buried his face between her breasts. God, she smelled good!

"I am a woman and you're a man," Luca contended. Her body needed little encouragement to respond to Morgan's touch. "And we are husband and wife. If only you'd allow yourself to . . ."

He stopped her words with a searing kiss. He didn't want to hear them. He refused to heed what his heart told him. If he listened to Luca and his heart he'd no longer be El Diablo, and he wasn't ready yet for that. Maybe he'd never be. For his own peace of mind he needed to remember that he was a man driven by hatred for his Spanish enemies. He intended to remain that man for a very long time.

Morgan's thinking process broke down completely as his rampant desire for his Spanish wife manifested itself in the aching hardness of his loins. Bloody Hell, Luca set his pulses racing, and she tested his control. Just looking at her stoked his desire to a raging inferno. He should have sent her back to her father in disgrace after he'd taken her virginity instead of keeping her for his own selfish enjoyment. Or better yet, he should have taken one look into her innocent eyes and not touched her at all. If fortune favored him, he'd have his fill of her tonight and go off to London with a clear mind and sated body. In the sexually charged atmosphere of Elizabeth's court it would be easy to forget he had a wife, he told himself.

Unable to wait a second longer, Morgan nudged Luca's legs apart, flexed his hips, and thrust deeply. The moment he felt her slick heat surround him he gave up his dark thoughts and let pleasure overwhelm him. The kind of pleasure only Luca could give him. He lowered his head and sucked her nipples.

Luca gasped and cried out, wanting desperately to be more to Morgan than a warm body. Then her thoughts scattered. The race toward ecstasy was too compelling as she exploded in violent climax. When he had coaxed everything from her she had to give, he grasped her bottom and thrust wildly. His own explosion was no less turbulent than Luca's.

Luca came to her senses slowly, feeling thoroughly sated. She glanced at Morgan and saw that he appeared as overcome as she.

"Morgan . . ."

His eyes opened slowly, dark with confusion, as if the very structure of his life had crumbled and he had learned something too disturbing to share. "Bloody Hell!" He leaped from bed, staring at her as if his world had been torn apart. "I've got to get the Hell out of here! You've sucked the soul from my body. I don't even know myself anymore!"

"Morgan, what is it?"

"I'm leaving, Luca, now. I'll keep in touch by messenger." He shoved his fingers through his tousled blond hair and turned away, muttering something beneath his breath about witchcraft and wives. He left the way he had come, through the dressing room, slamming doors behind him.

A short time later Luca heard the brisk tattoo of footsteps on the stairs and realized Morgan had been serious. He actually did intend to leave in the dead of night, regardless of highwaymen and other dangers awaiting him on the road to London. *Dios!* It was as if he'd glimpsed Hell and was fleeing for his life.

Luca slept late the next morning. She had remained awake for hours in hopes that Morgan might change his mind and return, but eventually sleep overcame her. A weak morning sun was streaming through the windows when Daisy roused her abruptly from a deep sleep. "The captain is gone,"

Daisy charged reproachfully. " 'Tis strange that a bridgroom would leave his new bride so soon. 'Tis obvious you do not please him." The smug smile died on her lips and her eyes widened when she spotted Luca's torn shift lying on the floor beside the bed. She tried to hide her surprise as she picked up the torn garment and tossed it over her arm. "Do you want this mended?"

Luca gasped in outrage. "You are brazenly disrespectful." If she couldn't put the impudent Daisy in her place now she'd never be able to control any of the servants. "Of course I want the garment mended. And see that it is returned within the hour."

"You'll have to speak more clearly," Daisy taunted, "your English is difficult to understand." She sauntered out the door, hips swaying jauntily.

Luca fumed in impotent rage. Never had she been so insulted, and by English heretics, no less. And adding insult to injury, Daisy made her wait over two hours for her crudely mended chemise. After breakfast the dressmaker arrived with the first of her dresses. When Luca met with Morgan's steward later, she looked quite fetching in a deep red velvet gown that accentuated the slim curves of her elegant form.

Clyde Withers was not what Luca expected. He was quite young, not much older than Morgan, and he had been hired by Morgan shortly after Morgan's return to London after his years of captivity. The queen had returned Morgan's estates almost immediately, and he needed someone to run them while he was off plundering Spanish galleons. Withers was an intense man, large and capable, with ruddy good looks and a serious nature. He appeared to be all business as he conferred with Luca in the library, the only room besides her bedchamber in which she felt comfortable.

"Your husband presented me with specific instructions before he left, Lady Scott," Withers said with a hint of embarrassment. "If you need anything, you're to come to me and I'll take care of it."

"Did my husband say how long he'd be in London?" It stung to have to ask a stranger what she should have learned from Morgan.

"No, but he promised to keep in touch by messenger. I'm sure he's told you all this. The captain rarely remains in the country when he's in England. The queen is a demanding monarch who insists her courtiers lavish her with their attention."

"So I've heard," Luca said sourly. "Is there anything else I should know, Mr. Withers?"

Clyde Withers felt a pang of pity for the

lovely Spanish woman whom Morgan Scott had married. He was aware of gossip circulating among the servants. It was rumored that Morgan was a reluctant bridegroom, but after finally meeting Morgan's bride he could well understand his master's fascination with the sultry beauty. He very much doubted Morgan would take a Spanish wife unless he truly wanted to. Yet he sensed in Luca an innate sadness, as if she hovered close to a breaking point. She appeared fragile and vulnerable. Something was desperately wrong in her marriage, Withers deduced.

"Captain Scott mentioned that you might have problems with the servants. Sometimes they can be uppity with foreigners." Suddenly he flushed, realizing what he said. "I'm sorry, Lady Scott, I didn't mean . . . I'd be happy to handle any difficulties you might encounter."

Luca gave a deprecating laugh. "No offense taken, Mr. Withers, I'm accustomed to it by now. By your standards I am a foreigner. I appreciate knowing that I can count on you, but I must learn to handle the servants on my own."

Withers's admiration for Luca grew in leaps and bounds. He wondered how Morgan could abandon such a compelling woman, who appeared fragile yet exuded confidence.

"I would be grateful if you'd inform me each time a messenger arrives from London with word from my husband."

"Of course," Withers agreed. "Oh, I almost forgot. Captain Scott left the coach for your convenience. Let me know if you wish to go to the village or visit the crofters, and I will see that it is made ready for you."

The interview ended on that note, and Luca was almost sorry to see the affable man leave. So far, he had been the only person in the entire household to exhibit kindness or offer the respect due her as Morgan's wife.

During the following days Luca learned her way about the hall. She knew instinctively that the house had been much loved by its former occupants. There was little, if anything, she would change. The rooms were large, airy, and filled with ghosts of the happy family who had once roamed the lofty halls. She sensed that there had been much laughter in this home. But, above all, she felt sad because she could never truly belong to this house, or to the man who now owned it.

Luca missed Morgan desperately. Though she had received no personal message from him, she knew he kept in touch with Clyde Withers, for he dutifully informed her whenever a message was received. He appeared embarrassed when he was forced to admit that no personal message had been included for Luca. Christmas arrived with little fanfare. Luca ordered the house decorated in hopes that Morgan would come home for the holidays. Instead, he sent a messenger with a gift.

A gift! Of what use was a gift when it was Morgan she wanted? She eyed the expensive emerald necklace dispassionately and promptly put it away. He hadn't even had the courtesy to include a note of greeting with the gift.

Early in January a messenger arrived with a thick packet of papers for Withers. Luca waited anxiously for Withers to tell her if Morgan had included a message for her. Of course he hadn't, and her disappointment was a bitter pill to swallow. She decided to disregard her pride and question the messenger, hoping he could tell her what, besides the queen, was occupying Morgan's time. A hot-blooded man like Morgan wasn't likely to deny himself a woman's comfort, and the thought of Morgan in another woman's arms shattered her.

She found the messenger in the kitchen

surrounded by the household servants. Luca heard them talking and gossiping among themselves and paused in the hall outside the door when she heard Morgan's name mentioned. Cracking the door open, she peered inside. The messenger was sitting at the table holding court. What he was telling them must have been fascinating, for he had their rapt attention.

"The captain is the most popular man at court with the ladies," the messenger bragged between bites of bread and cheese. "They fairly swoon over him."

"Tell us more, Tom," the cook encouraged, bribing him with a thick slice of roast beef. "Which ladybird does our captain fancy?"

"He fancies them all," Tom said importantly. "But when he's not with the queen he's seen most in the company of young Lady Jane Carey. A toothsome morsel, all eyes and tits. And an heiress to boot. Old Bess throws them together every chance she gets, and our captain ain't one to pass up an opportunity, if ye catch my meaning." He guffawed.

Chuckles and knowing smiles were exchanged all around while Tom tore off a piece of succulent beef and chewed with obvious enjoyment.

"Tell us what Bess said when she learned Captain Scott married without her approval?" Daisy asked eagerly.

"Rumors has it she was furious," Tom revealed. "Told him he could have the marriage annulled or seek a divorce, she did. Wanted to send the Spanish baggage packing and give him Lady Jane as a reward for his enriching her coffers with Spanish gold." He cackled uproariously.

"I knew it!" Daisy exulted. "We'll soon be rid of the Spanish whore."

Luca rested her head weakly against the wall. Their heartless ridicule made her physically ill. Tears threatened to spill from the corners of her eyes, and bitter bile rose up in her throat. It was no secret that Morgan had no use for her as his wife, and now she knew how little she meant to him. With Lady Jane waiting eagerly for Morgan to end his marriage, it would only be a matter of time before she was out of Morgan's life for good. If she returned to Spain her father would dispatch her to Havana and Don Diego. She was nothing but a pawn in the hands of men. Stifling a cry, she turned and fled. Had she remained to hear what Tom said next, she would have been heartened.

"Don't count on gettin' rid of yer mistress

yet. Gossip has it that Captain Scott still hasn't told the queen whether or not he will pursue an annulment. Can ye believe it? With him and Lady Jane so cozy everyone thought he'd jump at the chance to dump a woman everyone says he was forced to marry."

"Forced to marry!" Several voices joined in to voice their surprise.

"Aye, that's the rumor. Don't know the details, but ye can bet they're juicy." He rose abruptly, patting his stomach and belching. "Well, it's back to London."

Alone in her room, Luca paced the length of the floor and back. *The lecherous bastard,* she muttered beneath her breath. How dare Morgan cavort at court with another woman. How dare he make a laughingstock of her before his queen and all of England. She'd be damned if she'd stay in the country to be ridiculed and reviled by his servants. *Oh, no,* she vowed. She'd make Morgan Scott and his paramour sorry they frolicked behind her back.

She knew exactly what she had to do, and she was angry enough to do it.

14

It was mid-March before Luca was able to implement her plan. The weather these last weeks had been abysmal, making travel abroad over muddy, rutted roads all but impossible. She had been to the village several times during the winter, but the time hadn't been right for her to leave for London.

"You wish to go to the village again?" Forsythe asked frostily.

"*Si*. Please inform the coachman that I want the coach brought around at ten o'clock tomorrow morning."

"Is there a particular reason you wish to go to the village today?"

Luca raised her brows and gave him the best condescending glare she could muster. "Do I need one?"

"Of course not." His hands fluttered helplessly at his sides. "Daisy will accompany you as usual."

"That won't be necessary," Luca said tightly. "Send along a footman if you think there is danger."

"Madam, I simply cannot allow you to leave the estate without a maid in attendance."

Luca eyed him coolly. "I do not care what is proper or not. Have the coach waiting at precisely ten o'clock tomorrow morning." Turning abruptly, she left him standing with his mouth agape as she strode away.

Later that day, when Clyde Withers arrived at the house, Luca resigned herself to another battle. Evidently Forsythe had enlisted the overseer's help to dissuade her from going to the village without her maid.

"How can I help you, Mr. Withers?" Luca asked when she met with the overseer in the library.

Withers cleared his throat, obviously distressed at having to deal with so delicate a matter. "Forsythe informed me that you wished to go to the village. That is perfectly all right with me, but we cannot allow you to go alone. 'Tis not proper."

"I do not need a chaperon," Luca insisted curtly. "None of the servants like me, and I do not care to spend my time with them." If one of the servants tagged along, it would spoil all her plans.

Withers's face reddened. During the weeks and months Captain Scott had been in London, he'd not sent one personal message to his wife. Withers felt pity for the poor woman and couldn't understand why his employer had married the Spanish beauty if he intended to neglect her. If the messenger from London could be believed, Captain Scott was having the time of his life in London wooing Lady Jane Carey and playing the courtier. He could tell that Captain Scott's lady was lonely, but he was powerless to remedy the situation.

"I have no objection to your outing," Withers relented. "Is there anything else you'd like?"

"I do not like to travel about with an empty purse," Luca said, sending Withers a winsome smile.

"You may charge whatever pleases you, as you did before."

"Did my husband make no provisions for a monthly allowance?"

"He did say I was to give you whatever you needed."

"I need some coins for my purse."

Withers gave her an uncertain look, then shrugged and walked to the desk. Taking a key from his pocket, he unlocked one of the drawers and pulled out a small metal box.

Luca heard the jingle of coins and walked closer to get a better look. The box was crammed full of silver and gold pieces. Withers counted out several silver coins and looked askance at Luca.

"Perhaps one or two gold coins," Luca suggested brightly. "Morgan would want me to have enough to buy myself a few geegaws without charging them to his account. Of course anything major will be billed to my husband."

Always a soft touch for a woman's winsome smile, Withers readily acquiesced, handing Luca several gold, as well as silver, coins. He'd never known his employer to be a stingy man, so he doubted Morgan would begrudge his wife a monthly stipend. Had he known what Luca had in mind, he wouldn't have been so free with Morgan's blunt.

The following morning Luca left the hall at precisely ten o'clock and found the coach waiting outside the door.

"What time will you return, madam?" Forsythe asked as he handed her into the coach.

"Perhaps I shall visit the crofters after I'm finished in the village. Do not be alarmed if I don't return before dark. The day is unusually fine, and I am tired of being cooped up in the house. Signs of spring are everywhere, and I wish to enjoy them."

Luca waved gaily as the coach clattered down the road. There had been no rain for several days, and most of the puddles in the road had evaporated. Luca's spirits soared; the weather was cooperating beautifully. She had expended considerable time and thought on what had to be done and how to go about it. Weeks and months had passed, bringing no personal correspondence from Morgan. What little she'd heard had been gleaned from gossiping servants. She'd learned that more ships had gathered at Plymouth, and that England was preparing for the anticipated Spanish Expedition to reach their shores. A system of beacons had been set up, ready to flash along the coast and inland to every county when the Spanish fleet sailed into sight.

Every piece of ordnance available was being brought up to fortify the south coast and eastern counties. Town ditches were cleaned and deepened, breaches in town walls were repaired, and stone curtain walls were banked with earth against a possible barrage of artillery. Despite all this, Luca refused to believe an attack by Spain was forthcoming. The Catholic Queen Mary of Scots, having plotted for nineteen years to wrest the English crown from her cousin Elizabeth, had been tried for conspiracy against the crown, found guilty, and executed. Now that she was dead, there seemed no reason for an invasion.

The village came into view, and the coach slowed down to accommodate the heavier flow of people and carts. Today was market day, and farmers converged on the city in droves. This unexpected event suited Luca's purposes perfectly. At her signal, the coachman pulled up to the curb and jumped down from his box to open the door.

"Will this do, madam?"

"This will do just fine." Luca gave him an ingratiating smile. "You and the footman may visit the grog shop if you wish — I expect to be engaged for several hours."

"I'll send the footman along to carry your packages, Lady Scott." The coachman had orders from Mr. Withers to keep close tabs on the mistress since this was her first venture abroad without a maid.

Luca frowned. She neither needed nor wanted a bodyguard, but realized it was fruitless to gainsay Morgan's faithful servant. She acquiesced gracefully, hastily revising her plan.

Luca strolled about with little purpose until she found the dressmaker's shop. After instructing the footman to wait outside, that she'd likely be a long time ordering summer frocks, Luca entered the shop, which was crowded with market day customers. Mrs. Cromley was busy with another customer and did not notice Luca. Sidling around to a curtained doorway, Luca ducked through, pleased to find herself in a storeroom with a door leading into an alley. Everything was going so smoothly she couldn't believe it. It was almost as if God was watching out for her.

The coins jingled comfortingly in Luca's reticule as she picked her way through the filth-littered alley. Ditching the footman had been easy, but finding transportation to London was going to be more difficult. But once again luck was with her. In the alley she came upon a wine vendor unloading his cargo at the rear of a grog shop. She heard the vendor telling the shop owner, who had come out to pay him, that he was returning to London to pick up another load of wine at the warehouse. Luca waited until they had bid one another good-bye before approaching the vendor, who was busily spreading a canvas over the bed of the dray.

"Did I hear you say you were going to London, sir?" she asked as the man climbed into the wagon.

The vendor eyed her curiously. "Aye, lass, ye did. What's it to ye?"

"I'll make it worth your while if you take me with you."

The vendor spat in contempt. "What are ye, a whore? I'm a married man, faithful to me wife. I have a daughter older than ye. Find yerself another mark."

Luca drew herself up indignantly. "Indeed no, sir, I am no *puta*. I am merely in need of transportation to London and am willing to pay in coin for a ride."

The vendor stared narrow-eyed at Luca, finding her accented English highly suspicious. "Ye be a foreigner? Mayhap yer a spy."

"I am Spanish but certainly no spy. Please," Luca pleaded, "I am desperately in need of a ride to London."

"Spanish! I carry no Spaniards in me dray. Sorry, lass, find another way to London." He slapped the reins against the team's rump, and the dray jolted forward.

Unwilling to take no for an answer, Luca waited until the vendor was busy negotiating the narrow alley, then she hoisted herself onto the wagon bed and crawled beneath the canvas before the vendor could realize he had a passenger. By the time the dray pulled out onto the crowded street,

Luca was settled cozily beneath the canvas. Eased by the sun's warmth and lulled by the steady plodding of the horses, Luca promptly fell asleep.

London
March, 1588

The queen's Presence Chamber was teeming with men and women, all elegantly attired in silks, satins, and brocades. Both sexes were regally adorned with powdered wigs, rings on every finger, and shoes sporting jeweled buckles. But the brightest star in the large chamber was the queen, reigning among her courtiers and ladies. She was flirting outrageously with one courtier in particular, a tall, broad-shouldered man whose bronzed countenance gave mute testimony to many hours withstanding the glaring sun and blustery wind. Obviously a ceremony had just taken place, for dignitaries and privy councillors filled the chamber.

"Sir Morgan Scott. It does have a nice ring to it, does it not, Sir Scott?" the queen said, tapping Morgan playfully on the shoulder with her fan.

Aging but still vibrant, Elizabeth doted on

all the handsome men of her court. But if they strayed or displeased her, she made her displeasure known in many, and diverse, ways. None of them pleasant.

Morgan smiled at the queen in genuine warmth. Elizabeth's gratitude had been boundless when Morgan presented her with her share of Spanish plunder. In appreciation for his loyalty, she had bestowed knighthood upon Morgan, dubbing him Sir Morgan Scott. His diligent and single-minded pursuit of Spanish shipping had swelled her coffers.

"Your Majesty is most generous," he replied. " 'Tis more than I deserve."

"Mayhap you are right. We are gratified with your contribution to our coffers but nonetheless displeased with your disastrous marriage. Have you changed your mind about accepting our offer to dissolve your marriage to that Spanish woman? The marriage was performed under duress, if We have the right of it. The Lady Jane is a far better match for one of England's beloved heroes."

Morgan shifted uncomfortably under Elizabeth's steady perusal. The queen had not been pleased with his regrettable marriage and was quick to denounce it. After Morgan had explained how he had been forced to marry a Spaniard, the queen had ordered Morgan to seek an annulment, insisting that it was not legal. Some perverse imp inside Morgan made him balk. Morgan's resistance nearly caused the queen to change her mind about bestowing knighthood on him. But public clamor had been on Morgan's side, and Elizabeth had graciously conceded.

"Lady Jane is lovely," Morgan allowed, "any man would be honored to have her as his wife." Actually, Morgan considered the Lady Jane a hot little piece who was no stranger to a man's passion. Though the queen guarded her ladies-in-waiting jealously, she couldn't be with them every minute of every day and often had no knowledge of their shameful behavior.

Elizabeth sent Morgan a pleased smile. She hated the thought of one of her favorites married to a Spaniard, and with proper incentive felt certain Morgan would see things her way. "Is that not Lady Jane standing across the room? She looks lonely. Why don't you join her? We promised Sir Drake a private audience. This business with the Spanish grows worrisome. We have no idea where the Spanish fleet will strike, or when it will leave Lisbon, if at all. Sir Drake and the admirals want our navy to sail out and destroy them before they are within striking distance, but I see no reason to act precipitously. I would much rather settle things through peaceful negotiations."

"I have spoken with Sir Drake," Morgan said, "and I agree with him. Reports indicate that our navy is better armed and provisioned now than it has been in a very long time. If we strike first we can destroy the fleet before it leaves Lisbon."

"We must use caution," Elizabeth advised. "After We have spoken with Sir Drake, We will decide on what course to take."

"My ship is at your service, Your Majesty," Morgan offered generously. "I but await your command."

"We are aware of your loyalty, Sir Scott, except for your stubbornness concerning your marriage. Go now, Lady Jane is anxious for your company."

Morgan bowed and took himself off, but not to Lady Jane. He stealthily exited through an anteroom to the gardens beyond, deliberately avoiding the persistent Lady Jane. From the day he had arrived at Whitehall, Lady Jane Carey had latched onto him like a bloodthirsty leech. If he sought another woman's company, Jane's jealousy was awesome to behold. He had lost count of the times Jane had invited him to her bed, and a time or two he had actually considered accepting her brazen invitation. Lord knows he wanted to. But to his chagrin, something beyond his control prevented him from easing himself between Jane's white thighs.

Luca. Her name lingered on his lips like a precious memory.

Luca. Luca . . .

The first few weeks in London had been busy ones for Morgan, leaving little time to think of Luca. He and Stan Crawford had met almost daily with the queen and her privy council, who listened avidly to Stan's description of the great armada he'd seen gathering at Lisbon. And when Morgan wasn't dancing attendance on Elizabeth, he was conferring with such notables as Sir Francis Drake and Lord Burleigh. The situation with Spain was growing volatile, and the queen was deliberately dragging her feet in provisioning her navy. Sir Drake constantly bemoaned the fact that he should be sailing to blockade Lisbon instead of sitting with the navy at Plymouth.

Before Morgan knew it, Christmas arrived. He had the presence of mind to send Luca a gift. During those busy weeks Morgan thought he'd succeeded in purging

Luca from his mind, so he had no idea why he balked at annulling his marriage. To say that the queen was displeased with his marriage would be putting it mildly, but when she heard the circumstances she'd relented somewhat. But she was still miffed with Morgan for resisting her efforts to free him from an unfortunate match.

Then Elizabeth had offered Lady Jane as a reward for his service to England, and a rich prize she was. All Morgan had to do to receive the reward was discard his present wife. Morgan considered it, going so far as to pay court to Jane, but of late he found excuses to avoid her. Her pale blond beauty might be tempting to some, but Morgan found he preferred dark, sultry women with exotic features, fiery eyes, and shiny ebony curls shorn disgracefully short.

December gave way to January and a round of balls, routs, and boring musicales featuring Italian divas who sang off-key. Morgan visited dens of iniquity with cronies who drank themselves senseless and woke up with whores. Morgan might frequent the lowest hells in London and drink to excess, but he balked at cavorting with whores. He gambled excessively, sometimes losing, but more often winning, large amounts. February came and went and March arrived on the wings of spring. Twice he was enticed into visiting a high-class whorehouse and ended up playing cards below while his friends pleasured themselves with the best and most expensive whores in London. And each time he cursed himself for a fool.

Morgan couldn't deny he needed a woman. It angered him that he couldn't be satisfied with just any woman. And in his eagerness to free himself of Luca's image, Morgan had danced and flirted away the entire season in London. He knew Luca was faring well, for Withers kept him informed of his wife's well-being. Through it all, Morgan did learn one important fact in London. He learned that Luca would never fit into this kind of life.

Her dark, exotic beauty betrayed her Spanish heritage. She would be accepted by neither his friends nor his queen. If she were French instead of Spanish it might have been different, but she wasn't. The fact that Luca carried in her veins the blood of those he had dedicated his life to destroy was impossible to forgive. That fatal flaw made a mockery of their marriage. Yet he couldn't deny that his arms ached to hold her, that he yearned to hear her soft moans when he brought her to ecstasy. He missed unbearably her sweet response to his loving, which was without guile or pretense. If he didn't know better, he'd think they were made for one another.

Morgan shook his head to clear it of such disturbing thoughts. Wanting Luca only complicated his life. Elizabeth was urging him to obtain an annulment, and in the end he supposed he'd be forced to acquiesce and marry Lady Jane, or another woman equally appropriate. He recalled the times Luca had entreated him to send her home to the convent. She probably would be happy if he did so now. She couldn't be enjoying her circumstances, dumped amid hostile servants and neglected. He'd settle a sum on her and give her a choice of destinations. Perhaps, he thought dismally, she'd prefer to return to her former fiancé. That thought was not a pleasant one.

That's not what you want, an inner voice reminded him.

"Nevertheless, I shall do what's best for all concerned," he said aloud.

"Who in the world are you talking to, Morgan? What are you doing out here alone? I've been looking all over for you."

Morgan forced his fierce expression into a welcoming smile and turned to greet Lady Jane. "Jane, you startled me. I fear you've caught me in a pensive mood."

"Lord Henley said he saw you slipping out the door. Whatever are you doing here by yourself?" The smile slipped from her face, replaced by an ugly scowl. "You're not having an assignation with another woman, are you?"

"Jane, you wound me," Morgan protested gallantly. "I was merely seeking fresh air. You know you're the only woman who appeals to me." Lord, how he tired of the inane niceties required by society. He'd much rather be straddling the deck of the *Avenger* than reciting pretty phrases into a woman's ear.

Jane smiled and sidled closer. Her blond, unpowdered hair shimmered like tawny gold in the waning light. She lifted her face, her lips parted and inviting, aware that few men could resist her beauty. Unfortunately, the formidable Morgan Scott was proving to be one of the few. He wasn't like most men. It made scant difference to Jane that Morgan already had a wife, for she knew Elizabeth was pressing Morgan to obtain an annulment or divorce, and few men had the courage to disobey a vengeful queen.

But Morgan had been deliberately difficult. A few kisses and intimate caresses were all she'd gotten from him, though she'd tried to entice him to her bed on more than one occasion. Rumor had it that his had been a forced marriage, so there was no question of his being in love with his wife. Morgan rarely talked about the Spanish woman, yet Jane was hard put to explain the mysterious yearning in his eyes she noticed at odd times. But that didn't worry Jane, she was confident the dark-faced Spanish woman couldn't hold a candle to her own golden beauty.

"I know a place where we can be alone if crowds bother you," Jane said in a throaty whisper. " 'Tis not far." She grasped his hand. "Come, I'll show you."

Morgan hesitated but a moment. Why in the Hell shouldn't he take what Lady Jane so freely offered? He needed a diversion right now. He needed someone to replace Luca's image in his mind. Jane was beautiful, shapely, and no simpering virgin. Simply put, he needed to expend his sexual frustration in a woman's soft flesh.

Morgan was close on Jane's heels when she led him to a secluded gazebo located in a remote section of the garden. He could see it had fallen into disrepair, a fair indication that few people visited the isolated spot. Few people except Jane, mayhap, and her various lovers. And now she was going to add him to her list of conquests.

"Won't Queen Bess miss you?" Morgan asked as he followed Jane inside. He noted with dim interest that the interior was furnished with several benches covered with faded pads and little else. The screens were protected by canvas blinds, which could be lowered to ensure privacy.

"She is conferring with Sir Francis Drake," Jane said as she released the blinds, plunging them into a shadowy world that invited intimacy. "She will not miss me. We have many hours in which to enjoy ourselves." Sending Morgan a coy smile, she reclined invitingly on one of the benches and held out her arms to him.

Morgan regarded her through slitted lids before joining her and taking her into his arms. Jane sighed happily. She had every reason to believe she would soon be the wife of the handsome pirate who had become one of England's heroes. She shivered delicately, eagerly anticipating his rough handling. A man who plundered and killed for pleasure would not be a gentle lover, and she would be his willing slave. Didn't every woman dream of being ravished by a handsome pirate?

Slowly Morgan peeled the dress away from Jane, baring milky white, fleshy mounds. He grimaced in distaste, thinking

Jane pallid and unappealing compared to Luca's golden-skinned beauty. Forcing himself to continue, Morgan released her chemise and corset and took one pale breast in his hand. Jane moaned and grasped his head, pulling it down to her breast. Morgan obliged, taking her nipple into his mouth and laving it with his tongue.

He nearly gagged. Her flesh reeked of strong perfume. Sweet, cloying, and oppressive, it did not appeal to him. Perhaps it was the woman herself who did not appeal to him. Would any woman ever appeal to him after Luca? He tried. Lord knows he tried to purge Luca from his mind. But even as he sucked and strained over Jane's breasts, he remained unmoved by her moans and passionate writhing. It was as if he had detached himself from what he was doing and watched from afar.

"Oh, Morgan, please, I want you inside me," Jane panted as she spread her legs and reached for him. When her greedy fingers closed around him, she gasped and looked at him in total confusion. "You're not ready. What can I do to help?"

Morgan sat back in disgust. There was nothing Jane could do to make him ready for her. He couldn't force himself to perform when his flesh was unwilling. This had never happened to him before, and he didn't like it. What kind of spell had the Spanish witch placed on him? He had always prided himself on his sexual prowess. His ability to perform had never been in doubt, often giving and achieving satisfaction many times in one night. It wouldn't be fair to blame Jane for his lack; it would probably be the same with any woman except Luca.

"This is a mistake," Morgan said, trying to extricate himself from Jane's clutches. But Jane would have none of it. She fumbled with his clothing until she found his flaccid manhood. Before Morgan realized what she intended, she pulled it free and took him into her mouth.

"Bloody Hell!" He shuddered violently, thickening and hardening instantly. "Where did you learn that whore's trick?"

The more diligently Jane worked over his flesh, the angrier Morgan became. No one manipulated him without his consent, and he wasn't about to let a hot little baggage do it now. Grasping her shoulders, he pushed her away. Jane fell back on her rump, her eyes wide with disbelief. Her surprise soon turned to fury.

"What kind of man are you, Morgan Scott? Or are you a man at all? You were almost ready. Would you prefer using force?

You are a pirate, and I heard they treat women savagely. If you prefer ravishment I would be most happy to oblige. You may take me as roughly as you please, be as savage as you like, I'll not complain." Just thinking about it made her breathless with need.

Morgan's expression grew cold as he stretched to his feet and hastily straightened his clothing. "I do not like hurting women. As I said before, this was a mistake."

Jane rounded on Morgan, her face mottled with rage. "Is this the kind of treatment I can expect after we're married? I won't put up with it, Morgan. What has that Spanish bitch done to you?"

"I wish I knew," Morgan muttered distractedly. "When you and I marry, if we marry, you will have nothing to complain about in regards to my performance."

Jane smiled coyly. "Come and show me then. I felt you harden in my mouth; I know you wanted me."

"I'm only human," Morgan replied. "But this is neither the time nor the place. I'm conceited enough to want to pick the time and place myself. Perhaps we should return to the Presence Chamber before we're missed. Our good Queen Bess can be a tiger if she suspects one of her ladies is misbehaving. She is already angry with me. No need for you to earn her wrath as well."

"She wouldn't be upset with you if you agreed to set aside your Spanish wife so you can wed an Englishwoman," Jane grumbled crossly.

Morgan heaved a weary sigh. He'd heard it all before. Not only from the queen but from his friends as well. "Let's not go into that again. My marriage is not open for discussion. Are you ready to leave?"

"I look a sight," Jane complained, trying without success to rearrange her hair like it was before entering the gazebo. Finally she gave up and pushed it into a semblance of order. When she and Morgan entered the queen's Presence Chamber, they looked as if they'd just returned from an illicit rendezvous.

Luca lingered at the edge of the crowd, having arrived at Whitehall only moments ago. When told she was Lady Scott, a footman directed her to the queen's Presence Chamber, informing her that the queen had just knighted Sir Morgan Scott and that she'd find the entire court gathered for the ceremony in honor of her husband. When Luca arrived the room was teeming with people, all richly dressed in every manner of court attire. She felt drab and out of place in her travel-stained velvet gown and unpowdered hair. She searched the room for Morgan but did not see him. She started violently when she felt a hand on her shoulder. Turning abruptly, she was more than a little startled to see a black-clad Jesuit priest hovering at her elbow.

"Forgive me for startling you, daughter, but I could not help noticing that you are Spanish. What are you doing so far from your homeland? Elizabeth's court is no place for a Spaniard right now. Tempers are running high against our people." The Jesuit's fluent Spanish was music to Luca's ears.

"Are you from Spain?" Luca asked hopefully.

"*Sí.* I am with a delegation of Jesuits in England to convince the heretic queen to stop oppressing the Catholic population of England. We also carry assurances from King Philip and the pope that Spain has no intention of retaliating for Queen Mary's murder, though we condemn the act as a blatant miscarriage of justice and reprehensible in the eyes of God. What are you doing here, daughter?"

"It's a long story, Father," Luca said, sighing.

"You seem lost. Come with me, I will introduce you to the rest of our delegation, and you can tell us what brings you to England. We must all stick closely together in this immoral court."

Suddenly Luca spied Morgan, and her breath caught painfully in her throat. He had just walked into the chamber through a door across the room, accompanied by a beautiful woman who clung possessively to his arm. The woman was young, blond, regal, and charmingly disheveled in a way that was unmistakable. Luca's gaze returned to Morgan, who looked as if he hadn't had time to dress properly. His clothing was awry, and he appeared flustered. It occurred to Luca that she'd seen that look on his face many times in the past . . . after making love to her. Her fingers curled into fists. *Dios,* she wanted to kill the woman!

"What is it, daughter?" the priest asked as he followed Luca's gaze to Morgan and Lady Jane.

"Who is that?" Luca asked, nodding in Morgan's direction.

The priest scowled fiercely. " 'Tis the vicious pirate, Morgan Scott, and his *puta,* Lady Jane Carey. He's sent more Spanish galleons to the bottom of the sea than any other man living or dead. It was reported that he had met his death in Havana, then he turned up recently in England, very much alive. He's made quite a splash at court. The queen fairly dotes on him. The pirate was knighted today for his loyalty to England."

Luca's heart sank. Morgan was knighted, and she didn't even know about it. Clearly he chose to forget he had a wife. She was an embarrassment to him. When she saw Lady Jane whisper something in Morgan's ear that made him smile, a sob caught in her throat.

"Forget these godless people, daughter. Come with me, we will pray together for the conversion of England."

Too distraught to object, Luca meekly followed the priest from the chamber, away from Morgan and his mistress.

15

"Ah, here we are, daughter," the priest said as he opened the door to his chamber and ushered Luca inside. " 'Tis small but adequate. We are accustomed to simple pleasures."

Luca entered the chamber, and three other priests turned from their prayers to stare at her. "Sit, daughter," the priest said, motioning to the only chair in the room. "I am Father Pedro and these are Fathers Juan, Bernadino, and Raphael."

Luca greeted each in turn. "I am Luca Santiego, from Cadiz."

"Don Eduardo's daughter?" Father Pedro asked. "I know your father well. He is a benefactor of our order. I heard you had married Don Diego del Fugo, governor-general of Cuba. What in God's name are you doing in England?"

"I am here with my husband," Luca explained, recalling now that she'd heard her father speak of Father Pedro and his order.

The priests grew very excited, speaking among themselves in whispers. Finally Father Pedro turned to Luca and said, "We had no idea Don Diego was in England. We must confer with him immediately."

"Obviously you haven't seen or spoken to my father or brothers in a very long time. I am married to Morgan Scott."

Never had Luca seen such an open display of shock as evidenced by the expressions on the faces of the Jesuits. "El Diablo, the pirate? *Dios!*" They crossed themselves and looked at Luca as if she had suddenly grown horns. "How did such a travesty happen, my child?" Father Juan asked, reserving judgment until he heard the entire story. "Obviously there is more here than meets the eye."

"I'm not sure where to begin," Luca said, reluctant to bare her innermost secrets to the priests.

"At the beginning," Father Bernadino prodded gently. "Afterward, if you like, I will hear your confession and give you absolution. You may begin, daughter."

Luca swallowed past the lump in her throat and started with her abduction at sea and how she had assumed the guise of a nun in order to protect her virtue. The priests exchanged knowing looks when she admitted that the pirate had seen through her ruse. Without going into intimate details, she explained how her brothers rescued her and insisted upon an impromptu wedding ceremony. The Jesuits were dismayed when she described Morgan's escape from Havana on the eve of his execution and her abduction from Don Diego's home.

"You poor child," Father Pedro said, shaking his head in commiseration. "You have experienced Hell. How you must hate the pirate for what he has done to you. We will pray for you. Are you aware that your husband is committing adultery with immoral women? Since we've been at court, we have seen Captain Scott and Lady Jane together often. Rumor has it they will wed soon, that the queen is pushing for the marriage. Surely these heretics aren't allowed two wives, are they?"

"Morgan will probably annul our marriage and send me back to the convent."

"You are married in the eyes of God. No heretic marriage can take place without the Holy Father's approval of an annulment. What God has joined no man can set asunder," Pedro quoted piously. "Do you wish to return to Spain, daughter?"

Luca frowned. What she really wanted was to pull out every golden hair on Lady Jane's regal head. But if Morgan cast her aside, she'd be content to spend the rest of her days in a convent. One love in a lifetime was all she could tolerate.

"It might be best for all concerned," she admitted.

"We will be leaving England as soon as the Spanish Armada hoves into sight of English soil," Father Juan confided, lowering his voice to a whisper. "You must tell no one about this. If we are caught in England when the great armada arrives we will likely be imprisoned or put to death."

"Why are you here?" Luca asked curiously.

"We were sent by King Philip and Lord Parma to learn what we can of England's defenses and the queen's intentions."

"You're spies!" Luca said, aghast.

Father Pedro shifted uncomfortably. "That is a harsh term, daughter. We are on a peace mission. If you wish to return to Spain we will take you with us, and I will personally see that you are reunited with your father. We are entrusting you with our secret, but you must tell no one what we have just revealed. Shall we pray together for the success of the expedition?"

The Jesuits dropped to their knees, joining in prayer with Father Pedro. Luca scrambled quickly to her knees, but her mind wasn't on her prayers. She wondered if Morgan realized how close the armada was to sailing and if the queen's navy was sailing out to meet them. She had seen the fleet at Plymouth, but she had gotten the impression that no preparations were being made to leave the port any time soon.

After a long interval of prayer, Luca rose to leave. "We will keep in touch, daughter," Father Pedro said. "If you wish to leave England you must be prepared to move at a moment's notice. Meanwhile, you can perform a great service to your king and God by relaying anything of importance to us that you learn through your husband. When we reach Spain we will encourage the pope to declare your marriage to the heretic pirate invalid."

Luca left the Jesuits' chamber in a state of confusion. She had been surprised to learn that the Jesuits were Spanish spies and even more shocked when Father Pedro asked her to spy on her own husband. Morgan might be ruthless and utterly unscrupulous, but she could not force herself to spy on him.

In the first place, she doubted Morgan would reveal anything of importance to her.

In the second, he'd probably be so angry at seeing her in London he'd send her forthwith back to Scott Hall. Her presence here would definitely hamper his activity with the ladies, particularly Lady Jane. *I certainly hope so,* she thought with a hint of malice.

Luca wandered down the corridor, having little idea where she was going, and caring less.

After the queen left the Presence Chamber the crowd began to disperse. Having grown bored with Lady Jane and her possessiveness, Morgan excused himself politely.

"Where are you going, Morgan?" Jane asked, refusing to release his arm.

"To my room, my lady. Then to Billingsgate to meet my first mate aboard the *Avenger.*"

"You may escort me to my chamber," Jane suggested coyly. "Since the queen hasn't summoned me I'm free to do as I please."

Finding no ready excuse, Morgan offered his arm, and they strolled off together. They had to pass Morgan's chamber before arriving at Jane's. When they reached Morgan's chamber Jane stopped abruptly and dragged him toward the door.

"Show me your room, Morgan."

"I think I'd better . . ."

"That's your problem, you think too much."

Morgan groaned in dismay when Jane turned the knob and stepped inside. Morgan had no recourse but to follow. Was there no discouraging the hot little bitch? He'd had his fill of court intrigue and calculating women and wished himself aboard the *Avenger* instead of wasting his time playing court to a woman for whom he cared not a wit. Or in West Sussex with Luca, who managed quite nicely to dispel his boredom.

"This isn't wise," Morgan said in an effort to discourage Jane. "Think about your reputation."

"Since when did a woman's reputation matter to you?" Jane asked huskily. "We're in the privacy of your room, there's no one to stop us from enjoying one another. What better place than here and now? The queen expects us to wed, there's no reason to wait."

"Probably not," Morgan allowed, "except that I'm pressed for time. I must leave very soon to meet with Mr. Crawford aboard the *Avenger*. There isn't time to do us both justice. When I bed you I want to do it properly." He stroked her breast, hoping his intimate caress would convince her of his sincerity.

His words seemed to pacify Jane, who writhed passionately against him. "When?" she asked breathlessly. "I can hardly wait. I want you to make me yours."

Morgan nearly snorted in disgust. He thought about all the other men who had made Jane theirs. "Soon," he promised with as much fervor as he could muster. It would be sooner than he liked if he allowed Queen Bess her way. Luca would be his past, and Lady Jane, his future.

"Kiss me good-bye," Jane said, molding herself against the hard wall of his chest.

Morgan complied, aware that it was the only way to rid himself of Jane without a fuss. He really did need to meet with Stan and was anxious to be on his way. Lowering his head, his lips moved over hers, grimly aware that his kiss was tepid compared to what it would be if it were Luca in his arms.

"Are you lost, madam? Perhaps I can direct you to your room."

Luca stopped abruptly. Distracted by her thoughts, she had nearly run headlong into a handsome courtier. "Oh, I am sorry, my lord. I did not see you."

"These corridors are rather complex and

confusing if one isn't familiar with them. I don't think we have met. I am Dennis Burke, Viscount Harley, at your service." He executed a pretty bow. "And you are . . . ?"

"Luca . . . Scott," Luca said, stumbling over the name that was now hers by right of marriage.

"Good heavens! You're Sir Morgan Scott's Spanish bride. We were wondering when Scott was going to introduce his wife at court. I can understand his reluctance. You're a rare beauty, my lady. I would guard you jealously were you mine. Let me escort you to your husband's chamber. Or would you prefer looking for him in the Presence Chamber? Did you miss the ceremony? I don't recall seeing you there earlier."

"I would prefer to wait for Morgan in his chamber, my lord," Luca said. "I am travel weary and not dressed properly to attend a grand function. My husband did not know I was coming to London."

Luca thought Viscount Harley quite elegant, attired as he was in hose that hugged his shapely legs, satin pantaloons, and brocade doublet. He appeared courteous enough and harmless. She accepted his arm as he guided her through a maze of corridors.

"I'm betting your husband will be surprised to see you at Whitehall," Harley said with disguised glee. Scott's blatant affair with Lady Jane was common knowledge, and Harley wondered how the pirate would handle the situation. Queen Bess wanted to dissolve his marriage and bundle his Spanish bride off to Spain, freeing Morgan to wed the English heiress. Harley couldn't wait to spread the word of Luca's arrival among his cronies.

Luca did not reply to the handsome English lord's remark. No one knew better than she the extent of Morgan's temper. Her own temper could be just as formidable when provoked. And God knows Morgan had given her every reason to dislike the dissolute, licentious life he was living at court.

The corridors seemed endless, Luca thought, but Lord Harley appeared to know where he was going. He chatted excessively during their stroll, expecting no reply and receiving none. Finally they stopped before a door, and Lord Harley released her arm with marked reluctance.

"Here we are, my lady. I do not think the door is locked, for 'tis unnecessary here at Whitehall. Perhaps I will see you anon," he murmured, raising her hand and kissing it with a flourish. Luca watched as he swaggered down the corridor, thinking him quite the dandy.

Luca considered knocking before entering Morgan's chamber, but she decided there was no need. Morgan was probably still in the Presence Chamber paying court to his mistress. Besides, she was Morgan's wife and had every right to enter his chamber at will. The door opened on silent hinges, and she stepped inside. The scene that met her eyes brought a gasp of dismay to her lips. The sound prompted the chamber's occupants to spring apart.

"Who are you?" Jane asked, outraged at the intrusion. "How dare you enter Sir Scott's chamber without knocking? I must speak with Her Majesty about having you evicted from Whitehall. You're a brazen baggage."

"Luca." Morgan shuddered in awareness.

Dismissing Jane with a frosty glare, Luca's gaze collided with Morgan's. The silence between them stretched as Jane watched their reaction to one another with growing dismay. In that poignant silence, Luca saw Morgan's expression change from fury, to stunned disbelief, to guarded pleasure.

"Who is this woman, Morgan?" Jane demanded to know.

Both Luca and Morgan seemed oblivious to Jane's presence.

"Morgan, answer my question." Jane had a sneaking suspicion who the dark beauty was and needed only Morgan's confirmation.

Finally Morgan could ignore Jane no longer. "Leave us, Lady Jane."

"What!" Jane's rage was boundless. Turning to Luca, she boldly announced, "I am Morgan's fiancée. What right do you have to intrude upon a private moment?"

Muttering in annoyance, Morgan realized how shamelessly vocal Jane was in her pursuit of him, not that he hadn't known that all along. Until now he didn't care enough to let it annoy him. Seeing Luca now drew him from polite boredom into stark awareness. It disgusted him that he had put up with Jane's possessiveness all these months. Furthermore, he had conducted his days at court indiscreetly and carelessly. He had gambled, flirted, drunk excessively, and visited the most disreputable sorts of gentlemen's clubs with careless disregard for the consequences. He had told himself he had fallen into dissolute ways in an effort to erase Luca from his mind and heart, but it hadn't worked. And by some miracle Luca was here, and all he could think of was making love to her for long, blissful hours.

Tearing her gaze from Morgan, Luca turned to Jane, her eyes hostile with fury. "You may be Morgan's fiancée, but I am his wife. If you do not leave immediately I will cut out your heart and feed it to the pigs." As if to reinforce her threat, she stepped menacingly toward Jane. Jane gave a squawk of dismay and fled in terror for her life.

When they were alone, Luca rounded on Morgan in splendid rage. Morgan thought her anger daunting. "The same goes for you, Morgan. Your faithlessness is appalling. I will cut your heart out as easily as that of your mistress."

Morgan struggled to contain his mirth but failed. Laughter rolled from his chest as he stared at Luca in astonishment. "I believe you would, my fiery little bride." Then his amusement ended as quickly as it began. "What in bloody Hell are you doing in London? I left orders that you were to remain at Scott Hall."

Luca sent him a disgruntled look. "Did you think I would stay there while you cavorted shamelessly at court with your mistress? If you plan on dissolving our marriage, Morgan, do it now, but do not shame me by conducting your scandalous affairs while we are still husband and wife." She eyed him narrowly. "We still *are* husband and wife, are we not?"

"We are still married, Luca," Morgan said quietly.

Luca relaxed visibly.

"You still haven't told me what you are doing in London and how you got here. I'm amazed that Clyde Withers let you leave after I instructed him to keep you in West Sussex."

Not wanting to get Withers in trouble, Luca declared, "Mr. Withers had nothing to do with my being in London. I found my own transportation."

Dismayed, Morgan's mouth gaped open. "Bloody Hell, woman, do you realize the danger you exposed yourself to by traveling unescorted? Whatever possessed you to leave?"

"Rumors travel rather fast, and servants do gossip. Did you think I wouldn't hear about your licentious behavior at court? Why didn't you write me, Morgan? I've heard nothing directly from you since you left Scott Hall."

Morgan's hungry gaze literally devoured Luca. He was happy that she had reached London safely, but he was still angry at her for traveling alone. Just thinking about the danger she could have encountered made him shudder in dread. She risked all manner of mishaps, particularly since she was a stranger to England. That she made it to Whitehall safely spoke volumes about her courage and resourcefulness.

"I've kept in touch through Withers and Forsythe. Did they not inform you when my messages arrived?"

"Withers was good enough to inform me, but I would have preferred a personal message. You deliberately left me in the country so you could act the libertine at court. I thought your mistress quite amusing."

Morgan flushed, unable to deny Luca's charges. He deserved Luca's resentment. But to his credit he hadn't actually made Jane his mistress. He had hoped the old adage "Out of sight, out of mind" would apply to Luca once he had left her disrupting influence, but it hadn't worked that way. Prolonged absence made him realize how desperately he wanted Luca. Lady Jane, with her pallid English beauty, couldn't begin to compare to his vibrant wife. Luca moved him in mysterious ways. There was something deep and disturbing about her; something indescribably tempting.

He needed her.

Having her alone in his room made him tremble with anticipation.

"I have no mistress," he said truthfully.

Luca snorted derisively. "Regardless of what you think, I'm no fool. I saw you and Lady Jane earlier when you entered the Presence Chamber from God only knows where. Only a blind man would not notice your shameless state of disarray. It was obvious you had been engaged in an illicit affair. And what about just now, when I walked into your chamber and saw the lady in your arms? You looked as if you were ready to toss her skirts over her head and have at her."

"Think what you like, Luca, but I'm telling the truth. I've not bedded Jane or any other woman since I met you. I'm not proud of my celibate state, or the fact that none of the court ladies appealed to me. As long as I'm being honest I may as well admit that you are the source of my misery. I can't stop thinking about you long enough to bed another woman. I should punish you for coming to London without my permission, but I suddenly find myself hungry for the taste of your kisses. I want you. I want to be inside you, surrounded by you. And God help me, I don't want this feeling to stop."

Luca opened her mouth to hurl a stinging

retort, but Morgan halted it effortlessly by pulling her into his arms and seizing her lips with frantic urgency. The hot sweep of his tongue across the seam of her lips sent a jolt of raw pleasure surging through her veins. She had yearned for this for so long that her emotions were raw and exposed. His touch was like magic, rendering her vulnerable to his erotic seduction. She melted against him and opened her mouth to him. Despite his lies about his numerous infidelities, Luca was helpless to resist the man she loved more than life.

Morgan's kiss deepened, his tongue dueling with hers in a passionate exchange that left Luca breathless. She moaned beneath her breath when he sucked her tongue into his mouth and ravished it thoroughly, roughly, grasping her bottom and pulling her more solidly against the hardening cradle of his loins. With senseless abandon she gave herself up to his bruising kiss, thick with the taste of his hunger and mindless desire. With deliberate slowness he mated his mouth with hers, thrusting deeply with his tongue while he caressed her breasts.

Luca submitted to his passion, letting it surround her in a bright, shimmering haze. She felt giddy with the scent of his arousal, strong and tangy and infinitely male. He had unleashed some primitive impulse deep within her, and she ground her hips against him in wanton response. This wasn't mere lust; this madness went deeper, was more enduring. What she felt for Morgan was love, the kind that happened only once in a lifetime.

"Witch," Morgan muttered as he worked frantically to release the ties at the back of her dress. "Sultry witch." The sweet taste of her surrender excited him beyond endurance.

"I'm no witch," Luca challenged as her bodice slipped past her shoulders. "I'm your wife, Morgan. Witchcraft is sinful and wicked."

"Aye, sweetheart, wife," Morgan agreed as his lips slid down the slender column of her neck, raining gentle kisses against the upper portion of her breasts. "My wicked, sinful wife."

A sound of strangled pleasure escaped her when he peeled her corset and chemise away and took her nipple into his mouth. She was panting by the time he tugged her remaining garments from her body and knelt before her, stroking her bottom with consummate tenderness, nipping and licking her exquisitely sensitive nipples. When he had satisfied his hunger for her breasts, his mouth blazed a trail of fire across her stomach. Before continuing his downward path, he looked up and gave her a wicked grin. Then he lowered his mouth to the shiny nest of ebony curls below.

Luca shuddered violently, clutching his head in an effort to stop the sinful thrust of his tongue. "Morgan, no!"

"Aye, sweetheart, let me do this for you." Holding her tightly against him, he spread her legs slightly and inserted a finger into her slick sheath.

Luca thought she would die of rapture as he brushed his lips and tongue over her most sensitive flesh while creating a delicious pressure with the thrust and withdrawal of his finger into her intimate channel. She felt herself drifting, spiraling out of control, and suddenly her legs could no longer hold her. Morgan sensed the moment that weakness overcame her, and he swept her from her feet. Luca cried out in deprivation when his hands and mouth left her, but he crooned into her ear, telling her he'd not leave her, that he'd give her the pleasure she craved. Then he placed her on the bed and tore off his clothing. He joined her before Luca could fully appreciate the masculine beauty of his aroused body, but she felt him, full and heavy and hot as he pressed her down into the mattress.

Her arms came around him, wanting him inside her, raising her hips to give him free access, but he ignored her silent plea as he slid down her body and hooked her knees over his shoulders. Then he lowered his head and feasted on her with bold strokes of his tongue while his hands roved demandingly over her thighs, breasts, and bottom. She bucked wildly, but Morgan held her tightly, anchoring her against his mouth as she moved against him. Soft sobs shook her. He sucked her deeply, relentlessly, until she cried out her climax.

Releasing her knees, he watched her face. Her mouth was open, her eyes glazed, her body rosy with shattering ecstasy. With splintering insight he realized they shared something special. If not for the Spanish blood she carried in her veins, he could readily give a name to those feelings.

Luca looked into Morgan's eyes and recognized his confusion. But she saw something else. Something deep and abiding and caring. She smiled dreamily and opened her arms to him. "Come into me, Morgan." Her fingers curled around his distended staff, bringing him to the very portal of her softness.

Morgan groaned out his eagerness, lifted her hips, and slid full and deep inside her. The pleasure was pure agony. He was heavy and hard and throbbing. He felt her incredible heat squeeze and surround him, felt her tilt her hips so she could take him deeper, felt her arms clasp and hold him, and he gave himself up to the magic of their joining. He filled and stretched her until she was taut, ready to burst with throbbing pleasure.

Hot ecstasy flooded Luca's senses as Morgan suddenly shifted positions, sinking even deeper inside her as he brought her atop him. "Ride me, sweet Luca," he urged, pounding into her with wild fury. She sobbed her delight, threw her head back, and let her instincts guide her.

Heat and friction combined to drive her inexorably toward another powerful climax. It was heaven, it was Hell, it was the most perfect paradise Luca had ever known. Love such as she had never imagined welled up in her heart at the sounds of Morgan's groans and cries, pleased that she was giving him the same kind of rapture he was giving her. She moved against him wantonly, offering her aching breasts to the hot possession of his mouth. He licked and sucked greedily, tasting paradise. Then he was soaring, breaking free of his earthly bonds, taking Luca with him as he drove into her with deep, riveting strokes. She cried out her climax. He absorbed the sound with his mouth, adding his own piercing cries to the melody of love.

Tears blurred Luca's vision. Morgan's loving had touched her profoundly, and she feared he didn't feel the same about her. With a grim sense of recognition, Luca realized Morgan couldn't accept her love. Revenge was like a slow poison, filling his heart with hate and resentment. *Dios!* Was there no hope for them? She gazed at Morgan, wanting to ask him if he felt anything for her but lust, yet fearing she wouldn't like the answer. They were still joined intimately; Morgan held her tightly against him, as if reluctant to release her.

Suddenly he opened his eyes and met her searching gaze. He brushed a wisp of dark hair from her damp forehead and gave her a wry smile. "I missed you."

Luca gave a snort of disbelief. "Is that why you sent me so many endearing messages?" She tried to disengage their bodies, but Morgan seemed content to have her resting atop him.

"You can't possibly understand what drives me, or imagine the pain I suffered at the hands of your countrymen. You've seen the marks I carry on my back. They're not a pretty sight."

"Morgan, I . . ."

He continued as if he hadn't heard her. "Do you think it is easy watching your entire family being wiped out by murdering bastards insensitive to human suffering? Spanish bastards, Luca. You are the first Spaniard for whom I've felt anything but intense hatred. Wanting you the way I do confuses and angers me.

"Lord knows I've tried my damnedest to work you out of my system. Admitting my weakness for you is excessively painful. I don't like feeling this way about any woman. I always thought I'd have children one day, but having children with Spanish blood sickens me. God forbid that you should quicken with my child, for I don't know if I could accept that. That's one of the reasons I left you in the country. Out of sight, out of mind."

Morgan had no idea how profoundly his words hurt Luca. She too wanted children, but in her mind she pictured miniatures of Morgan. If he didn't want her to bear his children, she could see no future for them. After his candid confession she realized that Morgan would be better served wedded to

Lady Jane. Annulling their marriage seemed the only solution, for she could not tolerate the thought of Morgan despising a child of their union.

She had to leave Morgan. If she remained, a child was an inevitable result of their craving for one another. Luca thought it a miracle she wasn't already carrying his child.

With concentrated effort she drew the shattered remains of her dignity around her, discarding her dreams of a future with Morgan. "Out of sight, out of mind," she repeated bleakly. "I must leave you, Morgan."

Morgan's expression hardened. The play of light from the window made a sinister landscape of his face. "Like Hell! You're not leaving me, now or ever."

His arms tightened, and he thrust up into her with renewed vigor. After a few minutes' rest, he wanted her again. All his conflicting emotions were perversely at odds with one another, but of one thing he was certain: While he was buried deep inside her, the thought of letting her go was a denial of his heart's desire. The aching need for Luca was raw and bleeding and could be healed by no woman but his wife.

"But what if . . ."

"Don't talk, sweetheart, just feel."

Luca felt. She felt the pain of his rejection and the joy of his need. And she prayed they would not make a child.

16

The night was still young. Luca lay sleeping in Morgan's bed as he dressed and left to keep his appointment with Stan Crawford aboard the *Avenger*. When Morgan and Stan were sitting in the captain's cabin sharing a bottle of brandy, Morgan announced, "Luca is in London."

"You sent for her?" Stan asked, startled by Morgan's disclosure. "The queen won't be pleased. I thought you were considering the queen's proposal to dissolve your marriage and wed the Lady Jane."

"Hell no I didn't send for Luca! Besides, an annulment is Queen Bess's idea, not mine. I tried my damnedest to play by the queen's rules. You have no idea how bored I am with conniving court ladies and prissy courtiers. I don't belong here, Stan. Playing the courtier doesn't suit me. Dancing attendance upon the queen isn't my idea of a rewarding life. Bloody Hell! Why couldn't Luca have remained in the country? Now I am forced to introduce her to society and stand helplessly by while she's shunned and ridiculed. Her Spanish blood will make her an unpopular subject."

"We could leave," Stan suggested. "The *Avenger* is fully provisioned and ready to sail."

"I'm tempted, Stan, but I can't leave while England has need of my ship. We both know the Spanish Expedition is very real and an imminent threat to England's shores. I'm taking the *Avenger* to join Sir Frances Drake's fleet the moment the armada is spotted in English waters."

"What about Luca?"

"She'll remain in London," Morgan said tersely. "I'll introduce her to the queen and hope for the best."

Crawford searched Morgan's face, wondering if his captain knew he was in love with his own wife or if he was just too stubborn to realize it. Crawford thought Morgan a bloody fool to let Luca's Spanish heritage destroy what could be a happy marriage.

"Do you still believe Luca ordered your beatings in Havana? If you believe she hated you enough to advocate your death, I seriously doubt you'd still want her. Forgiveness isn't one of your virtues."

"I have few virtues, as you well know, Stan." Morgan took a healthy slug of brandy before continuing. "But you're correct in assuming I no longer believe Luca became del Fugo's mistress and ordered my beatings. If I did I would have devised a punishment worthy of the crime. If I was to admit . . ." His words fell off, and he gazed absently into the amber liquid in his glass.

"God help me. I've spent my entire adult life hating Spaniards and suddenly I find myself doubting my motives for revenge, my very sanity. I know Luca and I are an unlikely couple, that we've been thrown together by fate, but no other woman pleases me like Luca."

He stretched to his feet, embarrassed that he'd revealed so much about his innermost feelings. He was seldom driven to discuss matters of the heart. " 'Tis time I left. Luca will be awake now, and I still have an errand to attend to. Luca left Scott Hall without baggage, and her wardrobe will have to be replenished before she can be presented at court."

"Don't worry about the *Avenger*, Morgan. She's ready to sail when you are."

"Keep the men on a tight rein," Morgan advised. "It will do us little good if they are all in grog shops when we need them."

Luca awoke feeling indolent yet strangely content. She stretched languorously and smiled, recalling the rapturous hours spent making love with Morgan. After a moment of blissful recollection, she suddenly frowned, remembering how Morgan had cruelly renounced any child they might conceive. Leaping from bed, she dropped to her knees, fervently praying that no child had been conceived from their tempestuous mating. After a long interval of prayer, she rose unsteadily and began to dress, all the while contemplating her dismal future.

She had no idea when Morgan had left their bed or how long she'd slept, but her growling stomach reminded her that she hadn't eaten a decent meal since leaving Scott Hall. It had grown dark while she slept, but Luca surmised it wasn't late for she could hear strains of music drifting through the corridors. She'd heard that Elizabeth's court was a frivolous place where dances and such were held nearly every night. *Is that where Morgan went?* she wondered. *To dance with his mistress and play the gallant? Did he enjoy hopping from bed to bed?*

Another loud rumble reminded Luca of her empty stomach and she decided to find a footman who could direct her to food. The corridor was empty when she stepped from the chamber; no footman was in sight. She followed the sounds of music, hoping to find someone who could help her.

"Lady Scott, how wonderful to see you again so soon. Are you looking for your husband? Don't tell me he hasn't returned to his chamber."

Luca started violently, then relaxed when she recognized Lord Harley. "Lord Harley, you startled me. I've seen Morgan, but he seems to have disappeared again."

"Well, then," Harley said, his eyes sparkling with mischief, "allow me to escort you."

"Oh, no, there is no need," Luca declared, drawing back in alarm. "I'm merely looking for something to eat. Perhaps you can direct me. Anything will do."

"Indeed not," Harley said indignantly. "Not just anything will do for you, my lady. A woman of your great beauty and charm deserves a feast fit for a queen. Come," he said, offering his arm. "I know a private place where you may enjoy a meal."

He led her to a small anteroom off a deserted corridor. It was furnished with a table, chairs, and a brocade settee. A fire burned merrily in the hearth, making it a cozy haven for lovers. Ignorant of Harley's deviousness, Luca saw it merely as a quiet room where the frivolity of court could not intrude.

"Wait here, my lady, I will return shortly with a plate from the buffet table."

Luca thought Lord Harley a thoroughly likable man, and helpful besides. It occurred to her that Morgan had left her without a thought for her well-being, while Lord Harley seemed most solicitous of her welfare. Morgan should have inquired about her needs instead of sating his lust and then abandoning her, she thought crossly.

Lord Harley returned bearing a heaping plate of food, more than Luca could eat. He had also included a bottle of rich red wine and two glasses. He set the plate down on the table with a flourish and watched her hungrily, his eyes alive with anticipation. On his way back to Luca he couldn't resist stopping two of his friends and bragging about his intimate rendezvous with Sir Morgan Scott's Spanish bride. Nor could he help waxing poetic about her sultry beauty and lush charms, leaving his friends envious of his conquest.

"I've already eaten, but I'll share the wine with you," he told Luca. "It's an excellent vintage." He poured them both a glass and raised it in salute.

"Everything looks delicious," Luca declared, returning the toast. She took a sip of wine, realized she was quite thirsty, and gulped it down. Harley refilled it while Luca dug into the food, washing it down with more of the excellent wine. Whenever her glass was empty Harley refilled it, neglecting his own empty glass. He wanted keen wits about him when he enjoyed the Spanish morsel.

By the time Luca finished eating, the wine bottle was empty and her head was swimming. If not for the copious amount of food she'd consumed, she would have been drunk as a skunk.

"You're a beautiful woman, Lady Scott," Harley murmured huskily. "Come sit beside me on the settee. Unlike your husband, I will be most attentive to your needs."

Suddenly Luca was struck with the impropriety of being alone with a man she hardly knew. She must have been mad or really starving to permit such an intimate situation to develop. It occurred to her that her ignorance of court intrigue and her inexperience had allowed her to fall into this situation.

"It's getting late," Luca demurred. "I must return to my husband's chamber. Thank you again for assisting me."

"Your husband doesn't deserve you," Harley said, grasping her waist and tugging her toward the settee. "You are smart enough to know that he and Lady Jane are an item. 'Tis no secret that Jane is hot for him. She was hot for me at one time, but I wasn't wealthy enough."

Luca winced. Lord Harley was merely voicing what was common knowledge, but still it hurt. She let her mind wander and suddenly found herself sprawled across Lord Harley's lap, being thoroughly mauled.

"Lord Harley, let me go this very minute! I thought you were my friend."

"Oh, I am, Lady Scott, I am. I'm going to prove how true a friend I am as soon as I can get your clothes off."

Luca had to admit Lord Harley was adept with women's clothing. She no sooner shoved his hands away from one part of her anatomy than he pawed her in another, trying to get her out of her clothing. Were all men such lecherous pigs?

Morgan opened the door to his chamber, expecting to find Luca still sleeping. He carried a plate of food he had purloined from the buffet table, concerned that she hadn't yet eaten. He had completed his chores in town and was ready to confront their seemingly insurmountable problems. His chamber was dark, and Morgan carefully set the plate down and struck a flint to a candle. He cursed loud and long when he discovered that Luca was gone.

He stormed from the room in a rage. She knew virtually no one at court and could get herself into serious trouble. Luca was a beautiful woman, yet dangerously innocent in the ways of the world. Any one of the unscrupulous men or women at court would take advantage of her without blinking an eye. His feet seemed to sprout wings as he fled down the corridors in search of his wife.

It seemed as if Luca had disappeared into thin air, for Morgan could find her nowhere in the palace. His greatest fear was that she had left as mysteriously as she had appeared. The thought of Luca wandering alone in the streets of London filled him with dread. He was hurrying past the Presence Chamber when he was hailed by an acquaintance with whom he'd spent many hours drinking and gambling.

"Morgan, I say old chap, why didn't you

say your wife was at court? I hear she's a raving beauty."

Morgan stopped dead in his tracks. "You saw her, Pierce?"

"Not I, but Harley has described her in glowing terms. I for one don't care if she is Spanish. All women are the same beneath the sheets," he said, winking broadly. "I envy Harley right now."

Suddenly Morgan's control snapped. How dare he speak of Luca as if she were a common strumpet. Grasping Pierce by the lapels, he lifted him off his feet, bringing them nose to nose. "What about Harley and my wife? Do you know something I don't?"

Pierce sputtered fearfully. "I say, old chap, I meant no harm. With you and Lady Jane so cozy I thought Lady Scott was fair game. Everyone knows that yours was a forced marriage. It isn't a love match, so what is the problem?"

"The problem is that Luca is my wife," Morgan said through clenched teeth. "Where are they?"

Pierce swallowed visibly. "They're supping privately in a small anteroom off the west corridor."

"The one commonly used for private assignations?" Morgan asked. His control shattered, and he flung Pierce aside like a rag doll. He made directly for the chamber he had reason to know well. He had often met Lady Jane there for private conversation, though Jane would have had it otherwise. But he knew that it was used for more than conversation, much more, and the thought of what he'd find nearly destroyed him. An innocent like Luca would be putty in the hands of a womanizing scoundrel like Harley.

Luca wrested herself from Harley's lap in a tangle of arms and legs. Desperately trying to shake off the dizzying effect of the strong wine, she fell to the floor with a jolt that rattled her teeth.

"The floor is a wonderful idea, Lady Scott," Harley chuckled as he dropped to his knees beside her. "The settee is much too confining for what I have in mind." With a predatory grin he lowered himself atop her. Protesting vigorously, she scooted from beneath him and tried to rise. He grasped her ankle and pulled her back down.

"No, let me go!"

"You heard her Harley, release my wife."

Harley scrambled to his feet, his face drained of all color as he sought to placate Morgan. "I wasn't doing anything Lady

Scott didn't want," he insisted weakly. "She came here with me quite willingly."

Morgan sent Luca a withering look. "Is that true, Luca?"

"I left your chamber because I was hungry. Lord Harley offered to bring me a plate of food and suggested I eat in here, away from the crowds. I did not expect him to . . . to accost me. Are all Englishmen so crude?"

"Get out of here, Harley," Morgan hissed. Harley didn't wait for a second command. He fled the room as if the Devil was after him. A Devil named Morgan Scott.

Morgan's gaze never wavered from Luca, but he seemed to know the moment Harley was no longer with them. "Are you all right?"

Luca's head wobbled up and down. "Morgan, I had no idea Lord Harley would try to take advantage of me. Am I so naive that I do not know when I am in danger? The good sisters did not prepare me for court behavior, where a man's wife is fair game to unscrupulous men."

"Why did you leave my chamber?"

"I told you, I was hungry. I thought you had abandoned me after we . . ."

". . . made love?" Morgan supplied. "Why would I do that?"

"Perhaps Lady Jane . . ."

"I don't give a fig about Lady Jane, I thought I made that clear. I had an appointment with Stan Crawford aboard the *Avenger*. I returned as soon as I could, expecting to find you sleeping peacefully in my bed. I was nearly beside myself when I found the room empty. How did you meet Lord Harley?"

"When I arrived at Whitehall he was kind enough to direct me to your chamber. I thought him charming and . . . and . . ."

"He's a blackguard, just like all the other dandies at court. Stay away from them, Luca. You aren't equipped to handle their kind."

Luca had difficulty trying to focus on Morgan. There seemed to be two of him. The wine was playing havoc with her equilibrium, and she had the Devil's own time keeping her balance. "Am I equipped to handle you, Morgan?"

"More than equipped, witch," he growled, pulling her hard against him. "Keep away from other men, I won't stand for it."

Her response was a bubbly hiccup that sent Morgan's eyebrows skyward. "Are you tipsy, Luca?" He spied the empty wine bottle and groaned. "Bloody Hell, the bastard tried to get you drunk!"

"Morgan, I think I'm going to be sick."

"Bloody Hell." Sweeping her from her feet, he carried her out the door and down the winding corridors to his chamber.

Luca giggled all the while Morgan undressed her. When she finally kicked free of her last garment, she fell upon the bed, asleep before Morgan had time to tuck her in. He stood back and stared down at her, stunned at the trick life had played on him. Marriage to a Spanish beauty had never been part of his plans for the future, yet nothing short of death could convince him to part with Luca. His weakness for her was confusing and annoying, and so exciting that just looking at her made him rock hard and ravenous.

Morgan had no idea what fate had in store for them, or even if they had a future together. Fate was probably laughing at him this very minute. His lips twisted wryly as his gaze wandered to the soft nimbus of dark curls that drifted around her temples and neck. Her hair was growing; soon it would be long again. He recalled how shocked he had been when he'd first seen her shorn locks. He was accustomed to seeing her like this now, realizing that she'd always be beautiful to him no matter what she did to make herself unattractive. He'd always remember that drowsy, voluptuous look, the lush curve of her swollen red lips and heightened color, her gentle smile of surfeit after he made love to her.

God, she was magnificent! It was unfortunate she was Spanish. With stubborn perversity he realized that unless he wanted children tainted with their mother's Spanish blood, he had to keep his hands off her. When he touched her his lust for vengeance deserted him; he lusted only for his wife. But he'd pursued revenge against her family far too long to stop now. His hunger for Luca was elemental, yet arousal and completion were only a part of his need for her. His feelings made a mockery of the name El Diablo. If he didn't know better, he might think he actually loved Luca.

He groaned as if in pain. If love meant this gut-wrenching agony at the thought of giving Luca up, he wanted nothing to do with it.

"Wake up, Luca, there is much to be done before you can be presented to the queen."

Morgan gave Luca a none too gentle nudge, but she merely groaned and burrowed deeper beneath the covers.

"Luca, Queen Bess knows you're here and requests that you be presented to her this afternoon."

Morgan's last sentence brought an instant response from Luca. Shaking off her grogginess, she opened her eyes and stared at Morgan. "I'd prefer not to meet her at all."

Morgan shook his head and pulled the covers away, baring her naked body to the cool air. "One simply does not refuse the queen. Up with you, the dressmaker will arrive in an hour with an assortment of gowns that some of her clients were unable to pay for and left unclaimed. We should find something proper for you to wear that won't take much alteration. I've requested a tub and hot water for your bath."

Luca sat up, realized she was naked, and grabbed for the blanket. Morgan's magnificent eyes swept the length of her nude form as she tried to cover herself. She loved the way his eyes changed from blue to gray, depending on his mood. They could be piercingly aware, languidly shuttered, or deceptively calm. His harsh features were diffused now by those keen eyes as his gaze turned smoky with desire.

"I don't feel so good," Luca protested. "My head hurts and my stomach is churning."

Morgan's mouth pursed with displeasure. "Now that you're at court you'll have to learn whom to trust. Are you so naive that you didn't know what Lord Harley wanted? Or did you invite his attention?"

Luca's eyes narrowed in fury. "Think what you like, Morgan, you usually do. Why must I always explain myself to you? You probably still blame me for what happened to you in Havana, though I've denied it repeatedly. For your information I did not invite Lord Harley's attention, not knowingly, that is. I admit that court behavior is beyond my limited comprehension."

Morgan's expression softened as he eased down beside Luca, careful not to touch her. If he did he'd spend the rest of the morning in bed with her. "I've had abundant time to think during the past months and have come to the conclusion that you aren't capable of those things del Fugo accused you of. I absolved you long ago of any wrongdoing in Havana.

"As for your behavior last night with Lord Harley, I blame that bounder for assuming you were fair game. The only thing you were guilty of was trusting unwisely. Don't let it happen again, Luca. You are my wife, and I guard what is mine. So don't get any ideas about testing your feminine wiles on Elizabeth's smooth-talking courtiers."

Luca's eyes widened, stunned by Morgan's words. "If you feel that way, why are you paying court to Lady Jane?"

Morgan searched Luca's face, contemplating her question. She deserved an answer, but he could think of nothing that would ease the truth. She already knew how he felt about the Spanish blood flowing through her veins.

"Queen Bess was furious with me for marrying against her wishes and is pressing for an annulment on grounds that our marriage was forced. Lady Jane is to be my reward. She offered Lady Jane's hand as a reward for my obedience. Lady Jane is wealthy and titled and eager to become my wife."

Luca swallowed past the lump in her throat. " 'Tis common knowledge. West Sussex isn't so far from London that gossip doesn't reach Scott Hall. If it's the queen's wish that our marriage be dissolved, why haven't you done so?"

Morgan's eyes darkened with an emotion Luca didn't recognize. "Why, indeed?"

Their gazes collided and clung, reluctant to part as Morgan's eyes made love to her. Luca shuddered. The intensity of his glittering gaze made her breasts ache and flesh tingle. She felt as if he had stroked her intimately without actually touching her. After the space of a dozen heartbeats, Morgan cursed and looked away.

"Bloody Hell, Luca, how can I let you go when I still want you?"

He stood abruptly, as if startled by the admission.

"Servants will arrive soon with your bath. When the dressmaker arrives she will help you choose something appropriate for your audience with the queen. I'll return for you promptly at three o'clock."

Before Luca could catch her breath, Morgan was gone. He may have been confused about his feelings for her, but she knew exactly what she felt for her exasperating husband. Little good it did her to love him, when he continued to deny what was in his heart. And if there should be a babe, she shuddered to think how the poor child would suffer with a father who would despise him for his Spanish blood. Although her morose thoughts scattered when servants arrived with her bath, she couldn't help but note fleetingly that her first day at court had been anything but auspicious.

Morgan eyed Luca critically and nodded with satisfaction. Wearing a yellow brocade gown embellished with yards of lace and a high ruff collar, she outshined every court lady he knew. Morgan hoped she wouldn't outshine the queen, for Bess took pride in being the center of attention amid the bevy of beauties orbiting around her. No one dared shine brighter than Bess if they hoped to gain her good graces.

"You look lovely, Luca," Morgan said, meaning it. "Come along, the queen is waiting."

The corridors still confused Luca, but Morgan seemed to know where he was going as he conveyed her through the maze of hallways. Surprised when she found the Presence Chamber empty, Luca looked askance at Morgan.

"Bess is waiting in her Privy Chamber. She preferred to meet privately with you."

A footman announced them, and Luca felt her knees go weak as she entered the chamber on Morgan's arm. His strength lent her courage, for she discovered that they were not really alone. The room was crowded with spectators, most of them la- dies-in-waiting and courtiers. *Is this what private means to the queen?* she wondered. Then her thoughts scattered when a path cleared and she saw the queen sitting on an ornate carved chair at one end of the Privy Chamber.

The queen was a small woman, Luca

noted, but her stature was enhanced by her regal bearing. Her red wig was fashioned in an elaborate headdress, and her starched ruff emphasized her striking white skin. Nothing about the queen was ordinary. Luca saw immediately that Elizabeth was born for the role of sovereign and played it to the hilt.

"Your Majesty," Morgan said, executing a deep bow. Luca immediately dropped into a graceful curtsy.

Elizabeth bade them rise and offered her hand to Morgan. He clasped it and brought it to his lips, then introduced Luca. Elizabeth stared disconcertingly at Luca, immediately aware of Morgan's reason for steadfastly resisting her effort to dissolve his marriage. She thought the Spanish woman a rare beauty, but that knowledge failed to influence her thinking where Morgan's marriage was concerned. Sir Morgan Scott deserved an Englishwoman for a wife, not a Spaniard who brought nothing to the marriage.

"We did not summon your wife to court," Elizabeth said coolly. "We are not pleased, Sir Morgan. You know our wishes in this matter. It has been brought to our attention that your wife made threats against one of our ladies-in-waiting."

Luca wanted to sink into the carpet. The queen was daunting, and when she saw Lady Jane glaring at her, Luca knew the woman had taken her threat seriously. Without volition, Luca's chin climbed higher. She refused to be cowed by this ruthless monarch who had ordered the death of her own cousin Mary.

Morgan groaned beneath his breath. Damn Lady Jane for running to the queen with her tales. Couldn't they see that Luca's threat had been pure bravado?

"You must forgive my wife, Your Majesty. She is a stranger in England and new to our ways. She meant no harm."

Elizabeth directed her haughty gaze at Luca. "What say you, Lady Scott? Did your threat to commit murder have no teeth?"

Gathering her wits, Luca stared the queen in the eye and said, "I meant every word, Your Majesty. I will cut Lady Jane's heart out and feed it to the pigs if she does not leave my husband alone."

A collected gasp arose from those standing close enough to hear. None louder than Morgan's. Thus he missed the brief spark of admiration visible in Elizabeth's eyes.

"We have seen and heard enough from your Spanish bride, Sir Morgan," Elizabeth said dismissively. "We will remind you that your marriage does not please us. We had someone else in mind for you."

"I know, Your Majesty, and I will consider your wishes most diligently." He bowed and backed from the chamber, dragging Luca with him.

The moment they were out of earshot, he swung Luca around and glared at her. "Did you have to repeat that ridiculous threat to Elizabeth? Bloody Hell, Luca, what am I going to do with you? I don't know why I don't send you packing and marry Jane like the queen wants."

"Don't you?" Luca asked provocatively. "Think about it, Morgan."

Bloody Hell, he had already thought about it!

17

During the following weeks Luca met secretly with the Jesuits, who were still at court waiting for the Spanish Armada to hove into English waters. They moved about court like somber specters, tolerated by the queen in an effort to maintain peace between England and the powerful Catholic countries to the south. A wary eye was being kept on the Duke of Parma in the Spanish Netherlands, who was reported to be gathering troops in Spain's defense on the Flemish coast.

April arrived, bringing no changes for Luca at Elizabeth's hostile court. She still was regarded with suspicion. Morgan was deeply involved in preparations for the coming sea battle and during May traveled frequently to Plymouth to confer with Sir Francis Drake on the queen's behalf. Elizabeth seemed to be dragging her feet in preparing for a Spanish invasion. Had she forced matters by ordering her fleet to sea to destroy the armada before it left Lisbon, the battle would have ended before it began.

During Morgan's long absences in the month of May, Luca was drawn deeper into the Jesuits' confidence. Because they were the only people at court who valued her company, she felt comfortable with them. Having grown up in a convent, it seemed only natural for her to seek the company of priests.

To Luca's chagrin, Morgan continued to treat her with cool disdain when he was around long enough to take notice of her at all. Though she didn't want to believe Morgan was bedding Lady Jane, she couldn't be sure. She took nothing for granted where Morgan was concerned. If he was available, he escorted her to the buffet table at night, but more often than not she chose to have her meals brought to her. When she tried making friends with some of the court ladies, her efforts were promptly rebuffed. Only the men offered a semblance of friendship, and she knew where that would lead. Sometimes sheer boredom drove her from the chamber, and once she dared to venture out on the London streets. Morgan scolded her soundly for her reckless escapade. She wouldn't remain at court or even in England if there was a safe way for her to travel to Spain alone.

Any closeness she and Morgan may have shared at one time became nearly nonexistent now that Morgan was more deeply enmeshed in political intrigue. He rarely slept in their chamber, and when he did, he arrived so late and was so exhausted that he fell asleep immediately.

Luca worried about him excessively. She knew he intended to sail with the English fleet when they engaged the armada, and she feared he might lose his life in the battle. Yet he refused to talk about it, as if revealing England's plans to a Spanish woman would somehow betray his country. The reason for Morgan's remoteness was not difficult for Luca to understand. He still desired her, but it was obvious that his fear that she would conceive his child sufficiently chilled his ardor.

The month of June brought tensions at court to a breaking point. Rumors abounded. It was whispered that the armada had already sailed. Some said the ships carried nearly a hundred thousand troops equipped to invade England. Only Luca knew that the Jesuits had spread most of these rumors. Then, one sunny day in June, Morgan made a rare appearance in their chamber in the middle of the afternoon. Luca was more than a little startled when he stormed into the room in a state of great agitation.

"Morgan, what is it? Has the Spanish Armada been sighted?"

"Mayhap you know that better than I."

Luca drew back as if she'd just been slapped. "What are you saying?"

"Have you been consorting with spies behind my back?"

Luca drew herself up indignantly. "Certainly not!"

"It's been brought to my attention that you are spending a great deal of time with those Spanish priests who were sent here to spy for King Philip. If not for Elizabeth's good graces they would never have been allowed into our country." His eyes narrowed accusingly. "Have you turned spy, Luca?"

"I've done no such thing! Is it so unusual that I'd prefer the company of my own kind? These cold-blooded Englishmen hate me. At least the priests will talk to me, unlike you, who seem to have forgotten I exist. I've tried my best to stay away from the queen and her cohorts, since they seem to dislike me so."

Morgan scowled but said nothing. Unbeknownst to Luca, he had defended her time and again to Elizabeth, who continued to object strongly to one of her favorite courtiers being married to a Spaniard. Lady Jane had been quick to add her own disapproval to that of the queen. Jane tenaciously clung to the hope that she would soon be the wife of a national hero.

The past months had been as difficult for Morgan as they had been for Luca. Morgan would have liked to have pleased Elizabeth in regards to his marriage, but his emotions could not be forced. His heart was divided between duty to his queen and his increasingly tender feelings for his wife. His mind knew that Luca's Spanish blood would always be a barrier between them, but his heart told him it was time to forget the past and put the memory of his family to rest. Anger had a way of twisting and hardening a man's heart, and he'd carried the burden far too long. Revenge was a possessive mistress.

"Morgan, why are you staring at me like that?"

Morgan gave her a crooked smile. He had already forgotten why he wanted to speak with her. Looking at Luca made him forget his own name. "You're beautiful. Your hair is growing, it's nearly down to your shoulders. I rather liked it short."

"I could cut it again."

"Over my dead body." He stepped closer, closer still, until he felt her soft breath wafting across his cheek. "You haven't had an easy time of it, have you, sweetheart? Queen Bess doesn't like being crossed, and when she is, her displeasure can turn vicious. Perhaps I should send you back to the country, away from court and all this turmoil."

"Why *have* you disobeyed the queen, Morgan? And don't even think of sending me away, for I shall return. Your servants like me even less than your friends at court do. Perhaps," she said thoughtfully, painfully, "it would be best if I return to Spain."

Morgan's lips were but inches away when he said, "Of course it would, sweetheart, but since when have I ever done what is best? Letting you go would be like losing my right arm. I don't understand it, I don't even like it, but it's true."

Morgan had spent the past ten years schooling himself to hate Spaniards, and in a few short months Luca had taught him there was something more to life than revenge. She had elicited from him searing joy, fierce anguish, sweet passion . . . and heat. He felt the wall he'd built around his heart crumbling.

His mouth slanted across hers, hot and demanding as his tongue probed her sweetness. He groaned and grasped her bottom, pulling her into the hardening ridge of his desire. He couldn't begin to understand why he had denied himself all these weeks, when he would have given his soul to hold Luca's naked body in his arms and make love to her as his body demanded. For months he had tried to obey the queen's wishes instead of listening to his own heart. He had allowed his lust for revenge to destroy the only thing important in his life. It occurred to Morgan that he could live quite nicely without the queen, but he seriously doubted he could live without Luca.

Luca felt the swift, responsive rise of heat coil around her innards, tense and raw and as brilliant as the rising sun. Morgan's words had been a balm to her flagging spirits. He cared for her, she felt it deep within her soul, but he had built his lust for revenge into a wall she couldn't breach no matter how hard she pounded on it.

"Sweet Luca," Morgan groaned against her mouth. "You may not be a sorceress, but you come damn close. What you do to me is pure witchcraft."

"What you do to me is pure magic," Luca returned breathlessly. "And to think I wanted to be a nun. Had I never met you I would have missed the joy of being with you. Oh, Morgan, I lo . . ."

The words never left her mouth as Morgan's lips plundered hers ruthlessly and his hands left a trail of fire along her flesh. When he picked her up and carried her to the bed, Luca felt the kind of happiness that came only once in a lifetime. And now, with Morgan on the verge of admitting he loved her, she could finally confide a secret she'd only suspected these past few weeks. She felt certain she was carrying Morgan's child, but she had been too fearful of his response to tell him. The times he'd told her he didn't want a half-Spanish child were too numerous to count, but suddenly she felt confident in his affection for her.

In moments they were both naked, worshiping each other with hands and lips and mouths, bodies writhing with the need to consummate this new beginning. Morgan aroused her slowly, gently, with great care and expertise, bringing her to the brink of rapture, then denying her release. Luca shyly brought her mouth to his velvet hardness, tasting, savoring, surprised to find the slight saltiness of his essence pleasing to her palate.

Morgan arched violently and grit his

teeth. "Bloody Hell! No more, sweetheart, no more."

He pinned her to the bed, sliding down her body and touching his mouth to her intimate channel. His tongue probed deeply, savoring the musky scent of her arousal. With relentless purpose he drove her toward climax. Luca cried out and rode to a crescendo of raw bliss. He waited until her breathing returned to normal, then began arousing her again, until she was hot and wet with pearly moisture, until she begged him to come into her. Driven now by his body's urgency, he positioned his straining erection at the portal of her sex and thrust sharply forward. He nearly lost control the moment her softness closed around him, but he clamped his jaw tightly and flexed his hips, burying his throbbing length to the hilt. She felt the hardness of his sweat-drenched body quiver against hers, as if the effort for control was costing him dearly.

"Come with me, sweetheart," he murmured hoarsely into her ear. "Come with me . . . *now!*"

Crying out his name, Luca was nearly overwhelmed by the shattering ecstasy of her second climax.

Morgan gave a hoarse shout, thrust once, twice, then pulled out and spilled his seed onto the bedclothes. Luca watched in horror as his hand kept pumping until he was drained. Then he dropped down beside her and closed his eyes.

Though still dazed with passion, Luca wasn't too overcome to know that what Morgan had done was unnatural. When her breathing slowed to a steady pounding, she rolled to her side and stared at him. "Why did you do that?" she asked querulously.

Morgan opened his eyes and gave her a look that was more grim than apologetic. "You mean withdraw? It's one of the ways to prevent having children. We've been fortunate thus far, but our luck can't last forever."

His words effectively laid to rest Luca's foolish dream of living in contentment with Morgan and their child. He might want her sexually, but he had just proven that he abhorred the thought of having a child that carried her Spanish blood. The heartless rejection of their child brought a pain so severe that Luca clutched her stomach and turned away lest Morgan see how cruelly he had hurt her.

Had Morgan known the kind of devastation his words had wrought he would never have uttered them. His reasons had been quite different and far more simple than Luca's interpretation. He wanted children, what man didn't? The time had come to put the murder of his family to rest and get on with his life. Vengeance had been the driving force in his life for so long that he had excluded all else from it, including love. But now he wanted love. Luca's love. And he wanted to have children with her, but not now.

Very soon he would join the English fleet and engage Spaniards in battle. What if he lost his life and left Luca behind with a child in her belly? Knowing the queen's penchant for swift retaliation against those who displeased her, Morgan couldn't even be sure his estates would go to Luca if he lost his life at sea. In the past, Elizabeth had seized property from those who went against her wishes, and Luca could end up destitute, with his child to raise. He couldn't take that chance.

Of course it would be easier if he just stayed out of her bed, but their passionate natures made such an arrangement unworkable. *More like impossible*, he thought wryly. He could deny himself no longer, but he *could* be very careful to avoid leaving his seed inside her.

"Don't turn away from me, Luca,"

Morgan said, pulling her around to face him. "I can no longer deny my feelings for you. To Hell with the queen. To Hell with Lady Jane. 'Tis my life, and I'll damn well do what I please with it."

He touched her face and felt her tears. "Why are you crying, sweetheart?"

Luca saw no reason now to tell Morgan she was carrying his child. He might even make her get rid of her babe. She'd heard such things were possible.

"Did you hear me, Luca? What's the matter?"

Fortunately Luca didn't have to invent an answer. A loud rapping on the door interrupted what might have been a very awkward moment for Luca.

"Bloody Hell! Who could that be?" Tugging on his breeches, Morgan flung the door open, surprised to find Stan Crawford standing on the threshold.

"Stan! What is it? Has something happened to the *Avenger*?"

"Relax, Morgan, the ship is fine. The Spanish Armada left Lisbon some weeks ago. It was badly mauled and scattered by storms and perverse weather but reunited at Corunna and is now on course. It has been spotted off the coast of France."

"How do you know this?"

"A message arrived from the man you sent to track the armada. I imagine the queen has received the same intelligence."

"I must confer with the queen immediately," Morgan said, excited at being able to end this long period of inactivity. "I'll join you on the *Avenger* directly. Call all the men in from shore leave."

Morgan closed the door behind Crawford and turned to Luca. "You heard?"

She nodded weakly. "You're leaving."

"As soon as I've spoken with the queen. I'm sure she has her own intelligence out gathering information, but I need to know her plans now that the invasion is a virtual certainty."

He dressed quickly, then turned to Luca. "I'm afraid there is no time to send you back to the country now. If I place you in the queen's care, she won't dare let anything happen to you." He pulled her up by the shoulders and kissed her hard. His throat ached so he could hardly speak. "Luca, there are things I wanted to tell you, but they'll have to wait. Take care of yourself, my love."

"Be careful, Morgan. I will pray for you. I lo . . ." She started to say she loved him but thought better of it. It was far better that he hate her for what she had to do.

Queen Bess paced her Privy Chamber in a state of agitation. She was surrounded by members of her privy council and advisors, including Morgan.

"Intelligence just arrived indicating that the Spanish Expedition has encountered adverse weather but regrouped at Corunna and is nearing English shores," she confided. "We are ordering victuals and supplies sent to our fleet and have issued warrants granting permission for Howard, Drake, and Hawkins to intercept the armada before it reaches our shores."

"My ship is ready to sail," Morgan informed her.

"Can you carry our warrants to the fleet?" Elizabeth asked.

"Aye, Your Majesty."

"My scribe will give them to you. We wish you good sailing and happy hunting, Sir Scott."

Morgan hesitated. "May I speak freely, Your Majesty?"

"Is there something else you wish to discuss?"

"Aye. 'Tis about my wife. I know how you feel about her, but I am placing her into your keeping during my absence. I trust you will see that she is kept safe."

Elizabeth's eyebrows shot upward. "Your audacity is boundless, Sir Scott. Do you think Our good will is without limit where you are concerned? Men of higher rank than you have fallen when they demanded too much of Us."

"I realize I might be overstepping my boundaries, and, if I am, I beg your forgiveness. Luca is an innocent in many ways, and I ask only that you take her under your protection until I return."

Elizabeth tapped her fan impatiently against her chin. "You have contributed generously to our coffers, therefore I shall honor your request. But do not expect too much of Us."

"Thank you, Your Majesty," Morgan said, grateful for whatever protection she could offer Luca.

"God go with you, Sir Scott," Elizabeth said, bringing their conversation to an end.

Feeling in need of prayer and consolation, Luca dressed and hurried to the Jesuits' chamber. She found them in the midst of packing their meager belongings. Father Pedro greeted her with an air of distracted concern.

"Daughter, come in, come in. The time has come for us to leave. We received a message just today that the armada is finally within sight of English soil, and the queen's navy still sits idle at Plymouth."

"The queen will move quickly now," Luca surmised.

"The queen is a dithering old fool," Father Bernadino said scornfully. "We must leave immediately. A boat is waiting at Dover to carry us across the channel to Calais. From there we will travel by coach to Brest and board a ship for Lisbon."

"You must come with us, daughter," Father Juan urged. "We know you were forced into marriage and could never love an Englishman. It won't be safe for you at court once your husband leaves to join the English fleet. You must trust us, just as we trust you."

Luca looked at him in astonishment. "How do you know Morgan is leaving?"

"Ah, we have our ways, daughter. We know your husband carries warrants from the queen to the fleet. We expect the fleet will move against the armada very soon."

"We also know something not even the queen is aware of," Father Juan confided. "Once the armada enters the English Channel it will stop at Dunkirk. The Duke of Parma has amassed twenty-five thousand troops from the Spanish Netherlands. They will join the twenty-five thousand troops already deployed aboard the ships in Spain. The troops carry sufficient arms and powder to ensure victory."

Luca was dismayed by the numbers Father Juan had just quoted. "So many?"

"The size of the forces involved and the nature of their armament are unprecedented in either Spanish or English history," Father Pedro bragged. "Spain will emerge victorious, for God is on our side."

Luca's heart froze. The number of ships, men, and arms was mind-boggling. But even more frightening was the fact that Morgan could be rushing toward his death. Did he know what the English fleet was up against? She had to tell him before he left London. She knew nothing would change his mind but her information could be extremely valuable. Her love for her husband far surpassed her love for her homeland.

"How soon must we leave London?" Luca asked.

"Tomorrow," Father Pedro said. "Your suffering is nearly over. I will loan you one of my robes — no one will recognize you garbed as a priest. I will contact you later with the details."

"I must pack," Luca said, anxious to find Morgan and tell him what she had just learned.

"Go in peace, daughter," Father Pedro said. "Soon you will know the comfort of your father's home."

Luca hurried down the corridors, which had become quite familiar in the weeks she'd been at court, arriving in the queen's Presence Chamber out of breath. The chamber was crowded and, from what she could glean from snippets of conversation she overheard, the approaching armada was being widely discussed. A visual search of the room revealed no sight of Morgan. Then she spied Lady Jane and, swallowing her pride, approached the woman with chin held high.

"Have you seen my husband, my lady?"

Lady Jane gave Luca a dismissive wave. "Does Morgan tell you nothing of his plans? Everyone knows he left to join the fleet at Plymouth Sound." Her voice was cool and patronizing. "He asked me to wait for him. He said he had reached an important decision about his marriage and was anxious to tell me. Unfortunately he had no time to elaborate."

Her words had the desired effect on Luca. She knew she shouldn't believe Lady Jane for she probably spoke from jealousy, but it still hurt. Besides, it might be the truth.

"I am not here to argue about Morgan. I want to know if you've seen him in the last few minutes."

"You are too late," Lady Jane informed her. "He left over an hour ago."

Uttering a cry of dismay, Luca turned and fled. When she reached the front gate she questioned a footman stationed nearby. Her worst fears were confirmed when the footman told her that Morgan had left some time ago. It was useless to follow, for according to Stan Crawford, the *Avenger* was waiting only for Morgan to step aboard before hoisting sail.

Nothing was left to Luca now but prayer. If God was merciful, Morgan would return unscathed. She had to believe it, even though she would never know for certain. She and Morgan had no future together. Lady Jane could give him what she couldn't — an heir whose English blood was as pure as Morgan's. The child Luca carried might not be what Morgan wanted, but she would cherish the only part of him she was ever likely to have.

The following day five Jesuit priests were seen leaving Whitehall. The queen was happy to be rid of them. In fact, she breathed much easier knowing they were

404

gone. If they hadn't left of their own accord, she would have politely asked them to leave the country. When they filed through the corridors of Whitehall and out the gate into the waiting coach that would take them to Dover, all five had their cowls pulled low over their foreheads.

Luca hesitated before stepping inside the coach, close to changing her mind. Leaving Morgan was the most difficult thing she would ever be called upon to do, and perhaps the noblest. Her motives were pure and in the best interest of Morgan and their child. She could not bear the thought of raising their child in a hostile atmosphere. She prayed she had built enough memories of Morgan to last a lifetime. The terrifying thought that she hadn't done so brought a moment of panic, and she froze. Once she left London her relationship with Morgan would be irrevocably severed. There would be no turning back.

"Hurry, daughter," Father Pedro urged. "The boat won't wait forever."

Luca hesitated. That final step was so traumatic she was paralyzed, unable to think, unable to move. The decision was taken from her when Father Juan and Father Bernadino, who were waiting inside the coach, grabbed her arms and pulled her inside. Father Pedro quickly entered behind her and slammed the door. The coach left Whitehall behind in a rattle of hooves and wheels.

"You do not belong among these heretics," Father Pedro said when Luca started to protest. "Your father will be grateful to have you home safely. Perhaps grateful enough to endow our order."

Too numb to reply, Luca gazed wistfully out the window, recalling how tenderly Morgan had made love to her the day he had left. Everything had seemed so wonderful for a short time, until he had shown his contempt for her by releasing his seed onto the bedclothes. That one simple act had ended their relationship as effectively as if he had severed it with his sword. Morgan had made it abundantly clear that he would hate their child. Sighing in resignation, she turned her dismal thoughts to the future, no matter how bleak it might be without Morgan Scott in her life.

Morgan reached Plymouth with the queen's warrants and delivered them to the admirals. Two days later, after a spell of foul weather, a fair, fresh wind sprang up from the northeast. The admirals halted the loading of stores and ordered the fleet out for a quick run to intercept the armada. The *Avenger* joined the ninety-odd armed ships, great and small, which comprised the gallant and valorous fleet.

Five days later they were back in Plymouth Sound. In the middle of the Bay of Biscay, the wind perversely hauled round to the south, and they were forced to turn back. During the following week the fleet encountered problems with the same kind of rough weather that had plagued the Spanish Armada. Some of the merchantmen had strained themselves and sprung leaks, and some needed new spars and cordage. And as with most ships too long at sea, there was much sickness. During the lull the commanders did what could be done in the short time they had, replenishing their ships with fresh water, stores, ammunition, and provisions.

Morgan chafed impatiently. The delays were proving disastrous to men and ships. Morgan wanted to defeat the Spanish Armada as quickly as possible, rush home to Luca, and tell her that he loved her. Not even the queen's disapproval could convince him to give up Luca. Not for all the Lady Janes in England.

Just as talk circulated that the Spanish Armada had given up the expedition for this year, the *Golden Hind,* one of the ships as-signed to cruise in the mouth of the Channel, arrived to report that a large group of Spanish ships had been sighted near the Scilly Isles with sails struck, appar-ently waiting for the rest of their fleet to come up. Word was immediately sent to the queen, and finally, on July 19, the order was given for the main army to assemble at Tilbury and the second army to report to St. James for the purpose of defending the queen's person.

At ten that night the fighting English fleet sailed out of Plymouth. The next day the wind freshened from the southwest, and the fleet, including the *Avenger,* began to beat out to sea to avoid being caught by the enemy on a lee shore.

The armada, somewhat spread out but still making haste, bore away westward to get sea room. Morgan stood at the helm of the *Avenger,* tracking the armada's progress through the glass.

"My God, Stan, look at them!" he said, handing the glass to his first mate. "I've never seen anything like it."

Holding its course up the Channel, the ar-mada of over one hundred and thirty vessels hove into sight. In front sailed the main fighting force, in line abreast; behind it the smaller and less defensible ships; and on each flank and somewhat to the rear moved a smaller fighting squadron.

"I can't believe the armada survived intact given the inclement weather they've encountered these last weeks," Morgan commented, amazed.

"Where do you think they'll make landfall?"

"Hard telling. Drake's last message indicated that we were to let the Spanish pass to their destinations. Then we will hit them with everything we've got."

For seven breathtaking days the floating army plodded on toward its imaginary goal, continually harassed by Drake's fleet but not brought to a halt by its nimble foes. Two days later off the Isle of Wight, a general action took place on July 23. The armada made for the opposite coast, anchoring at Calais, hoping to establish contact with Lord Parma and his promised army. It proved to be their undoing. The English fleet attacked, scattering them for miles along the coast. That day proved to be the decisive battle of the campaign.

The *Avenger* was in the midst of the fray, holding its own against the mighty armada. It sustained minor damage and lost a few good Englishmen, but on the whole escaped virtually unscathed. Neither Morgan nor Crawford was hurt.

When the armada tried to escape to a friendly haven, they found only a hostile coast. There was nothing left for them but to return home in defeat. It became clear that returning by way of the Channel was out of the question, for the battered ships would be picked off one by one by the English navy. In a desperate move the admirals took the only route open to them, north around Scotland and Ireland. Less than half the ships of the armada, and perhaps one-third of the men, returned home. Many of the survivors died later of injuries or sickness, having endured everything and achieved nothing.

18

The *Avenger* sailed up the Thames and docked at Billingsgate on August 15, after several days of sea battles in which the fleeing armada had been consistently battered by English ships following doggedly in their wake. But once it became obvious that the armada was broken and taking a northern route home, the English fleet backed off and returned to their home port to celebrate their victory. The entire country was in a jubilant mood. The navy and their commanders were hailed as heroes, and the queen's popularity rose to an all-time high.

Though happy to have been a part of the glorious victory, Morgan eagerly anticipated a joyful reunion with Luca. He had missed her dreadfully. He had been at sea nearly six weeks, most of that time spent waiting for the enemy rather than engaging in battle, until the final days of July and early

August when the English fleet and Spanish Armada clashed repeatedly.

The defeat of the armada was a stunning personal victory for Morgan. His decisive triumph over his lifelong enemy banished for good his vendetta against Spaniards. For the first time in years he felt free to follow his heart. His future with Luca had never looked brighter. He felt at peace with his decision and capable of dealing with Luca's Spanish heritage with complete honesty.

He loved Luca. He'd loved her for a very long time but had sealed his heart against everything but his need for revenge. He prayed she would forgive him for his many sins against her and hoped that one day she would come to love him as much as he loved her. By some miracle he had emerged unscathed from battle and looked forward with relish to the life and to the children he and Luca would create together.

Stan Crawford approached Morgan quietly, hating to interrupt his reverie but finding it necessary. The ship had already docked, and Crawford was awaiting instructions. He cleared his throat, waiting for Morgan to acknowledge him. Morgan heard him and turned abruptly.

"Is the ship in order, Mr. Crawford?"

"Aye, Captain. In order, and awaiting your instructions."

"Give the men shore leave, all but a skeleton crew. They deserve it. And see that the wounded are cared for."

"What about the damage the *Avenger* sustained in battle?"

"Make a list of the damage. I'll return after I've seen Luca. Meanwhile you can hire carpenters and sailmakers to begin repairs."

Morgan arrived at court in the midst of a joyous celebration honoring the defeat of the Spanish Armada, the greatest naval flotilla in history. Just the size and magnitude of the huge armada was incomparable. Had things gone as planned and the weather had not been a factor, the Spanish Expedition might have succeeded. Those who sailed the ships realized it, but the majority of Englishmen failed to comprehend the very real danger that had threatened their shores.

Queen Elizabeth, her regal, black-clad form striking amid the peacock-hued clothing of her courtiers and ladies, was holding court in the Presence Chamber. Morgan scanned the room for Luca but failed to find her. He was on the verge of leaving the chamber to search for her when Lady Jane saw him and called out his name. Heads turned and Morgan found himself surrounded by well-wishers, congratulating him on the victory and demanding details. He drew so much attention that the queen noticed him and sent a page to summon him.

Morgan frowned in annoyance. The queen and her court dandies were the last people he wanted to see right now. He wanted to find Luca. He wanted to hold her, make love to her, tell her what a fool he'd been to deny what his heart had known all along. But when one was summoned by the queen, one did not refuse. The crowd cleared a path for him as he approached Elizabeth's carved throne. Lady Jane clung tenaciously to his arm.

Before Morgan could shake himself free, they had reached the dais. He executed a bow, and the queen gave him a brilliant smile.

"We are most pleased with you, Sir Scott. As We are with all our brave men and their admirals. You are the first to return. Tell us what transpired."

Finding no way to escape gracefully, Morgan spent the next hour relating details of the battles fought and the armada's route of escape, which would take them around Scotland and Ireland.

"The Spanish won't have an easy time of it," Elizabeth predicted. "They are likely to encounter dangerous weather this time of year in northern waters and along the Irish coast."

The queen's prediction proved all too true. It was later reported that countless ships had piled up on the rocky Irish shores with few survivors.

"We have received reports that our losses were minor compared to those of the enemy. We have brave men like you to thank. We will think of an appropriate reward," Elizabeth said grandly.

"I desire no reward," Morgan said, "except the freedom to claim my wife and retire to my estate."

Elizabeth scowled her displeasure, and the room grew unnaturally quiet. Morgan felt a chilling premonition and fought the urge to find Luca and flee London in all haste. He waited for Elizabeth to speak and instinctively knew he wasn't going to like what he heard.

"We fear that is the one thing We cannot grant you. Your wife no longer resides at court."

Morgan gasped in outrage and disbelief. "You sent Luca away?"

"Nay, We did not send her away. She disappeared a day or two after you sailed to join the fleet. No one knows exactly when she left, only that she is no longer with us."

"Is this how you keep your promises?" Morgan lashed out. "You said you would protect Luca. What have you done to her?"

"We have done nothing!" the queen said indignantly. She was unaccustomed to being addressed in so disrespectful a manner, and her temper flared dangerously. "We suggest you hold your tongue and remember to whom you are speaking."

"Morgan, please," Lady Jane urged, "say no more. You are incurring the queen's ire and that is not wise."

Morgan shook free of Jane's clinging grip, his expression hard and resentful. "Where is my wife? You and your ladies made her life a living Hell, and your courtiers considered her fair game for their vile attentions."

Elizabeth rose majestically from her chair, her rage daunting. "You go too far, Sir Scott! We do not know where your wife went and had no hand in her disappearance. We intended to fulfill our promise to you. After her disappearance was noted We sent a messenger to Scott Hall to inquire after her. But she was not there. It is our opinion that she has returned to Spain."

"Alone?" Morgan scoffed. "Luca had no

money; she knew no one in London to ask for help. How could she have gone to Spain?"

"The priests," Elizabeth said with haughty disdain. "The Jesuits left the day after you sailed. Though no one can verify it, We believe your wife accompanied them. 'Tis for the best."

Morgan's hands clenched into fists, wanting to hit someone or something. "I will go to Spain immediately and bring her back. Luca would not leave without good reason."

Morgan blamed himself as much as Elizabeth for Luca's disappearance but couldn't hide the fierce resentment he felt for the English court. Everyone in the Presence Chamber had heard him insult the queen, and they waited expectantly for Elizabeth to exact retribution.

"Nay, you will not leave England!" the queen declared, stamping her foot to give emphasis to her words. "The Spanish woman is where she belongs. Look to Lady Jane for solace, she will be a wife worthy of your name. We have taken the liberty of asking the bishop to prepare annulment papers. They await your signature."

Morgan exhaled slowly. "And if I refuse?"

"Your properties will be confiscated and

you will be imprisoned in the Tower until you regain your senses. Is that your wish?"

"It appears my wishes are of no consequence in this matter."

" 'Tis in your best interest, Sir Scott. You know We were never pleased with your marriage. Not only were you forced to take a wife totally unsuitable to your station but the marriage was performed by a Papist priest, reason enough for annulment. Lady Jane brings with her enormous wealth and numerous estates. 'Tis our fondest wish that our beloved hero wed the Lady Jane. You have much to lose by denying our request and everything to gain by accepting it, the least of which is a lovely wife who is smitten with you." Her words sounded suspiciously like a threat, and Morgan did not take kindly to threats.

After delivering her ultimatum, the queen sank gracefully into her chair, waiting complacently for Morgan to submit to her wishes. She would not accept refusal; she never did.

"Is that Your Majesty's last word?"

"Aye, 'tis my final word on the subject."

"Then I have no choice," Morgan ceded graciously. It was quite a feat keeping his temper on an even keel while inside he seethed with resentment and rage, but somehow he managed. The queen might guess but would never know the cost to his pride.

"Oh, Morgan, you won't regret it," Lady Jane squealed delightedly. Morgan gave her a wintry smile. "I knew you would make the right decision, that's why I went ahead with the plans for our wedding. We will be married one week from today with the entire court in attendance. We can spend our honeymoon at my remote estate in Cornwall. I've already sent word to have it prepared for our visit."

"You've thought of everything," Morgan observed coolly.

"You have made a wise choice, Sir Scott," the queen said, more than pleased with Morgan's capitulation. Few of her subjects were so foolish as to thwart her wishes.

"So be it," Morgan said, eager to escape the queen and Lady Jane. "If you will excuse me, Your Majesty, there is much I must do before the wedding. I still have a damaged ship and wounded men to attend. I must send word to Scott Hall and acquire a proper wardrobe to honor my bride."

Elizabeth gave an imperious wave of her hand. "You are excused, Sir Scott. Weeks at sea with our victorious fleet must have left you exhausted."

Morgan withdrew with as much grace as he could muster. He had no idea Lady Jane was following until he sensed her at his side. "I really am exhausted, Jane," he repeated for her benefit. "Tomorrow would be a better time to discuss plans."

"I don't want to talk." Her voice held a sultry note of promise. "There is no reason for restraint now. Our wedding needs only the ceremony to make it legal. Your wife has deserted you, and I already feel like your wife. Make love to me, Morgan."

Morgan gritted his teeth in frustration. Damn Bess and damn Jane for pushing him into something he did not want. He still had a week and he intended to make good use of it before . . .

"Not now," Morgan hedged. "I'll come to your chamber tonight. I'll be of little use to you if I fall asleep the moment my head hits the pillow. I'm filthy and in need of a bath. Please excuse me."

Jane pouted prettily. "I'll help you with your bath. Who knows what will happen once you are refreshed."

"I know. I intend to take a long nap."

"Morgan, I'm beginning to think you're trying to avoid making love to me." Her voice took on a hard edge. "All I need to do is suggest to Queen Bess that you intend to back out of the marriage and she will promptly seize all your holdings and lock you in the Tower until you come around."

"Ah, Jane, I believe you would enjoy that," Morgan said softly, too softly, sending a shiver racing down Jane's elegant back. He pulled her into his arms, kissing her hard, roughly, transferring all his anger to the harsh possession of her mouth. Jane shuddered, welcoming his brutal kiss with ravening hunger.

"Morgan, oh, Morgan, yes, I like you this way." She moaned mindlessly against his mouth, breathless with anticipation. "I don't care how rough you get."

A sound of disgust gurgled deep in Morgan's throat. Jane's mouth was wet and slack beneath his. He suspected that he could take her on the floor, in the corridor, and she wouldn't protest. But he didn't want her, not now, not ever. Luca was the only woman he wanted, and he'd have her if he could get rid of Jane without forfeiting his life. Time was of the essence. He had but a week to get his affairs in order, and it was going to be damn difficult with Jane panting after him. How in the Hell was he going to keep her satisfied without actually bedding her?

"Tonight," Morgan whispered against her mouth. Giving her breast a teasing caress that promised long hours of bliss, he turned and strode briskly away.

"Morgan . . ." Jane stamped her foot angrily, her body still thrumming with unrequited desire. "Damn that man," she muttered beneath her breath. If he didn't fulfill his promise this time, there would be Hell to pay. Her family was a powerful force in England. She'd personally see that Morgan Scott was rendered penniless if he disappointed her. By the time she finished with him he'd have nothing, not even his ship, which he seemed to value so greatly. Spinning on her heel, she returned to the Presence Chamber.

A short time later Morgan slipped out a side entrance, hailed a passing hack and arrived at Billingsgate a short time later. Crawford was waiting for him aboard the *Avenger.*

"That didn't take long, Morgan." His eyes gleamed with mirth. "I assumed you'd spend more time with Luca, knowing how anxious you were to see her."

"Luca is gone," Morgan said tersely.

"Gone! Where in the Devil has she gone?"

"My guess is Spain. I'm assuming she accompanied a group of Jesuit priests who returned to Spain shortly after we sailed."

"You know that for a fact?"

Morgan's expression altered subtly, conveying his uncertainty. "No. No one saw her leave, but it's the only lead I have. Bess already ascertained she's not at Scott Hall. There's nowhere else she could go. She had no one to turn to at court but the Jesuits — everyone else ignored her, and I was too busy or too stubborn to be much of a husband to her. I'm going after her to beg her forgiveness."

"When?"

"How badly is the ship damaged?"

"Not badly. Our own carpenters can repair the rudder and riggings, and our sailmakers can mend torn canvas with no problem. Shouldn't take over two weeks."

Morgan sent him a bleak look. "I don't have two weeks. Everything has to be done in six days or less."

"Six days! You expect miracles, Morgan."

"Aye, can you do it?"

"What happens if it can't be done?"

"I'll either be forced to marry Lady Jane or lose all my possessions to the crown and spend the rest of my days in the Tower. I'll be destitute, Stan. I won't even have a ship to take me back to Andros."

"Not exactly destitute, my friend. Have you forgotten the plunder hidden on Andros?"

"I've not forgotten, but it's insubstantial compared to what's in the bank in London."

"What are your plans?" Crawford asked, sensing another adventure.

"We're going to Spain," Morgan confided, "but first . . ." In a low voice he outlined his plan to Crawford.

Crawford listened intently, nodding eagerly as Morgan's plan unfolded. "It could work, but what if Luca isn't willing? What if she wants nothing to do with you? And your plans concerning Lady Jane are risky at best. 'Tis obvious she intends to have you in her bed before the ceremony. And last but not least, there is the queen to contend with. If you pull this off, she'll likely never forgive you. You'll be arrested and imprisoned."

"I've considered everything, Stan, and it's paltry compared to a life without Luca. All the riches in the world are worthless without Luca to share them with me."

"Those are strong words from a man who can't abide Spaniards. The little nun got under your skin, didn't she?"

"Aye," Morgan admitted, "more than you'll ever know. Otherwise I'd do my duty to the queen no matter how distasteful. But now I'll rot in the Tower before becoming the queen's pawn and signing those damn annulment papers. But I need your help."

Crawford chuckled. "What you're asking of me is a little unorthodox."

"Desperate times call for desperate measures. If you have no stomach for it . . ."

"It isn't that," Crawford contended, still grinning. "The lady is bound to know the difference."

"Not if you use the darkness to your advantage. We are enough alike in looks and build to raise no suspicion. Just make damn certain you perform adequately. I want no doubts about my virility. I do have a reputation to uphold."

Crawford gave a shout of laughter. "As arrogant as ever, I see. Don't worry, my friend, I'll raise my mast high in salute to the lady. We have shared women many times throughout the years, but this is the first and last time I'll be doing it in your name."

"Start the men on the repairs, Stan. There is much to be done before we hoist sail. I'll see you later tonight in my chamber at Whitehall."

Morgan left, going directly from the *Avenger* to his solicitor's office. Morgan had engaged Sylvester Thornhill shortly after returning to England as a young man, following his escape from slavery. Thornhill had proven his worth time and again during the years Morgan sailed the high seas in search of Spanish plunder. He was trustworthy, discreet, and above all, competent to handle all aspects of Morgan's business. And Morgan trusted Thornhill to divulge nothing that went on within the confines of his office.

"Do you have any qualms about doing what I ask?" Morgan inquired once he had laid his plans before the lawyer.

"Let me get this straight," Thornhill said slowly. "You wish to pension off your servants at Scott Hall and give them a generous severance. Are you planning on closing the hall permanently?"

"I'm leaving the country, perhaps for good," Morgan confided. "I'll be honest with you, Thornhill, because you deserve it. 'Tis likely my estates will be seized by the crown. I don't want my servants to suffer, especially Clyde Withers. He's a good man, and loyal."

Thornhill's eyes widened. "You're a hero, Captain, why would your estates be confiscated?"

"It's a long story, and I certainly will tell you, but first, are you willing to follow my instructions?"

"Of course, did you doubt it? What else can I do for you?"

"Plenty. I will be turning all my assets into gold and transferring it aboard the *Avenger*.

If you can find a buyer for Scott Hall within a week's time, fine, but if not, it's of no consequence."

"It may be difficult, but not impossible. Several prospects have already come to mind. Is that all?"

"No. I want you to continue as my London broker for the lumber I ship from Andros. Take your fees from the profits and bank the rest under the name of my first mate, Stan Crawford. He will be free to come and go from England at will."

Thornhill searched Morgan's face. "This certainly sounds like you are severing ties with England, Captain Scott. Are you certain this is what you want?"

"Circumstances make it necessary. I would not have chosen this course if the queen weren't making it all but impossible for me to remain in England." He stretched to his feet. "Time grows short, and there's much yet to be done. Send word around to the *Avenger* when you've completed the tasks I've set for you. Nothing is private at court, and I wish to keep my plans secret."

"You'll be hearing from me soon, Captain Scott."

Later that day Stan Crawford made his way to Morgan's chamber with little fanfare.

His discreet knock was answered immediately, and he slipped inside the moment the door opened.

"I hope to God this works," Stan said, grinning mischievously. "I still say you should do your own dirty work."

Morgan sent him a quelling look. "It's not as if you won't be pleasurably rewarded for this night's work."

Crawford raised a well-shaped brow. "I'll let you know later. Are you sure this is what you want?"

"I need to buy time, Stan, and I certainly don't want to bed Lady Jane. I couldn't touch her without thinking of Luca every minute I was with her. I don't want to betray my wife. This is the only way I can think of to placate Jane and not to betray my marriage vows. Jane's a hot little piece. I think you'll enjoy her. I was sorely tempted to try her on more than one occasion, but something always stopped me."

" 'Tis a foul trick, but I understand. Don't worry, I won't disappoint the lady."

"Just one thing, Stan," Morgan reminded him. "I don't want you to leave Jane with a babe in her belly when neither you nor I will be around to claim it. I don't want to hurt her, she's not a vicious person, just a determined one. She's not a virgin, so you won't

428

be stealing anything from her that she hasn't already given away. Just be sure to give her enough pleasure to satisfy her."

The corridors were deserted. It was long past midnight; a time when the darkest hours of night pulled a blanket over the sleeping world. Stan and Morgan slipped quietly from the chamber and crept down the hallway to Lady Jane's room. They paused outside the door for the briefest moment, then Morgan turned to Stan and placed a finger over his mouth. Stan stood aside as Morgan opened the door and stepped inside. A single candle, burnt nearly down to a stub, cast the room into a shadowy haven for lovers. The flickering flame was dangerously close to sputtering out.

"Morgan, is that you? What took you so long? I've been waiting for hours." Her pouty tone revealed her vexation.

"Aye, 'tis me, Jane." He moved toward the bed, pausing near the dancing candlelight a few seconds so Jane could get a good look at him.

"Hurry, love," she breathed raggedly, "and for God's sake close the door."

Turning swiftly, Morgan made certain he created enough breeze in passing to douse the dying flame. The room was plunged into darkness.

"Morgan, what happened?"

"Nothing," Morgan assured her. "The candle sputtered out. We don't need a light. I'll be with you as soon as I close the door." He walked to the door, slipped into the hall, and motioned for Stan to take his place. Once Stan was inside the chamber, Morgan closed the door.

"I'm waiting, Morgan," Jane said peevishly. "Can't you light the candle, I want to see you."

The bed dipped and Stan eased beneath the sheets beside Jane. "Forget the light, I want to learn you with my hands." His voice held a rough edge of anticipation, so Jane did not question the slight change in tone. She was experienced enough to recognize the gruff impatience of a man's passion.

Stan did not disappoint Jane, nor did his lovemaking damage Morgan's reputation. If anything, Morgan's virility was enhanced by Stan's magnificent performance as a lover. Stan knew immediately that Jane was well-acquainted with passion, for her performance left him breathless. By the time he'd aroused Jane to stunning rapture, he was blessing Morgan for giving him this enjoyable chore. Not only did Stan please Jane exceptionally well, he did it more than once. Unlike Morgan, there was no other woman in his life, and he enjoyed Jane to the fullest, keeping in mind Morgan's warning about not leaving Jane with child. He crept from her bed just before dawn, after Jane had lapsed into an exhausted sleep.

Stan returned to find Morgan pacing his chamber with a marked lack of patience.

"Well, how did it go? Did Jane suspect anything? You sure as Hell stayed long enough."

Stan stretched and yawned. "Lady Jane isn't a woman you can easily leave once she has you in her bed. Bloody Hell, Morgan, she came damn close to wearing me out."

Morgan suppressed a grin. "Are you complaining?"

"Not bloody likely. You have nothing to worry about, my friend, I gave us both a good accounting. Your reputation with the ladies will flourish after last night."

Morgan gave a shout of laughter. "A modest fellow, aren't you? Nevertheless, I'm grateful. There is only one woman for me, Stan, and she's in Spain."

"I should be getting back to the ship," Stan said, staring longingly at the bed. He hadn't slept a wink. "If you have need of my services again, let me know. I'll be happy to oblige."

"You're a true friend," Morgan chuckled. "I hope I'll have no need of such a deception again. Now that I've proven myself, Jane can't accuse me of avoiding her bed."

"You're an amazing lover," Stan said, tongue in cheek. "Well, I'll be off then. Any instructions?"

"Keep the men working on the ship. We'll slip from Billingsgate on the evening tide the night before my wedding day. Meanwhile, I'll make all necessary arrangements and try to avoid Jane. Trunks should be arriving daily with the bulk of my wealth. Store them in the hold with the cargo."

Later that day Morgan tried to slip away from Whitehall without being noticed. As luck would have it, Lady Jane hailed him as he approached the gate. Having run all the way to catch up with him, she was panting for breath when she reached him. Morgan could not help but note how her eyes sparkled; her lips appeared slightly swollen and red from her night's exertions, no doubt. Stan hadn't exaggerated, Jane looked like a woman who had been thoroughly tumbled.

"Morgan, where are you going?"

"Business, Jane," Morgan replied. The corners of his eyes crinkled with amusement as he bent low and whispered, "Are you displeased with me?"

"Displeased? God, no! You lived up to my expectations and more. You were magnificent, Morgan, I cannot begin to tell you how well you pleased me. Will you return tonight?"

"Greedy, aren't you? I have pressing business in West Sussex. Don't look for me until the day before the wedding."

"But Morgan, the queen says you haven't signed the annulment document yet. And what about the prenuptual festivities?"

"I will return in plenty of time to sign the document and attend the festivities, Jane. Unless you keep me here talking and delaying my journey."

"Hurry back, darling," Jane said, grasping his head and pulling it down for a hard kiss.

Jane remained at the gate until Morgan stepped into a waiting hack. When she finally turned away, she walked into the arms of Lord Harley.

"Where is your betrothed going?" Harley asked curiously.

"To West Sussex."

Harley gave her a leering grin. "Does he intend to stay long in West Sussex?"

Jane tilted her head, regarding him with

interest. "Long enough. What do you have in mind?"

"You should be marrying me, you know."

"I am but following the queen's wishes. Perhaps she'll find you another heiress."

"Do you suppose you might take pity on a poor rejected suitor?"

"Whatever do you mean?" Jane asked coyly. She had nothing against Harley. He was a good lover, though not as good as Morgan, but then Morgan was not here, was he?

"Tonight," he whispered urgently. "After the queen releases you from duty. Meet me in the arbor, it should be deserted at that late hour."

Executing a courtly bow, he pressed a kiss into her upturned palm and took his leave. Harley knew Jane would meet him. Their past relationship had been of a passionate nature, and he had learned during their association that she was a hedonist who derived great enjoyment from sexual encounters. Besides, Harley thought as he strolled away whistling a jaunty tune, he would gain enormous pleasure from making a cuckold of Morgan Scott.

19

Morgan hastened along the quay to the *Avenger*, where he had been staying since leaving Whitehall six days before. He ventured out into the streets of London only when it was necessary for him to conduct business. It would be dangerous to risk recognition when he was supposed to be at Scott Hall. He had made a fast trip to Scott Hall to confer with Clyde Withers and had returned the same day. After Morgan explained his predicament to his faithful steward, Withers promptly asked for and received a berth aboard the *Avenger*, expressing his willingness to throw in with Morgan rather than remain behind and look for a new employer.

During his short visit to Scott Hall, Morgan gathered up a few family heirlooms and pictures he couldn't part with and had them sent on to the *Avenger*. When he returned to London he found an urgent message from Thornhill, his solicitor. A buyer had been found for his property, and the transfer deed awaited his signature. As much as he loved Scott Hall, Morgan felt little remorse over selling it, for he knew how unhappy Luca had been there. Finding no reason to delay the inevitable, Morgan called on Thornhill immediately.

Within a short time the transaction was completed to everyone's satisfaction, and the documents now rested safely in Morgan's vest pocket. With his house sold and his gold safely transferred aboard the *Avenger*, Morgan knew he could no longer delay his return to Whitehall. If he failed to return at the appointed time, the queen would quickly figure out what Morgan intended and dispatch the palace guards to Billingsgate to apprehend him. Morgan didn't want the queen or anyone else to know that the *Avenger* was taking on stores for a very long journey.

Unbeknownst to Morgan, someone did know. Lord Harley and Lord Bainter, out for a drive, had seen him leave his solicitor's office. Since both men were of a curious nature, they decided to follow. Harley knew that Morgan was supposed to return to Whitehall today to attend his prenuptual festivities and wondered why he was still wandering around town. When Morgan's hired hack turned toward Billingsgate, they followed in their own conveyance. They watched as Morgan strolled up the gangplank and disappeared into his cabin.

"What do you suppose he's doing?" Harley wondered.

"Damned if I know," Bainter drawled, "but I'd like to find out."

"Wait here," Harley said, springing lightly from the coach. "There seems to be a lot of activity taking place around Scott's ship."

Walking swiftly toward a group of dockhands, Harley watched in silent scrutiny as they loaded stores and ammunition aboard the *Avenger*. Having seen enough to raise his suspicion, he approached one of the dockhands. "Looks like the *Avenger* is preparing for a long trip."

The man barely glanced at Harley. "I get paid to load ships, not answer questions."

"Do you know where the *Avenger* is going and when she will sail?"

"I told ya, mate, I get paid to . . ."

"I know, load ships not answer questions," Harley echoed. "What if I make it worth your while? You can use some extra blunt, can't you?"

That finally got the dockhand's attention. "What bloke can't? How much ya offerin'?"

Harley pulled a handful of shillings from his pocket and shoved them under the man's nose. "Will this do?"

The man licked his lips greedily. "What do ya want to know?"

"When is the *Avenger* sailing?"

"No one has actually said, but the scuttle is she sails on tonight's tide. All stores are to be loaded and stowed by dusk."

"Interesting," Harley murmured. "One more thing. What's the *Avenger*'s destination?"

The dockhand scratched his balding head. "Don't know, the captain never said."

Harley's attention sharpened. "Captain? You dealt with the captain directly?"

"I never actually spoke with the captain, we dealt with the first mate. But I understand his orders came directly from El Diablo. I seen the captain around all week, though, comin' and goin' at odd times of the day and night."

"All week? You're sure?"

"Aye, as sure as I can be. Ya think he's goin' after Spaniards again? I doubt there's any of 'em left after our fleet scattered the bastards from here to eternity."

Harley smiled smugly. "He's going after Spaniards, all right. One Spaniard in particular, unless I miss my guess. Thank you, my friend." He tossed the coins at the dock-hand's feet and returned to the coach.

"I hope you're satisfied," Bainter yawned as Harley settled into the seat beside him. "Can we go back now? I promised Lady Camille a dance at tonight's celebration and I need a nap to fortify myself for the ordeal. She's a clumsy bitch, but entertaining enough beneath the sheets. The queen is hosting the celebration to honor the marriage of Sir Scott and Lady Jane, you know."

"I know, and I'm going to make damn certain the reluctant bridegroom is brought to heel. Back to Whitehall it is," Harley said, grinning hugely. "I wouldn't miss the celebration tonight for all the gold in the queen's coffers."

Morgan returned to Whitehall at dusk, after he'd seen to the loading and storing of cargo. He wanted nothing to go wrong. His entire future was at stake, and he didn't intend to spend it leg-shackled to Lady Jane. He already had a wife, one he loved, and no one, not even the queen of England, was going to take her from him.

Morgan was surprised to see Jane waiting for him inside his chamber. She threw herself into his arms. "Morgan, darling, you're back! I've been frantic with worry."

"You shouldn't be here, Jane. Shouldn't you be dressing for tonight's festivities?"

"Yes, of course, but I wanted to be here to greet you when you returned." She sent him a searing look. "After what transpired in my bed the other night I thought you'd be glad to see me. Was naught amiss at Scott Hall?"

"Everything is fine, Jane, but it grows late. You'd better hurry. Wear something fetching for me."

"Oh, I will, Morgan, I will!" Blowing him a kiss, she ducked out of his chamber.

Morgan breathed a sigh of relief. But it was short-lived, for almost immediately a summons came from the queen. She requested his presence in her Privy Chamber, at once. Morgan had a pretty good idea what Bess wanted and had hoped to avoid it. He reached the Privy Chamber and a warning chill slithered down his spine when he saw Lord Harley engaged in earnest conversation with the queen. Elizabeth turned at Morgan's entrance, her eyes glittering with anger.

"You summoned me, Your Majesty?" Morgan asked blandly.

"We are glad you returned from West Sussex in time to celebrate the occasion of your wedding. But alas, you neglected to sign the annulment document prepared by my bishop. It is our wish that you sign it now so there can be no question of legality tomorrow."

The queen's secretary approached Morgan and presented him with the document.

"You will find quill and ink on the writing table," Elizabeth directed.

Morgan grasped the document, strolled casually to the writing table, and carefully unrolled it. Stretching it out on the smooth surface of the table, he dipped the quill in the ink and signed it with a flourish. Then he carefully rolled it up and handed it back to the secretary, who bowed to the queen and left the chamber.

"Well done, Sir Scott," Harley sneered. "Now perhaps you can explain why you lied about your visit to West Sussex? I have it on good authority that you were staying aboard the *Avenger* this past week. You weren't in West Sussex at all, were you?"

Morgan gave Harley a look of intense dislike. "You may check if you like, but you will find that I was indeed in West Sussex to confer with my steward. I returned a day early and stayed aboard the *Avenger* to make sure all the work I ordered was completed to my satisfaction."

"Stores are being loaded aboard the

Avenger," Harley charged. "You were seen aboard the ship when you were supposed to be visiting your estate."

"My first mate and I are often mistaken for one another. We have the same look about us. Mr. Crawford is taking command of the *Avenger* in my absence. Do you have a problem with that? What am I being accused of?"

"Lord Harley seems to think you intend to leave your bride at the altar," the queen accused. "We would be most unhappy if you attempted anything so foolish."

"Nothing is further from the truth, Your Majesty," Morgan lied. "May I go now?"

Elizabeth searched Morgan's face, apparently satisfied that he meant what he said. After a tense silence, she dismissed him with a wave of her hand. "We will see you anon, Sir Scott. 'Tis most upsetting that you appear to be a reluctant bridegroom when you have so much to lose if you do not go through with the wedding."

Elizabeth's thinly veiled threat made Morgan's hackles rise. He had no idea how Harley had learned about the *Avenger*'s sailing plans but leaving England was going to be more difficult than Morgan had anticipated. Somehow he had to sneak away from his own party before high tide tonight, reach the *Avenger*, and raise anchor without anyone being the wiser.

The festivities that night were a test to Morgan's control. Jane clung to him tenaciously, and Queen Bess watched him with hawklike intensity. Through it all he acted his usual self, talking, flirting, and paying courteous attention to Jane. When the hour approached for Morgan to duck out of the festivities, he waited for precisely the right moment. It came when Lord Harley asked Jane for a dance.

"I'll be at the card tables," Morgan said as Harley led Jane away. When the couple strolled onto the dance floor, Morgan ambled into the card room. But he didn't stop there. He exited through another door into the anteroom and slipped cautiously into the corridor.

A few minutes later he was exiting through a side entrance, where he'd had the foresight to order a hackney to stand in readiness for his departure. The alert driver pulled the hackney to the entrance, and Morgan leaped inside, directing the driver to Billingsgate. They reached the docks without mishap despite the dark night and rain-slick streets, and Morgan leaped out. The hackney rattled away, Morgan having paid the driver in advance.

Morgan sprinted toward the quay, where the *Avenger* was moored. He took but a few short steps before halting abruptly in his tracks. He was more than a little shocked to see that the *Avenger* had slipped her moorings and rode at anchor a short distance out into the Thames. But even more astounding was the company of palace guards patrolling the area.

"Damn Bess and her distrustful nature," Morgan muttered beneath his breath as he hid behind some barrels piled in front of a warehouse. She'd obviously suspected that he'd try to duck out of his commitment. He could only guess at Stan Crawford's reason for moving the *Avenger* into the Thames, but he would be willing to bet it had something to do with the patrolling guards. Morgan's mind worked furiously. Crawford was an astute man. He probably figured it would be easier to escape the patrol if the ship rode at anchor in the Thames, where it would be more difficult for the queen's men to board. It was also out of range of musket fire. The drawback was that Morgan had to find a way to reach the ship before the tide went against them.

Suddenly Morgan's attention was diverted as a rider clattered down the cobbled street and hailed the captain of the guard.

They spoke at length, and when he left, the captain called his men together for new instructions. Morgan knew without being told that his presence had been missed at Whitehall and that Bess had correctly guessed that he'd head for Billingsgate and his ship. Suddenly the patrol scattered and began searching in earnest along the quay. Morgan cursed violently. If he didn't do something fast, he'd be caught like a rat in a trap.

He had no choice but to make a break for it and trust his luck, unless he wanted to spend the rest of his days locked in the Tower. Morgan waited until a cloud drifted across the moon, then crept from behind the barrels. He ran as if the Devil was nipping at his heels. The sound of his bootheels striking the cobblestones echoed loudly in the darkness, and he waited in dread for an alarm to be raised. He had nearly reached the end of the quay when he was spotted.

"There he is, get him!"

Footsteps thundered after him, and bullets whizzed over his head and all around him. He shed his coat before he reached the end of the quay and dove into the foul, refuse-strewn water. Bullets flew furiously as he hit the water, where he dove deep. But not deep enough. A bullet found its mark in the back of his thigh. He heard a sickening crack, and then pain shuddered through him. The icy water kept him from blacking out as he gritted his teeth against the agony and struck out for the ship. Fortunately he was now out of musket range. But when he glanced over his shoulder he saw the patrol searching the bank for a boat.

Trying to ignore the burning agony of his wound and the dead weight of his useless right leg, Morgan stretched his arms and swam for his life. On one of his upstrokes he saw lights blinking on the *Avenger* and guessed that the crew had heard the commotion on shore. Then he heard the splash of oars behind him and realized his pursuers had found a boat and pushed off after him. He swam harder. Lanterns appeared at the rail of the *Avenger*.

"Morgan, where are you?" Crawford bellowed toward the dark water below.

Morgan called out a reply, surprised that his voice sounded so weak. But Crawford must have heard, for he cupped his hands around his mouth and yelled, "The anchor chain, Morgan. Hold onto the anchor chain and we'll pull you aboard!"

His strength nearly depleted, Morgan reached the ship and found the anchor chain. He clung desperately to the cold metal, aware that there was no time for his crew to lower a boat with the queen's patrol hard on his heels. The pursuers were so close now that he could hear their voices. He expected them to start shooting again and braced himself for the brutal impact of another bullet.

Slowly but surely the anchor began to rise, hoisting Morgan out of the polluted water. Then hands were lifting him over the rail while crewmen scurried about to secure the anchor and unfurl the sails. A welcome puff of wind filled the canvas, and high tide carried the *Avenger* down the Thames and into the Channel. From the distant shore, the queen's guards shook their fists and sent curses flying after their prey. The queen would not be pleased.

"That . . . was . . . close," Morgan said, shaking from pain and weariness.

"Are you all right? We moved out into the Thames when we saw the palace guards patrolling along the quay. I figured they were looking for you and hoped you'd find a way to reach us. It seemed our only chance of escaping. I worried that the patrol would come aboard and prevent us from leaving."

"I knew . . . I could count on you," Morgan grunted as he tried to rise. He screamed in agony and crumbled to the deck. Crawford rushed forward to help him.

"I think . . . my leg . . . is broken." Those were his last words before he blacked out.

Cadiz, Spain
July, 1588

Luca played nervously with the lace adorning her dress as her father paced back and forth across the elegant room. Father Pedro stood by the door, his hands folded piously inside the long sleeves of his robe. Luca had arrived home just yesterday and had immediately taken to her bed, exhausted from the weather-plagued trip from England. Her father had seemed delighted to see her but expressed shock when she told him she'd come from England, not Havana. All these months he had assumed that Luca was wed to Diego, and that El Diablo had been sent to meet his maker.

"You say that the Englishman kidnapped you from Diego's palace?" Don Eduardo repeated in disbelief. "I can't believe he had the audacity to attempt such a thing. A most amazing man," he allowed grudgingly.

"Morgan is indeed an amazing man, Father," Luca agreed. "The queen pressed for an annulment of our marriage so he could wed an English heiress, but I do not know if Morgan did as she asked."

"It does not matter," Father Pedro interrupted. "I have business in Rome and will petition the Holy Father in your behalf while I am there."

"I will be eternally grateful, Father Pedro," Don Eduardo said earnestly. "I am in your debt for bringing my daughter home from that heathen country." He shook his head regretfully. "All these months I thought she was married to Diego del Fugo."

"I will take my leave, Don Eduardo. I must report to my superiors before I journey forth again."

"Tell your superiors that I will bestow a grant upon your order in appreciation for your help. In addition, you will personally be rewarded for your service in my behalf. Please keep me informed on the Holy Father's progress concerning Luca's annulment."

"Well, Luca," Don Eduardo said once the Jesuit was gone, "you seem to have gotten yourself into quite a predicament. Arturo and Cordero thought they had solved everything by wedding you to that pirate, never suspecting that he would live to claim you as his wife."

"Where are my brothers?" Luca asked.

"With the armada," Don Eduardo said

449

proudly. "We have received little word on the expedition's progress, but I suspect by now they have joined with Parma's ground forces and are on English soil."

Luca withheld judgment. In her estimation the English fleet was a force to be reckoned with and would not be easily defeated.

"But we are here to discuss you, my dear. I am at a loss where you are concerned. What am I to do with you? Perhaps Diego will still be willing to marry you once your annulment is in order."

Luca's eyes flared angrily. "Diego is a rutting pig, Father! He duped my brothers into believing he would wed me but instead planned to make me his mistress."

Don Eduardo was flabbergasted. He found it difficult to believe an upstanding man like Diego would act in such a vile manner. "Surely you misunderstood his intentions."

"No, Father, I misunderstood nothing. It's just as I said. I will not marry Diego even if my marriage to Morgan is dissolved. I would prefer to retire to the convent and devote my life to prayer."

Luca deliberately refrained from telling her father about the baby. She feared he would insist she give the baby up, but once she was safe inside the convent and out of his sight, she felt he would forget all about her. She knew her father well. He was a busy man, too involved with his own life to concern himself with her. She prayed she could persuade him to provide generously for her upkeep, and the good sisters would let her live in anonymity within their walls.

"I will send my swiftest ship to Havana and apprise Don Diego of this latest development. He still has your dowry. He may not be willing to part with it. I suspect that is why I have heard nothing from him about your abduction from Havana," Don Eduardo said astutely.

"I do not care about the dowry. Give it to the sisters if it is returned; they will put it to good use and provide a home for me as long as I live."

"I will compromise, daughter. You may go to the convent for the time being and I will see that the nuns are recompensed for your care. But if Diego still wants you after your marriage is dissolved, I will give you to him. But you will never become his mistress, daughter, I will see to that. He must either wed you by proxy or do it properly in person before I allow you to take ship for Havana. Everything must be legal and binding. He will not make you his mistress."

"I do not like Diego. He is a despicable man."

"You judge him too harshly, daughter. You must remember that he expected a virgin bride. I'm sure he would have done right by you. It would have been expedient if Diego had made you a widow immediately upon reaching Havana. I am most grateful that you did not conceive the pirate's child. I could not have borne such an insult. My pride would never recover."

"I will leave tomorrow, Father. I truly think the convent is the best place for me."

Don Eduardo's mind had already turned in another direction. "What? Perhaps you're right, *querida*. I'll make arrangements for your departure and instruct the Reverend Mother to treat you as a guest. I never intended that you join the order."

"*Gracias*, Father." She kissed his cheek and quickly departed.

A plethora of thoughts raced through Luca's mind after she left her father. Since she was carrying a child, becoming a nun was no longer feasible. The Reverend Mother had always liked her, and Luca knew she would protect her secret. It wasn't the first time a wife sought refuge behind convent walls. Sometimes a husband banished his wife to a convent if he thought she had been unfaithful. Nor would hers be the first child born under such circumstances. Luca had every intention of telling the Reverend Mother about her child when the time arrived. In a few months she would have no choice. After the birth she would decide whether she would raise the babe in the peaceful atmosphere of the convent or strike out on her own.

Luca, astute enough to realize she must plan ahead for the future, would take all her mother's jewels, which rightfully belonged to her, and hide them among her belongings. One day she might want to leave the convent with her child and live independently from her father. The valuable jewelry would keep them for life if they lived frugally.

But Luca was wrong about her father forgetting about her. Within an hour after their conversation, Don Eduardo had written a letter to Diego del Fugo and dispatched it to Havana on his swiftest ship. If his missive didn't fetch Diego from Havana, nothing would. Don Eduardo knew his intended son-in-law well. Diego Del Fugo would not willingly return a dowry as valuable as Luca's.

Andros Island
August, 1588

Morgan tossed restlessly on his rumpled bed. His fever-ridden body and bloodshot eyes gave grim testimony to his illness. A musket ball had shattered a bone in his thigh, and raging infection had followed, the result of contamination from river water. It kept him bedridden for many weeks. The bullet had been successfully removed and his bone set while they were aboard the *Avenger*, but nothing could prevent the onset of fever that struck Morgan almost immediately.

Stan Crawford had made the decision to take Morgan to Andros, where Lani could take care of him, instead of sailing directly for Cadiz. Morgan's grave condition had given Stan the authority to alter their course, but when Morgan recovered to the point where he realized he was on Andros, he became livid.

"Bloody Hell, Morgan, you were in no condition to go to Spain. You can't even walk." Crawford's attempt to placate Morgan was met with a splendid display of temper.

"Damn you, Stan! I'd have found a way." A nerve twitched in Morgan's taut jaw. Though he'd never admit it, the pain from his broken bone was excruciating, and his infected wound was slow to heal.

"Like Hell," Crawford said, shaking his head. "Luca will wait. You should be damn grateful that Lani saved your life. The native medicine she gave you was potent; we had nothing aboard ship to match it. We will go to Spain when your leg is healed enough to walk, perhaps in five or six weeks."

Morgan recognized the wisdom of Crawford's words but didn't accept them lightly. Every day he spent lying in bed meant another day without Luca. *Where was she now?* he wondered despondently. Was she happy? Did she think about him at all? He cursed the fates for having denied him the right moment to tell her that he loved her. The notion had been so new to him, so utterly astounding, that he had been reluctant to share his feelings. He had failed Luca, and for that he would never forgive himself.

Had she left England thinking he cared nothing for her? He'd be the first to admit he hadn't been the best of husbands. He'd tried to do his duty to his queen and in so doing had lost the woman he loved. Bloody Hell! It had been difficult to come to grips with the knowledge that he loved a Spaniard. He'd hated Spaniards for so long that he couldn't even recall when he hadn't. Being with Luca had taught him a lesson in humility. It was a terrible burden to live with such a passion for revenge.

Luca was sweet and giving and incapable of committing atrocities such as he'd experienced at the hands of her countrymen. Perhaps not all Spaniards were like the ones who had killed his family and enslaved him, he admitted grudgingly. Granted, the ship on which he'd spent five miserable years of servitude belonged to Luca's father, but Morgan had evened the score many times over. He'd plundered more ships of the Santiego line than any other. It was time now to forget and move forward with his life. His gnawing concern was that Luca would refuse to put the past behind them and spend the rest of her life as his wife. His little nun was not meant to be a holy woman. She had too much passion, too much fire inside her to wither and die behind cloistered walls. He needed her; he ached for her; his heart wept for her.

Wedded bliss. Morgan almost laughed aloud at that supposition. Together he and Luca were explosive. Both in bed and out. Life would never be dull with his fiery wife keeping him on his toes. Where other men might become bored with marriage, he was held spellbound.

Of course there would be children, he waxed enthusiastically. Morgan cursed himself for a fool when he realized how he had hurt Luca by claiming he wanted no child with her. What an arrogant bastard he had been. He would never forgive himself if his heartless words had cost him his wife.

The weeks sped by. Chained to his bed by his injury, Morgan cursed his weakness and inability to leave Andros. Unable to go to Spain and claim his wife, he worried that in the interim Luca would forget him and he would lose his Spanish bride forever.

20

"I'm going ashore with you, Morgan, no matter how vigorously you protest. I know you think your leg is healed, but you still don't have complete freedom of movement. You need me to pick up the pieces."

Morgan sent Stan an exasperated look. "Bloody Hell, Stan, except for this limp my leg is as healed as it will ever be. I don't need a keeper."

"Argue all you want, I'm coming along. My Spanish isn't as good as yours, but I'll leave the talking to you. If Luca isn't at home with her father, we may have to travel to the convent. You haven't sat a horse since your injury."

"The ship . . ."

"There is little danger. The *Avenger* flies the Spanish flag, and Withers is capable of controlling the crew should the need arise. Enough of our men speak Spanish to avoid raising suspicion should they be challenged by port authorities. Besides, Spain is in such chaos after the failed expedition that no one will be paying attention to another ship in the harbor."

"Very well," Morgan said, impatient to debark. His plaguing injuries had delayed him too long already. "Let's go."

Luca stared morosely out through the small window of her tiny cell. Days were somewhat cooler now, but within the ancient stone walls it was always cool and slightly damp. Luca pulled the shawl closer about her shoulders, her mind straying toward forbidden thoughts of Morgan. She had prayed long and hard to extinguish the lingering embers of passion she felt for him, but her pleas were met with only limited success. The babe she carried beneath her heart served as a constant reminder of the love she bore her child's father. She had not been prepared for the intense love she bore this small life who would so completely depend on her.

In the three months she had been at the convent, her pregnancy had made itself known in the most basic way. With Renalda's help she had let out nearly all of her dresses. The Reverend Mother had been shocked when told of Luca's pregnancy, but she had accepted it with good grace, just as Luca knew she would. As Luca had anticipated, her father neither visited her nor inquired after her well-being, though he continued to contribute to her care.

Her brothers had come to see her shortly after returning to Spain with the remnants of the broken armada. Their stunning defeat at the hands of the English had been a demoralizing blow, and they'd told Luca they were leaving immediately on a voyage to the New World, where they'd heard the streets were lined with gold. When they'd described the suffering and adverse winds encountered by the ill-fated expedition, Luca had thought they were lucky to have arrived home alive.

After their visit Luca had languished in welcome boredom, devoting her days to prayer, but not even prayer could heal the ache in her heart. Then she was befriended by another woman who had been banished to the convent by her father.

Renalda had been born into a rich and powerful family. She'd been betrothed at birth to a man her equal in station and would have been married at eighteen if she hadn't done the unforgivable and fallen in love with Antonio, a vaquero's son. Desperate to find happiness, they had run away, intending to be married by a priest in a small village where no one knew them.

Her father and fiancé had followed them. Antonio had been killed when their carriage overturned during the chase. As luck would have it, Renalda suffered only bruises. Because she and Antonio had spent one night together, her fiancé had backed out of the marriage, and her father had beaten her and packed her off to the convent. Renalda, like Luca, was neither a nun nor a postulant. But unlike Luca, who was there by choice, Renalda was a prisoner within the convent walls, unable to leave without her father's consent. For her part, Luca knew she would never love again, so she chose to remain with the holy sisters.

A knock on the door roused Luca from her reverie. The door opened almost immediately, and a slim young woman with lustrous black hair, dark eyes, and skin as translucent as fine porcelain entered. Luca greeted Renalda with a smile and beckoned her inside.

"Is there anything you need before you retire?" Renalda asked with concern. She worried that Luca wasn't eating enough to nourish both herself and the child she carried.

"Nothing, thank you," Luca replied, "unless you care to stay awhile and visit."

Renalda sent Luca a wistful look. "You are lonely for your babe's father." It was a statement, not a question.

"I have to learn to live without Morgan," Luca said brokenly. After all this time it was still painful to talk about the man she loved. "If he'd cared for me he would have come after me. He'd done it before, with great danger to himself." She shook her head sadly. "No, Renalda, by now Morgan is married to Lady Jane. It's what his queen wanted for him."

Renalda took Luca's hand in hers and gave it a squeeze. "After your child is born you can leave here and find a new love, but I will likely die of old age without ever setting foot beyond these walls."

"If I decide to leave I will take you with me," Luca promised.

Renalda sighed dispiritedly. "I fear that is impossible, but your friendship means everything to me. It is the only thing that has kept me sane. At least you will have a child to remind you of your love, while I . . ." She shrugged expansively. "I must go. I promised Sister Maria that I would set out the bread dough for tomorrow's meals."

"Good night, Renalda, go with God."

"Bribing Don Eduardo's servant was a wise move, Morgan," Stan said as they left Cadiz behind. "You're a wanted man with a price on your head. Had you revealed your identity to Don Eduardo, he would surely have reported you to the authorities."

After learning that Luca was living at the convent, they had passed the night at an inn outside Cadiz and started out bright and early the next day. Morgan drove a rented carriage. To his chagrin his leg hadn't been able to bear the strain of mounting a horse. Stan rode in the carriage beside him, tying a horse behind the carriage to take him back to the *Avenger* when Luca replaced him in the carriage with Morgan.

"That's why I approached the servants first. Most men will do anything for a price. All I want to do is find Luca, convince her that I care about her, and get the Hell out of Spain as fast as possible."

A formidable task, Morgan thought but did not say. So much time had elapsed since Luca left that she probably thought he had forgotten her. He was going to need all his wits about him if he wanted to convince Luca she was the only woman he'd ever wanted.

★ ★ ★

Renalda sighed tiredly as she placed a clean cloth over the last pan of bread dough. By morning it would be ready to bake in the oven. One of her favorite tasks was helping in the kitchen. Keeping busy helped to relieve the boredom and sameness of each day. Sister Maria had already retired, and she was headed in that direction herself. The halls were dark and deserted. The sisters rose early and usually retired immediately after evening prayers. Renalda looked forward to her own hard bed, for only in sleep could she forget that she had been the cause of a young man's death.

Renalda had truly believed she was in love with Antonio, but they had both been so young. She'd never forget his sweet smile and gentle nature. Causing his death had been traumatic. The convent had seemed a welcome haven at first, but it had soon become her prison. She was young, she yearned for life beyond these confining walls. She prayed most diligently that her father would relent one day and come for her, ending her isolation. It was the only way she would ever leave the convent, until death freed her.

Renalda's footsteps echoed sharply down the silent hallway as she made her way to her bed. She started violently when she heard a ruckus at the outer gate. Visitors were rare this time of night and never admitted. Whoever was rattling the gate was most insistent. If it didn't stop, Reverend Mother and all the sisters would be rudely awakened. Renalda didn't want that to happen.

Concerned only with maintaining peace within the convent walls, Renalda pulled open the heavy oak door and hurried out to the gate. The night was cool, and she shivered. Suddenly she realized she was not shivering from cold but in anticipation. She had never felt this way before and approached the gate with a sense of destiny. Or was it dread she felt? The feeling was beyond definition.

The bolted gate was constructed of solid oak. A small hinged door in the center of the gate opened from the inside, allowing the gatekeeper a glimpse of the visitors. Renalda's hands shook as she opened the small door and peered into the darkness beyond the gate. A full moon allowed her a shadowy glimpse of the large man standing on the other side of the gate.

"What do you want? It's late, everyone is abed. No visitors are allowed after dark."

Responding in fluent Spanish, Morgan said, "It's imperative that I see my wife."

"Your wife? You are mistaken. No one here . . ." Her words faltered. Luca was the only married woman in the convent at the present time. Could this man be Luca's husband? Was the handsome man demanding entrance the pirate referred to as El Diablo? *Madre di Dios,* no wonder Luca had fallen in love with him.

"I know Luca is here. Luca Scott, my wife. Perhaps you know her as Luca Santiego."

"You are Luca's pirate?"

Morgan smiled wryly. "*Sí.* Now will you open the gate?"

"No. It changes nothing. It is much too late for visitors. The Reverend Mother does not admit visitors after dark. You will have to return tomorrow."

"Perhaps we should find a bed in the town we rode through earlier and return tomorrow," Stan suggested as he stepped into Renalda's view.

Until Stan made his presence known, Renalda had no idea that Morgan had a companion with him. She stared at Stan in the dim light, thinking him nearly as handsome as Luca's husband. Neither of them appeared as fearsome as rumor made them out to be.

"No, I will not leave," Morgan said with

grim determination. "I want to see Luca, and I want to see her now. Will you let us in, Sister, or must I scale the wall?"

Renalda swallowed convulsively. She knew instinctively that nothing would keep the Englishman out if he was determined to gain entrance. But she had to make certain that admitting the pirate was in Luca's best interest.

"Why do you wish to see Luca? I am her friend, I do not wish to see her hurt."

"Look, Sister . . ."

"I am not a nun. Like Luca, I am a guest here."

"Very well, senorita . . ."

"Renalda. Renalda Cortez."

"Senorita Renalda. My wife does not belong here. She belongs with me. I've come to take her home."

"Home? To England?"

Morgan and Stan exchanged meaningful glances. "No, not to England. I am no longer welcome there. I am taking Luca to Andros Island in the Bahamas. Now, Senorita, will you let me in?"

Renalda was torn. She knew Luca still loved her English pirate, but according to Luca, Morgan hated Spaniards and wanted no children with Spanish blood. She debated whether to allow the Englishmen entrance without Luca's consent or to insist that he come back tomorrow.

"Senorita, if you are worried that I might harm my wife, you can put your fears to rest. I care deeply for Luca. I don't know what she told you, but I've changed. By a quirk of fate Luca became my wife and I . . ." He found it difficult to bare his soul before strangers, but he wanted Luca's friend to know how deep his feelings for Luca went. "I love Luca. If she will forgive me, I will spend the rest of my life making her happy."

Morgan's sincerity impressed Renalda. Something in the pirate's expression told her that his love for Luca would endure the ages. If a man were to love her like that, she'd be the happiest of women.

"Very well, senor, I will let you in to see Luca, but I will probably earn severe punishment from Reverend Mother for this night's work."

She slid aside the heavy bar and swung the gate wide. Morgan stepped inside; Stan followed close on his heels.

"How do I find Luca's room?" Morgan asked. He'd waited so long for this day that he could barely contain his excitement.

Renalda regarded Morgan through narrowed lids. Suddenly she viewed Morgan's appearance as a sign from God. Her keen mind saw it as a way to escape the impossible situation imposed upon her by her father. Her eyes glowed with dark defiance as she lifted her chin to challenge Morgan. "I will not tell you. And you cannot find it on your own without awakening the entire convent. The halls are a maze of tiny cells, all housing sisters and postulants."

Morgan's eyes narrowed angrily. Grasping Renalda's shoulders, he gave her a violent shake. Renalda flinched but remained stubbornly mute. "Why did you let me inside if you had no intention of leading me to Luca?"

"Morgan, you're hurting her," Stan warned. His tone was gentle as he spoke to Renalda. "My name is Stan Crawford. You must have a reason for refusing Morgan's request." His Spanish was halting and not as good as Morgan's but Renalda appeared to understand him.

Renalda's mouth went dry, unable to form a reply.

"Renalda, do you understand? Why won't you take Morgan to Luca?"

"I will storm every room in the convent if I have to," Morgan promised.

Renalda stared at Morgan. She had to wet her lips with the tip of her tongue before she could speak. "I will tell you where she is only if you promise to take me with you."

"What! Surely you jest." Astonishment colored Morgan's words. "What would your family say?"

"I am dead to my family," Renalda said sadly. "I committed a terrible sin. They disowned me and sent me here as punishment. I will probably spend the remainder of my days behind these walls."

"You are so young. What terrible sin have you committed?" Stan asked.

Renalda hung her head in shame. She couldn't find the words to tell virtual strangers what had caused her family to disown her.

"My sin is of no importance. I ask only that you take me with you. Luca and I are friends. I can be of great help to her. She will need a woman's attention."

Morgan stopped short. "What do you mean?"

Renalda remained silent. It wasn't her place to tell Morgan that he was going to become a father.

"Bloody Hell! Just tell me where to find Luca. I can't take you with me, it's impossible."

"I say we take her," Stan said quietly. Something about the girl reached out to him. If Renalda was so desperate to escape the convent, Stan could see no reason not to help her.

Morgan's eyes narrowed. He'd never seen Stan so adamant about aiding a distressed woman before. "I won't accept responsibility for her. There is a price on my head, and danger abounds in this foreign country."

Morgan spoke to Stan in English; Renalda looked from one to the other, wishing she understood what they were saying. Obviously they were talking about her.

"I will take full responsibility," Stan argued.

Morgan had neither the time nor the inclination to stand there exchanging words with Stan. Impatience gnawed at him. He was so close to attaining his goal, that he would have agreed to anything.

"Very well, but make sure she causes no trouble. I noticed an inn in the town of Lebrija as we passed through earlier. Engage rooms for us. I will follow with Luca as soon as possible."

"Thank you, Morgan. I don't know why, but I feel strongly that this is right." He turned to Renalda, explaining to her gently, "We will take you with us."

Renalda's eyes glistened with tears. Until

these Englishmen arrived she had despaired of ever finding her way out of the convent. She was so grateful that she threw her arms around Stan and proceeded to blubber on his jacket.

Impatience got the best of Morgan. "The directions, Senorita Renalda. How do I find Luca?"

Renalda dried her eyes and gave precise directions to Luca's tiny cell. "The door will not be locked, senor," she said. "We are allowed little privacy."

Morgan nodded curtly, turned on his heel, and limped off into the darkness while Stan then led Renalda through the gate, lifted her onto his horse, and mounted behind her.

"Where are we going?" she asked breathlessly.

"I'm taking you to town, where we will wait for Morgan and Luca," Stan explained. His arm tightened possessively around her waist, and suddenly Stan wanted this woman. He hardened immediately, wondering if Renalda was still a virgin, or if her "terrible" sin had resulted in her loss of innocence.

Morgan crept through the deserted corridors, following Renalda's directions to the letter. It was dark except for candles left burning at each intersection, but they allowed Morgan sufficient light to make the right turns and count the doors lining each side of the long hallways. When he finally reached the door indicated by Renalda's directions, he paused, sucked in a steadying breath, and lifted the latch. The door opened noiselessly, and he stepped inside. A shaft of bright moonlight spilled through the window. Since his eyes were already accustomed to the dark, they needed little adjustment to see Luca kneeling beside the bed, wrapped from neck to toe in a voluminous white nightgown.

Engaged in prayer, Luca failed to hear the creak of the door opening and closing, or the sound of Morgan's approaching footsteps. Mesmerized by the play of moonlight upon her bent head, Morgan stood perfectly still, staring at her with desperate longing. He noted with pleasure that her hair had grown, falling around her shoulders like a shimmering black curtain. Her feet were bare, and her perfect pink toes were all that was visible of her body except her hands and head. Starved for the sight of her, he seemed unable to move or think.

Luca prayed fervently, a habit she faithfully followed each night before retiring.

She prayed that Morgan was happy and well wherever he was, that her unborn child would be born healthy, and that Renalda would be released one day from her forced imprisonment. Though Luca had resigned herself to an austere life, she knew Renalda yearned for something more.

Suddenly Luca sensed that she was not alone. Her first thought was that Renalda had returned. "I'm glad that you decided to return for a visit, Renalda," she called out. "I will be finished in a moment."

Her words released Morgan's frozen limbs, and he moved silently toward the bed where Luca knelt in prayer. He smiled, recalling that she had been on her knees most of the time during their first days together.

He stood behind her now, close enough to reach out and touch her. Her special scent, sweetly seductive yet subtly elusive, enticed him beyond endurance. His hand shook as he placed it with great gentleness on her right shoulder. He sensed the precise moment when she realized it was him and not Renalda in the room with her. Her body tensed, and she sucked her breath in sharply. Then she turned slowly, his name leaving her lips on a trembling sigh.

Luca knew the precise moment she became aware that Morgan was in the room with her. She sensed the powerful allure of his presence, felt the heat of his body. She breathed in the heady scent of leather, horse, and something else uniquely his. Then she felt the jarring current of his touch and knew she wasn't dreaming. Turning slowly, her lids fluttered upward, stunned by the look of raw hunger burning in the depths of his eyes.

"Luca . . ." Raising her to her feet, he stared into her eyes, his own dark and seeking, and suspiciously moist. But he didn't try to embrace her. Not yet. Not until he knew how she felt about him. "Thank God I found you. I've been living in Hell since you left. Why? Why did you leave me?"

Luca's mouth went dry. How could Morgan ask such a question when everyone at court knew he'd been pursuing Lady Jane as if he'd been a free man?

Her voice was bitter. "Where have you been all this time, Morgan? Are we still married? Have you already made Lady Jane your new wife? The queen must be ecstatic. Lady Jane told me you wanted an annulment so you could marry her. Why are you here? I thought I was doing you a favor by leaving."

"Favor!" Morgan all but shouted. "I was worried sick about you. All those weeks that

I lay helplessly in bed I imagined all kinds of terrible things that could have happened to you."

"You were ill? Were you wounded at sea? Oh, Morgan, I'm so sorry." Her hands roamed over his shoulders, his arms, his chest, searching for signs of injury. She felt nothing but hard-muscled flesh, and she let out a shaky sigh. She couldn't have borne it if he had been gravely wounded.

"I took a musket ball," Morgan said without elaborating. " 'Tis nothing, it's healed now . . . well, almost," he added, thinking about the limp he might never lose.

"Oh, Morgan, why have you come? What about Lady Jane?"

"I don't care about Lady Jane. I never wanted her. You're the only woman I'll ever want."

Luca wanted to believe him, truly she did, but there were so many unresolved differences preventing their happiness. And there was still the baby he couldn't accept.

"I'll always be Spanish, Morgan," she reminded him.

"It no longer matters. I've lived with the burden of hatred too long, 'tis time I put the past behind me and concentrate on the future, our future. You gave me incredible pleasure each time we made love, Luca, but it was guilty pleasure. Because of my vendetta against the Spanish, making love to you stripped my pride and filled me with anguish. I wanted you so desperately, but I felt as if I were betraying my family and myself. Thank God I no longer harbor those feelings, Luca. My heart is now free to love you as you deserve. I do love you, sweetheart. Will you forgive me for all those terrible things I did and said to you?"

Luca regarded him with astonishment. "You love me? You want me?"

"I've always wanted you. What do I have to do or say to prove it to you? Will you trust me in this?" The moment the words left his mouth, Morgan branded himself a fool. How could Luca trust him when he'd done nothing to gain her trust?

Trust was an awesome burden, Luca decided. Especially when it involved an innocent child. How would Morgan feel about a son or daughter who carried her Spanish blood?

"Bloody Hell, Luca, I need you! Let me take you home to Andros. I'm giving up the sea for good."

The need to have Luca in his arms, to feel her softness melting into his hardness, became a raging inferno within him, one he had kept banked until he could no longer contain it. His arms came around her and his lips found hers, kissing her fiercely, delving into the deepest recesses of her mouth with a soul-destroying sweep of his tongue. Cupping her rounded bottom, he pulled her against him, aware of every lush curve of her fertile body.

Morgan blinked in confusion. Memory must have failed him, for he felt curves Luca hadn't had before, curves that . . . The breath slammed from his throat and he stared at her with a dazed expression.

His hands slid downward. By the time they reached the unmistakable bulge of her stomach, they were shaking. He made a sound of strangled delight deep in his throat. Luca mistook the sound for disgust and tried to shove his hands aside.

"My God, you're expecting my child!"

Luca finally succeeded in freeing herself. She stepped back and glared up at him. "I know you didn't want a child with me, Morgan, but I'm not sorry. I'll love this child even if you won't. Under the circumstances the convent is the best place for me."

Morgan exhaled sharply. He had only himself to blame for Luca's mistaken belief that he didn't want their child. Bloody Hell! He was going to be a father, and Luca never intended to tell him. If he hadn't come to Spain he might never have known. The thought was frightening in the extreme. He prayed he'd find the words to convince Luca that he wanted their child. That he would love it as much as he loved her.

"Luca, listen to me, it's true I didn't want to get you pregnant before I sailed out to meet the armada. But that was because I feared I might not come back and worried that you'd be left in a strange land with a child to raise. I didn't mean to imply I never wanted children with you."

Luca made a sound of disbelief deep in her throat. Morgan quickly added, "I won't deny I felt that way once, but I'm not the same man I was when we first met. I've said a lot of things I've since regretted, sweetheart."

Luca touched his face, his eyes, his mouth, her fingertips moving lovingly over his dear features. He grasped her hand and held it to his mouth, placing a kiss on her palm and closing her fingers around it.

"Luca, come with me now. You're my wife. You're carrying my child. I need you both desperately. The *Avenger* is waiting in the harbor at Cadiz. The longer we delay, the greater the danger."

He kissed her again, his mouth gently

coaxing. She tasted his desperation, felt his need, and answered with a need of her own, her lips clinging to his in profound yearning. When he finally broke off the kiss, she was gasping for breath. She loved him! *Dios,* she loved him.

"Tell me you'll leave with me now, sweetheart," Morgan pleaded. "Tell me you love me. You and our child are all I have left in the world that mean anything to me."

His sincerity touched a place in Luca's heart where slim hope had survived. The moisture glistening in the corners of his eyes and his heartfelt declaration of love convinced her that miracles do happen.

"I love you, Morgan. I've loved you for a very long time. I left because I didn't want to burden you with a child you didn't want and couldn't accept. I thought you would be happier with Lady Jane."

"I can be happy with no one but you. Now get dressed, Stan is waiting for us in town."

"I can't leave without telling Reverend Mother," Luca protested. "She's been very good to me. And Renalda. She's my friend. I promised I'd take her with me when I left. I want to . . ."

"Leave a note for Reverend Mother," Morgan interrupted. "As for Renalda, she's with Stan. You'll see her very soon. Hurry, there's bound to be a fuss if I'm discovered here. I'm still a wanted man in Spain." And in England, too, he thought but did not say.

Luca gave Morgan a startled look. "Stan abducted Renalda? Whyever for?"

Morgan gave her a wicked grin. "I would suspect for the same reason I abducted you, only Stan did not have to resort to force. Renalda was quite eager to leave."

Luca smiled. "You never cease to amaze me, Morgan Scott."

21

The small town of Lebrija boasted only one inn. Stan Crawford engaged three rooms, earning a suspicious glare from the innkeeper for his faulty Spanish. But since Stan offered hard coin in payment, the innkeeper grudgingly handed over the keys to the foreigner.

Renalda fidgeted nervously, wondering what the English pirate expected in return for helping her escape the convent. No matter what the price, she would willingly pay it in return for the opportunity to experience life outside convent walls. And she would be with Luca; that fact alone gave her courage. Not that Stan Crawford was hard to take. Besides, she was so steeped in sin now, one more improper act wouldn't hurt, if it came to that. She prayed that it wouldn't. She was no *puta* and hoped the pirate realized it. The fact that he had paid for three rooms gave her hope.

"I'll take you to your room, you must be exhausted," Stan said, guiding Renalda up the stairs. "I'll wait below in the common room for Morgan and Luca."

Renalda's sigh of relief was so loud that Stan nearly laughed aloud. Clearly she thought he intended to bed her and was apprehensive about it. The thought was not too far-fetched, Stan admitted somewhat guiltily, but this was not the time. First he wanted her to trust him and feel comfortable with him.

Stan opened Renalda's door and handed her the key. "Lock the door," Stan advised. "I'll awaken you in the morning. If you still wish to come with us, we will take you aboard the *Avenger*. If you change your mind after sleeping on it, I will arrange transportation back to the convent."

"I will not change my mind," Renalda vowed resolutely.

"Then I wish you good night."

Stan waited until he heard the key turn in the lock before walking away. Just being with the dark-eyed minx gave him a painful erection. He couldn't recall when he'd felt such urgency, such overwhelming desire to bed a woman. Renalda's fathomless black eyes, her courage to change her situation, her willingness to cast her lot to fate, enticed and beguiled him. He was attracted to her in a way that frightened him. He'd wanted to take her to bed so desperately that he'd given her the key to lock him out. No matter how much he wanted her, she was too vulnerable right now to be taken advantage of. He could tell by her expressive eyes that she had suffered, and he didn't want to add to her distress.

Mother of God Convent

No one awoke to stop them as Luca and Morgan crept down the hallway and out the front door into the convent yard. Luca had left a note for the Reverend Mother, then gathered up her clothing, which Morgan bundled in a sheet and carried under his arm. The gate hung slightly agape, and Morgan closed it noiselessly behind him. As they walked to the carriage Luca suddenly realized that Morgan was limping. She stopped abruptly.

"What is it?" Morgan asked, alarmed when Luca suddenly halted.

"You're limping. You were injured more seriously than you let on."

"The musket bullet shattered a bone in my leg. It's mended now, but I may always limp. Does it matter?"

"That you limp? It matters only that you suffered pain and I was not there to ease your suffering. How did it happen?"

Morgan's brow furrowed. Now was not the time to divulge the information that he had been wounded by Englishmen as he tried to flee England. "I'll tell you later, sweetheart. Right now it's more important that we meet Stan in town. Come on, I'll help you into the carriage."

Within a few minutes they were traveling down the road to the town of Lebrija. Luca didn't regret leaving the convent. It had provided her a safe haven when she thought Morgan didn't want her, but now that she knew her husband loved her and wanted their child she was eager to follow him wherever he wished to take her.

They arrived at the inn during the small hours of the morning. Luca had fallen asleep with her head resting on Morgan's shoulder. His arm wrapped around her, he held her tightly against him; he could feel her sweet breath brushing his cheek and her swollen stomach pressing against him. He was still reeling from shock. A child! Luca was carrying his baby. He could picture the child now; a girl with dark curly hair and fiery eyes like her mother.

Morgan pulled the carriage to a stop in

the courtyard. A groggy stableboy roused himself and stumbled out to greet them, rubbing sleep from his eyes. After giving the boy instruction as to the care of his rig, Morgan carefully lifted Luca and carried her into the inn. The innkeeper had already retired to his bed, leaving a banked fire in the hearth and Stan Crawford keeping vigil. The moment the door opened, Stan shook himself awake and rose to greet Morgan. He smiled broadly when he saw the sleeping woman Morgan carried in his arms.

"I was beginning to think you were having difficulty," Stan said. "Here, let me have Luca. I'll carry her upstairs. I can tell by your aggravated limp that your leg is paining you."

"My leg is fine," Morgan said tersely, though in truth his leg trembled from exertion. "I'll carry my wife. Just tell me which room is ours."

"I'll show you," Stan said, more than ready to seek his own bed. "It's between mine and Renalda's."

"Ah, yes, Renalda," Morgan said, suddenly recalling the woman Stan had insisted they bring along. "Is she still determined to leave the convent?"

"Aye, more determined than ever. And

I'm equally determined to take her with us, just in case you have any ideas to the contrary."

Morgan's answer was forestalled when Luca stirred in his arms and opened her eyes. "Where are we?"

"At the inn, sweetheart. Stan is here and so is Renalda. You'll see them soon." Content, Luca settled back in his arms.

Stan opened the door to Morgan's room and handed him the key. "It isn't much, but it's clean. Take care of your wife, Morgan, she looks exhausted."

"I intend to. Nothing is going to happen to Luca and our child."

Stan's eyes widened. "Luca is carrying your child? Bloody Hell, we didn't get here any too soon, did we? You're a lucky dog, Morgan Scott. Someday I hope to have children of my own. Good night, my friend. Sleep well."

Stan turned away. For the first time in his recent memory, he was jealous of Morgan. He envied Morgan's happiness, the child he had conceived with Luca, and the love they obviously shared. Later, as he lay in bed staring at the ceiling, the only woman he could picture as the mother of his children was a raven-haired beauty with sultry black eyes and skin as pale as camilla blossoms.

Morgan carefully placed Luca on the bed and turned to light a candle. He heard her sigh, and when he looked at her he was startled to find her staring at him, her eyes luminous with the love she bore him.

"You're awake. Go back to sleep."

Luca sent him a beguiling smile. "I'm no longer tired. I slept nearly all the way here." She held her arms out to him. "Make love to me, Morgan. It's been so long."

Her words sent instant heat rushing through his veins, and he felt himself grow heavy and thick. Despite her invitation and the swollen need rising taut and hard between his legs, he was reluctant to take her, fearful of hurting her or their child.

"You're in no condition," he reasoned. "The babe . . ."

"It won't hurt the babe, Morgan. I'm not all that knowledgeable, but I don't think husbands and wives stop loving one another when a child is expected. At least not until the last month or so. Please, Morgan, I need you."

Her plea snapped the slim thread of Morgan's restraint. He unbuckled his sword and lay down beside her, holding her with bruising desperation. "It makes me ill just thinking how close I came to losing you and our child."

"You'll never lose us, Morgan. I'll never leave you again. I love you too much."

His arms closed around her, and his mouth came down on hers with a primal growl of raw need. He kissed her ravenously, reticence fleeing as he peeled away her clothing so he could feast on the succulent flesh beneath. Luca moaned, pressing against him, touching and caressing him, undulating against the inflamed ridge of his manhood with wanton abandon. When she could no longer endure the barrier of his clothing between them, she began tearing at them in frustration.

Morgan made a gurgling sound deep in his throat and tore off the offending garments, flinging them on the floor to join hers. Her cool skin absorbed his warmth as she pressed against him, and she knew that she was nearly driving him over the edge. He gritted his teeth visibly as she touched him reverently; his shoulders, his chest, his stomach, the throbbing ridge of his sex. His skin was smooth and silken yet as hard and unyielding as steel. When her hand closed around him, he jerked violently against her palm. A drop of lubricant appeared, and Luca lowered her head to lick delicately. He tasted slightly salty and delicious.

"Bloody Hell, Luca!" he cried out mindlessly. "Enough! You're killing me. Lay back and let me love you."

He cupped her full breasts and lowered his mouth to tease and warm each nipple until they peaked into rigid buds. His skilled hands roved over her body, caressing her with loving tenderness. She exhaled sharply when his lips followed, moving down her stomach, kissing the taut skin shielding their child. After thoroughly worshiping the bulging mound, he glided lower into the down beneath, and further still, his hands and tongue probing and titillating the slick folds of her femininity.

Luca moaned softly and moved fitfully, arching into the wet heat of his mouth, her hands mindlessly reaching for him as he diligently plied his tongue to her tender fount of pleasure.

Fury inflamed Luca as Morgan's lips and tongue caressed her. It was primitive, mindless abandon. It was pure magic. It was surrender. Release came with the sucking force of a swirling tornado, robbing her of wits and stealing her soul.

Gasping for breath, Luca tumbled back to reality. Morgan watched her, his eyes gleaming brighter than silver. "Are you all right?" Concern colored his words and Luca smiled, easing his mind considerably.

"I'm going to come inside you now, sweetheart. I'll try to be gentle, but I'm so hard I'm afraid I'll hurt you."

"You won't hurt me," Luca murmured. "I want you inside me. I ache to feel you inside me again."

Raising himself up and over her body, his hands found her warmth, and his fingers penetrated her, preparing her for his entry. Deliberately he dragged the swollen tip of his arousal against her dewy folds while caressing the hidden hood of flesh with his thumb. He aroused her slowly and with gentle thoroughness, and when she was gasping and writhing beneath him, he glided into her wet, lubricated warmth, then rocked gently back and forth, slowly forcing himself deeper with each successive stroke. "Jesus, this is the closest I'll ever get to heaven," he whispered raggedly.

Luca's legs came up to grip him, and she rose eagerly to meet each thrust. His hips flexed and he shoved himself deeper, moving faster, all restraint crumbling as her tight sheath sucked him deeper inside her. He ground himself against her, grasping her buttocks and lifting her to meet his thrusts. Wanting to prolong their pleasure, he cupped her face and kissed her fiercely. He could feel the tension building within her as she panted against his lips. Sensing she was close to the brink, he quickly brought her to climax before his own control shattered completely.

Luca was awash with sensation, responding to Morgan's kisses by twining her tongue with his and raising her body to the thrust of his swollen shaft. Suddenly lightning struck in her heated center, stars exploded behind her eyes, and ecstasy shuddered through her.

The end came to Morgan so violently he nearly lost consciousness. Jerking and moaning, he expelled his seed deep into Luca's core. Fearing he would hurt her, he fell back onto the bed and drew her against him, reluctant to let her go.

"That was . . . spectacular," Luca said shyly.

Morgan gave a shout of laughter. "Merely spectacular?" Suddenly he grew serious. "Did I hurt you?"

"How could something so . . . spectacular hurt? You gave me great pleasure, Morgan, and you know it. It's been so long that I'd nearly forgotten how wonderful it could be. I tried not to think about it in the convent, because I was so sure I'd never experience that kind of addictive pleasure again."

"I would have come sooner, but my damn broken leg and resulting fever laid me up weeks longer than I expected. If not for Lani's medicinal skills I would not be here now."

"Lani? You went to Andros? I don't understand."

"It's a long story, love."

"Tell me, I'm not at all sleepy."

Settling down beside her, Morgan explained how he came to be wounded. "I survived the sea battle without a scratch. So did most of my crew."

"Then how . . . ?"

"I was wounded by one of the palace guards. Bess didn't exactly give me permission to leave England on the eve of my wedding to Lady Jane."

Luca stared at him, her eyes wary. "You were going to marry Lady Jane?" Her eyes clouded. "Am I to assume we are no longer married?"

Morgan smiled and kissed the tip of her nose. "We are still very much married, love. Instead of signing the annulment document with my real name, I signed it El Diablo and hoped no one would inspect the signature. Clever of me, wasn't it?"

"What need was there for subterfuge?" Luca wondered. "If you didn't want to end our marriage, you should have made it clear to the queen."

"Easier said than done, my love. To defy the queen deliberately is to invite disaster. 'Tis common knowledge that those who earn her displeasure end up in the Tower. She threatened to imprison me and confiscate everything I owned if I did not marry Lady Jane. I have an aversion to closed-in places. I planned my escape carefully, but I did not count on Lord Harley's spying on me."

"You did all this for me?"

"For us. How could I wed Jane when I love you? You did make it rather difficult when you left England so abruptly. Had you stayed and told me about our child, 'tis possible the queen might have relented."

Luca looked so remorseful that Morgan wanted to kiss her sweet lips until their corners lifted into a smile. He did, bringing not only the desired smile but also a contented sigh. "Will you ever be able to return to England?"

"There is nothing left in England for me. I sold Scott Hall and withdrew all my assets from the bank. Everything I own is now on Andros."

"You sold Scott Hall? Oh, Morgan, I'm so sorry. I know you loved the place."

"I love you more," he said so earnestly that Luca had no reason to doubt him. "I love Andros, too. It won't be long before we'll have neighbors. Some of my crewmen expressed the desire to marry and settle down on the island. The village will grow, and soon there will be children for our little ones to play with."

Suddenly a shadow passed before Luca's eyes. Morgan couldn't help noticing the change. "What is it, sweetheart?"

"Will El Diablo continue to ply the seas in search of Spanish plunder?"

"Those days are over, Luca. My vendetta against the Spanish ended the day I married you. It's taken me a long time to realize that there are more important things in life than revenge. Living with hatred made a bitter man of me, and until I met you I didn't know the meaning of love. From now on I will concentrate on my plantation. England still needs the lumber I export aboard my ships. My London solicitor has agreed to handle my affairs in England. I seriously doubt Queen Bess will bother us on Andros. She is not a young woman. Her heir will likely offer amnesty to people like me if we wish it."

"I don't care where we live, Morgan, as long as we're together. What about Stan Crawford?"

"He knows of my decision to retire El

Diablo. He hasn't told me yet if he intends to carry on where I left off or if he wants to settle down. I've offered him one of my ships if he still wishes for adventure on the high seas. He's certainly rich enough to settle down should he desire."

"About Renalda. You won't regret bringing her along with us. She's my friend. I'll take care of her."

Morgan gave a snort of laughter. "Stan beat you to it. He's already accepted responsibility for her. In fact, he seems quite taken with her, and she with him. But forget them, I'm famished for you again. Every day without you was an eternity. I want to love you again . . . if you're not too tired," he added hopefully.

"That's what I want, too," Luca sighed, pressing against him in blatant invitation.

Morgan took his time arousing her, kissing her lips, her face, her breasts, stroking the tender folds between her legs. Suddenly he rolled onto his back, dragging her atop him. Bringing her face down to his, he cradled the back of her neck in one hand and kissed her hungrily. He lowered his head to nuzzle her throat. She shivered in response.

"Morgan, *Dios* . . ."

Her fingers threaded through his hair,

holding him in unmistakable urgency as his sex throbbed against her stomach. He cupped her sweet breast in his hand and flicked her turgid nipple with his thumb. She cried out when he took her nipple into his mouth and suckled gently.

"I want you inside me!" Her plea made Morgan swell and thicken to nearly painful proportions.

Acting upon her most fervent desire, she raised slightly, grasped the jutting length of his staff, and guided it inside her, at the same time lowering herself upon him. Unable to remain passive, Morgan thrust violently upward, sheathing himself completely.

Pleasure shuddered through Luca, relishing every nuance of his lovemaking — the warmth of his slender hips against her inner thighs, the feel of his strong hands spanning her buttocks, holding her immobile for his upward thrusts. The throbbing heat of him inside her, thick and hard, surrounded by her own wetness, the feel of his slick, hard-muscled flesh beneath her hands. Never would she grow tired of the magic of Morgan's loving.

Then suddenly she was weightless and powerless, drifting into oblivion as ecstasy shuddered through her. She called out his name, but Morgan was too consumed with his own climax to respond. Jerking violently, Morgan pulled her down and seized her lips, thrusting his tongue into her mouth in perfect harmony with his thrusting below. He stiffened and gave a hoarse shout as he spun out of control.

After a long interval, Morgan pulled Luca into the curve of his body. "Go to sleep, sweetheart." Luca sighed contentedly as she relaxed against him and drifted off to sleep.

Morgan awakened early and went down to the common room, discovering that Stan and Renalda had already broken their fast, and now waited for him and Luca. "Where is Luca?" Renalda asked worriedly. "She is all right, isn't she?"

"She's fine," Morgan grinned, "just exhausted. I think she should rest today. You and Renalda go on ahead and wait for us aboard the *Avenger*."

"Are you sure, Morgan?" Crawford asked anxiously. " 'Tis dangerous to linger in a hostile country."

"According to Luca, she is free to leave the convent whenever she chooses. We are still husband and wife, and no one can stop me from taking what is mine."

"Very well, Renalda and I will leave immediately. If you don't join us within twenty-four hours, I'll come looking for you."

Morgan grinned, realizing how fortunate he was to have a faithful friend like Stan Crawford. "Luca and I will leave first thing in the morning. I promise we will be with you well within the allotted time."

They made their farewells. Before returning upstairs to his sleeping wife, Morgan ordered breakfast to be served in their room.

Luca was grateful for Morgan's concern. She was indeed exhausted. Seeing Morgan again, learning that he loved her and spending long hours last night making love with him had been too much excitement for a pregnant lady. She seemed to tire so easily these days. It took little urging on Morgan's part to persuade Luca to spend the day in bed, and she welcomed the opportunity to be alone with Morgan for an entire day without interference.

"Tell me about Renalda," Morgan asked as they shared dinner that night in their room. "She said her parents disowned her. Was she lying?"

" 'Tis the truth," Luca vowed. "Renalda fell in love with a young vaquero, and her father forbade her to see him. She was soon to marry a man she'd been betrothed to since childhood. Renalda and her vaquero ran away, intending to marry, but her lover was killed before the deed was done. After learning that Renalda and Antonio had spent one night together, her fiancé refused to honor their betrothal. Her family became very angry. She had dishonored them and was banished forthwith to the convent."

"Why didn't she leave if she was unhappy?"

"You don't understand our customs. Where would she go? What would she do? She had no money, no family to take her in, and no way to support herself. She is not a *puta* and could never become one. A young girl has little choice regarding her future. She is but a pawn in the scheme of life. I suppose when you and Stan came along, Renalda saw a way out of her dilemma and took it."

"I hope Stan doesn't take advantage of Renalda," Morgan mused. "He seems quite taken with her and can be very aggressive when he wants to be."

"Why not let nature take its course," Luca advised. "I haven't spoken with Renalda yet, but I do know she is a woman who knows her own mind and isn't afraid to take chances. If Stan oversteps the bounds of decency, Renalda will set him straight. Unless," she added cryptically, "she is of the same mind as Stan."

"Then I won't worry about her," Morgan said. "Are you finished eating? We should retire early, for tomorrow will be a long day. I promised Stan we would join him on the *Avenger* within twenty-four hours, and I don't want him to worry if we are late."

"Morgan, would it be possible to bid my father good-bye before we leave Cadiz? 'Tis unlikely I'll see him again. He's always done what he thought was best for me, even if I didn't agree. I regret that a ship of his line sank the one carrying your family, but that was a long time ago. I'd like Father to know that I'm going to have his grandchild."

Morgan didn't think it was a good idea, but Luca looked so hopeful that he hadn't the heart to refuse her. "If it means so much to you, love, we'll stop."

"*Gracias*, Morgan, now I'm ready for bed." Her eyes glowed darkly, hinting of mischief and pleasure . . . mostly pleasure.

"You need your rest, Luca," Morgan warned in an effort to restrain the erection straining against his codpiece.

"There will be plenty of time for rest once we are aboard the *Avenger*." She reached for him, and Morgan was lost.

They made love gently, tenderly, each

aware that there were many more days of loving one another left to them in this lifetime. And perhaps more in the next.

The sound of steps pounding in the hallway outside their door awakened Morgan. He reached for his sword, cursing violently when he noted that it lay across the room atop the pile of clothing that he had shed hastily and left carelessly on the worn carpet. He jerked upright, grateful that he'd had the foresight to lock the door. But before he could rise from bed, the door was battered open and men spilled into the room.

Frightened from a sound sleep, Luca shrieked and pulled the sheet up to her chin. Her eyes were wild, her heart pumping furiously.

"My mistake was in not killing you in Havana," one of the men sneered, as he surveyed the rumpled bed and disheveled couple occupying it with disdain.

Luca stared at the two men standing on the threshold, blanching when recognition dawned. "Father! Don Diego! What are you doing here?"

"Bloody Hell," Morgan muttered beneath his breath. If it wasn't for bad luck he wouldn't have any luck at all. How in the

Hell had they found him? Who'd told them he was in Spain? And why wasn't del Fugo in Havana?

22

Morgan did not like the odds stacked against him. Standing behind Don Diego and Don Eduardo were two armed henchmen. Morgan glanced at Luca and swore beneath his breath. She was pale and shaking like a leaf.

"I'm sorry we did not arrive in time to prevent the pirate from hurting you again, daughter," Don Eduardo said, thinking that he had truly saved Luca from the Devil. "Father Pedro returned from Rome a week ago. The Holy Father has granted an annulment of your marriage. I was preparing to journey here to tell you the good news when Diego arrived."

"Morgan did not hurt me, Father," Luca protested. "Please leave us."

Morgan kept his eyes trained on del Fugo, whose right hand was poised over the hilt of his sword. The Spaniard's glowering expression did not bode well for Morgan. Morgan glanced wistfully at his own sword with no hope of recovering it. Without it and his clothing, he was as vulnerable as a newborn babe. He was at a most definite disadvantage.

"Diego came all the way from Havana to make you his bride. He is willing to overlook your past indiscretion with the Englishman. Before you leave Spain I will see you properly wed to Diego."

Luca's eyes burned with indignation. "Why is everyone trying to destroy my marriage? I don't want an annulment. Diego is a man without scruples. He doesn't want me, 'tis my dowry he craves. He'd do anything to keep it for himself."

"You wrong me, Luca," Diego said contritely. "I was overset when I realized you were not the virgin bride I expected, but I would have done the right thing by you once my anger had cooled. I've apologized profusely to your father, that's why I came all the way to Spain. We will speak our vows before sailing to Havana."

Morgan's rage escalated as Diego spouted his lies. No piece of paper could simply dissolve what he and Luca shared. The deceitful bastard would never get his hands on his wife or their child. Heedless of his nudity, Morgan surged from bed and took a menacing step toward Diego.

"Get out of here, all of you! Luca is my wife and will remain my wife."

Diego smiled nastily and stepped aside, allowing his henchmen into the room. Morgan's jaw tightened as he made a wild dash for his sword. Alas, it was not to be. Diego's men were on him in seconds. Though he fought bravely, he was overpowered when Diego joined the fray, bringing the hilt of his sword down with crushing force on Morgan's head. Luca screamed as Morgan crumbled to the ground.

"Shall we kill him, *patrón?*" one of the henchmen asked, pressing the tip of his sword against Morgan's exposed throat.

"Noooo!" Luca screamed. "Father, if you love me, don't let them kill Morgan."

Don Eduardo looked at his frantic daughter and relented. "Luca is right, Don Diego. It is not up to us to kill the pirate. Take him to Cadiz and turn him over to the authorities. There is a generous reward for his capture. I will follow with Luca when she has calmed down. Come to the house tomorrow, and we will make plans for the wedding."

Luca was sobbing softly, wanting to go to Morgan but unable to because of her nudity.

"Don't hurt him, please. He was wounded recently and hasn't fully recovered from his injuries."

"We will find a nice comfortable *calabozo* for him," Don Diego laughed. "Bind him with drapery cords," he ordered. By the time the henchmen finished, Morgan was beginning to stir. "Take him away."

"Wait, give him his clothing," Luca pleaded. "Allow him some dignity."

Diego paid her no heed, but Don Eduardo gathered together Morgan's clothing and handed them to one of the henchmen. "Take him out into the hallway and help him dress."

"Bah, you are too soft," Don Diego spat. "The authorities will put him before the firing squad within twenty-four hours."

Don Eduardo had never considered himself a particularly tenderhearted man, but Luca was so distraught that he was suddenly stricken with guilt. Perhaps his daughter really did love the rogue pirate. He remembered what it was like to love someone. When Luca's lovely mother had died, he had lost something precious. Still, El Diablo had been the bane of Spanish shipping for too long to be set free. If he hadn't boldly abducted Luca in the first place, none of this would have happened.

"What the authorities do with El Diablo is out of our hands," Don Eduardo said. "His death will not be on my conscience. Go now, Diego. I will bring Luca home."

The moment Don Eduardo turned his back on them, Diego sent Luca a look that caused the hair to rise on the nape of her neck. His scathing glance conveyed the seething contempt he felt for her. Only a fool would fail to see that she was naked beneath the sheet, and only a simpleton would think she and Morgan had been merely sleeping. Don Diego was neither. The room reeked of sex, and the rumpled bedclothes gave mute testimony to the activity in which the couple had been engaged. It was beyond bearing and a mortal blow to Diego's pride.

"Until tomorrow, Luca," Don Diego said in a voice that gave hint to his anger. *Sí*, he would marry the pirate's *puta* in order to keep her enormous dowry, but he would give up none of his mistresses. Once Luca gave him an heir or two, he would banish her to a convent and promptly forget her.

Luca was sobbing silently, unable to stop the huge tears coursing down her cheeks. It seemed that even God was against her and Morgan. Fortunately she had a secret that she hoped would change things in her favor. Once Diego learned she was pregnant with

Morgan's child he would not want her. Of course there was one hitch. She hadn't figured out yet how revealing her pregnancy would help Morgan. Morgan was on his way to the *calabozo,* and Diego would see to it that he was punished to the fullest extent of the law.

"Get dressed, daughter," Don Eduardo said kindly. "I'll wait out in the hallway while you dress and pack. Perhaps we can get a decent breakfast from the kitchen before returning to Cadiz. I do not like to see you so upset."

"How can I not be upset, Father, when the man I love faces death? Diego holds a grudge against Morgan. What guarantee do I have that Morgan will reach Cadiz alive?"

"Diego is a gentleman. He would not harm an unarmed man. It is up to the authorities to demand punishment."

Luca gave a harsh sound of disgust. "You do not know Don Diego if you think that."

Don Eduardo merely shrugged and made a hasty exit. He wasn't good at handling hysterical women. Once she was alone, Luca rose from bed and dressed quickly. She retrieved a cloak from her bundle of clothing and wrapped it around her, carefully concealing her protruding stomach within its generous folds. It wasn't the right time to tell her father she was carrying Morgan's child.

Once Morgan was hustled into the hallway, groggy and disoriented from the vicious blow to his head, he was thrust into his trunk hose and dragged down the stairs. If the innkeeper felt the least bit of compassion, he carefully hid it beneath his bland expression while Diego arranged for a wagon to haul Morgan to Cadiz. Within minutes Morgan was forced into the wagon bed, trussed like a Christmas goose and bleeding from a head wound. One henchman climbed in beside him, while the second leaped into the driver's box and took up the reins. At Diego's signal the wagon jerked forward, sending Morgan crashing violently against the side. Excruciating pain exploded through his bad leg, up his spine, and into his head. Then he knew no more.

Luca eyed the food on her plate with disinterest. How could she eat when she had no idea how badly Morgan was hurt? What if Don Diego took justice into his own hands and killed Morgan the moment they left the inn?

"I know you think you love the pirate, Luca, but Diego will soon make you forget him, I swear it. He will be a good husband to you. Soon you can put all this nasty business behind you."

"How can I forget Morgan when I love him, Father? I will never marry Don Diego, no matter what happens."

Don Eduardo patted Luca's shoulder awkwardly. "Trust me to know what's best for you."

"Did you send for Diego? Why is he in Spain?"

Don Eduardo's glance fell away. "I wrote to Diego the day you returned from England. I explained that Father Pedro was on his way to Rome to petition the pope for an annulment of your marriage. I urged Diego to come to Spain immediately if he still wanted you. If not, I told him I expected full restitution of your dowry."

Luca gave a mirthless laugh. "Surely you did not think he'd return my dowry, did you? No, I can see you didn't."

"Diego left Havana immediately upon receiving my missive. When he arrived in Cadiz he was overjoyed to learn you are a free woman. We left Cadiz together to impart the good news to you. We had no idea Morgan Scott was here."

"How did you find us at the inn? How did you learn Morgan was in Spain?"

"Pure luck, daughter. We stopped at the inn to quench our raging thirst; we had ridden hard, you see, and the innkeeper, a loquacious man, told us about the foreigners staying at his inn. Diego seemed interested to learn that a fair-haired man and a Spanish woman were asleep above stairs, but he had no reason to suspect anything.

"We made haste for the convent and learned that you and another woman had left without permission the night before. We put two and two together and returned to the inn."

Good luck for Diego and Father but bad luck for me and Morgan, Luca thought glumly. "May I see the annulment document, Father?" Luca asked, holding out her hand.

"It is perfectly legal, Luca."

"Please, Father."

With marked reluctance, Don Eduardo retrieved the document from his pocket and handed it to Luca. Luca's hands shook as she unrolled it and read the contents. She had nearly reached the end when she let out an audible gasp. Excitement coursed through her.

"Father! Have you read this?"

Don Eduardo frowned. "Of course. Is there something you do not understand?"

"It states that if I am carrying Morgan Scott's child the annulment becomes invalid. It further states that a child of the union will be considered legitimate issue since the marriage was performed by a priest and is legal in the eyes of God. Is that true?"

"I believe the document specifies the Holy Father's wishes in this matter. As long as there are no children to complicate matters, the annulment is a simple matter." He gave Luca a shrewd smile. "Thank God you have no worries on that score. If the scoundrel managed to impregnate you in the last two days there will be no way to tell if the child belongs to him or Don Diego, for your marriage to the governor-general of Cuba will take place immediately."

Luca returned his smile, only hers was more radiant than the sunrise. She rose clumsily to her feet and slowly unclasped the cloak she'd donned to disguise her condition. She let it slide to the floor and stood proudly before her father. There was no mistaking the protruding roundness of her abdomen.

Don Eduardo inhaled sharply. "*Madre di Dios!* Who did this to you?"

Luca gave him a blissful smile. "No one at the convent, Father. I suspected I was carrying Morgan's child when I left England."

Don Eduardo cursed violently. "Why in God's name did you leave the pirate if you were carrying his child?"

"A misunderstanding. I thought Morgan did not want our child. The queen was pressing for an annulment, and I did not wish to be a burden to him. When one loves, one cannot always see clearly or distinguish between right and wrong. I chose the wrong course, but thank God Morgan found me and set me straight. We love one another. You and Diego have destroyed any chance we might have had to find happiness."

Don Eduardo could not take his eyes off Luca's bulging stomach. Carefully he removed the annulment document from her hand and tore it into tiny pieces. No man in his right mind would want a woman far gone with another man's child. Certainly not a proud man like Diego del Fugo, regardless of Luca's sizable dowry.

"Father, you must do something," Luca pleaded. "Morgan has changed. He has abandoned his vendetta; never more will El Diablo plunder Spanish ships. If you love me, you will help Morgan."

Don Eduardo shrugged helplessly. "What can I do? Your pirate's fate is up to God."

"No! There must be something you can do. Morgan loved me enough to risk his life for me. He came to Spain knowing the danger involved. Do you want to see the father of your grandchild die an ignoble death?" She hugged her stomach protectively. "This may be your only grandchild. My brothers might never return from their adventures. And if they do, they are unlikely to settle down long enough to raise a family. They'd rather sail the world searching for gold and riches."

Don Eduardo realized the truth of Luca's words. With his mother's solid Spanish stock and his father's English courage, his grandchild would be strong and resilient and brave. But he truly saw no way to help Luca's husband, even if he wanted to.

"I'm sorry, daughter. Morgan Scott is Diego's captive, and Diego is a vindictive man."

"We must not let him turn Morgan over to the authorities. If we hurry, we can catch them."

"Even if we did, Diego would not let him go. Resign yourself, daughter. There is no way to free El Diablo. Once Diego learns you are carrying the pirate's child, his anger will know no bounds. He will feel cheated and will take revenge on the man responsible."

"Tell him he can keep my dowry for the trouble I've caused him," Luca suggested. "Is my happiness not worth it? Throughout the years my welfare did not concern you, until it came time to marry me off to Diego. I've asked little from you and received even less."

Her words had the desired effect. It was true he had neglected his daughter in favor of his sons, but he had always loved Luca despite her high-spirited antics. He just never knew how to handle her, nor had he had the time to learn. He sincerely thought marriage to Diego was the best course for her.

"I will see what I can do," Don Eduardo promised, though he held little hope of saving the pirate's life. Diego del Fugo was a powerful man, with more political clout than the Santiego family. Don Eduardo didn't let on to Luca, but in his estimation Morgan Scott was as good as dead.

Rudely jarred into consciousness, Morgan was aware of every excruciating pain suffered by his bruised body. He moaned, trying to shift into a more comfortable position. All he earned was a kick in the ribs for his trouble. Over the rim of the wagon bed he could see del Fugo riding slightly ahead of the rig. Morgan cursed the man with raw, consuming hatred.

"What happened to my wife?" Morgan asked the brutal henchman who seemed to derive great pleasure from abusing him.

The man laughed nastily. "You mean your *puta?* Her father is taking care of her. 'Tis a pity Don Diego has to marry the bitch to keep her dowry."

Morgan struggled helplessly against his bonds, vowing to make the man eat his words. "Where are you taking me?"

"Don Eduardo thinks we are taking you to the authorities, but I doubt you will reach there alive." He gave a nasty bark of laughter and aimed another kick at Morgan's middle. Morgan saw it coming and rolled into a ball to protect his vulnerable parts. The guard's booted foot connected with Morgan's bad leg, and Morgan bit his lip to keep from screaming in anguish.

Morgan could live with the pain, but the thought of Luca's future life with del Fugo brought a far greater agony. *What will happen when he learns about Luca's pregnancy?* Morgan wondered desperately. He hoped her father was strong enough to protect her from del Fugo's violence. His own death he could accept, but he could not bear the thought of either Luca or their child suffering on his account.

After years of denying there even was a God, Morgan closed his eyes and prayed. Prayer was Luca's strength, and Morgan tried to make it his. Another vicious kick to his head sent Morgan spinning into oblivion.

"I'm not sure this is wise," Clyde Withers said as he rode beside Stan Crawford toward Lebrija. "Neither of us can speak Spanish well enough to avoid trouble. And what about the men?" he asked, motioning toward the four armed seamen riding in the bed of the rented wagon. "There is no mistaking them for anything but what they are, seasoned seamen. We're going to look silly when we meet Morgan on the road and he and Lady Scott are both hale and hardy."

"From the moment I left them at the inn I've had this premonition," Stan said slowly. "I tried to ignore it, but this morning it was stronger than ever. 'Tis better to be safe than sorry. If we find Morgan and Luca well, we've lost nothing. But if something unforeseen has happened to them, we'll be prepared." He paused to get his bearings. "If Morgan and Luca left this morning, we should be meeting them on the road soon."

As the morning progressed and they failed to cross paths with the carriage carrying Morgan and Luca, Stan's nagging fear increased. They were nearly half the distance to Lebrija when they heard the sound of approaching horsemen. Within minutes a horse hove into sight, followed by a wagon rattling along the narrow dirt road. Stan did not recognize the man charging toward them on horseback.

"Get off the road, peasants!" he ordered haughtily. "Make way."

Stan understood the harsh Spanish words and politely pulled his horse to the side of the road, motioning for Withers and the wagon to do the same. He wasn't looking for trouble with the local dignitaries. Diego rode by without a second glance at the men he assumed were lowly peasants unworthy of his attention. When the wagon drew abreast, Crawford nearly fell off his horse, so great was his shock.

Withers saw Morgan's battered body curled into a ball in the wagon bed nearly at the same time Crawford did. They exchanged startled glances. Scant moments later the four crewmen in the wagon became aware of the situation and awaited orders from Stan.

The wagon carrying Morgan rattled past. At Stan's wordless gesture the sailors jumped from their wagon and ran to catch up with the wagon carrying Morgan. They overpowered the two Spaniards at the reins, while Stan and Withers pounded after the leader, who had galloped ahead, unaware of the ruckus behind him. The scuffle was brief and bloody. Outnumbered two to one, the Spaniards soon succumbed to the Englishmen. One Spaniard was slain outright, and the other lay dying on the grass. The men quickly untied Morgan, who showed no signs of regaining consciousness. Meanwhile Crawford and Withers approached Diego from behind.

Diego didn't realize he was in trouble until it was too late. Having grown impatient with the slow-moving wagon, he had ridden far ahead and hadn't heard the brief battle being waged behind him. Diego spat out a violent oath when Crawford and Withers rode up, sandwiching him between them and jerking the reins from his hands. He reached for his sword, but it was too late. Two primed pistols were aimed at his head.

"What's the meaning of this?" he blustered as his mount was brought to a halt. "Do you know who I am? I am Diego del Fugo, governor-general of Cuba. The king will have your heads for this."

"What in the Hell is he talking about?" Withers asked.

"Damned if I know, except that his name is Diego del Fugo, governor-general of Cuba." Suddenly comprehension dawned. "This is the bastard who nearly beat Morgan to death in Havana. Wonder what he's doing in Spain."

"What do you suppose happened to Lady Scott?" Withers asked worriedly.

"Perhaps Morgan can tell us," Stan suggested.

Stan's attention wavered briefly, and Diego seized the opportunity to bolt. He dug his heels cruelly into his mount's flanks, and the abused animal shot forward.

"Son of a bitch! Don't let the bastard get away!" Stan shouted. Both men brought up their pistols, took aim, and fired. At least one of the bullets found its mark. Diego hit the ground and lay still.

"Do you think he's dead?" Withers asked.

Stan slid from his mount and knelt beside the fallen Spaniard. "He's still breathing. We'd better get the Hell out of here fast. I hope Morgan can tell us what happened to

Luca, for 'tis too dangerous to dally any longer."

Morgan was still unconscious when they returned to the wagon. "What in the Hell did they do to him?" Withers wondered.

Stan made a hasty examination and found a nasty head wound in addition to several purple bruises on various parts of Morgan's body. "The bloody bastards. Transfer Morgan into our wagon," he ordered. "Be careful, we don't know the severity of his injuries yet."

"What about del Fugo?" Withers asked.

"Leave him, and let's get the Hell out of here."

"What about Lady Scott?"

"We have no idea where she is and can do nothing until Morgan regains consciousness and tells us. Obviously del Fugo is in no condition to tell us anything."

Two sturdy sailors hopped inside the wagon bed with Morgan and kept him from being jolted as the wagon bumped along the rutted dirt road to Cadiz, where the *Avenger* awaited.

23

Luca and her father left Lebrija in the carriage Morgan had rented in Cadiz. Don Eduardo tied his mount to the back, placed Luca's bundle of clothing and Morgan's sword, which had been left behind, inside, and set off at a brisk pace on the road to Cadiz. It couldn't be too fast for Luca. Morgan's life was at stake. She didn't trust Diego and feared he would kill Morgan before they reached their destination.

"Calm down, daughter," Don Eduardo urged. "I told you I would do what I could for your pirate."

"My husband, Father. Morgan is my husband."

"*Sí*, Luca, though it is difficult to think of the Englishman as your husband."

Luca peered anxiously into the distance. Diego had a good two-hour head start but she knew the lumbering farm wagon carrying Morgan traveled much slower than their lighter carriage. "Shouldn't we encounter them soon, Father? Can't you go any faster?"

"I'm being careful of your delicate condition, daughter. I don't want to harm your child."

Luca fidgeted impatiently. "I don't think . . ." Her words slid to a halt as she spied something down the road. "Father, look! Isn't that the wagon? *Sí*, I'm sure it is. And there's Diego's horse grazing nearby. Why have they stopped?" An ominous premonition slithered down her spine. "Stop the carriage, Father!"

Heedless of her condition, Luca leaped from the carriage before it came to a full stop and ran awkwardly toward the wagon. Her scream brought Don Eduardo immediately to her side.

"What is it, daughter?"

"Look!" she gasped, indicating the body lying in the bed of the wagon. Her heart constricted painfully until she saw that it wasn't Morgan.

Don Eduardo hoisted himself into the wagon bed and bent to examine the man. "He's dead."

"There's another man lying in the grass," Luca exclaimed.

Don Eduardo eased down from the wagon bed and quickly ascertained that the second man was beyond human intervention. "He's dead, too. I wonder what happened to Diego?"

They found him lying beside his horse a short distance away. "Is he dead?" Luca asked.

"He seems to have a minor head wound. The bullet grazed him. I suspect he will come around soon and tell us what happened. Who would have thought your pirate could overpower three men in his condition," he mused thoughtfully.

"He couldn't," Luca replied. "Someone else was responsible, and I have a good idea who it was. Quickly, Father, you must take me to Cadiz without delay."

"Very well, Luca, as soon as I get Diego into the carriage. He needs medical attention."

Luca grasped his arm, urging him away from Diego. "No, Father, we can't take him with us. Don't you see? If we do, he'll notify the authorities. We have to leave him here until someone comes along or he makes it to Cadiz under his own power. It's Morgan's only chance to escape Spain and certain death."

Don Eduardo stared at his daughter in

consternation. "But, daughter, Diego is my friend. I cannot leave him."

"You said yourself his injury wasn't serious. If we're fortunate, we'll reach the *Avenger* before he revives. Please, Father, do this for my child's sake. My baby needs a father to love and nurture him to adulthood."

Don Eduardo was torn. It was true that Diego probably suffered from nothing more serious than a mild concussion, but his honor demanded that he aid his countryman. Yet with Luca, his own flesh and blood, beseeching him so earnestly, he hadn't the heart to deny her. He had ignored her wishes once, and look what had happened. She was now the wife of an English pirate and expecting his child. If he had allowed her to become a nun, none of this would have happened.

"Very well, Luca, I will do as you wish. But we must hurry if we are to reach Cadiz before Diego. Once he revives he will be hard on our heels. His horse is bred for speed and will catch up with us in no time at all."

"Then we must take his horse with us," Luca said firmly. "Morgan must be given every opportunity to escape. Quickly, tie Don Diego's mount to the back of the carriage."

"Luca, this does not sit well with me."

"Even when you were stern and uncompromising I loved you," Luca said, growing desperate. "And I know you loved me. Prove it now. Leave Don Diego. It's not as if you're leaving him stranded. He can drive the wagon to Cadiz, it isn't all that far."

"I will do as you wish, but I like it not."

Within minutes they were jouncing down the road with Diego's horse tethered to the back of the carriage next to Eduardo's.

It was nearly dusk when the wagon bearing Morgan wound its way through the streets of Cadiz to the waterfront. Morgan had drifted in and out of consciousness several times but hadn't been coherent enough to reveal Luca's fate or how he'd ended up as Diego's prisoner.

"Be careful with him, men," Stan warned as he quickly located the boat they had left tied up at the quay, guarded by a couple of men. "He might have internal injuries."

Morgan was placed into the boat and settled so that he was resting against Withers. Two men manned the oars, while the others pushed off. Stan breathed a sigh of relief as the boat cut smoothly through the water toward the *Avenger*. The boat was hoisted aboard by a system of pulleys, and in a short time Morgan was lying in his bunk, waiting for the cook, who doubled as the ship's doctor, to arrive and treat his wounds.

"Feels like he has a cracked rib," the cook said as he examined Morgan's bruises. "There's a lump the size of an egg on his head, and his leg appears to have been injured in the same spot where it was broken."

"How serious is it?" Stan asked anxiously.

"The leg's not broken, just bruised. The captain is tough, he'll heal right properly, I suspect, if he doesn't try to get out of bed too soon. I'll dose him with laudanum."

"No, no laudanum." Morgan's voice was weak but determined. "I need all my senses if I'm to go after Luca."

"Where is she?" Crawford asked, leaning close to Morgan.

"Home with her father by now," Morgan guessed. "I don't remember much. What happened to del Fugo and his henchmen? How did you happen to be on the road, when you were supposed to wait for me aboard the *Avenger*?"

"Call it a wild hunch I couldn't shake. Thank God I followed my hunch. What in Hell is del Fugo doing in Spain?"

"That's something I don't understand myself," Morgan croaked. Pain coursed through him; his entire body was an aching mass of flesh and bone. He was in so much agony that he could barely speak. But he fought it with every breath he took. He couldn't surrender to pain until he had Luca safely aboard the *Avenger*. Trying to rise, he fought the blackness closing in on him, and his face turned white as a sheet.

"What in bloody Hell do you think you're doing?" Stan asked, vexed at Morgan's stubbornness. "You're in no condition to get out of that bed."

"Help me, Stan, I have to find Luca before del Fugo gets to her."

"Don't worry about del Fugo," Crawford remarked. "His henchmen are dead, and he's in no condition to travel any time soon."

"You killed him?"

"No, at least I don't think so. He was breathing when we left him, but I doubt he'll feel like traveling for a while."

"Don't underestimate the bastard, Stan. Are you going to help me up?"

"No."

"No? As your captain I order you to obey my order."

"No."

Morgan felt so damn helpless he wanted to scream in frustration. "I could have you put in irons for insubordination."

"Try it," Stan challenged.

Morgan turned to Withers. "I guess it's up to you, Clyde. I'll deal with Mr. Crawford later. Ready the longboat, I'll be going ashore."

Withers shook his head regretfully. "Sorry, Captain, I agree with Mr. Crawford."

"Then I'll damn well do it myself." It took him three tries, but he finally gained his feet. A jolt of raw agony caused him to double over, but he quickly gained control and righted himself. His own injuries didn't matter. He had to save his wife and unborn child from del Fugo.

Withers and Crawford exchanged worried looks, then reluctantly moved to help Morgan. "Very well, Morgan," Crawford said, "we'll help you. You always were a stubborn ass. But I seriously doubt you'll make it to shore. Don't worry, Clyde and I will go after Luca. I know Don Eduardo's residence."

"No, I'm Luca's husband. She's my responsibility." Morgan moved slowly, with great effort. "Just get me to shore and find me a horse. And give me a sword and pistol."

"Damn hardheaded fool," Crawford muttered beneath his breath. "We'll help you, but I'm going with you no matter what you say." Withers went in search of a sword and pistol, while Crawford helped Morgan make his way on deck and into the longboat.

"You're not getting rid of me that easily," Withers said as he jumped into the longboat with Crawford. "I'll help row." He shoved the sword and pistol at Morgan and directed the crewmen to lower them down to the water.

Crawford watched Morgan closely. He had no idea what kept the man upright. The severe injuries he had sustained would keep most men in bed for days. But Morgan was not most men. Still, Crawford seriously doubted that Morgan could withstand the pain of mounting a horse. He fully expected to haul him back to the ship unconscious. But he wouldn't fail Morgan. He vowed to find Luca no matter what it took.

Diego regained consciousness a short time after Luca and her father left him behind to fend for himself. His head throbbed painfully, and it took him a few minutes to remember what had happened. Rising groggily, he staggered to the wagon and let out a violent curse when he discovered his dead henchmen. He had been foolish not to pay closer attention to the peasants, for clearly they were not peasants at all but El Diablo's crewmen. The ambush had been successful; his oversight had cost him dearly. El Diablo had fled with his men, and Diego realized he had to get to Cadiz as quickly as possible if he wanted to prevent the pirate from escaping once more.

Diego's anger was boundless when he looked for his horse and found him missing. He had brought the horse with him from Havana and had trained the steed himself. He knew his horse wouldn't wander away on his own; someone had to have taken him. What an overconfident fool he had been. The delay was not to be tolerated. It was imperative that he reach Cadiz and alert the dragoons before the pirate's ship sailed.

Diego eyed the nag hitched to the wagon with obvious distaste. The horse was past its prime, but riding it to Cadiz was a damn sight better than pulling a wagon filled with dead men. An excellent horseman, Diego didn't balk at riding without a saddle. Fortunately he was familiar with the area, having lived there during his youth, and knew a shortcut to town through fields and olive groves.

Diego waited a moment for the stunning pain in his head to abate before unhitching the nag and dragging himself onto the horse's back. Grasping the leading reins, he kicked the nag's skinny flanks and took off through the fields to Cadiz.

★ ★ ★

Luca and her father reached Cadiz and made directly for the waterfront. Luca shook with excitement when she saw the *Avenger* lying at anchor in the bay. She had made it! Soon she and Morgan would be together forever.

"A boat, Father, I have to find a boat to take me to the *Avenger*."

Don Eduardo sighed resignedly. "I'll take care of it, Luca. Wait in the carriage. There should be someone around willing to row you out to the ship."

"No, Father, I'll come along." Clutching her bundle of clothing and Morgan's sword, she waited for her father to help her down.

Suddenly Luca's attention focused on a longboat discharging passengers on the quay. A thick gray fog rolled in from the sea, obscuring the figures in swaddling mist. Fog and waning daylight prevented Luca from recognizing the men scrambling onto the quay from the boat. But when two men bent to assist a third from the boat, she dropped the bundle of clothing and the sword, screamed Morgan's name, and started running.

Don Eduardo scooped up the possessions and followed close on her heels.

Sitting upright in the longboat had cost Morgan dearly. He wondered how in the Hell he was going to sit a horse without passing out, but he was determined to do it or die trying. Luca belonged to him. She and his child meant everything to him. Without them he had no future.

"Are you all right, Morgan?" Crawford asked anxiously.

"I'm fine," Morgan said with a gasp of pain. "Just get me on a horse."

The horses and wagon they had rented earlier were still hitched nearby. No one had taken them back to the livery, since settling Morgan aboard the *Avenger* had been their primary concern. Withers unhitched one of the horses and held it so Morgan could mount. He seriously doubted Morgan's ability to sit a horse but nevertheless did as his captain ordered.

Morgan's head felt as if it had a thousand Devils with pitchforks inside it trying to get out. His body was on fire and his leg throbbed with unbelievable pain, but he managed to lift his leg into the stirrup without passing out. He prepared himself for the searing agony of being boosted into the saddle. When neither Crawford nor Withers moved to assist him, he glanced over his shoulder to question the delay and saw that both men were staring down the length of the quay.

He heard her call his name before he saw her, her voice frantic but jubilant. Then he saw her emerging from the fog, her cloak billowing around her and her tousled, windblown hair flying wildly about her pale features.

"Luca!" Morgan used the last of his reserves to bring his foot down from the stirrup and start toward her. He collapsed in Luca's arms when they came together halfway down the quay. Don Eduardo, huffing and puffing from the unaccustomed exertion, reached them in time to help support Morgan's body. Crawford and Withers arrived seconds later.

"Is he all right?" Luca asked, beside herself with worry. "He looks so pale."

"Morgan suffered severe injuries," Crawford replied. "Now that you're here we can get him back to the ship and in bed, where he belongs. He insisted on going after you himself. He was crazed with worry and refused to listen to reason. Thank God you're here. There is danger all around us. I can smell it." He looked pointedly at Don Eduardo.

"Father brought me here," Luca explained. "He won't stop us from leaving."

"You must hurry," Don Eduardo urged. " 'Tis possible that Diego is hard on our heels."

He had no sooner uttered the words than a commotion on the quay shattered the murky night. Luca gasped in dismay when she spied Diego and a patrol of armed dragoons charging down the cobbled walkway.

"Stop them! Stop the pirate!" Diego cried, wielding his sword like a battle-ax.

"Hurry, oh, please hurry," Luca urged breathlessly as they half-dragged, half-carried Morgan to the longboat.

Luca stumbled clumsily, hindered by her pregnancy. Without missing a step, Withers scooped her into his arms and placed her into the boat. Then he helped Crawford and Don Eduardo settle Morgan beside her. The boat shoved off without a moment to spare. Tears streamed down Luca's cheeks as she bid her father a rushed good-bye.

"I love you, Father. You will always be welcome on Andros. I want my child to know his grandfather."

"I will come, daughter," Eduardo promised. "I may not have always shown it, but I love you."

The longboat slid into the dense fog just as Diego and the dragoons reached the end of the quay. Diego rudely shoved Eduardo aside, cursing the thick, gray mist that aided the pirate's escape.

Froth gathered at the corners of Diego's mouth as he vented his rage. "They're getting away! Shoot!" he ordered as the dragoons watched the boat disappear into the thickening mist.

"Stop!" Eduardo cried, desperate to protect his daughter. Ignoring Eduardo, the dragoons shouldered their muskets and fired blindly, reloading and firing until it became obvious that their prey was out of range.

"What have you done?" Diego shouted, rounding on Eduardo.

"For the first time in my life I considered my daughter's happiness," Eduardo said, choking back a sob. "She carries the Englishman's child, you would not want her in that condition. She belongs with her husband. Luca gave her word that El Diablo will pose no danger to Spanish shipping in the future."

"And you believe her?" Diego spat contemptuously.

"*Si*, I believe her. Let them be, Diego. As a consolation for your loss you may keep a generous portion of Luca's dowry. Find yourself a wife worthy of your station."

Diego recognized defeat and tried to

make the best of it. "You are right, Eduardo. As much as I would have liked to have caught the pirate and presented his head to the king, I will settle for what you offer. I am too proud to want a woman carrying another man's child. Unless El Diablo takes to the sea again, I will consider the matter closed."

Eduardo bit back a smile. "Come back to the house with me and we will drink a toast to your health and prosperity."

Wringing her hands, Luca hovered over Morgan like a mother hen, waiting for him to regain consciousness. Crawford, Withers, and Renalda stood behind her, lending their support.

"He'll be fine, Luca," Renalda assured her. "Stan said your Morgan is a strong man and has suffered worse in his time."

Luca sent Renalda a watery smile. She had been too distraught to greet her friend properly, but after she was certain Morgan was out of danger they would have a joyous reunion.

Luca spoke to Renalda in rapid Spanish, which she knew neither Withers nor Crawford could follow. "Do you regret leaving Spain, Renalda? I know you were unhappy in the convent, but leaving the country of your birth can't have been an easy decision to make. You still have family here."

Renalda smiled wistfully. "I love my family, but I know them well. They will never change their minds about disowning me. I would have grown old and died in the convent before they relented. You and your pirate have given me a chance for a future. I will always be grateful. I hope you're not angry with me for pressuring Morgan to take me with him. I have no money and nowhere else to go."

"I'm glad, Renalda; it's what I wanted. One day soon Andros will be populated with towns and people, and you will find a man to love. I'm sure of it."

"I'm sure of it, too," Renalda said, casting a shy glance at Stan.

"What are you two jabbering about?" Stan asked, placing his arm around Renalda's narrow shoulders. His gesture was so possessive that no one could doubt Stan's feelings for the Spanish miss.

"The future," Luca said cryptically. "It suddenly looks very bright."

"Aye," Stan agreed, his arm tightening around Renalda. He was startled to realize that he wanted the woman in his arms. Perhaps he and Renalda would find happiness together.

Moments later Morgan opened his eyes and smiled at Luca. When it became obvious that Morgan had eyes for no one but his wife, the others excused themselves and quietly exited.

Morgan reached for Luca's hand, bringing it to his lips. "How did you get here?"

"We have my father to thank. He isn't the demon you think he is. When he realized I carried your child and that I could be happy with no other man, he relented. We are still husband and wife, Morgan. I read the annulment document. It states that the terms are invalid if I am carrying your child."

"It doesn't matter, I would have married you again."

"I regret that one of Father's ships was responsible for your family's death and your enslavement, but I beg you to put that behind you and try to forgive him. It isn't fair to hold him responsible for what each and every one of his ships did during their voyages."

"I don't want to talk about your father, sweetheart," Morgan murmured. "I'm willing to let bygones be bygones if he is. He brought you to me, and for that I'm grateful. Did I hear gunfire before I passed out?"

"*Sí*, Diego brought the dragoons, but fog and darkness worked in our favor. We're safe now. Stan has set a course for Andros. I can't believe you came to Spain for me when the danger to you and your men was so great. You've given my countrymen no reason to love El Diablo."

Morgan stared at Luca as if she had lost her senses. "Not come for you? How could I not, loving you as I do? You belong to me. I've risked my life for you many times in the past and will do so again should it become necessary. When you love someone the way I love you, no sacrifice is too great. Now I'll have our child to love, too."

Luca gave him a glowing smile. "I can't believe you truly want our child. I was resigned to raise it by myself and love it enough for both of us."

Tenderly he placed a hand on her swollen stomach. "I want this child as much as you do, sweetheart. Finally I'll have a family of my own. Until I met you, that hard, bitter mass that beat within my breast couldn't even be classified as a heart. Vengeance ruled my life and hatred dwelled in my soul. Now I am so filled with love I can find no room in my heart for any other emotion."

Luca's dark eyes sparkled wickedly. "Some things have not changed, my love. You are the same handsome rogue who came into my life like a whirlwind and carried me to rapture. If not for you I would never have known such bliss existed."

"If I recall correctly, you wanted to become a nun," Morgan said with a twinkle in his eye.

Luca sent him an impudent grin. "I did not know then that I would burn so hotly for you." She bent down, kissing him full on the lips. "All I want now is to be your wife forever."

"From the beginning I recognized the passion you tried desperately to deny. Even as you fell to your knees in prayer, your sultry dark eyes hinted of a boundless desire just waiting for release. I love you, Luca."

Luca's eyes glowed happily. "I love you, Morgan. Once you are well I'll show you how much."

"Lie beside me," Morgan urged, holding back the covers. "I need to feel you in my arms."

"I don't want to hurt you."

"I can't love you properly yet, I just want to hold you."

The urgency in his voice shattered her resolve. Gingerly she sat on the edge of the bed, preparing to slip in beside him.

"No, not like that, take off your clothes."

"Morgan, I . . . it's not a good idea. You need to rest."

Morgan smiled crookedly. "It's a wonderful idea. I want to feel our child move against me when I fall asleep."

Luca didn't resist when he lovingly undressed her and made room for her on the bunk. When he curved his bruised body around hers, he felt renewed vigor surging through him; he felt whole again.

Epilogue

"Isn't it spectacular, Morgan?" Luca sighed as they watched the sun slowly sink below the sparkling water. Luca rested her head on Morgan's shoulder as the sky turned from brilliant orange to subdued gold to mauve, sprinkling a blanket of glittering diamonds on the placid sea stretched out before them.

"Every sunset is spectacular when I'm with you," Morgan replied, hugging her tightly. "Do you regret coming to Andros with me?"

"I love it here," Luca replied dreamily. "It's what I always imagined paradise would be like. And the village is growing by leaps and bounds. There are plenty of playmates for Richard. Stan and Renalda's daughter is but a year younger than our son, and Renalda is expecting again."

"Were you upset when Clyde Withers brought Rouge to Andros?" Morgan wondered. "I have to admit it came as a shock to learn that he had met Rouge on one of his voyages and fell head over heels for her. Do you want me to send her away?"

"They seem truly taken with one another," Luca allowed. "As long as Rouge doesn't set her sights on you, she's welcome to stay."

Morgan laughed. "No need to worry about that, I'm well and truly taken and she knows it. I do believe Rouge has found true love with Clyde."

Luca nodded, her thoughts turning to their other friend. "I'm glad you made Stan part owner of the lumber business," she said, quickly losing interest in Rouge and Clyde. "He and Renalda have been such good friends to us throughout the years. Isn't it ironic that two men who hated Spaniards would end up with Spanish wives?"

"Stranger things have happened. I never thought I'd be content without a deck beneath my feet," Morgan contended. "You and Richard make every day an adventure; I no longer feel compelled to roam the seas. Did you enjoy your father's visit? He appeared quite loath to leave yesterday."

"Very much. I know you still don't feel comfortable around Father, but he enjoys his grandson so much that he wants to return in a few months. He wants to bring Cordero and Arturo next time. On their last visit home they expressed their desire to meet their nephew."

"I'm reconciled to the fact that your father and brothers are a part of our lives."

"Morgan, do you regret being banished from English shores?"

"Not in the least," Morgan said earnestly. "One day the Bahamas will be populated beyond our wildest expectations. The islands have been more or less ignored since being discovered, but I foresee a time when people will flock to our private paradise.

"Perhaps we can return to England in time, for a visit. The queen is ailing. My solicitor informed me that Bess sent envoys to his office inquiring about my well-being. I think she'd welcome us back to England if we wished to return."

Luca wrinkled her nose. "I do not like England."

Morgan chuckled. "And I'm not welcome in Spain. We seem to have the best of two worlds right here on Andros. Shall we go back home and rescue our son from Lani? She spoils him outrageously."

Luca gave him a provocative smile. "Not yet." She took his hand and led him along the beach to a thick stand of palm trees. The grass beneath was thick and spongy, and she pulled Morgan down beside her.

"What do you have in mind, wife?"

"It's been a long time since we've made love beneath a swaying palm on a balmy night. Make love to me, Morgan."

Morgan's eyes glowed darkly. "An invitation like that is hard to resist."

His lips sought hers, taking satisfaction in the hungry joy of her response. Luca had come a long way from the frightened girl whose ambition in life was to become a nun. He pressed her down into the moss, slowly undressing her and then himself. They came together in splendid passion, their naked bodies vessels of adoration as they stroked and caressed and worshiped with hands, lips, and mouths. A gasp of splintered wonder sent Luca's teeth sinking into his shoulder when he thrust mindlessly between her thighs.

"My God, this is madness," Morgan gasped as her heat surrounded him. "I want you as much today as I did five years ago. Sweet nun, you've held me spellbound since the moment I set eyes on you."

"Don't talk, Morgan. When you're inside me I can't think clearly. I can only feel." He flexed his hips and drove himself deeper. She arched upward, rejoicing in his hunger, his unbridled passion, in his expanding thickness. Deep rapture stole her breath and her thoughts, and she cried out her pleasure.

He covered her mouth with his, her hoarse, gusting cries of ecstasy joining with his as she convulsed around him. The ferocity of her climax triggered his own tempest as utter fulfillment coursed through him.

Their mouths still clinging, Morgan shifted to lie beside her. He drew her into his arms as the last pulsebeat of pleasure shivered through them.

"We might have made a baby tonight," he whispered into her ear. He tried not to sound too hopeful, but their son was over three years old and he thought it was time to give Richard a brother or sister.

"That's impossible," Luca said with certain knowledge.

Morgan tried to hide his disappointment. Didn't Luca want another child with him? Renalda was already expecting a second child. "What makes you say that? How can you be certain?"

Luca touched his face with exquisite tenderness. Then she took his hand and held it against her flat stomach. "It's impossible to make a baby tonight because I'm already carrying your second child."

A slow smile lifted the corners of his mouth. "Are you sure?"

"As sure as I can be."

"I can't recall a time in my life when I've ever been happier."

"Nor I," Luca vowed. "Let's go home, my love, our son is waiting for us."

About the Author

Connie Mason is the bestselling author of more than thirty historical romances and novellas. Her tales of passion and adventure are set in exotic as well as American locales. Connie was named Storyteller of the Year in 1990 by *Romantic Times*, and was awarded a Career Achievement award in the Western category by *Romantic Times* in 1994. Connie makes her home in Tarpon Springs, Florida, with her husband, Jerry.

In addition to writing and traveling, Connie enjoys telling anyone who will listen about her three children and nine grandchildren, and sharing memories of her years living abroad in Europe and Asia as the wife of a career serviceman. In her spare time, Connie enjoys reading, dancing, playing bridge, and freshwater fishing with her husband.

The employees of Thorndike Press hope you have enjoyed this Large Print book. All our Thorndike and Wheeler Large Print titles are designed for easy reading, and all our books are made to last. Other Thorndike Press Large Print books are available at your library, through selected bookstores, or directly from us.

For information about titles, please call:

(800) 223-1244

or visit our Web site at:

www.gale.com/thorndike
www.gale.com/wheeler

To share your comments, please write:

Publisher
Thorndike Press
295 Kennedy Memorial Drive
Waterville, ME 04901